Once more Jagger inhaled her sweet scent deep into his lungs as his question hung in the air between them.

"*What* are you?"

That question caught her off guard. "What kind of game is this now? You are joking, right? Why didn't you kill me when you had the chance?"

"Kill you? Killing you was the last thing on my mind—in case you didn't notice."

Her gaze dropped down the length of his naked body. Her blue eyes flew back to his and the force of the emotions that colored the brilliant orbs nearly took his breath away.

"I'm the only thing standing between you and about twenty jaguar warriors."

Worry furled her brow and he felt like groaning as her tongue absently licked the luscious red of her lips . . .

By Juliana Stone

His Darkest Embrace
His Darkest Hunger

JULIANA STONE

His Darkest
EMBRACE

AVON
An Imprint of HarperCollinsPublishers

This is a work of fiction. Names, characters, places, and incidents are products of the author's imagination or are used fictitiously and are not to be construed as real. Any resemblance to actual events, locales, organizations, or persons, living or dead, is entirely coincidental.

AVON BOOKS
An Imprint of HarperCollins*Publishers*
10 East 53rd Street
New York, New York 10022-5299

Copyright © 2010 by Juliana Stone
Excerpt from *His Darkest Salvation* copyright © 2011 by Juliana Stone
ISBN 978-0-06-180880-7
www.avonromance.com

First Avon Books paperback printing: November 2010

Avon Trademark Reg. U.S. Pat. Off. and in Other Countries, Marca Registrada, Hecho en U.S.A.
HarperCollins® is a registered trademark of HarperCollins Publishers.

Printed in the U.S.A.

10 9 8 7 6 5 4 3 2 1

This book and every book I write
is dedicated to my family:
my husband, children,
Mom and Dad,
and yes, Shelby the dog.
I love you all.

acknowledgments

Since I was lame and didn't get this into the first book, I will try my best to get it right!

First off, I know I wouldn't be here without the support of these women: Lauren Hawkeye, who told me once that rules are meant to be broken; Nini, who was brave enough to be the first person to ever read my work; Amanda Vyne, who has a sharp eye, biting wit, and is a great roommate to boot; Sue, whose love of spreadsheets is legendary; the other Sirens: Barbara C., Barbara H., Linda (Star Girl); and the newest, Dara Snow. You guys are all so generous and amazing, I am lucky to have such a great group of writing friends.

I need to say that I am thankful to have such an amazing agent, Laura Bradford, and an editor, Esi Sogah, who not only has legs to die for, but is beautiful, funny, and great to work with. You ladies have helped me achieve my dream and for that I am grateful.

Thomas Egner, you so rock the cover world. Wendy Ho and Pam Jaffee, you guys are not only pros at your job, you're also very talented, bright women. Tessa Woodward and all the many people I'm not even aware of who have worked on these books, I totally love you all! For reals!

I need to mention the Bradford Bunch ladies, who have always, always, been there with their knowledge and support. You guys so rock and I truthfully think I hit the jackpot the day I signed with Laura.

I want to thank Christine Feehan for writing her amazing books. My world changed the day I picked up *Dark Prince*.

Finally, to all my friends and family, the Mudslides in particular, I truly am blessed.

Chapter 1

Skye Knightly was knee-deep in shit. In fact it was way past her knees and sitting up near her ass.

And *that* was putting it mildly.

Only an idiot would be caught at night, alone in the jungle so far from base camp. What the hell had she been thinking?

She inhaled a ragged breath as she melted deeper into the thick stand of trees. Her heart was banging against her chest like a freaking jackhammer and Skye rested her forehead against a tall pine tree, her skin slick with the humid jungle air.

She was tired, hungry, and now she could add scared as hell to the list. She peered out into the thickening gloom, back toward where she had just come from.

She was pissed and had no one to blame but herself. She knew how dangerous things were. *Especially now.* But the damn cave had been incredible and she'd been so caught up in exploring and recording that she'd lost all track of time.

If Finn were here, he'd kick her ass. Hell, she'd kick her own ass if she could. *Number one rule: always return before dark.*

When Skye heard a *snap* echo from the dense grouping of trees, across the small clearing to her right, she stilled. Her breaths shot out in small staccato bursts as the fear inside of her burrowed its way deep into her heart.

She gritted her teeth as another sound followed the first. Bastards weren't even trying to hide their presence, and she might very well pay the ultimate price for her stupidity.

She'd become aware that she was being followed soon after exiting the cave. Usually she didn't have a problem losing trackers but these men had proven ruthless, which led her to believe they were not your average hired guns.

They were not looking for tourists to rob. They wanted something.

Her heart flipped over and she tried to calm her nerves. Were they jaguar?

Her razor-sharp eyes normally could pick out a target hundreds of feet away, but sadly, her raptorlike qualities only shone in the daylight. Her powers to shift and morph into her eagle form faded as soon as the first inky fingers of night crawled up from below the earth.

Such was the curse borne by all eagle knights. They could only function to the fullest of their abilities with the caress of heat on their backs and the kiss of sun on their faces. Unfair really, considering Skye's many enemies had no such problems.

The jaguar, nocturnal creature that it was, could shift, hunt, and kill whether it be night or day, and the magicks, they could spell and charm whenever the fancy struck.

It was one of the reasons her people had been hunted to near extinction hundreds of years ago. She thought of the band of jaguar warriors that had until recently lived not too far from the archeological dig in Caracol.

They were a particularly vicious bunch.

She should know. They'd captured her and held her prisoner for several months. Skye bit her lip and tried to push back the rush of memories that always accompanied thoughts of the DaCosta jaguars. She broke out into a sweat and felt panic begin to take hold of her belly.

The DaCostas could never know that she'd survived the destruction of the compound, and subsequent battle, at the Mayan ruins in Caracol. If they had even the slightest inkling that an eagle knight was still messing about in the Belizean jungle, they would never stop looking for the portal. They would assume, correctly so, that the portal had been moved from its original resting place in Mexico to a safe place here in the vast mountains of Belize.

Only her father had known the precise location. He'd been murdered while trying to carry out his final mission—to seal the portal forever—and with his passing the final resting place of the portal had vanished.

Hatred, thick and nasty, threatened to choke her airway as her thoughts slid to Cormac O'Hara, the man who'd killed her father. She felt the rage swell but quickly shoved all emotion aside. There was no time for that.

The Sorcerer would meet his fate one day. Michael Knightly was gone from this earth and Skye was determined to see Cormac follow.

Tears threatened as she slipped into the heavy thicket of trees. She would not fail her father or her people now. She was so close to the portal she could taste it. She *had* to find it before the DaCostas and O'Hara got their hands on it. The bastards were now in league with each other, and she felt the noose of their evil tightening around her, each and every day.

She swallowed back bitter tears and feasted on the anger that lay inside. To fail would mean that her father's death had been in vain.

And that, simply, was not an option.

Silently she began to move deeper into the cool cover of pine trees, her breath held tightly as two men appeared in the small clearing a mere twenty paces from her. They were both tall, heavily muscled, and carried deadly weapons that even now were circling about.

Looking for her.

The taller of the two stopped short and his nostrils quivered excitedly. "She's here. I can smell her."

A lump of panic fell from her throat to land heavily in her gut. Skye held on with gritty determination as her mind frantically worked out plausible scenarios. Hopefully, ones that didn't end with her butt being served up on a platter to the two hard-bodied mercenaries.

The second soldier dropped to his knees and studied the ground she'd trod upon only minutes earlier. His head snapped up and she shrank behind a large tree. His eyes seemed to glow an eerie bluish yellow and her senses roared to life as adrenaline flooded her veins.

Both of them were dressed head to toe in black and she could just make out the beginnings of an intricate tattoo along the left side of the neck of the one closest to her. Skye bit her lip as the fear deep in her gut began to surface. The man's eyes continued to search along the path she'd taken and his mouth split into a grin, one that somehow didn't creep into his eyes.

He was jaguar—of that there was no mistake—and probably one of the DaCostas.

Fuck. This was worse than she'd first thought.

She eased her feet away from the tree trunk, and she dared not move her eyes from the clearing as she continued to disappear deeper into the interior. Slowly she adjusted the satchel that hung from around her neck. She might not be able to shift and fly out of this situation, but she was gifted with extraordinary speed, strength, and stamina.

Skye inhaled deeply, turned to the left and bolted up a steep incline with all the speed she could muster.

Dark laughter followed behind and she swore as one of the hunters' words drifted on the air to mock her.

"Run little bird, it only makes the hunt that much more interesting."

She ignored the taunt even as the import of his words washed over her. They knew what she was!

Panic, fear, and anger mingled together until they became a tight knot of pain that encircled her gut. She ignored it and mentally fought for the ice-cold calm that she knew resided deep within her psyche. Her body answered the call and she welcomed the ruthless strength that flooded her body.

Everything faded away. She was aware of her heartbeat and she visualized the muscle, encouraging it, cajoling more energy as her lungs expanded. Her legs became a blur as she sped through the verdant jungle, leaping over dead logs and vast arrays of flora, almost flying, so fast was her body moving.

A loud roar colored the night and she stumbled as it echoed into the quiet blackness that surrounded her. Up ahead, mist began to pour over her and the thunder of a waterfall became crystal clear as she sped toward it.

The entire area was awash with waterfalls, caves, grottos . . . it's what made the Maya Mountains so incredible. But they were dangerous and she continued along, picking up speed as she ran toward the deafening sound.

Skye knew it was her only chance to survive.

Her long legs covered the distance in no time and she burst through the thick foliage, skidding to a halt as she quickly scanned the perimeter.

To her right was yet another cave, the dark opening covered with a protective mist that seemed sinister as it fingered and clawed its way over the rock face and out toward the low-hanging canopy. Out of its mouth water rushed with a fury toward the ledge to her left, where it disappeared into the night.

From where she was perched, Skye had no clue how far down the waterfall trailed, but from the sounds she could hear, she anticipated a long drop.

The mist was heavy and it clung to her skin, molding the white tank top to her breasts. Her hair had long since fallen from its pony tail into thick strands of caramel down her back, where it clung, full of humidity, to her sweaty skin.

Her sapphire blue eyes pierced the night, but once again the curse of the sun prevented her from seeing any other means of escape.

She could try the cave or jump over the falls. Desperately she swiveled her head around as she continued to search for a way out, her large eyes widening at the sight of both jaguar hunters as they burst through the trees into the small clearing. One was in human form. The other growled deep from its chest and paced back and forth in all its majestic animal glory.

The large jaguar was black, signaling its status as something other than a regular shifter. They were of the warrior class. And they both looked at her like she was a tasty morsel they wanted to sample . . . before the real games began.

The one in human form laughed outright as his gaze raked over her body, lingering salaciously on her breasts before settling on the juncture between her legs. Skye's eyes darkened as a slow anger began to burn through her. When he licked his lips, she spit into the ground, which elicited a harsh laugh.

"That's good. I like a woman with spunk almost as much as I like to play with my food. It's so much more palatable when its essence is spirited." He continued to laugh while the jaguar at his side roared in triumph. His eyes glowed eerily. "Hell yeah, this is gonna be fun."

Skye tried to ignore his words but truthfully, she was more terrified than she'd like to admit. And that was saying a lot. In her young life span of twenty-six years she'd seen and done a lot, but her current situation was about as bad as it could get.

She was trapped with few options, alone in the jungle and facing two very ruthless, deadly jaguar warriors.

Enemies that her people had faced for eons.

She felt the flush of blood hit her cells as she grabbed onto all the power she could muster. She needed more time. She needed to think.

"Who the hell are you?"

The jaguar growled at her words and she flinched slightly at the intensity of its vocalization. The tall man to its side smiled once more, and through the thick mist his white teeth flashed at her, the canines seeming to glisten with an unholy shimmer.

"I think you know exactly who and what we are." He snorted as he began to slowly move toward her. "And you should be very afraid, little bird."

Skye began to inch to her right; the darkened interior of the cave was looking a tad more inviting than it had seconds ago. The jaguar warriors were too close to the edge of the waterfall, effectively cutting off that escape route.

Her eyes narrowed and she made a face. "Siegfried and Roy's lost cousin?"

Loud laughter echoed her words and the warrior in human form began to clap slowly, methodically. The sound grated on her last working nerve and Skye grimaced as she continued to move toward the cave.

"I think our little eagle deserves some sort of award for her acting skills." He looked to the jaguar at his side and then winked through the mist at Skye.

"What do you think, Christo? Should we reward her with some play time before we get down to business?"

The cat licked its lips as its tail flickered back and forth. Skye felt bile begin to rise in her throat and she swallowed thickly. She needed to keep them occupied and away from her, at least until she was close enough to the cave to make a run for it.

"Keep talking to that cat on steroids and I'm gonna have to call the crazy police, which might be kinda hard since we're out in the middle of the jungle."

"Enough!"

Skye jumped, nearly slipping upon the wet rocks as his voice tore through her. His eyes began to glow in earnest and the air around him shimmered as it darkened considerably, encircling him in a blanket of malice.

"We know exactly who you are, Skye Knightly." He laughed once more and she felt every hair on her body rise as the danger of her situation tripled. *"And we know what you are."*

Skye bolted, leaping over the large boulder that stood between the cave and her body, reaching into her satchel as she crested the rock to land hard, knee-deep in rushing water.

A splash sounded behind her, and she whirled around, releasing a deadly blade—one that was charmed and dipped in poison—in a hard arc that struck the jaguar dead center in its massive chest. The beast roared in pain and the man at its side snarled in rage as he, too, jumped toward her, his anger and bulk carrying him forward in a rush.

Skye tried to twist away, but the warrior was too powerful and his momentum crashed his large body into hers, knocking them both into the fast-moving water that fled the cave. Her head went under and she sputtered wildly as she came up for air, her feet churning fast in an effort to get away from her enemy.

His fist came from nowhere and connected with her head in a hard ringing slam that brought stars to her eyes. She flew back and once more was under water. Skye kicked with all her might, hoping to ride the current over the falls, and felt tears of frustration rise as something gripped her calf painfully and she was hauled out of the water and thrown back onto the embankment beside the mouth of the cave.

To the furious man above her, she weighed little more than a doll. His heavy frame covered hers, the muscled thighs gripping her body as his hands encircled her head. Her arms were trapped against her sides and the sheer weight of him made breathing difficult. Skye ceased her struggles, aware that it both inflamed and excited the man.

His eyes were as black as tar but the tinge of blue light that shone from behind them was eerie and he smiled at the fear that briefly graced her features. He ground his body against hers, laughing as she bucked her hips, the reaction instant as a sickening lurch went through her.

"You're not going anywhere, bitch."

His hands tightened cruelly against her cranium but Skye held on and uttered not a sound as he continued to apply pressure, his fingers sharp with their clawlike nails, biting deep into the skull. She watched in silence as his eyes began to shimmer and the blue light that lit them churned brighter and morphed into a deep red color.

His mouth opened to a slash of white teeth and his tongue reached down toward her. He growled menacingly and Skye tried to arch away, but she was held fast, and shuddered as he licked her face from her forehead down to her chin.

She was going to be sick. She could feel her gut rolling over as a mixture of dread and fear settled in the shadows of her soul.

"It's a shame really, how this night will end. You

taste like the sun. And make no mistake, I will taste every inch of you, but first I need to know where the portal is."

"Screw you, dickhead." Skye spit in his face and cringed, expecting some sort of physical retaliation. Instead laughter echoed across the stillness of the night.

She closed her eyes as he howled at the top of his lungs, "The jaguar will once more feast upon the flesh of the eagle." He moved slightly and she was able to breathe a little easier. "But first things first."

The bile that had been sitting at the back of her throat rose quickly and even though Skye was a warrior in her own right, an eagle knight, she felt shame wash over her at the fear that began to beat through her body as his eyes raked over her curves.

Her mind began to close in on itself and a vision of her father drifted before her. How had it come to this?

Her father's eyes sliced through her, full of love and encouragement but alive with the fire of battle. It was all she needed, and once more she began to struggle against the monster. A surge of adrenaline hit her hard as her heart answered the call, and she continued to struggle, ignoring his harsh laughter.

Her blue eyes sought the black of his and her hatred for the jaguar sizzled. "I will never submit willingly to such filth."

"I wouldn't dream of you submitting willingly . . . that would take all the fun out of it, don't you think?" His laughter fell over her like sharp glass and she felt the heat of his breath on her face.

Skye closed her eyes. She wasn't strong enough physically to defeat the bastard on top of her. She braced herself and sought the place of calm that resided in her mind. He would use her body, but she would plot and find a way out of this.

There was no other option.

An unholy roar rent the air and bounced off the rock face. It was full of power and Skye felt the warrior atop her go still. Something new stalked this evening and she waited, hoping an opportunity for escape would present itself.

Her eyes cracked open and she watched as a furious snarl erupted from the man on top of her. His large hands ground into her skull once more and he cracked her head hard against the rock she lay against. The pain was immediate and Skye felt her sanity slip away as the scent of blood filled the air. A deep sadness leeched from her heart into every cell of her body, but she could do nothing about it.

She would fail her father and their people.

And she would die this night.

The heavy weight left her as the warrior sprang from her, his body shifting into the mist. She fought the darkness that lingered around the edges of her mind, knowing her one chance for survival was fast slipping away. But her body wasn't working and her mind was slow.

She could hear the sounds of battle: screams, roars, and a fight that sounded savage in its simplicity as flesh pounded against flesh. Skye inhaled deeply and forced her brain to work through the fog. She urged her limbs into work mode and lurched forward, her eyes automatically seeking out the enemy.

What she saw left her speechless. Two large jaguars were locked in a fight to the death.

To her left was the body of the jaguar she'd killed. Her gaze flew back to the two snarling animals and she began to inch away. Her legs slid down the slippery rock and she drifted into the water once more. Once she was in, she began to swim toward the ledge of the waterfall.

An insane and painful roar erupted from behind her and Skye quickly glanced back in time to see one of the jaguars crushing the skull of the other. The beast stood above its kill and its eyes sought hers through the mist and dark that enveloped her.

Something slithered through her as she locked onto the strange green eyes that shone brightly like beacons. The jaguar stood there, panting and barking its victory. It started pacing along the embankment, and it growled deep from its belly but never broke eye contact with her.

If Skye didn't know better, she'd say it felt as if the animal were warning her of danger. She shook her head. All jaguars were evil. They lived to hunt and kill. They could take human form, yes, but there was nothing remotely human about them.

Her feet scraped along the shallow bottom as she neared the edge of the falls, and slowly she stood. The animal roared its disapproval and jumped into the cool depths of the water, its body encircled with mist as it glided toward her. Skye glanced below and tried not to acknowledge her fear of the long, dark, and dangerous drop.

Her head felt dull, thick with pain, and she shook herself, her eyes once more drawn to the wall of mist. Sparks seemed to fly from within, and she was taken aback as a tall, lean, incredibly ripped and naked man slid from the fog to stand before her. His green eyes glowed with a feral fire and her heart began to beat a rhythm that left her breathless.

He moved toward her with sinuous grace and Skye panicked. She took a step back and teetered on the edge, feeling the water twirl around her feet as it cascaded below. The man stopped and she noticed his tattoos through the darkness that separated them.

They clawed their way up abs that looked as if they were carved from stone. Black symbols that caressed taut muscle.

He was a jaguar warrior. She had no other choice.

Skye inhaled a ragged breath and murmured to herself, "Watch over me, Daddy," before closing her eyes.

And then she jumped.

Chapter 2

The tall, powerful male shook his head aggressively. His skin shimmered as the last remnants of jaguar slipped from his limbs, the soft black fur rippling away in silence. Water sprayed out into a fine mist around his body and settled in a silvery sheen that coated his flesh in an eerie glow.

Jagger Castille had not taken his human form in almost two months. *Hell, it could have been six months.* He'd lost track of time and quite possibly his grip on reality.

His eyes burned with a fire that lit them with an intensity that seemed frenetic. The scent of the woman lay heavy in his mind, and he felt an unmistakable twinge as his body hardened with a need long denied.

Thin tendrils of fog crept forward from the mouth of the cave he'd called home for the past two months, and lapped at the water that rose up to his thighs. A few drops of moisture fell into his eyes and he impatiently wiped them away as he slowly moved toward the edge of the falls.

His hair had grown since he'd been in the jungle and was now touching the tops of his shoulders. The blue black waves were a far cry from the crisp military cut he normally sported.

He snorted; that seemed like a lifetime ago.

His ears perked and he listened intently, waiting for a splash. He knew the terrain here well, and if the female survived the fall, it would be a miracle. There was not a lot of room from the center of the falls out to the sides and there were large boulders below that would break her body into pieces if she landed on them. The pool at the bottom was deep where the water circled before heading toward yet another waterfall that went straight down the mountain, well over one thousand feet.

If she were to have a chance of living, he'd have to act now.

He moved forward, frustrated because his body seemed sluggish as it took time to adjust to his human form. Jagger was well over six feet in height, and his center of gravity was extremely different from that of his jaguar.

He stood atop the falls, on the precipice of indecision. His mind was at war with his body and he shuddered as images began to assault him, ones he cared not to revisit ever again. Small slivers of his past rippled through his brain and he cursed at his weakness.

He could literally taste hot desert in his mouth, the sand so thick he felt like choking. He once more saw explosions, blood, his brothers; all of it converged and formed a collage of confusion.

And Eden, the one he'd tried to forget the most. Her face, deathly pale as her life fled quickly. Even then, she'd looked at him like he was some kind of hero.

He almost took a step back.

But the woman's scent triggered something buried inside of him, a protective instinct that was only enhanced by the fact that the two jaguars who had attacked her belonged to the DaCosta clan. Just thinking of them brought a savage snarl to his handsome face. His mouth broke into a smile that not wholly conveyed pleasure, but nonetheless fit his mood.

Without further thought Jagger ran forward and leapt over the edge of the slippery cliff, his body streaking down three hundred feet, until water closed over his head.

The water was chilled but refreshing, and he welcomed the purity of it as it slithered over his long body. He was heavy and went deep, but with a few quick, strong kicks his body rose to the surface seconds later, and he broke through.

The night had become quiet. He noticed the lack of sound immediately and his eyes automatically scanned the perimeter of the large basin, running over the rock face and embankment in quick succession as his arms began to slice through the wetness that surrounded him. There was no moon this evening, but his eyes penetrated the gloom, his enhanced vision moving along quickly as he searched for any sign of the woman.

He was almost to the side when a sliver of something caught at his peripheral vision and he swung closer to where the water gathered and moved quickly toward the second drop.

There! Near the edge!

Long blond hair snaked out, riding the top of the water and drifting toward certain death. Without pause, Jagger accelerated and grabbed the woman's arm just as the tug of the stream would have lifted her over the edge.

She was unconscious, and his nose inhaled the scent of blood. He gathered her close and began to swim against the current, his eyes seeking out the path he'd used many times before. He could feel her heartbeat against his chest; it was faint but steady, and as he glided through the silent night, his eyes raked over the features he'd not seen clearly before.

Her eyes were closed but he didn't need to see them open to know she was one hell of a looker. A straight patrician nose was accentuated by high cheekbones, wide-set eyebrows and lush, killer lips.

Her breasts were crushed against him and he could feel their softness and the fact that they were a little more than a handful.

Just the way he liked them.

Even as the thought crossed his brain he could feel her nipples harden against his naked flesh, and his own body, already tense with need, answered in kind.

The animal inside, still so close to the edge, roared in frustration and his skin began to burn as his jaguar railed against being confined. He'd been too long in animal form and the savagery shocked him. He pushed the beast back, cursing the way his body was behaving. Not liking any of the sensations that pulled at him now.

Things were so much simpler when he'd become one with his jaguar. After the DaCosta compound attack and subsequent destruction, he'd woken up, deep in the jungle, and hadn't returned to his human form.

He'd not remembered his human side for several weeks after, but even when he did, Jagger had had no desire whatsoever to return to his old life.

He'd welcomed the fierceness of his jaguar blood, and thrived on the wild nature that was left wide open to roam and to hunt, and slowly he'd felt his grip on reality begin to fade. He truly thought he'd never answer the call from his other half again.

As time moved on, his humanity had slowly slipped away, and truthfully, he'd been happy to just be and live with the status quo.

He couldn't even explain why, he only knew he needed this. His body and mind were tired of war, tired of conflict, and he'd seen enough death and destruction to last a lifetime. Losing people you cared about just wasn't worth it anymore.

He was done with it.

He'd felt guilt as he thought of his family. His brother, Julian, along with Cracker and Declan, had come back several weeks earlier, and he'd avoided detection by them, wanting only to be left alone.

He had existed peacefully with the vast array of animals that inhabited the dense mountain terrain he'd come to love. He had even made his way north, down the mountains and into the lush rain forest that caressed the lower lands. A jaguar refuge was deep in the heart of the Cayo district and he had spent time amongst his animal kind.

They knew what he was—a shifter, neither fully animal nor human—and they'd steered clear of him. Jaguars were pretty much a solitary breed but he had enjoyed knowing they were nearby.

Yeah, his self-imposed exile had been a long time coming and he felt a flash of resentment run through him as he hauled his body out of the water, still cradling the unconscious woman. What the hell was he going to do with her?

The animal inside of him cried out at the thought, wanting only to do one thing, needing to free the tension that rode both of them hard. Jagger clenched his teeth and hissed as his body began to throb with a hunger that he wasn't sure he'd be able to control. His gaze passed over her face once more, and with superhuman effort, he managed to keep his emotions at bay and picked his way up the slippery, smooth rocks until his feet landed upon warm, moist earth.

His eyes were constantly on the move, and even though the surrounding forest was eerily quiet, he sensed no danger. He grasped the woman tightly and swallowed a groan at the sensation of her soft, wet skin sliding against his hard flesh.

Without further thought he climbed back up the side of the mountain, his long legs eating the distance in less than five minutes. Once he'd gained the top of the waterfall, the scent of the two dead jaguars clung heavily to the humid air and surrounding mist.

He strode forward, his shoulders squared and nostrils flared as rage simmered along the edges of his mind.

Dirty filth! How dare they creep into his domain and foul his small corner of paradise with their DaCosta stink. His eyes found themselves once more regarding the unconscious woman he held so close to his chest.

Her scent was tantalizing in its simplicity and he frowned slightly, sensing something a bit *off*. He lowered his head until his face was merely inches from hers and without thinking, closed the remaining space between them as his nose nuzzled the soft cheek that lay there.

Her skin was cool to the touch and he savored the feminine texture, drawing her essence deep into his lungs. There was no false scent clinging to her skin, no manufactured perfumes to cover the unique and musky odor that was all her own. She was of the earth, the sky, and his body began to quiver in excitement.

The cat clawed at him hard and his skin began to shimmer and burn. He felt his fingernails begin to grow and he growled loudly, pushing the animal back once more.

Jagger tore his face from hers and his eyes landed on the corpse near the edge of the pool of water. He jumped over a large boulder and quickly made his way inside the dark opening of his cave. Here the air was cool and he deposited the still form near the back where he usually slumbered.

Returning outside, he made quick work of the bodies, dragging them down the side of the mountain and into the thick, silent forest. He disposed of them, leaving the remains on display at the edge of his territory as a warning to all.

He would not tolerate any form of human jaguar in his domain. If the DaCostas were starting to make noise once more, he was more than ready to battle.

It was almost an hour later when Jagger returned to the cave, silently returning to where he had left the woman. She was still unconscious, and he found her balled into the fetal position, her skin damp, and shivering with cold.

He knelt down beside her, probing the back of her head with his fingers, and she winced, jerking uncontrollably when he passed over a wound at the back.

Her hair was matted here, stiff and sticky with blood, but the wound had stopped seeping.

Jagger sighed softly. What the hell was he going to do with her? He rocked back on his haunches, his face a mask of indecision.

There were still several hours until daylight, and while normally he was active at this time of night, he knew that the woman would become feverish and sick if he left her on her own. His gaze slowly made its way over her body. She was shivering and he briefly considered removing her wet clothes. Indeed the white tank top did nothing to hide her lush curves. In fact the dark circles of her hardened nipples were clearly visible.

He tore his eyes from her chest only to focus on the outline of her butt, where the wet shorts she wore cupped each delicious mound. Jagger groaned as his body once more reacted to such a display of feminine beauty. He glanced down at his own rigid hardness, realizing for the first time he had not one stitch of clothing with him.

He righted himself and frowned, feeling tension begin to trickle down his neck and settle in his shoulders. Resentment danced along his mind as well.

His mouth formed a thin line as once more his gaze raked over the shaking form beneath him.

He inhaled slowly and let his breath out, his hands combing through the thick waves of hair at his neck. He wanted nothing more than to leave and forget the woman even existed.

But he could never do that. His genetic makeup would not allow him to callously leave a defenseless woman alone out here in the jungle.

His eyes settled on her face and he kinked his head

to the side in an effort to better study her. A slight grimace creased the soft corners of her mouth and her eyes were moving rapidly behind the closed lids. Her arms were wrapped tightly about her midsection and long strands of dark blond hair fell in mass disarray well past her shoulders.

"Who the hell are you?" he murmured out loud, stunned to hear the sound of his own voice, husky and scratchy from months of silence.

Jagger glanced around what had been his home for the last two months and then without pausing slid his long limbs behind the slumbering woman. He clenched his mouth together tightly, biting the inside of his cheek at the feel of her against his nakedness.

It was pure torture . . . and incredibly erotic. His cock, already hard with need lay against the small of her back. Slowly he pulled her shivering form into his embrace and fought the urge to bury his face in the fragrant layers of hair that caressed her neck.

He felt her body tense but then, seconds later, relax. She sighed softly, welcoming the warmth his body provided, and wiggled her ass slightly in an effort to get closer to him. Jagger hissed at the sensations that exploded up from his groin and went straight to his dick.

Fuck. It was gonna be a long night.

Pain was the first thing Skye felt as she slowly muddled her way up from the deep recesses of sleep. Her mind was fuzzy, thick, and sluggish. It felt like a whole bottle of cotton balls had been deposited inside her cranium and they were deadening all sensation and warping her thought process.

The pain continued and radiated from the back of her skull outward. Her hands automatically tried to reach the back of her head but she was pinned beneath something. Her eyes flew open and she groaned as fragments of pressure burst behind them, and she squinted, trying to see clearly.

She felt something at her back. It was warm, solid, and as her brain began to function, a feeling of dread leapt up from her belly. She could *feel* and *hear* a heartbeat that was strong and steady against her flesh. It belonged to a male. Of that there was no doubt. The masculine hardness that gripped her soft curves could not be confused with anything other than what it was.

She stilled and looked downward. Two long arms encircled her from behind: one lay protectively underneath the swell of her breasts; the other was splayed out along the ground, palms up, fingers loose and relaxed. The flesh was much darker than her golden skin, like amaretto, and heat swirled quickly inside her belly.

She shook her head, trying to clear the cobwebs, extremely annoyed at her body's response.

She squealed softly as the arm that lay underneath her breasts moved slightly and she felt the shift of his body behind her as one long leg slowly covered her hip and moved her in closer to the ever-present hardness that was unmistakable against her back.

She held her breath and snuck a quick peak at the leg that lay so intimately against her own. Once again it was long, muscular and way too comfortably draped across her hip.

Where the hell was she? And who the heck was the naked man scrunched up against her butt? She sure as hell knew he didn't have a stitch of clothing on.

She could feel it.

Unease continued to pump inside of her, rushing

through her veins, as fear, confusion, and panic began to build.

She closed her eyes and struggled to remember how she had ended up here . . . wherever the hell *here* was.

Then it came to her in a rush and her heart took off as her lungs fed on the adrenaline spike. She sputtered as she tried to breathe. She'd been attacked by jaguars. The last thing she remembered was a tall, naked god of a man approaching her from the mist.

Softly Skye groaned and the slight movement sent sharp pains rushing through her skull. *He* was jaguar and she'd jumped over the falls.

And now she was . . . *Where the hell was she?*

Frantic, she searched the immediate area with her eyes, and she swallowed thickly when the arm around her midsection tightened, as if the man knew she was desperate to flee. The hand that had been relaxed on the ground slowly crept over her body and began to caress her belly.

Skye hissed softly as her mind began to run in circles. She clamped her mouth shut tightly and forced herself to calm. She needed to think and get herself out of this situation. But she had to be smart about it. Too much rested on her shoulders and there was no room for error.

His hands were rough, callused, and his scent filled her nostrils as he slowly turned her body. She closed her eyes and centered her mind as she calculated her odds. The man was strong, that she could feel, so she needed to time things properly.

He continued to slowly pull her up his body and suddenly her eyes flew open to stare into deep green eyes that at the moment were hooded, heavy with desire.

It was definitely the man from the mist and she tried not to let her panic show.

He was dark, with longish, wavy, blue black hair, a straight noble nose, chiseled cheekbones, and square jaw. He was incredibly male, totally sexy, but he carried the tattoos of her enemy. They shimmered against his flesh, caressing his neck as they flaunted their power in her face.

Skye held her breath and let her body relax into liquid as she stared directly into his eyes. He knew something was up. Wariness now clung to them, replacing the dark desire she'd first witnessed.

He was one hell of a male specimen, for sure.

But he was jaguar and even though he'd taken out a DaCosta the night before, in her world, that didn't mean squat. She couldn't take the chance that he was aligned with the wrong side. Cormac's side.

Without warning she kneed him sharply in the balls. Hard.

He roared in anger as his grip loosened and she rolled away from him, her legs churning as she wildly looked for escape. She was in a cave of some sort. Frantically she sought an exit, and she bolted toward long beams of light that beckoned from down the narrow tunnel.

Skye didn't bother looking back. She was down the passage in an instant and as the light became brighter, she tapped into her eagle, and felt the large raptor explode as she leapt out into the sun.

She made the shift seamlessly. As her large wings unfurled and her body rose high into the warm sky, she headed toward camp.

She heard a shout of rage follow her, but ignored it.

She had more pressing matters to attend to. The

DaCosta jaguars were on the hunt, and she needed to warn Finn and Sam.

Sam was human and dear to her heart. He'd been working with her for the past two years as she'd tried to locate the portal.

But Finn . . . he was of her blood, and if he was lost to her, then she'd truly be on her own. She'd be the last Knightly to walk the earth and soar free in the skies.

As her great wings carried her higher into the welcoming sunlight, she felt the elation of the shift leave her as a great sadness crept into her soul.

She would be the only eagle knight left to carry out her father's mission, one that would only succeed with the ultimate sacrifice.

She just prayed she'd be strong enough to carry it through to the bitter end.

Chapter 3

Jagger Castille staggered to his feet, trying to control his fast-rising temper. He inhaled sharply, his eyes darkening yet again, and this time desire had nothing to do with it.

Christ, his nuts were fucking killing him. He bent over, his breath ragged, and he couldn't decide what hurt more, his aching jewels or his pride.

He'd not had sex in a seriously long time, and the scent of the woman he'd held so close was still in his nostrils, taunting him. He felt his cock react, hardening even more at the thought of her perfect breasts in his hands. He stood straight and shook his tense muscles, cursing loudly as the pain between his legs refused to lessen.

What the hell had happened?

He growled his displeasure as his long legs carried him to the entrance of the cave. She was nowhere in sight. His head swiveled around but there was no trace of her.

What the fuck?

Jagger wasn't sure how long he stood there, cock jutting straight out like a bull about to charge. He knew he should let it go. But how could he?

Groaning, he let out a long breath and glanced down at his aching appendage. There was no way that was going away anytime soon.

He could take care of *those* needs the old-fashioned way if he had to. As his eyes quickly scanned the entire perimeter, her elusive scent caught at him, enthralled him with its sweetness. It was riding the wind and he found himself facing north, his eyes scouring the distance, searching for some kind of sign.

What the hell was he thinking?

The detached part of his human nature warned him to just leave it alone. But the cat hungered inside, wanting to taste her.

Savagely, Jagger snarled and plunged his overheated flesh into the cool water that fell from his cave. The refreshing wetness abated the fever he was feeling briefly, but he knew he would be walking around with a hard-on for days.

And so he stood, six feet, six inches of rock-solid muscle, pissed off that some random female had infiltrated his space and reduced him to a quivering mass of need.

Her scent still floated in the air and he inhaled the richness of it, feeling it burn through his veins as her unique odor caught at the very heart of him.

The satchel that he'd taken from around her shoulders lay against the pallet on the floor and quickly he opened it, hoping to find information about this mystery woman who'd been attacked by two jaguar warriors so close to his territory.

The small satchel was full of maps, notes, and intricately drawn recordings of caves. Detailed and precise, they aroused his curiosity.

He sat back on his haunches and quickly skimmed the renderings. Several small notes had been scribbled into one margin, and he felt the sting of anger hit him once more as one word stood out in stark relief.

DaCosta.

Fucking bastards just wouldn't go away.

His fingers gripped the pages and he felt a fire begin in his gut as he read on. There were several words and phrases highlighted. Caracol. Ritual. Cave of the Sun. But one word grabbed at him hard and he hissed when he saw it.

Libby.

He inhaled deeply as his thoughts turned to his brother Jaxon and the woman he loved. What the hell had happened after the sky had opened up and fire had rained down upon them, that night at the DaCosta compound? Did they make it out alive?

Fear of the unknown began to eat at him and Jagger jumped to his feet, suddenly filled with nervous energy and the need to act. Something at the bottom of the bag caught his eye, and he withdrew a small object carved from soft limestone.

It was an eagle, wings spread as if in flight, and there were markings on the bottom of it. The piece looked extremely old and well used, maybe a small toy for a child. He put it back along with the mess of papers and clipped the bag shut.

He stood there, lost in thought for several long moments, and then turned abruptly, bag in hand. His body reacted to what his mind was commanding and the cat purred with joy. He exited the cave once more and leapt over the water, making his way down the ledge that led to the second waterfall below. Before he'd cleared the bottom, mist had enveloped his body, and it was no longer that of a human male but a large black jaguar that swam across the water and emerged on the other side.

Jagger clutched the satchel in his mouth, turning his head to the sky, trying to catch a whiff of her scent. It was elusive, and he shook his head, clearly puzzled. His powerful paws made quick work of the muddy banks and he made it to higher ground before the smallest touch of *her* grabbed him.

He began following the trail and felt excitement pound through his body. Her essence was tantalizing and the cat growled from deep in his chest before he disappeared into the thick stand of trees that lined the water.

The next four hours proved to be somewhat of a chore for Jagger; he wasn't used to hunting something that he couldn't seem to find. Her scent kept disappearing and then reappearing as the wind picked up. It was confusing, but carefully he tracked her, wandering miles from what had become his territory, and the ridge changed as he left the thick pine forests far behind him and traveled lower, down into the heart of the jungle.

Here, he picked a path through the thick, lush underbelly, his heavy paws silent as his body slid through dense greenery. The jungle was so much a part of who and what he was, he felt his spirit soar.

He knew he wasn't far from the massive Mayan ruins in Caracol and he swung east as her scent continued to tease. It lingered just out of reach and drove him mad with the desire to find her.

What the hell he was going to do when he eventually did get his paws on her was another story, but he'd invested too much time and energy to just let it go at this point.

The sun was high in the azure blue sky, and he felt the heat of her rays filtering through the canopy high above him. He was just about to cross a small stream, when out of nowhere a new scent drifted over him, one that immediately brought to the surface the aggressive nature that was the jaguar.

He began to pant as it washed over him, his body quivering in anticipation. His mind recognized the testosterone-laden body signatures that were unique to his kind, and he stilled his trembling frame, trying to find its source.

It took only a few seconds, but he knew he was in close proximity to a large gathering of jaguar shifters. He sensed another scent that was unusual and felt his heart speed up as he realized it was very close to the mystery woman's signature.

Had she been taken?

Quickly he circled back, up a large hill, using the dense jungle for cover. He was downwind from their encampment, and as of yet sensed no other predators in the immediate vicinity.

Faint voices could be heard traveling up from below and Jagger homed in on them, but he realized that they could still be miles away. Quickly he started following them, and a half hour later he slowed to a crawl, his senses on high alert as his nose twitched impatiently.

He kept his body low to the ground and moved forward quietly, surprised that no guards had been posted so close to camp. As he nudged closer, he realized it was because there were at least twenty soldiers present, several bearing the tattoos that proclaimed their elite warrior status.

He settled in to listen and to observe, pushing the bolt of excitement to the back of his mind, knowing he needed to play it cool and smart, or else his life could be on the line.

A large male, clearly the one in charge, was pacing about, nervous energy clinging to his heavily muscled frame. He, too, bore the warrior tattoos, but they were unfamiliar to Jagger.

He grumbled softly as he continued to study the large man, not liking the fact that he was so outnumbered. To be discovered would mean certain death.

Abruptly the leader stopped, as a new player entered the camp from the opposite direction. He was panting heavily, his body dripping in sweat and trembling from exertion.

"Where are they?"

The newcomer took a few more seconds to catch his breath and the large male growled loudly, his stance aggressive as he quickly crossed over to where the panting warrior stood.

"They're dead."

The tall leader bellowed his rage, and his fists flew out into the chest of the bearer of such bad news, and both of them snarled as they began to shimmer, and mist fell upon their bodies. The rest of the pack stood back, most of them looking bored, as if the battle waged before them was an everyday occurrence.

From his perch behind the thick thatch of greenery that lined the perimeter of the camp, Jagger stilled.

The human part of his mind understood the words and their implications. Obviously, the two DaCosta warriors that had been killed near his cave somehow belonged with this dangerous bunch. The question was, why were two DaCostas out here working alongside several different clans of warriors?

Jagger's brain went into overdrive as he tried to puzzle it out. It was not normal for different jaguar clans to mingle, especially warriors. One thing was certain, something was up. Something big. And somehow the little slip of a woman he'd run across was mixed up in the whole mess.

The snarls subsided and when the mist cleared, the warriors had returned to their human forms. The leader slowly gained his feet, his face dark with anger. He walked a few paces away, collected himself before turning back toward the messenger.

"How?"

The one-word question was uttered harshly and the other warrior spit into the ground, his growls slowly dying out as he faced his superior.

"One was knifed and the other's skull was crushed." The warrior's chest heaved in an effort to slow his breathing as he continued, "I picked up her scent. The bitch is still alive but there was another jaguar there, and by the look of the attack I don't think it was a regular shifter."

"Fuck! Where the hell is she?" the leader exploded loudly as his temper erupted. He crossed over to a stand of trees and Jagger strained his head in an effort to better see. When a tall, thin man with graying hair was yanked forward he sighed silently, glad to see it wasn't the female he'd been hunting.

The urge to protect was building steadily, but Jagger held back, listening intently, hoping to find out what the hell the large gathering of warriors was up to.

The leader threw the man to the ground and kicked him hard in the chest. The effort produced a grunt of pain, and Jagger was impressed at the fire of hatred that burned brightly in the man's eyes.

"Where the hell is the eagle bitch?"

The man remained silent, earning another quick kick to the gut and a backhand to the face. Blood spurted out and several teeth flew from his mouth, but the man smiled up wickedly at his adversary, licking the thick red substance that was slowly trickling from the side of his mouth.

"You'll never get your black paws on her," the man sneered. "And she'll make sure of it."

The warrior roared in fury, his foot colliding hard with the side of the man's head, effectively quieting him as his body slid to the earthen floor. The other warriors dispersed and Jagger noiselessly retreated far back into the underbrush.

Questions pummeled his brain: who was the woman and what were the DaCostas seeking? But there was no time to seek answers. The warriors would be on the hunt and he needed to kick it up a notch.

His heart began to pound and the rush of blood that flew through his veins pushed him to a relentless pace as he headed east, away from the jaguars.

The blond woman was in danger, and his need to get to her, while foreign, nevertheless had his powerful frame streaking through the jungle in an effort to locate her scent once more. He had to reach her before the pack of jaguars did.

If he was too late, there would be no telling what they'd do to her once they had her in their hands. The DaCostas were a nasty bunch, and the thought of anyone touching the blonde brought such anger crashing through him that his growl reverberated loudly, and several wailer monkeys flew along the canopy above, yelling their encouragement.

His powerful legs ate up a considerable range of lush jungle and he kept up a harsh pace for well over two hours. It was getting late in the afternoon and the sun's warmth was definitely decreasing when he began to close in on her location.

Jagger had just crested a small hill as a warm breeze picked up, coming in off the Caribbean Sea and filtering inland. His nostrils quivered in excitement as the elusive scent he'd been searching for all morning and into the afternoon flew at him. He drew her essence deep into his body and his green eyes quickly scoured the area immediately below him. Off in the distance he saw what looked like a small clearing, a break in the thick foliage that carpeted the entire area.

He knew it was only luck that brought her scent to him. For whatever reason she was riding the wind and it wouldn't be long before it drifted downward, to where the warriors were.

He took off, quickly disappearing deep into cover, and as her scent became stronger, he slowed to a crawl.

He paused as he closed in on the area where he thought she was and scented the air. His nostrils quivered in distaste, and he shook his head as the sickening aroma of death cloaked any sweetness that had been riding the wind.

Panic gnawed at him, but the hunter that lived inside clung to an air of caution. Methodically, he inched forward, keeping his body well hidden.

Jagger didn't sense any enemies close at hand, but the powerful feeling that something tragic had occurred hung thick in the humid jungle air. His lungs inhaled it deeply and his mouth hung open as he panted hard in an effort to hold himself from rushing headlong into something that could prove to be very dangerous.

Silently he slipped through the abundant flora and fauna that covered the jungle floor, his stare transfixed directly in front of him where the mess of foliage thinned, and the obvious clearing could be seen.

He stopped, just at the edge, and felt his heart begin to beat erratically once more, as a camp of some sort had come into view. There were two tents, or rather what was left of them; the contents were scattered in disarray, adding to the chaos he'd sensed earlier.

He was inundated with the scents of several jaguar shifters, and his mouth watered as they mingled with the overlying odor of death. It permeated the entire area, and quickly his eyes scanned the immediate vicinity, trying to locate its source.

He could see nothing.

Cautiously Jagger crept forward, his powerful frame low to the ground, his great head moving about as his eyes took in every single detail of the mess in front of him. Dark stains along the edges of a ruined tent drew his attention, and cautiously he moved closer, his nose to the ground as tension hung low in his belly.

It was definitely blood, but he felt a huge wave of relief when he realized it didn't belong to the woman he was seeking.

It wasn't human, that he was sure of, and he shook his head slightly as he once more tried to puzzle out the subtle differences. It wasn't something he'd ever come across before.

The camp appeared deserted, and for a few seconds the black jaguar contemplated his next move. There were too many scents intermingled with the sickly stench of death, and it was hard for him to filter out the singular trace he was searching for.

He continued forward and when he spied the body of a downed jaguar, his massive frame froze, as the putrid odor of violence clung to the carcass.

Something terrible had happened here, and his gut roiled at the leftover feelings of terror and pain that shrouded the encampment like a fine mist of misery. His need to find the mystery woman was paramount, and his senses went on high alert.

He had just made it to the far end of the clearing when a sound caught at him, and he whipped his head toward the thick jungle that lined the perimeter opposite him.

Adrenaline rifled through his veins and he loped forward until he cleared the immediate perimeter and plunged into the thick interior once more.

The jungle quieted, and he growled softly as the pangs of frustration threatened to spill out. He slowed his heart rate and concentrated, all of his senses open to any movement whatsoever. He edged toward a rotted mess of downed trees, and when he came abreast of it, his heart took off like a rocket as his body shot a second load of adrenaline hard through his veins.

A struggle had recently occurred and the smell of fear and rage was heavy in the air. He sniffed at a large dark stain that was obviously blood and his mouth lolled open as he tried to force the bitterness of it from his nasal passages.

He studied the ground, and from the looks of things, three different warriors had attacked a single person, a male judging by the footprints.

Jagger followed them, but when they disappeared,

he held back, clearly puzzled. It was as if the person who'd been attacked had vanished into thin air. A feeling of unease washed over him, and for the first time in a long time, he was truly stumped. He couldn't make sense of the clues left in the jungle.

Some serious shit had gone down here recently, bad mojo all around. He had a feeling black magick was at play, maybe heavily involved.

He barked once, low and soft. The need to find the blond woman gnawed at his gut with a burn that wouldn't go away. But was it worth it? Should he not just turn around and hightail it back to his cave and forget he ever laid eyes on her?

Any other smart man probably would, but as the late afternoon sun began to wane, Jagger knew he wasn't out here playing it smart. He was out here because *he needed to be*. He knew that his self-imposed exile was about to end. He could feel it, deep in his bones, and surprisingly, he was okay with it.

His gut clenched in excitement. In fact, he was more than okay with it.

Should he run away? Move on?

The questions flew into his mind and were discarded equally as fast. He snarled and flexed the powerful muscles in his body.

He was a Castille and would not leave a lone woman out here in the jungle at the mercy of the pack of shifters he'd come across. Indeed the blood that pounded through his body literally sang the warrior chant.

He realized then that he'd been too long from the fight. He craved it like food, and as a loud growl erupted from deep within his chest, he welcomed the chance to meet it headlong.

Fortunately for the great cat, the battle was about

to land in his lap, as a scream that could wake the dead sliced through the quiet jungle and a flash of blond streaked at him from his right.

He had no time to react. He took the hit, cushioning the body that had lain so close to him only hours earlier.

They rolled together into the warm moist earth, and Jagger twisted in an effort to avoid the deadly looking machete that was aimed, straight and true, toward his groin. It wasn't easy. The satchel was still entwined along his body and he immediately called the mist to him, his great paws doing their best to avoid slashing the soft, creamy skin that was now trapped between them.

The little hellion was swearing viscously, and he felt the burn of metal through flesh as she successfully nicked his left leg. His growl erupted into a full-blown curse as his human form shimmered and the fur fell from his limbs to reveal a long expanse of muscled limbs.

"Jesus Christ, hold still."

She tried to bite his forearm and Jagger felt his patience wear thin, as her leg aimed for the delicate area between his legs.

There was no way in hell he'd let her get anywhere near his balls again.

He grunted as he tossed her onto her back, and was on top of her in less than a second, her arms splayed out above her head and held captive by his own.

She struggled and he was surprised at the strength she possessed, but he tried not to hurt her as he looked down into the bluest eyes he'd ever seen. They were huge, startling in their clarity, as if cut from a sapphire.

And they were pissed.

Christ, pissed didn't even come close to describing the fury that shadowed the beautiful depths a much darker shade. A fury that only deepened as the seconds ticked by.

He studied her in silence, noticing for the first time the pain that clung to her features as well. Her emotions were laid bare for him and they caught at his gut. Slowly he relaxed his grip on her arms and felt a tug of admiration as her eyes flashed resentment and she continued to struggle against him.

He had to admit, the woman had spunk. But spunk wouldn't keep her safe from the jaguars that were hot on her trail.

"You're going to have to kill me, asshole. I'll never let you take me again."

The words slipped from her tongue with a snarl. Jagger kept the smile he felt inside from manifesting itself. He somehow knew that would piss her off even more.

Instead he remained quiet and took his time studying her features before his gaze traveled down to where her chest heaved against the thin fabric of a faded T-shirt. A vision of her straining breasts, plastered to the white tank top she'd worn the previous night, danced in front of his eyes and he tore his gaze away, needing a moment to collect his thoughts.

When his eyes met hers once more he felt a perverse pleasure as her heart rate increased with rapid precision, and her cheeks flushed pink as she took notice of his nakedness, pressed so intimately against her body.

He couldn't help himself and a sly grin wavered around the corners of his mouth, but the rush of heat that flooded his dick soon took the smile away.

"You're the shifter from last night." Her eyes narrowed and while still ringed with fear, they seemed confused.

Jagger paused and then nodded. "Yeah, and uh, you're welcome for saving your ass." His face darkened slightly as he continued. "And thanks for the knock in the nuts this morning, nothing like a shot to the balls to really wake you up."

The woman beneath him again struggled and cursed loudly, and Jagger applied just enough pressure with his powerful thighs and arms to keep her still. He didn't trust her one bit, and ignored the slight wince that crossed her delicate features.

He didn't understand any of what was going on, but he knew one thing for sure. The feel of her beneath him was pulling at all sorts of long-repressed desires and his skin burned hot with them.

The more pressure he applied, the more she struggled, and after a few moments she exploded as frustration and fury ate at her.

"What the fuck are you waiting for? Just do it and get it over with. It's not like you left anything for me to come back to."

The misery in her voice gave him pause, and Jagger relented. He leaned back and jumped to his feet, pulling her body along, up with him. They stood close together, her blond head just reaching the top of his shoulder. Her sweet scent clung to his nostrils and he fought the urge to bury his nose in the wild curtain of hair that fell well past her shoulders.

What was it about this woman that called to him so?

He felt her body tremble and a small gasp escaped from between her lips as she spied the satchel that was strung across his powerful shoulders. He watched as her eyes studied the tattoos that were so proudly on display, and the muscles in his abs tightened as her gaze slid over his body.

"You're not DaCosta."

She inhaled raggedly and he felt a bolt of electricity shoot through him as her eyes slowly traveled up and met his. She'd successfully hidden her emotions in the blue depths, but the telltale blush of pink still stained her golden cheeks.

She was like a goddess straight from an island of sunshine, all tawny, lush curves, golden skin, and liquid-gold hair.

Her mention of the jaguar shifters rudely brought his fantasies to a halt. The woman was in danger, inviting the wrath of one of the most ruthless warrior clans that existed and he didn't even know her name.

Seemed he should, considering he was about to plunge headlong into another war with the DaCostas, and he didn't even know why. He only knew that this woman needed his help and protection.

And he was willing to give it. Hell, every cell in his body was electrified at the thought of battle.

"Who are you?"

Once more Jagger inhaled her sweet scent as his question hung in the air between them.

She ignored it, and tried to grab the satchel away from him.

He easily kept it from her, and frowned as once more her trace signature felt foreign to him. She wasn't wholly human, that was for sure. But what the hell was she?

"*What* are you?"

That question caught her off guard, and she stilled, her eyebrows rose incredulously.

"What kind of game is this now?" she huffed, and laughed harshly as she repeated his question: "*What am I*? You are joking, right?"

Her surprise soon sobered as she continued to study him, and for the first time he felt her relax somewhat.

"Why didn't you kill me when you had the chance?"

"Kill you? Christ, killing you was the last thing on my mind—in case you didn't notice."

Her gaze dropped down the length of his naked body and rested briefly on his already tightening cock. Jagger bit his lip and forced his body to calm. He was starting to feel like a yo-yo and this woman was pulling his string.

Her blue eyes again met his and the force of the emotions that colored them nearly took his breath away.

"You don't know what I am." She moved away, her eyes never leaving the precious satchel that he still held. "How can that be?"

"Look, I don't give a shit what you are." He frowned and his voice deepened. "The DaCostas have been a pain in my ass for a long time, and by the looks of it, I'm the only thing standing between you and about twenty jaguar warriors."

Worry furled her brow and he felt like groaning as her tongue absently licked the luscious red of her lips. "They must have attacked when I was exploring the cave yesterday." Frantically her gaze wandered the ruined camp and she whispered softly, "If they've killed Finn . . ."

Her voice trailed off and he could see she was upset.

"They had a prisoner; he looked pretty roughed up but was alive."

"Was he a tall blond man?"

The look of yearning in her eyes left a bad taste in his mouth and Jagger swallowed hard before answering.

"No, it was an older gentleman."

Her audible sigh of relief was short lived; she quickly ran to what was left of a large tent. She reemerged a few moments later and tossed a worn pair of jeans, boots, and T-shirt at him.

"These belong to Finn. You're about the same height and build."

He raised his eyebrows but accepted the clothes nonetheless. The small flesh wound she'd inflicted on the inside of his thigh was already healing, and he caught a blush forming as they locked eyes. She looked away, muttering, "don't expect an apology."

Once he was fully clothed, he stood silently watching her while she gathered up a few more things from the scattered remains of the camp. Jagger could tell she was trying to act nonchalant, but it was obvious she was dying to get her hands on the satchel and all of the maps and detailed notes that were safe inside.

When she was done, he held out the satchel, his dark green eyes holding hers with a direct stare.

"Do you want this?"

He could feel her heartbeat and the rush of blood begin to churn throughout her system, and it only confirmed what he was starting to suspect. The notes held information that the DaCostas were willing to kill for.

She paused as if afraid to speak and jumped when he continued speaking. "I'll give it to you, on one condition."

"And what's that?"

"I need a name, I want to know what the hell you are, *and for the record* you still owe me."

Her blue eyes flashed in anger and she very nearly

spat at him. "Owe you? What the hell do I owe you?"

Jagger smiled softly. "If we're gonna be working together I'm thinking we need to start this operation *even Stevens*." He watched her eyes narrow as he moved toward her, and admired her spunk when she refused to move.

"You sound like we're fifth graders out playing some stupid game at recess." Her gaze fell to his lips and he smiled.

"It may be stupid, but I'm thinking my earlier injury requires a bit of payback." Her eyes lowered and his grin widened even more.

Her voice was husky. "What is it that you wanted?"

"Let me show you," he murmured, and without hesitation claimed the mouth that had been taunting him, *calling to him*, awakening a hunger that was so deep it was almost painful.

He groaned softly into her sweetness, and deep inside, the cat growled in pleasure.

Chapter 4

The feel of his lips against hers was like the sweetest sin imaginable.

What the hell was she doing?

Skye opened her mouth in protest and his tongue immediately plunged inside. To say she was shocked would have been an absolute understatement. She was stunned. Horrified, actually. And *that* was because the sensations that slid over her body sent shivers spinning out from deep inside, until her flesh broke out in a mess of goose bumps.

She *liked* the feel of his mouth skating across hers. *A lot.*

Reality had taken a vacation.

An alien had invaded her body.

Surely that was the reason she had lost control of her faculties. If she *were* in control, there was no way she would let the jaguar get this close to her. *Again.*

And man, he was close. His scent was potent, pure,

raw and full of power. To make matters worse, he tasted even better than he smelled. She fought against the waves of pleasure that sprang to life, and against her will, she felt her insides melt at each pass of his tongue.

For a second, everything faded away, and there was nothing but his hardness, *his incredible maleness*, and a raw need that clawed at her in a most painful way.

But then, like a slap in the face, reality came crashing through the dense fog that had clouded her judgment, and she fought him, her fingers digging into his forearms in an effort to push him away. She could feel his reluctance and sighed raggedly when his arms left her body and his mouth slowly fell from her lips.

What the hell was wrong with her? Skye knew that she should be running as fast and as hard as she could in the other direction.

Jaguars bad—eagles good; plain and simple, they were her enemy. That's what she had grown up believing.

It had been her mantra for as long as she could remember. But, there was something about this particular jaguar that gave her pause. And that was rare.

This tall, dark, sexy specimen . . . what was it about him that changed all of that? She couldn't explain it, even if she tried. There was an intangible feeling that he could be trusted, and truth be told, it's not like she had any other options at this point.

The camp had been attacked. Sam was a prisoner, and Finn? A sob caught in her throat as she thought of her brother. She could only hope and pray that Finn had managed to escape unharmed and at this very moment was hidden in the undergrowth—waiting and biding his time.

She took a few more moments to catch her breath and watched him move away, his hands still holding fast to the satchel.

"I believe you have something that belongs to me."

At her words the jaguar warrior raised an eyebrow and smiled rakishly. "I believe I need a name first."

She narrowed her eyes, not liking the little game he was playing, but she answered him, the word falling from her lips softly. "Skye."

"Does Skye have a last name?"

"Knightly." She reached for the satchel but it was held just beyond her fingertips.

There was no time to waste and if she had to beg, so be it.

"Please, I . . . I don't have a lot of time." She knew she sounded desperate but didn't care. She watched his green eyes darken as he regarded her in silence, and then he handed the bag over.

She grabbed it quickly to her body. The soft leather felt good against her skin and a plethora of emotion threatened to break free as her fingers clung to the worn satchel.

The man continued to study her with his dark, fathomless eyes. They were unsettling.

His voice when he spoke was low and the timbre that rang through his words was full of strength.

"We need to get going. The jaguars are furious that two DaCostas were killed last night." He paused. "Guess we're both responsible for that."

"We?" she asked softly, not liking where things were headed.

Skye felt the beginnings of panic in the pit of her stomach. It was like a lead ball that stuck hard and fast to her insides, and she felt queasy from the force of it. She tried to quell her anxiety, but her breaths came short and fast and she was beginning to feel light-headed. She closed her eyes and centered herself, reaching deep for a sense of calm.

Now was not the time to fall apart and as the moments ticked by, she welcomed the brave eagle that lay in wait, so very deep inside of her. It was time to meet her fate head-on, and to carry through her mission.

There was so much left for her to do and if she failed . . . Skye shuddered at the thought, slamming the door shut on the wanderings of her mind. She couldn't go there. She *would not* fail.

She would succeed or die trying.

She grimaced at that thought. How ironic, really, considering she would *have* to die in order to succeed. To seal the portal and keep the demon underworld from invading the human realm, she would have to give the ultimate sacrifice.

Her very life.

She turned away from the warrior, not wanting him to see any form of weakness, but when his warm hands grazed her back she froze.

"I won't let them hurt you."

For just one moment, Skye wanted nothing more than to fall back into his chest and wrap herself around his strong, warm body. *Just for one moment.*

But then she shook such feelings aside and pulled away from his touch. There was much to do. "We'll need some food . . . and I need a name too."

The smile that was still lingering around his handsome face was starting to irritate her, but when he spoke, there was no denying the animal magnetism the warrior possessed.

"The name's Castille, Jagger Castille."

Skye stilled and her eyes widened. The dude was a joker. Not what she would expect of a jaguar.

"I know what you're thinking, but what would you say if I told you my favorite drink was a martini, shaken and not stirred?"

She smiled in spite of herself. A Bond joke, no less. His electric green eyes seemed to glisten and sparkle as he raised his eyebrows questioningly.

"I suppose you drive an Aston Martin as well?" Crap. Was that her voice? What the hell was wrong with her? The grin that lit his face was devastating and Skye felt her mouth go dry. She gave herself a mental shake, and cleared her throat. "I'd say you were full of shit."

His laughter echoed into the quiet jungle. It was hearty, intoxicating in its freedom. "Actually, I prefer whiskey and I drive a battered pickup truck." He winked at her, and just like that, Skye admitted to herself that she, an elite eagle knight, would accept help from her natural born enemy.

She turned from him abruptly and ran to the tattered remains of one of the tents, reemerging a few minutes later loaded down with two large bags of supplies. She threw one at Jagger and hiked her satchel securely around her shoulder, grasping the remaining bag of supplies in her other hand.

"So, do you have a hideout or something? They already know of your cave."

She watched Jagger as he paused before answering, and tried to ignore the sexy ghost of a smile that touched his incredible lips.

"Yeah, or *something*."

Something caught his attention then and he whipped his head around, his entire demeanor suddenly changing. Power and danger clung to his hard frame like a second skin. He reeked with the potency of it. She could see a muscle working along his jaw and the air between them exploded with energy. It rippled through the air in waves. His nostrils quivered as an eerie howl rent the air, echoing down into the valley from the large mountain that loomed in the distance.

Skye swallowed thickly and tried to ignore the slash of terror that shot through her body. The jaguars were on the hunt and she had, *maybe,* an hour or so head start.

"We head east." Jagger spoke softly, but the steely resolve that laced his words lent credence to the severity of the situation. For the first time, she realized just how much shit this man was getting himself into.

"You don't need to come with me." She shook her head, trying to get him to understand. "In fact it might be better if we just parted ways—"

"You're going to have to try a lot harder than that to get rid of me."

Her eyes followed him as he turned to the east, his handsome face lit with a harsh smile that was anything but subtle. The man was certifiably crazy. He *looked* like he was actually enjoying the whole experience of being on the run with a total stranger, just one step ahead of a pack of rabid jaguar shifters. When he paused and raised his eyebrows at her, indicating that she should follow, Skye knew she was in trouble.

Christ, was she in trouble.

It had nothing whatsoever to do with that fact that her life was in danger, or that if she didn't complete her father's mission, well, mankind would suffer the consequences. Yeah, *that* was deep shit.

But this—this was something else entirely, and it had everything to do with the fluttery butterflies that were winging their way through her already unsettled stomach. Those pesky little butterflies were there because of the tall, dark man who was still staring at her in a way that made her insides tremble.

She exhaled softly and without another word followed him, praying to every god imaginable that she wasn't making the biggest mistake of her life.

He was fast and she was happy to see that she had no trouble whatsoever keeping up with him. They literally flew through the dense underbrush and more than once she silently wished she could call to her eagle and take flight, but the sun had already begun to fade and evening was fast approaching.

Besides, she believed that Jagger truly had no clue what she was. Oh, he was curious and he obviously knew that she was not human, but so far, he'd not pressed her further.

They began to make their way up the side of a steep mountain. The going was rough and the trail they took tricky, but they kept up a demanding pace, knowing that the jaguar warriors were somewhere below, hunting and tracking. They swam through several streams and one fast-flowing river, and Skye was confident that their trail could not be followed.

Well, at least not easily.

A few hours later, darkness had indeed fallen, coating the jungle in its velvety softness. Jagger stopped just ahead of her and she came up beside him, her chest heaving after the rough climb up. A flicker of annoyance crept over her features when she noted the man had hardly broken a sweat.

He pointed a few hundred feet higher, and even

though her raptor eyes afforded her enhanced vision, she was puzzled.

"I'm not sure what I'm supposed to be looking at."

Jagger grabbed her and pulled her after him, his enthusiasm reminding her of a child who had a secret to share.

"Where are we going?" Skye knew she sounded petulant but damn it, she was tired, running on fumes, and for some reason he was irritating the crap out of her.

"This is my *something*."

A flash of white drew her attention to his incredible mouth, and the smile that slashed through the night was devastating. Her belly did a little flip, as slowly, her eyes wound their way up to his, and she swallowed hard. The man was like a freaking god; all hard muscle and chiseled features. Why were the dangerous ones always so incredibly sexy?

"Um, *your something*?" God, did she have to sound like a complete idiot?

He actually laughed at that and she found an answering smile gracing her own tired features.

"My hideout."

A lightbulb suddenly went off in her head and she studied the rock formation more closely, for the first time noticing that the shadowing was different amongst the layers.

There was an opening there!

Adrenaline pumped through her body and she eagerly followed him up toward the entrance. After climbing along a steep ledge she followed him through an opening that was only wide enough to allow one body at a time. You could literally blink and miss it.

It really was the perfect hideout.

Once inside, cool air wafted over her and she was suddenly blind from a wall of darkness. It weighed heavily on her. She felt claustrophobic and her heart rate sped up as she struggled to inhale a deep breath.

"Take it easy, breathe nice and slow."

Skye felt Jagger's breath on her face and was startled at his close proximity. Heat spiraled up from her belly spreading fire in a slow burn. It didn't sit well with the intense feelings that were messing with her head. Instead of feeing reassured that such a strong ally was close by, she felt incredibly vulnerable. His fingers slid from her cheek to her shoulder and down along her arm until he grasped her hand tightly.

"You can't see around me but the opening gets wider a few hundred yards ahead of us. Did you throw flashlights in these bags?"

"Yeah," she whispered.

Jagger squeezed her fingers. "When we have more room, I'll grab one."

Skye let him lead her down the stone corridor and while grateful for the guidance, she was extremely resentful that she needed him so, and wanted nothing more than to wrench her fingers from his grasp.

She tried to clear her mind and not think about the dark, and the fact that thousands of tons of solid rock surrounded her. She did not do well in closed, confined spaces. The months that she'd been held captive at the DaCosta compound, chained like a dog in a small shack, had been some of the most trying and difficult times she'd ever gone through.

She was an eagle and was used to the open air, the sky and the kiss of the sun.

And though she'd been out in the jungles of Belize for the past two months, exploring caves of all sizes, she'd not been this tightly entombed within one before.

After a few moments the passage opened up a bit more and she was able to breathe easier. When they finally emerged into a small chamber, she pulled her hand from Jagger's.

She waited while he grabbed a flashlight from his bag and when he flicked it on she took a few steps away from him. Ignoring the amused look that swept over his handsome features, she slowly examined the room, grateful that she was finally able to see.

To say that she was disappointed would have been an understatement.

"This is it?"

The words slipped from her mouth before she had a chance to censor herself, and she winced at the childish tone that accompanied them.

A deep chuckle broke from the warrior and she felt his laughter fall over her like warm chocolate.

"No, Skye, this isn't it."

The sound of her name coming from his lips flushed every inch of her body in a wave of heat. He moved toward her, but she refused to back away, and clenched her hands together as his head lowered toward hers. She inhaled sharply as his mouth rested against her cheek, and his breath against her skin sent tiny shivers of electricity burning down her neck.

"A little patience."

He pulled her after him once more, and just like that, his warmth and the tingles that had spread in little shock waves over her limbs receded. They began to navigate around a large piece of stone that was circular, which suggested the influence of man, and it was also smooth on top. It looked somewhat like a ceremonial altar, and she paused, running her fingers over the cold stone, wondering what it had been used for, so many years in the past.

Reluctantly she let go and they continued down another passageway that opened up into a much larger chamber, several hundred feet farther into the mountain.

It was magnificent and Skye clutched her satchel close to her body as she simply stood back and stared up into the enormous cavern. The air was cool, damp, and she shivered slightly at the shadows that played against the walls.

She could hear Jagger rustling about a few feet away, and when he lit a large torch, the natural beauty of the cave took her breath away. The firelight did so much more for the space than the artificial beam from the flashlight.

Skye had been searching through so many incredible caves in the last few months, and the sheer beauty and unique structure of each one she'd recorded never failed to impress her. Nature was an amazing thing.

There were remnants of pottery strewn about, but there was nothing to indicate that this was anything other than a cave used by ancient Mayans thousands of years earlier. Impressive from an archeological standpoint, yes, and at one time Skye would have been all over the importance of that, but her mission was simple. She needed to find one specific cave only.

Her gaze rested once more on the jaguar warrior as he set about building a small fire in the ancient pit that was dead center in the cave. He had obviously spent a great amount of time out here in the jungle, exploring. Would he know of the cave she sought?

Excitement sizzled through her as she thought of

the possibility that he might have knowledge of the Cave of the Sun. Could it be as simple as that?

The more important question, however, was, could she trust him?

He straightened suddenly, and his stare pierced hers with a directness that shot like a spike of adrenaline straight to her heart. It took off like a rocket, the muscle working hard and fast in reaction to the heated look that burned so deeply in his eyes.

Jagger Castille looked like a predator as he stood silent, watching her closely.

Something deep inside of her body was screaming to answer in kind, but Skye turned away abruptly and walked over to a long, low stone bench. She sat down and looked at her feet.

Who the hell was she kidding? Could she trust him. Please! The real question was, *could she trust herself?*

They shared a sparse meal in quiet, without further conversation, and after several long minutes Skye grabbed a blanket from her bag and laid it upon the hard stone surface. She frowned in dismay, but beggars couldn't be choosers, and quickly stretched out her tired body.

"So, you gonna tell me what this is all about?" he asked suddenly.

Skye bit her lip. There was so much to tell, but she couldn't share it. "It's complicated."

"Yeah, I got that."

Silence fell between them once more but Skye found her mind wandering and she surprised herself when she spoke aloud. "Why are you out here? I mean, in the jungle living in that cave."

"It's complicated," he answered, and she smiled to herself. *Touché.*

"Things had become too . . . hard and I just found it easier to chill in the jungle and try and forget." She heard him move restlessly before continuing. "It's been almost a year since I came back. I don't think I'll ever be able to forget."

"Came back?"

The warrior paused and his voice was rough as he continued. "Iraq. Afghanistan."

Skye turned her head and met his gaze, swallowing a lump at the pain she could see in his eyes. It was there and gone just as fast. Seemed her jaguar had his own demons to wrestle.

He turned from her and she settled back down, drawing the blanket up for warmth. She was tired, cold, and shaking. Her mind turned in circles, her thoughts a mad collage of her mission, the portal, Finn, and not surprisingly, the jaguar.

Jagger Castille was a man with many layers, and as she pondered them, her eyes began to get heavy and moments later she was asleep.

Skye wasn't sure how long she'd been out, and she wasn't entirely sure what woke her.

She'd been deep in dreamland, however, and it had not been a pleasant visit. Her skin was clammy and cold from sweat. She arched her neck and pushed away the damp mass of hair that was sticking to her flesh. Her fast-beating heart actually hurt her chest, and she pressed trembling hands against her rib cage in an effort to stop it.

She'd had nightmares on and off for as long as she could remember. She'd go weeks without one, months even, but they always returned. The nightmares were a constant in her life that she could count on, without fail. The dreams were always the same: blurred images and overwhelming feelings of despair, terror, and pain.

As a young girl she would crawl into bed with her brother Finn, and he'd tell stories until late into the night, and eventually the terror would fade and she'd be able to fall asleep. It was as much a part of her life as breathing, really, and she'd learned to deal with the terror, to compartmentalize the intense feelings it brought to the surface.

But even she was having difficulty dealing with the frequency of the nightmares and the abject horror that had accompanied them in recent months. They'd started to intensify when she'd been held captive in the DaCosta compound. Many a night she'd woken, drenched in sweat, and by the end of her captivity she had a name to go along with her dreams: Azaiel.

She was unsure if he was real, or what the dreams meant, but she'd woken several times with the distinct impression that he'd touched her. Lain beside her.

That her dream demon was calling to her. That he wanted something.

Tiredly, Skye opened her eyes. She blinked slowly, waiting for her sleep-deprived brain to adjust. The soft glow from the torch that had been lit earlier reflected weirdly against the uneven rock face of the cavern. Shadows danced wickedly and she shuddered, suddenly wanting nothing more than to leave. She was lying on a stone ledge, with only the comfort of a wool blanket to cushion the solid surface.

Turning her head she winced as sharp pains shot down her neck and across her stiff shoulders. A small groan escaped and echoed across the vast cavern. She was suddenly aware that she was very much alone, and she twisted her body around as she frantically searched for Jagger.

But he was nowhere to be seen. The pallet he'd made for himself in the corner, opposite where she lay, was empty.

Skye jumped off the hard ledge and stretched out stiff muscles. The silence in the large cave was deafening, and she found herself fighting the urge to cover her ears with her hands.

Suddenly remembering her precious satchel, she breathed a huge sigh of relief as her fingers felt the familiar strap slung across her shoulders. She opened it up, just to make sure, and was relieved to see that all of her maps and notes were safe and secure.

She was so deep into the mountain, it was impossible to figure out what time it was, but if she were to hazard a guess, she'd say it was a few hours before dawn. She reveled in the strength she gained as Mother Sun slowly crept through the darkness.

But where the hell was the jaguar? Had he betrayed her? Was he at this very moment colluding with the DaCostas? Certainly they'd pay handsomely for her capture. They needed her in order to get their slimy paws on the portal.

The panic she'd felt earlier resurfaced as her thoughts continued to swirl. Skye had never felt so desperate and alone in her entire life. She didn't like it. Not one bit.

She was an eagle knight, for God's sakes. She should not be counting on a jaguar to protect her.

What the hell had she been thinking? It was time for her to put her big-girl pants on and get the show on the road.

Quickly she gathered up the bag of supplies that

she'd dropped when she'd first arrived. She eyed the remaining bag that Jagger had carried, but realized it would just weigh her down. She'd travel much faster and farther, the less that she had to carry.

Once she had both her supplies and her satchel slung across her shoulders, Skye hesitated for a second. She needed to get a move on and leave before Jagger came back. Whether he was alone or with the entire Da-Costa clan, he'd be dangerous.

The sad fact was, she wasn't sure which scenario scared her more.

The thought of sliding her body back through the tiny opening didn't much appeal to her, and she swung curious eyes toward several chambers that led from the large cavern.

Moisture led her to believe that there was indeed another way out of the cavern. Walking toward the far end of the huge open space, Skye closed her eyes and concentrated with all her might, hoping for a sign.

She felt the briefest whisper of warmth flood her mind, and the feelings were so welcome they brought tears to her eyes. Her father always came to her in her darkest moments, and she believed with all of her heart that he was leading her in the right direction.

Her eyes snapped open and she turned to a tunnel that was half hidden by huge staccato slices of rock. Immediately, Skye grabbed the torch and exhaled softly as she disappeared into the dark depths.

Chapter 5

A soft breeze slipped through the underbelly of the jungle, ruffling the ferns, bushes, and branches of the low-lying greenery. Warm moist air caressed Jagger's face as he slid through the dark interior.

It was near daybreak. He could feel the change. It made him jumpy, nervous as all hell. He'd been too long in the jungle and the urge to get back to Skye was playing on him heavily.

Jagger had waited patiently for her to fall asleep the night before, and once he'd been certain that she was down for the count, he'd left.

Like the deadly hunter that he was, he'd slipped silently through the jungle, stalking the enemy, and he'd made quick work of three of them. Adrenaline from the kills still rushed through his veins and he trembled slightly at the intensity of it all.

He'd been much too long from the fight.

Jagger had spent the remainder of the evening dragging his ass over three square miles in an effort to engulf the entire area in his scent and throw the warriors off of his trail. Wearily, he ran a hand through the thick hair at his nape and stretched taut shoulders. He was exhausted and would love nothing more than to get some rest himself, but he knew that was impossible. The warriors were already on the move.

He needed to get Skye the hell out of the jungle.

From what he'd witnessed, the jaguar shifters would not rest until they had the elusive blonde in their custody.

Jagger rolled his head around, loosening the tense cords of muscle at his neck. She'd not given anything up the night before. He still had no clue why the Da-Costas were after her, but truthfully, he didn't care. It was enough that they were involved. He'd not felt this alive in a long time.

His eyes swept the immediate area one last time before he turned his body south. It was time to go.

The first shafts of sunlight were just beginning to feather their way across the horizon when he arrived at the foot of the rock face that led to his hideout. He paused and let the cool, damp mist crawl over his heated flesh.

Something tingled at the edge of his mind and Jagger stilled as a foreign scent rifled its way down his lungs. His nostrils flared and he felt his heart speed up as he recognized the scent for what it was.

Magick. *Otherworld magick,* and the darkness that accompanied it left no doubt whatsoever that it wasn't the friendly type. It was the kind that tightened his belly and raised his blood pressure.

Fear began to beat at him, not for himself but for the lone woman he'd left behind, and Jagger cursed as he quickly swept up the steep mountain and disappeared into the hidden crevice.

His nocturnal eyes quickly adjusted to the thick darkness and he immediately crept forward, his stealth and agility enabling him to glide through the gloom without making a sound. Every single muscle in his body was tense, and Jagger's agitation grew as the stink of otherworld magick became stronger.

It loosened up memories, long buried, and as he moved forward down the narrow passage a collage of images stumbled through his brain. Explosions. Blood. Black night. *And death.* Jagger stopped, his hands braced against the cold, damp wall of the cave.

He took a few seconds and slowly calmed his fast-beating heart, but the pain that the memories left in their wake was wicked. It knifed through him and even though he shook his head savagely, he couldn't forget the haunting images of another female, a member of his team in Iraq. Eden.

She'd foolishly trusted him with her life, yet had come back from war zipped tight inside a body bag.

Anger then replaced the pain and it flushed hard through his body as Jagger savagely pushed his bulk away from the cool rock wall. He would not lose another in his care.

He would die before that happened.

He let the anger feed his soul, snarling into the darkness.

Jagger turned quickly and slid through the blackness, his feet gliding over the floor in silence as he melted into the shadows. He retraced his steps from the night before, coldly putting aside the intensity of his emotions as he concentrated on the scents that lingered still.

He wasn't anywhere near the large cavern where they'd made camp but Skye's intoxicating odor drifted over him, teasing him with its subtle flavor.

It wasn't alone.

The smell of otherworld continued to grow stronger, and Jagger quickened his pace, his thoughts deadly, his intentions even more so.

Within minutes he reached the opening of the smaller chamber and sped past, disappearing through yet another passage before silently slipping into the huge cavern where he'd left Skye.

It appeared to be empty. Jagger paused, his senses on full alert. After a few seconds he was positive that there was nothing more dangerous than silence.

He quickly crossed to where he'd left his bag and withdrew a flashlight. Seconds later he turned around, bathing the cave in an eerie glow of artificial light.

His eyes quickly scanned the interior as he carefully made his way deeper into the chamber. The stone ledge where Skye had fallen asleep held no trace of the woman at all. He could sense nothing except the lingering scent of his enemies.

There was something strangely familiar about the trace signatures of the magick that hung in the air like a dark cloud. It gave him pause, but Jagger filed it away just as quickly. It was another piece of the puzzle that he would deal with later.

He had no time for the details. He needed to get to Skye.

Jagger knelt down, his fingers slowly caressing the earthen floor, and was barely able to make out the imprint of what was, undoubtedly, a large male footprint. It shadowed the smaller outline of Skye's. The evidence was unmistakable, and savagely he scattered the soft covering of dust until there was nothing left.

Jagger sprang to his feet as the urgency of the situation hammered at him. He grabbed his satchel, swung it over his shoulder, and turned toward the openings along the far side of the chamber.

Both sets of footprints led to the last one on the right, and he knew from previous explorations that it was the only other tunnel that led to the outside.

Jagger stowed the flashlight. His animal quieted as a deadly calm washed over him and settled against his chest. His eyes quickly adjusted to the dark again and he growled softly. He turned and crossed to the passage.

It was time to hunt.

The damp air that permeated the area was cooler inside the tunnel, its smell old and musty. Jagger inhaled deeply and slipped through the passage, his steps sure, his body tight with power and intent.

He'd trod the exact same steps not more than two weeks earlier, and he made his way through the narrow crevice easily, his senses inflamed as Skye's soft scent lingered in the air, urging him forward.

He wasn't sure how much of a head start she had and he pushed his body to a relentless pace, his thoughts centered on the otherworlder who was hot on her heels. He needed to get to her before the enemy did.

There was no other option.

It took him almost a full two hours to push through the passageway; sometimes he was barely able to squeeze his large bulk through the narrow chasm that led to the outside. By the time he neared the end of the tunnel, his body was slick with sweat and trembling with the need to act.

Up ahead Jagger could see the soft glow of light that fell in from outside and he slowed a bit, his mind and body cautious even as he fought the urge to rush forward.

Slowly Jagger approached the exit, his senses flying outward, looking for any hint of danger. Satisfied that the coast was clear, he slipped outside and stood near the base of the mountain, surrounded on all sides by lush jungle.

It was thick, green, and carpeted the landscape for miles. Overhead the blue sky held a radiant sun and Jagger's chilled skin welcomed the warmth as it enveloped him whole. It was early yet and already the air was filled with humidity.

Without a doubt it was gonna be a bitch of a day.

His gaze fell on the ground at his feet, and once more, footprints in the earth were like a beacon, leading him forward until the jungle swallowed him whole.

Once Jagger was deep into the undergrowth, he focused on the mission at hand. He knew he was gaining on Skye and the otherworlder, and Jagger's cool facade hid a growing anger that was building in his gut.

Anger at himself for leaving her behind. It would be the last time.

He followed the trail for well over another hour and as time marched on he began to feel panicked. What if he was too late? What if the otherworlder harmed Skye?

The need to get to her was clawing at his insides with such force that it was becoming a physical pain inside of him. When he crested a small knoll, Jagger paused and scented the air, adrenaline rushing through him in a dizzying assault when he realized he was almost upon them. He could literally taste the black energy that rode the wind and he knew the source of it was close at hand.

He swung his head back and forth and after a few seconds began to melt into the darkness that lay along the jungle floor. They were just ahead, to his right.

Everything but his target faded away and the calm that settled over him was like a neon sign, proclaiming to all the deadly predator that he truly was. This is what he was made for. The hunt. The fight.

Voices drifted on the air. The deep timbre of a male mingled with the distinct, melodic sound of Skye's.

Carefully, silently, Jagger crept along the jungle floor, his human body melting into the earth as easily as his animal. His eyes stared through the thick foliage, their piercing green countenance unwavering, and when he finally spied his quarry, his body stilled, poised to pounce.

But the scene before him was not what he'd expected. In fact the growing anger that clutched at his midsection shattered, erupting into a tangible, living thing and it took every ounce of control he had to maintain his silent presence.

Skye and the otherworlder were in profile and she seemed not to be scared at all. In fact, considering her hand rested upon his forearm, she seemed a little too comfortable. It pissed Jagger off and awakened an emotion he'd not felt in a long time.

Jealousy. Possessiveness. Call it what you will.

And *that* pissed him off even more. What the hell was it about this female that had him running in circles?

"Look, I'll make a deal with you. Tell me where Cormac is and I won't kill you."

Skye's throaty words hung in the air and the man

with her laughed softly before answering. "Chica, you always did have such spunk."

Jagger bit his lip and watched as the man lowered his head until his mouth was mere inches from Skye's.

Son-of-a-bitch! He frowned savagely. Why the hell did he care so much? He'd just met the woman and from what he could tell, she didn't give a rat's ass about him. He should turn and leave her to whatever the hell was coming down on her head.

And yet, he couldn't.

"I could perhaps be persuaded, but I'd require some sort of payment, no?"

"And what would that be?"

Jagger sucked in air, holding the growl at bay. What the fuck was she doing? The man reeked of black magic.

"Oh, I think you know." The otherworlder's voice had deepened and his arms crept up to Skye's shoulders.

The beast inside of Jagger erupted and the control that he'd had disintegrated in less than a second. The snarl that fell from his lips pushed him forward and he leapt to his feet, bursting from the underbrush with a fury that was only matched by the deadly intent in his eyes.

"What the hell?"

The otherworlder whipped his head around and pushed Skye away with a powerful shove. She landed hard and rolled over into a crouch. "Fucking bitch. You set me up."

The man was tall, muscular, with a nasty smile gracing features that were as cold as ice. He also held in his hand a deadly looking weapon and Jagger stalled, noting that the barrel of the gun was pointed directly at Skye.

The black magick Jagger had sensed earlier was

heavy in the air but it was layered with a subtle hint of something else entirely, and while it tugged at his mind, he couldn't quite put his finger on what it was exactly.

"Touch her and I'll rip your head off," Jagger growled.

The man turned his weird silver/gray eyes back to Jagger. They narrowed and he spit into the ground before he spoke. "You're jaguar." He nodded to Skye and shook his head, ignoring the warrior. "Feeling desperate, love? Desperate enough to bed down with the likes of him?"

"Tell me where Cormac is or I'll—"

"You'll what, Skye?" The otherworlder snorted. "Time's almost up and you're on the losing side of this war. He *will* find the portal, and this"—the man waved his hands as the air around him began to shimmer—"this will no longer exist."

Jagger fought the urge to attack. He needed to keep his cool. There was no way he could risk the fucker firing a shot at Skye.

"I wouldn't be so sure about that, Kragen," Skye said as she stood and faced the man.

Alarm shot through Jagger and he was primed to react, to do anything he could to protect the woman, but a vortex of wind, mist, and rain enveloped all of them. It was gone as fast as it had arrived, and with it the otherworlder.

Jagger's tense body shifted as he stood staring into the empty spot where the other man had been. His nostrils wrinkled as the smell of sulfur rent the air. It was putrid, metallic. He was just about to turn toward Skye when instinct had him dropping to the earthen floor, twisting his body as he rolled.

He narrowly avoided the deadly knife that arced through the air. It had been thrown with such force that it became embedded deep in the large trunk of a tree.

He whipped his head around, the snarl that erupted from his mouth matched by the fury that graced the blonde's beautiful features.

"You dumb-ass fucking idiot! Do you know what you just did?" Skye shouted hoarsely, so full of emotion was she. "Kragen could've led me to Cormac."

He watched in silence as she began to pace, shaking her head in agitation. "With Cormac out of the way things would have been so much easier, but now"— her eyes flashed as she whirled around toward him— "you've screwed it all up. What the hell was I thinking hooking up with you? You're a goddamn jaguar, nothing good can come of that!"

Jagger had had enough.

If anyone should be pissed off it was him, not her. Up until the day before his life had been a peaceful, if somewhat lonely, nomadic existence. She was the one who had blown all of that to hell.

He moved so fast, Skye had no time to react. When he grabbed her arms and pulled her in close, he expected to see at least *some* fear deep in her eyes. Instead, the vibrant blue that stared back at him was cloaked in something close to disgust.

Whether she was disgusted at herself or him, he couldn't say. But the fact that she stood rigid in his embrace, looking at Jagger like he was the biggest piece of crap on the planet, totally enraged him.

He could feel the blackness that lived inside of him tickle along the edges of his mind, and his skin began to burn. Energy sizzled along nerve endings, trailing a path of fire all over his body.

"Two things," he said roughly. "I want to know who the hell this Cormac dude is, but more importantly, *what* the hell he is." His hands gripped her tightly and he took some measure of pleasure as she winced in pain.

"And secondly, someone needs a lesson in manners." Jagger's voice dropped into a whisper and he watched closely, feeling a keen sense of satisfaction as she swallowed heavily. He could hear her heart rate increase and her mouth opened slightly as she tried to control the rapid breaths that filled her lungs. She flinched and turned slightly. "Take your hands off me."

Jagger pushed her back until she was trapped between his body and a large tree. He grabbed her chin and forced her to look up at him. "I spent most of last night covering the backs of our asses because I made a decision to protect you." He had to pause as his anger threatened to get the most of him. "Seems to me a little bit of thanks isn't much to ask for."

She spit at him, "Thanks? Are you for real? Well, thanks for nothing. I had a chance at Cormac and now you've totally screwed it."

Skye began to squirm and her face became flush with anger.

Jagger felt his own rage begin to boil and he thought he should do exactly as she wished and leave her the hell alone. Why was he risking his own neck for a total stranger?

And yet, as he held her body even closer, all he could think about was the intoxicating scent that fell from her, and the fact that her skin, slick with the humidity of the jungle, kept the tank top she wore molded to her curves.

His eyes dropped to her breasts and a new heat began to pulse through his body. It was hard, unrelenting.

It felt so fucking good, it was painful.

His body became rock hard and as his eyes bored into the depths of Skye's, he resented the hell out of what she was doing to him.

He could tell himself he wanted her so badly because he'd been alone in the jungle for months. That would make sense. He had needs that were long neglected.

Except there was more to it and he growled in frustration, as the biggest complication he'd encountered in as long as he could remember continued to struggle against him. What was it about her, this particular woman, that he craved so?

She was making him crazy, tapping into the dark part of him that was best left alone.

When she arched her back and tried to bite him, he swore and tightened his grip until she yelped in pain.

"You're no better than the DaCostas," she spit out in between ragged breaths.

"Sticks and stones," Jagger whispered.

"Filthy animal," she replied, and he watched her flinch as the anger he felt toward her words cloaked his face in a cold grimace.

He wanted to hurt her. He wanted her to feel pain.

Jagger flung Skye away from him, suddenly afraid that he would become the very thing she'd just accused him of. The air around him began to shimmer and he could sense the mist beginning to rise against his legs.

He was on the edge.

He closed his eyes, using inhuman strength to still the animal that raged inside of him.

"Get your shit together. We need to leave now if you want half a chance of getting out of this jungle alive," he managed to get out from between clenched teeth. His eyes flew open and he made no attempt to hide his fury. "Because it's crawling with an entire clan of *filthy animals*, and you've got a bull's-eye pretty much tattooed to that pretty blonde head of yours."

"I'm not going anywhere with you."

Jagger raised an eyebrow and laughed harshly. "Is that so?"

He moved toward her, enjoying the panic that was beginning to flicker across her face. "If you think I'm going to leave you at the mercy of the DaCostas you're sadly mistaken." His eyes raked over her form, causing a stain of red to flush her already heated cheeks. "You need my help, and fuck if I know why I'm still willing to give it, but *you will* come with me one way or another. If that means hog-tying you and carrying you out of here on my back, then so be it."

"I will die before I ever let a jaguar pull my strings again." Skye shook her head and Jagger couldn't help but notice how the sunshine played upon the long blond hair that fell around her shoulders. It looked like silken honey.

Her hands pushed the hair behind her ears impatiently and then fell to the edges of her top. Jagger stilled as she pierced him with a look that he couldn't quite read. Her long, elegant fingers began to pull the thin white fabric up over toned, tanned skin and the hard bulge between his legs ached with such a force that he nearly went down to his knees.

What the hell was she doing?

He continued to watch her in silence as the material was pulled up over perfect, luscious breasts, the nipples puckered, begging for his mouth. When she flung the top away and began to slip the loose shorts down over her hips, he hissed from between clenched teeth, not liking the smile that played around her lips.

It was calculating.

Seconds later she stood, basking in the sunlight, naked, wild, and incredibly seductive. Jagger's belly tightened into a nauseating ball as he pulled air into his lungs. His skin burned still and he had to force himself to remain calm. It was one of the hardest things he'd ever had to do.

Considering the only thing on his mind was the need to grab the seductress before him, throw her to the ground, and sink his aching cock deep inside of her.

"You will never have me," Skye said slowly, softly, enunciating her words in such a way that he was hypnotized.

He stepped back, astonished as mist began to curl over her, twisting around her frame, and swirling into a storm that wrapped her entire body in magick.

Seconds later, Jagger stood stunned as a large golden eagle flew from the mist, long deadly claws aimed straight for his head. He had to drop and roll in order to avoid a hit, and when he finally righted himself he looked up into the sky in wonder.

Skye Knightly was an eagle shifter.

And she was leaving him.

Jagger leapt to his feet, his eyes sweeping the area, looking for something, anything he could use to bring the eagle back, and when his gaze fell upon her satchel, he couldn't help the laugh that came from his lips.

The eagle was still circling overhead, her triumphant cry echoing eerily into the humid air.

But when he held the leather bag aloft and grinned up at the magnificent creature, its cries were silenced. Jagger swung the bag around his shoulders and grinned up at her.

"Forget something?" he shouted. He then saluted, before turning toward the mountains in the distance.

Beyond the vast ridge was the promise of warm shores and sandy beaches. The Caribbean Sea was calling to him and he was surprised that there was no reluctance to answer its call.

It was time to go. To leave this place he'd called home for the past three months.

With Skye's precious satchel held firmly in his hands, he cracked a smile and began to move.

He knew she would follow; the eagle couldn't fly forever.

When she eventually came down he'd be waiting.

Chapter 6

Skye's moment of jubilation—that second of *hell yeah, fuck you*—disappeared as quickly as it had come.

She watched helplessly as Jagger held her satchel.

She cursed in silence as he saluted.

And she continued to circle in frustration, feeling impotent rage engulf her, as he smiled up at her wickedly.

When he began to head east, she had no choice but to follow.

What the hell had she been thinking?

She'd not been thinking. That was her problem. She'd reacted entirely on emotion. The jaguar got under her skin, big-time, and like an amateur she'd let him goad her into making one of the stupidest mistakes ever.

For the *second time*, no less.

Furious, she cried loudly, ignoring the answering

laughter that floated on the wind from below. She'd follow the bastard, get her stuff back if it was the last thing she did.

If only she knew where the hell her brother was. Or if Finn was even alive.

Despair threatened to overwhelm her once more and Skye fought it off. There was no time for pity, sadness, or anything other than the task at hand.

She needed to locate the portal. And she needed to do it, like, yesterday.

Things were heating up and there wasn't much time. For Kragen to be involved at this point, Cormac was gearing up for the impending war. Of that there was no doubt.

The stink of demon was already drifting into the human realm, and if the portal was opened, the consequences would be horrendous. Unimaginable.

As she continued to float on the wind, easily following the jaguar below, Skye tried to keep her thoughts focused. But it was so hard. She really had landed smack-dab in the middle of the most important war that would ever affect the human world.

And they had no clue.

Skye continued to follow Jagger for the remainder of the day. He didn't stop once, and in fact kept up a relentless pace. She kept to the top of the canopy, flying low and keeping herself as hidden as she could. She didn't want the enemy spotting her high in the sky.

Off in the distance she could see that he was headed for the coast.

She needed to get her shit and return to her quest. Deep within the Maya Mountains of Belize, the portal lay, long buried, hidden from the eyes of man, magick, and indeed, the eagle shifters who'd been charged with its protection.

Why her father had decided to hide the portal without telling her or Finn was something she didn't understand. But he had died trying to close it and Skye wasn't leaving until she found it.

And sealed it forever.

A small sliver of sadness wove through her then, because truthfully, she was never leaving. Either way, her days were numbered.

If the enemy didn't get to her first, she'd be sucked far into the demon realm when she finally got her hands on the portal and closed it.

Skye tucked her dark thoughts far away into the little holes of her mind that hid such things. She had no time to dwell on them.

In fact as the fading sun began to affect her shifting capabilities, she realized she had no time at all. She was fast losing power.

As she dipped ever lower amongst the trees, Skye was aware that Jagger was a good mile ahead. Hopefully, he'd realize she was no longer following and stop, or she'd have a long night ahead of her, trekking through the jungle.

In the buff.

She felt the ancient magick take hold of her body as limbs elongated, feathers slipped into skin and her human body replaced that of her eagle.

Several seconds later Skye came to a running stop and she paused for a moment, her equilibrium a little out of sorts. She was always thrown slightly off balance when her raptor eyes returned to their much weaker human form. It only lasted for a few seconds, and in fact her eyesight was still much stronger than the average human, but the change threw her for a loop. It was as if a film of mist rolled across her vision and then cleared.

She blew out a deep breath and looked around.

The air was colder down here. It was much damper along the jungle floor and she felt her skin react. Her hands caressed the goose bumps that had spread like a rash across her flesh, and she began to shiver slightly as the heated flesh started to cool.

A howler monkey wailed from several feet away and Skye jumped nervously, her eyes straining to see past the thickening gloom.

Her belly grumbled loudly and she felt frustrated yet again. She was so freaking tired of being hungry, of being hunted, of being in a constant state of unrest. It really was time to get her ass in gear and end this all.

She felt the telltale prick of tears begin at the corners of her eyes and wiped them away angrily. There was no time for weakness.

Skye squared her shoulders, shook out her hair until it fell down past her shoulders in a mess of tawny waves. She turned toward the direction that would lead her to Jagger and seconds later was swallowed whole by the lush greenery that enveloped the jungle floor.

At least two hours later she stopped. Her legs were trembling from exhaustion and lack of food, and the need for water was pounding at her relentlessly.

Skye's skin was slick with sweat and impatiently she wiped her brow, lifting the heavy mass of hair that was now sticking to her neck in an uncomfortable tangle. She was very near the end of her rope, but forced her body to move forward.

She'd just cleared another ridge when she sensed

someone close by. Pulling herself up against a tall tree, Skye melted into the darkness as her eyes scanned the area in front of her. Panic was beginning to beat at her heavily. Was it Jagger? Or had he fled? Left her out here alone and naked?

Long, silent moments went by and Skye began to question her own sanity. Was there anybody out there? Had she imagined it?

She closed her eyes and tried to concentrate, but it was no use. She was done. Used up.

She leaned her body back, resting briefly against the tree as her mind continued to whirl in a jumble of chaotic thoughts.

Several moments later she detected a hint of water in the air and her eyes widened. The thirst that had been stuck at the back of her throat returned with a vengeance and she turned quickly, silently slipping back into the underbrush as she headed toward the water.

She opened up her senses and smiled harshly. The flow of water could be heard somewhere ahead to the right, and Skye quickly switched direction, making haste. She needed food and water, not necessarily in that order.

Seconds later she burst through the thick greenery and was rewarded with a sight for sore eyes.

To her left was a crystal clear flow of water that fell from the mountain that towered behind her. A mere trickle really, but it was enough to fill a rather large basin with the cool, refreshing liquid that her body was craving.

Skye licked her parched lips, whispered a prayer of thanks, and ran gracefully to the edge, her body arcing into perfect form as she dove deeply. The cool wetness slithered over her hot flesh and for a brief moment, her world was perfect.

Brief being the operative word.

She was just about to move forward when alarm bells began to ring from deep inside, her own personal "spidey sense," as it were, and a tingle of awareness shot up her spine.

She was no longer alone.

She held her body still and scanned the embankment along the water. It was empty, and as far as she could see the entire area was the same. But she knew that there was someone out there.

She just didn't know if it was friendly.

Skye treaded water in silence, her nerves as taut as the muscles that clenched her stomach. She slowly made her way toward the far end of the basin, her eyes constantly on the move.

Was it Jagger? Or one of the other shifters that had been hunting her?

She grabbed on to a rock ledge, conserving her energy while she waited. There really wasn't much else that she could do.

Long moments passed and just when she felt like screaming in frustration, movement drew her eyes toward the opposite side of the water basin. There, amongst the darkness, a shape appeared. Tall, undoubtedly male.

He moved toward her with a slow grace that had her heart rate increasing, and she struggled to breathe. Skye bit her lip and remained quiet. When the tall male stepped into a beam of moonlight, the relief she felt was nearly overwhelming.

It was Jagger.

Her relief was short-lived however, once she had an

opportunity to gauge his mood. To say that he was pissed would be an understatement. His handsome face looked down upon her, the features tight, the eyes hard.

Skye's belly did a little flip, and on top of the hunger and exhaustion that she felt, she could now add fear.

Filthy animal.

Her words echoed through her mind and she winced in embarrassment. It had been a cheap shot; she knew he was nothing like the DaCostas and she had a feeling her words would not be so easily forgivable.

Skye inhaled a shaky breath. Crap. Could things be any more complicated? All she wanted was her bag back and to be on her way.

She looked up at the warrior as he stood staring across the water and began to shiver, her teeth clacking against each other. Just because she was scared didn't mean the warrior had to know. She exhaled slowly and stilled her fast-beating heart, drawing on the strength of her eagle.

She gazed back at him boldly and for the hundredth time she had to ask, what in the hell had she gotten herself into?

Jagger's eyes narrowed as he stared down at Skye. She looked like a fucking sea nymph. Her long blond hair floated out around her shoulders, framing her body in a halo of long caramel spikes. Her classic features, enhanced even more with the beauty of the moon caressing her skin, taunted him.

She looked up at him and tilted her chin, just so. It really was a *fuck you* look and he felt a sliver of admiration roll through him, in spite of his dark thoughts.

She should be nervous as all hell. Her arrogance was really astounding.

He felt the anger—which he'd successfully banished in his relentless trek through the jungle—eat at him once more. Jagger clenched his teeth together hard as a muscle worked along the lean line of his jaw.

He could hear the chatter of her teeth and knew that she must be damn near dead on her feet from exhaustion, but it didn't matter.

He smiled wickedly and heard a small gasp escape from between her lips. It was time to teach Skye Knightly a lesson.

She needed to know who was in charge.

Slowly he shed his clothes, his smile growing wider as her eyes did the same. His long, lean body reveled in the feel of night as the humid air slid against his bare skin. When he was naked, he stood at the edge of the water, watching her tread water lightly.

"What . . . what are you doing?" she whispered hoarsely.

Jagger ignored her question and without warning dove into the water, his head cresting the surface before she'd had a chance to react. He heard her yelp and slowly his long arms arced out, slicing through the water, until a few seconds later he was within reach of her.

To her credit, Skye stood her ground. She held on to the ledge, the water slowly lapping at the tops of her breasts as her eyes met his in defiance.

Jagger's own narrowed as he studied the eagle shifter in silence.

He'd heard of them in stories passed down by his mother's family but he'd never come across one before.

Now he wished he'd paid more attention. If he remembered correctly, the eagles had been pretty much wiped out hundreds of years earlier in a war with the jaguars.

His very own ancestors.

For what reason, he couldn't recall but really, it didn't matter. He had no time at all for a history lesson. Major shit was about to hit the fan, and the woman who stared back at him was in the middle of it all.

He moved forward once more. It was time for him to not only teach Skye a lesson, but also to find out exactly what the hell was going on.

"I'm not afraid of you," she said, and though she tried to keep her voice neutral, Jagger could hear the subtle tremor that lay beneath her words.

He kept his mouth shut, enjoying the heaviness of the silence and the darkness it brought with it. He wanted her to feel on edge. Off center.

He stopped when his body was mere inches from hers. He was so close he could count the goose bumps that covered the flesh of her shoulders.

His feet touched the bottom easily here, but he could see that she still had to tread water in order to stay above the surface.

"Jagger, I . . ." Her words trailed off into a whisper and the only sounds that could be heard were the deep breaths falling from between her lips and the slow steady beat of his heart.

Her gaze finally fell away from his. "I'm sorry if I offended you this morning, but you have to understand I didn't mean—"

"Maybe you can enlighten me. What *exactly* did you mean?" he inserted, his voice low and dangerous.

He watched her flinch as he threw his words at her.

Jagger grabbed the ledge, his hands on either side of Skye, effectively trapping her between them. Her body was crushed against the hardness of his own. The feel of her soft breasts brought an immediate response and his cock roared to life, hardening quickly to rest against her midsection.

Her eyes grew large and she swallowed thickly but didn't look away. In fact she met his gaze dead on, and for the first time he became aware of an answering heat in the depths of her expressive orbs.

She cleared her throat and pushed her hands against his chest. "A little room would be nice."

Jagger raised an eyebrow and tilted his head to the side, but moved back a bit, letting cool water slide between them once more.

"I was angry. I'm sorry," she began, her voice building as she continued, "but I had every right to be pissed at you. I mean, for Christ sakes, I would have been able to make Kragen talk and give me Cormac's location."

"By screwing him?" Jagger answered dangerously. "Is that how you get things done?"

"What? No! Ew!" she replied quickly.

His eyes dropped to her lips and when her tongue darted out he had to work hard to stifle the groan that was caught in the back of his throat. "Who's Cormac?" Jagger asked suddenly, trying to throw her off balance a bit.

"What?"

"I think it's time you shared a little info with me, no? Starting with this Cormac dude. Who the hell is he?"

They stared at each other intently and Jagger fought the urge to grind his aching dick against her. His attempt at interrogation was lame. Everything about the situation was lame. How could it be otherwise?

All he could think about was sex. With Skye. His mind was alive with many, many different versions of how he'd like to screw the hot blonde that he held between his hands.

Teach her a lesson? Who the hell was he kidding? The only teaching he wanted to do right now involved his cock and the heated core that he could feel between her legs.

His eyes held hers and time seemed to stand still. Everything about the last few days faded away. None of it mattered. He was here, in the jungle, his hard body inches away from the most beautiful thing he'd seen in a long while, and the only thoughts that crowded his brain centered on seduction.

He wanted Skye in the worst way imaginable. More than he'd ever wanted a woman. Was it the jungle? The danger? Her spirit and beauty?

He sure as hell didn't know and he hissed from between his lips as he lowered his head. He just wanted a taste.

The groan that escaped from deep inside of him as his lips slowly swept across hers echoed into the air around them. Her soft lips trembled beneath his, but remained closed, even as his tongue flicked across the top one, seeking entrance to the mouth that had tantalized him for the last forty-eight hours.

She was stiff in his arms, but he smiled against her mouth as the pounding heart within her chest alerted him to the fact that she was just as affected by him as he was by her.

She tried to speak but Jagger reacted quickly, taking

advantage. He locked his mouth over hers and plunged his tongue deep inside her warmth. He could feel her fingers digging into the muscles at his shoulders and as he began to gyrate the hardness between his legs against the soft contours of her body, he was rewarded with the merest whisper of a groan.

She relaxed against him and he deepened the kiss, passing his tongue along the inside of her mouth, tasting everything that there was and going back for more. He could feel the pressure building inside of him, the need and the want to claim the woman as his. Jagger's skin began to burn and it added a torturous slash of pain that only elevated the pleasure to something he'd not felt before.

"Stop."

Dimly, Jagger was aware that she'd spoken against his lips and when she began to push at him in earnest he reluctantly pulled away.

"We can't do this." Her voice was barely above a whisper and he had to strain in order to hear her properly.

Jagger smiled down at her. Skye's lips were swollen from the assault of his mouth, and as she leaned back against the rocks, her chest heaving, he couldn't help but think she was the sexiest thing he'd ever seen.

And he'd seen a lot.

"You really have no clue what's going on, do you?" she managed to say between hearty intakes of air.

Jagger stilled at her words. He could play her game. They'd have a good long conversation about the shit they were in, and then he'd make her cry for the kind of mercy only he could give her.

He smiled rakishly, adjusting the heavy appendage,

which throbbed like a bitch, so that it pulsed against her belly. "Like I said, enlighten me."

He could see the internal struggle rifling through Skye. It was written across her face as clear as day. She was conflicted. Didn't know if she should trust him.

"There's a war coming and if it happens—if the gates of hell are thrown open . . ." her voice drifted off into silence and Jagger felt the icy fingers of dread climb up his spine. "If that happens," she began again, "then humanity is dead. Everything as we know it is dead."

"Trust me, there's always a war brewing somewhere in this world. And yeah, dark magick and those that would use their supernatural powers are usually at the heart of it, but it's just how things are. What's so different this time? And why the hell are the DaCostas involved?"

Skye closed her eyes and he felt his patience begin to fade along with his passion. "What are you not telling me?"

Once more she stared directly at him and he had the weird sensation that she could see into the very heart of him. Her eyes were massive, huge round bowls of blue sky hung in a pale, delicate face.

They wavered slightly and he heard her breath catch in the back of her throat.

"I can't, I . . ."

"Look, if I'm gonna lay my ass on the line and take hits from scum like the DaCostas you better damn well fill me in on everything."

"I really, I can't—"

Jagger cut her off savagely, no longer liking their little game. "What do you mean you can't? Open your mouth and speak."

Her body was tense and he could feel fear begin to beat at her, but when she spoke her voice was calm. "I can't because there's a jaguar on the bank directly behind you."

Jagger stilled at her words.

Slowly he turned around, his large body effectively keeping her hidden from the animal that stood looking at him, its long tail flicking back and forth in clean precise strokes. It growled low, deep from its chest, and barked a challenge.

"And I don't think it's friendly," Skye whispered from behind his back.

Yeah, Jagger thought as his body tightened at the new threat of danger. *No shit*.

Chapter 7

The animal was large, heavily muscled, and definitely a shifter. Its sleek lines were enhanced by a beautiful series of large rosettes clearly visible against the tawny hide. A spotted jaguar. Not of the warrior class.

Which meant nothing. Any animal with the power and hunting skills that a jaguar possessed was dangerous.

Jagger could sense the humanity locked deep inside even though the cat was at least a hundred yards from him. It paced back and forth along the embankment, its long powerful body humming with an energy that while expected, was more than a little puzzling to Jagger.

It almost felt like the animal was pissed. *At him*.

He continued to watch the cat as it barked, growled, and when it stood, looking as if it were about to plunge headlong into the water, Jagger's breath caught, and a pain long forgotten wrapped itself deep around his heart.

He had no time to react, however, for with a mighty roar the cat plunged into the water, its powerful limbs carrying it forward.

Jagger pushed Skye away, shouting at her to get out of the water. He felt her hesitate. Would the woman never listen to him?

He turned around, shouting, *"Now!"* his eyes already glowing with the change as mist began to crawl up his limbs. Once he was sure she would listen, he turned back, his body now completely enveloped deep within the magick that pulled the skin from his frame, leaving in its wake a beautiful, glossy black pelt.

He barked an answer to the challenge and bared his teeth at the spotted jaguar as it swam to within a few yards of him. The other cat's eyes were glowing a tawny, golden color and it growled loudly, hissing in anger.

It swung its massive head toward Skye and Jagger attacked, his long powerful body propelling him forward at blinding speed.

Jaguars were naturally great swimmers and his body sliced through the cool liquid with ease. Jagger bumped heavily into the spotted jag and took a swipe with his paws before twisting just out of reach of the counterattack.

He kept going, swimming toward the far side of the bank, knowing that the other jaguar would follow.

How could it not? The animal's quarrel wasn't with Skye. It was personal, its anger directed solely at Jagger. And he couldn't blame the cat. Hell, if he was in his position he'd be mad as hell.

It wasn't every day that you found the younger

brother who'd basically evaded you for three long months.

Julian Castille had every right to be pissed. Jagger had successfully hidden from him, Cracker, and Declan.

Jagger had initially been injured, but when he'd finally cleared the fog from his brain, he'd decided to say a big fat, *fuck you* to the human world and all the pain and suffering that went along with it.

Guilt ate at him, but it had never been enough to bring him out of hiding. He couldn't even explain it to himself. It just had been what it was.

And now his brother was hot on his ass, full of anger and feelings of betrayal, and Jagger had no one to blame but himself.

He reached the opposite bank, his sharp claws digging in deep as he hauled his body from the water, leaping up it in one graceful move. He began to head into the thick underbrush, knowing that Julian was hot on his heels. There was no need for Skye to witness the airing out of his family business.

'Cause it sure as hell wasn't gonna be pretty.

He'd barely cleared a hundred feet when the sting of claws ripped at his hindquarters. Jagger twisted his body as he whirled around in the air, kicking out with his powerful hind legs.

He managed to get Julian off balance and a low, mean growl erupted from deep within his chest. The smell of blood drifted in the air. His blood. It fed the demon that was always just underneath the surface and he charged at his brother, teeth bared, his mind black. The battle had just started but he'd had enough.

They hit each other, midair. The loud thump reverberated in the still night. And it was indeed quiet. All the nocturnal sounds of the jungle ceased. The only things that could be heard were the growls, barks, and savage wails that each of the jaguars spewed forth.

The two animals rolled over, falling down a small incline until they came to rest against the base of a large pine tree. Jagger's head hit it hard and he momentarily saw stars.

He snarled savagely, his hefty paws striking a line of red across Julian's chest as he shoved his brother away.

Enough! he roared, the word slipping from between his lips in a strange guttural way as the mist overcame him and he stood panting, staring down at his brother.

The golden jaguar hissed, moved away and began to pace back and forth slowly. Jagger could tell his brother was trying to calm the beast that was very much alive within him.

A strange thought that, considering less than four months ago, his brother had been leading the life of a rich and powerful corporate CEO, running Blue Heaven industries, the company their family owned.

Very white collar and a world away from what stood staring up at him.

Jagger shook his head. His father would have a fucking heart attack if he saw what his golden heir had become.

He continued to watch his brother in silence as the mist crept up and over the powerful cat and when Julian emerged from deep within the ancient magick, Jagger couldn't help but feel joy.

Slowly, the brothers took stock, each noticing the many changes the past few months had wrought.

"Where the fuck have you been?" Julian spit out, his face white with anger. "We've been looking for you. Cracker, Declan, all of us, busting our balls out here, looking for a sign, *anything* that would tell us you hadn't been blown to bits when the compound was attacked."

His brother glared at him and Jagger had the presence of mind to remain quiet.

"We did it because we knew you'd never leave one of us behind." Julian's voice dropped to a hoarse whisper. He growled and flexed his muscles.

Jagger noticed the considerable bulk that had been added to his tall frame.

Still he remained silent.

Julian began to pace. "I should kick your ass from here to Guatemala and back. Do you have any idea what we've all gone through? How guilty Libby feels?"

Julian stomped toward him, until the two men stood toe to toe. Jagger could tell that his brother was more than pissed. Something else was at play here. He could see it in the energy that shimmered in the air around Julian.

He'd changed. A lot. There was an edge of darkness that clung to his powerful frame. Something new. And Jagger wasn't so sure it was a good thing.

"Aren't you going to say anything?"

Jagger looked deeply into the golden eyes of his brother, and truthfully, he had so much to say that he didn't know where to start. So he remained quiet and took the hit to the chest when Julian pounded him in frustration.

"Who the hell is the blond whore you've been fucking with? Is she the reason you turned your back on the family?"

Jagger's eyes flattened to a dangerous hue, the green of his eyes morphing into a shade as dark as night.

The growl that hung low in his chest sounded deadly. "Don't ever refer to Skye in that way again." The words slipped from between tight lips.

Julian hissed, baring his teeth. "She's more important than family? That explosion must have scrambled your brain, because I sure as hell don't understand why you've been avoiding us."

Jagger held his ground as his brother pushed him, ignoring the burning pain that beat at him as his jaguar railed against the hostile energy in the air.

"And we've known for several weeks that you've been alive," Julian continued, his breaths coming in staccato bursts as his anger continued to grow. "I thought for sure you'd been injured, but to find you out here screwing some blond bitch while major shit is going down in the real world— "

Jagger had had enough. He growled loudly, his fury apparent. "I'm not gonna tell you again. Insult her once more and I won't hesitate to treat you like any other asshole that's pissed me off."

He stepped closer, until he was almost touching Julian. His lips were drawn back in a feral grimace and his eyes were lit from behind with an eerie glow. One that signaled he was close to the change.

Ready to do damage. To inflict pain if need be.

Julian shook his head in disgust. "You have no fucking clue what's going on, do you?"

For the first time a tingle of apprehension wove its way through Jagger's veins as his lack of information slapped at him hard. He took a second to gather his thoughts before speaking again.

His brother, corporate CEO, was out here in the jungles of Belize, three months after the DaCosta compound fiasco. That didn't make any sense. Shouldn't he be home taking care of business, instead of running around the jungle playing Rambo?

His mind began to work furiously. Where the hell was Jaxon? He swallowed heavily, feeling his anger dissipate as fear began to choke his airways.

"Where's Jax?" he asked hoarsely.

"If you gave a flying fuck about Jaxon you wouldn't have disappeared for three months," Julian answered, his eyes narrowing into tiny slits.

"Don't even go there with me. Where is he? He *did* make it out, right?" Jagger couldn't even contemplate the thought of Jaxon dead. It wasn't possible.

Jagger paced back and forth, the air around him shimmering in a dangerous manner as his emotions began to take over. He was losing control. He could feel it. He inhaled deeply and bent over to rest his palms against his upper thighs. His skin burned and the itch that clawed just underneath the surface was becoming unbearable.

"He's fine," Julian answered finally. "All of them are just fucking peachy."

"Thank God," Jagger muttered, ignoring his brother's sarcasm. "What about the baby?" he asked, slowly straightening.

"The child, Logan, was found and is safe with Jaxon and Libby." Julian shook his head. "Why are you out here?" he asked once more. "Why did you do everything in your power to avoid us?"

Jagger was silent for a few moments before answering honestly. "I had shit going on that you'd never understand." Jagger rotated his neck in a full circle, trying to alleviate the tension that had wrapped around him like a band.

"Why? Because I'm not like you? Because I'm not a

warrior?" Julian threw the words at Jagger furiously.

"Because you've never been to war," Jagger cut in bitterly. "Because you've never been to Iraq or Afghanistan or any of those hellholes I was sent to." He exhaled harshly, the sound of his breaths rough, uneven.

He could feel his canines erupting as the beast inside of him howled at the remembered pain and his voice became hoarse. "Because you've never watched people in your care being blown to bits, their bodies broken apart and spread over the desert like some sick buffet. Innocent civilians murdered for no reason . . ." His voice trailed off.

Jagger closed his eyes as the face that had haunted him for almost a full year rose up to taunt him. Again. Long crimson hair, eyes as green as the foliage at his feet, lips curved into a smile. Eden had trusted him and he'd failed.

She'd barely been old enough to vote.

He felt his heart harden as he pushed the emotion away. It was the only way to cope. "It's a hell of a lot different than sitting around a boardroom table making a deal. So don't get your ass all bent out of shape. It's nothing personal. You just have no fucking clue."

And that was the truth. Laid bare. Jagger had been haunted nightly, ever since he'd returned from overseas. War at any given time was horrible, but over the last twenty years the otherworld element had taken hold, and the tragedies and atrocities that had occurred every day in these countries tripled.

To some of these fringe otherworlders, humans were nothing more than chess pieces to be moved about. They didn't care how many of them died.

And what for? *Power.*

He was sick of it, and as soon as he could, he'd left and never looked back. Out here in the jungle he'd not once thought about the past or his human life. Of the mistakes that had cost him dearly. The men in his unit who'd died and sweet Eden who'd loved him though the feelings weren't returned.

He should have left her alone. Should have been stronger, maybe then she'd have made it out alive.

Wearily he rubbed his neck, feeling the energy drain from his limbs in one big swoop, as the effects of an all-nighter out in the jungle on top of a full day trekking through the thick underbrush began to take hold.

He really didn't want to get into it with Julian. Not now. When he was weak he couldn't control the cat inside of him. And that made him dangerous. Christ, he'd never forgive himself if he hurt his brother.

"Well, well, well. Look what the cat dragged in."

The sandpaper-rough voice drifted into the silence between them and Jagger turned to his right, a smile breaking across the tight features of his face.

Cracker! The craggy face looked a little worn, a few more wrinkles, a few more lines of worry on his forehead.

Not sure of his welcome considering his own flesh and blood had wanted to rip his head off, Jagger hesitated.

Cracker spit to the side, his light-colored eyes shifting up and down until they made contact with Jagger's.

"I never really took you for a fan of *The Jungle Book* and can't say as the whole Mowgli thing is working, but damn, I can't lie. It's good to see you." Cracker chuckled then, his gaze swinging to Julian. "Although I'd prefer to see a little less of you boys."

Jagger laughed heartily and crossed over to his old

friend. Cracker was a man of mystery, a former soldier who worked for his brother Jaxon. No one really knew much about him, other than the fact that he was loyal to the end.

And he wasn't quite human. Jagger had never been able to figure out just what was floating around in his DNA, and Cracker had never volunteered it.

"Yeah, well, sorry for the peep show but my clothes are back there." Jagger pointed behind him, unabashed and totally comfortable with his nakedness. He glanced at Julian. "Him, I have no clue."

"Yeah, well, I have his clothes." Cracker threw a small duffel bag toward Julian. "He's always stripping down and running off." He snorted and his eyes narrowed. "Seems to run in the family, more so for some of you."

The small rebuke didn't go unnoticed but Jagger remained silent as his brother quickly pulled on some clothes and slipped his feet into a sturdy pair of boots. Jagger couldn't help but stare. His brother looked more like a soldier than most of his crew from Iraq.

What had happened in the few months he'd been away?

He asked that very question and got more than a little spooked at the look between his brother and Cracker. The silence that fell between them did little to dispel his nervousness.

"All right, you guys are starting to freak me out. What the hell is going on?"

Cracker was the first one to answer, and the severity of the situation rolled over Jagger as the tone of his words set him on edge. "We're not sure, exactly. The DaCostas are on the hunt, for what we don't know, but you can bet your ass it ain't anything good.

They're forming alliances with shifter clans from all over and it's on a scale that's unprecedented."

Julian cut in, his face dark. "They've also hooked up with Cormac O'Hara, the bastard that had Libby's baby."

Jagger felt something inside of him shift at the mention of that name. Was it the same Cormac that Skye was after?

"O'Hara?" Jagger asked stiffly, not liking where this was headed. "Any relation to Declan?"

"The bastard is his father," Cracker answered roughly.

"What? But I thought his father was a nonissue, as in long gone and dead."

"After the banishment from his coven, he was presumed dead," Cracker continued, "but he's obviously very much alive and up to no good."

Jagger let the words sink in and his thoughts turned to Skye. What the hell was her connection to O'Hara?

He needed to get to her, and fast—before his brother did. There was no telling what the jaguar would do if he thought Skye was somehow involved in that whole mess.

He could feel Julian staring him down, and his brother's aggression was falling off him in waves. It called to the animal inside Jagger, and he could feel his control slipping again as thoughts of Skye in danger filled his mind.

He forced himself into a somewhat calm state and turned to Cracker. "You should know that there is a large contingent of warriors about a day's hike south of here. I took three out last night and laid down a shitload of false trails to confuse the rest, but I'm sure it will only slow them down for a day or so."

"Good to know," Cracker said softly. "So . . . you have somewhere you need to be, or can we count on your help?"

Jagger's hands fisted before he loosened and stretched out his tight fingers. He hesitated.

What the hell was he going to do? His gut told him that Skye was involved. He just didn't know if she was up to her neck in it, or over her head. Was she the enemy? Or was she in need of his help?

His insides began to tremble with the urge to get to her. The thought of her alone in the jungle touched off a protective instinct in him that he'd not experienced before, and he was beginning to think it was more than just fleeting.

Skye was one hell of an amazing woman.

Nervous energy rolled over his skin. "Why don't I hook up with you boys tomorrow morning? I've got to take care of something first."

Decision made, Jagger turned to leave, but stopped abruptly as his senses came alive, like a layer of film had just been pulled away. A rustling off to the right drew all of their attention and he felt his animal begin to make noise as a tall man appeared, his lean, muscled frame sliding into the clearing like he'd been pulled from the air.

He wasn't alone.

Jagger felt his animal explode so swiftly he nearly doubled over as he fought the change that threatened again. Declan O'Hara sauntered into the clearing, his arm gripped tight around none other than Skye.

He'd had the decency to give her his shirt, but it was the sight of his hands on her soft flesh that tore at him, and Jagger growled low, deep from his gut. He ignored the quick look that Cracker threw at him. Ignored the way Julian grew quiet.

At the moment all of his senses were focused on Declan and the blonde that stood at his side, chest heaving.

Skye's curves were barely covered and the thought of Declan, *of anyone*, looking upon her, or *touching* her, filled him with such anger that he began to tremble.

"Would this be what needs taking care of?" Declan asked, his voice deceptively light. He pushed Skye forward and she barely avoided falling.

Jagger leapt toward them and caught her in his arms, hissing a warning, his face blackened in anger.

"So," Declan continued his tone conversational, his manner anything but. "Let me get this straight. You've been MIA for the past three months, playing Tarzan and Jane with Cormac's whore?"

"I'm not . . . you don't know what you're talking about!" Skye shouted.

"No?" Declan said softly, his white teeth slashing through the gloom as he continued to smile at her. "Wanna explain to us all how you've miraculously come back from the dead?" He sneered and stepped away, totally disgusted.

Silence stretched long and hard. "Cat got your tongue, Skye? Doesn't matter. I have my own theory." Declan's voice dropped. "*I think* you and Cormac are working together. I think you wanted us to believe you were dead and that you in fact helped the bastard escape."

Jagger stilled at Declan's words. He felt Skye tense beneath his hands and he turned her around roughly.

Her eyes were huge in her pale face, the blue so dark it almost appeared black.

She kept them aimed straight at his chest, totally avoiding contact with his. Her action spoke volumes, and what it shouted to him was guilt.

The anger he felt earlier multiplied tenfold and he bared his teeth, his breaths coming hot and fast.

He sure as hell didn't know what was going on, but one thing was clear: Skye Knightly was playing him, and like an idiot he'd walked right into her trap.

Jagger's fingers bit into her soft flesh, his grip hard, and God help him but he enjoyed the small whimper of pain that escaped her lips. He ignored Skye and turned his attention to the men who stood staring at him expectantly.

There was no way he was turning her over to them.

He bent down and whispered into her ear, feeling a keen sense of satisfaction as she shivered at his words. "Seems as if my little bird has been leading me on a wild goose chase." He ran his finger down her clammy cheek, holding her steady when she would have moved away. "No matter. It ends tonight."

He was done playing games. It was time to find out exactly what the hell was going on.

Chapter 8

Skye pushed down the fear that pretty much clogged every single vein in her body. She was shivering, but in no way was she cold. In fact her body felt overheated, her limbs heavy and weak.

She could almost taste the anger that Jagger felt. It was potent enough to tie her belly up in knots for weeks. Months even. It was as if winter's kiss had blown down from the north and stolen the heat that had been there less than an hour before.

Her bizarre world had just shrunk a little more, and she was trapped.

How many obstacles were there in her immediate future? What hoops was she gonna have to jump through next?

God, she just wanted to close her eyes and wish everything away.

Her body was physically tapped out and her mind was pretty much toast. Not a good way to be when you were surrounded by a bunch of pissed-off shifters and the magick dude from hell.

Skye kept her eyes averted, her thoughts swirling furiously because, honestly, she had no clue what her next move should be.

She should never have turned back.

After the other jaguar had jumped into the water, she'd fled, running as fast as she could, using the last fumes of adrenaline that she had left. She'd been well on her way, too, but the unholy sounds of two large animals fighting filled the still jungle air, and she'd stopped dead in her tracks and turned around.

What if Jagger was hurt? She couldn't leave him out there alone. He was her only link to the satchel.

It was the only reason she turned back.

At least that's what she'd told herself.

Slowly she'd crept back and was almost to the water, when the hairs on the back of her neck had stood on end and she'd known that she was no longer alone. The air was thick with a darkness that'd sucked the heat out of the humid jungle. It felt empty, sinister. The terror that rose up inside of her was nearly debilitating.

It felt like old magick, black magick.

Dark arts!

Blindly, like a child caught in the middle of a nightmare, she turned, not knowing where to go, only knowing that she was in danger. She'd taken off running, ignoring the pain that clutched at her midsection, ignoring the low-lying branches that scraped at her nakedness. All coherent thoughts fled.

Then he was there. Right in front of her.

Skye's world spun out of control as she dug in her feet in order to avoid colliding with him. But it was too late. He had her.

She'd recognized him immediately. He'd been the one to pull her from the rubble of the DaCosta compound only three months earlier. The one they'd called Declan.

He'd changed in the last three months. There was a new layer to his skin, one that clung to his body like a second glove. It slithered in the air around him, mixing with his magick until the energy literally hummed.

He was incredibly strong.

It was familiar, his signature, but she couldn't connect the dots and felt a moment of frustration, thinking she was missing something important. It was no matter. The man was dangerous and she was in his direct line of fire.

Skye had tried to struggle but it was no use. There were no words spoken, only a look of dismissal as he'd slowly pulled the shirt from his powerful frame and handed it to her as if her nakedness made him ill.

"Cover yourself." And then he'd pretty much dragged her back the rest of the way, his eyes accusing and full of malice. When they'd come upon Jagger and two other men she recognized from before, her heart sank.

It suddenly became apparent to her that Jagger was tied to them and what had gone down three months earlier at Caracol. And now, as he held her tightly, painfully, within his grip, she refused to meet his gaze. Afraid of what she'd see.

Skye's thoughts continued to whirl into a tornado of panic. When had her life taken such a header directly into the shithouse?

She could feel tears once more stinging the corners of her eyes as she thought of her father, dead, and Finn most likely the same. Of the countless others that had given their lives in order to protect the portal.

Fucking magicks and shifters, she thought. None of them could be trusted. Not even the towering jaguar that stood before her.

Skye welcomed the anger that suddenly erupted from within as her eyes slowly met Jagger's, and she fed on it, closing off her mind and her emotions.

They would not win. She would find a way out of this situation. She would find the portal. Alone.

And she would seal it.

Only then would she be able to rest. And God knows, she was so very tired.

"Is it true?" Jagger asked harshly, his fingernails clawing at her flesh.

Skye ignored the pain, doing her best to keep her face neutral. There was no way she'd let them see how upset and rattled she was.

She remained quiet, her gaze never meeting his, not even when he began to shake her so hard that she began to see stars. What was the point? It's not like he'd believe her anyway.

"Stop it!" the older gentleman ordered gruffly. "We need her brain in working order, because she sure as hell owes us some answers."

Jagger let her go and this time she did lose her balance, unable to stop herself from falling to the ground. The tender skin on her knees took the brunt and she bit down on a groan as her aching body protested. Her head was pounding and she began to see white spots floating in the air.

She was so very hungry and thirsty.

A wave of dizziness caught her off guard and she

sucked in a deep breath, fighting the nausea that accompanied it. She closed her eyes for a few seconds, aware of the rumble of male voices. They rose and then fell. There were angry words, orders barked, but she paid no mind.

Skye needed to concentrate, to conserve that little spark of energy that was left inside her. It was the only thing that was going to carry her forward. She clung to it and when her arm was yanked nearly out of the socket as she was pulled up to her feet, she uttered not a sound.

She did not bow in defeat or weakness. She was an eagle knight and would hold her head high.

Skye met the eyes of the magick man, Declan, with a defiance that earned a ghost of a smile, one that didn't go anywhere near his eyes. She'd heard the whispers. He was Cormac's son.

He grinned down at her. "I wouldn't be so cocky if I were you. Honestly, I'd love to get a crack at getting inside that head of yours." Declan leaned closer and his voice dropped to a whisper. Skye had to strain in order to hear his words. "Magick does have a way of pulling thoughts and memories out, but methinks that in this case Jagger here will be much more effective." He winked at her then. "Or at the very least, he'll have way more fun."

Jagger moved into her line of vision. Skye held her ground and even though no outward sign betrayed her innermost feelings, she gulped back the fear that began to spread quickly.

Jagger's face held no emotion whatsoever, his features as cold as a slab of granite. Unflinching. Unyielding. It was amazing, really, that a face so incredibly arresting could look so aloof and bitter.

She swallowed thickly. It was obvious he'd made up his mind. She was now his enemy.

He'd donned a pair of pants and suddenly she felt exposed, vulnerable, as she stood there, her nakedness barely covered. Quickly her gaze passed over the other three men, but they all stared her down as if she had no right to be breathing the same air as they did. The older one, Cracker, spit into the ground and turned away. The other two followed, until they disappeared into the darkness, swallowed whole by the thick vines.

She was alone. With a jaguar warrior who not long ago would have thrown her to the ground and made love to her if she'd let him.

Yet now looked at her with no emotion at all.

Skye took a second to push back her fear, held her head high, and slowly moved toward him. There was no use trying to escape. She needed to be smart about this. It was the only way.

"This way," he said flatly.

They trudged through the jungle, swinging by the small pond of water where they'd been together less than an hour earlier. Jagger retrieved his clothes and pointed her in the direction he wanted her to take.

She didn't rate so much as a word, just the odd grunt and gesture.

The silence was almost unbearable. Truthfully, she'd rather he yell at her, pick a fight or something. Anything was better than the morose quiet that followed as she carefully trekked across the jungle floor, picking a careful path.

Several times the soles of her feet landed on sharp roots and she bit her tongue at the pain. Bitterly, she cursed in silence, thinking it was easy for the warrior since his feet were encased in heavy-duty boots.

Her brother's boots.

Skye's body began to drag, she could feel her energy depleting rapidly. When Jagger stopped suddenly, indicating that she do the same, relief washed over her.

She wiped the sweat from her brow, lifting the heavy waves of hair that were stuck to her neck and shoulders. Her chest was heaving and she ran her tongue over parched lips as her gaze wandered the immediate area.

She wasn't sure why they stopped. As far as she could see, there was nothing here. Anxiously she looked at Jagger, wondering, not for the first time, where the hell her satchel was.

His hooded eyes were looking straight at her and her breath caught in the back of her throat. The man stood like a stone god, all hard angles and sculpted features. The animosity that he felt was so thick she could taste it and she swallowed painfully, her dry throat protesting.

Her gaze fell to the jungle floor. Darkness had fallen several hours earlier, but her eyes had adjusted and she could see quite clearly through the thick gloom. The foliage was knee high and there wasn't much room to maneuver, no path that was evident.

Jagger nodded toward a thick stand of trees, a grouping that was made of several trunks that had twisted and melded together to form one solid form.

"Up," was the only word that fell from his lips, but either her mind was too tired to understand or he wasn't making any sense. Skye remained where she was, tottering on the brink of exhaustion, her limbs trembling.

Jagger cursed, his voice low, almost guttural. He crossed over to her in two long strides until he was so close she could see the pulse that pinched at his temple. She could feel the heat from his body slowly evaporating into the air and she welcomed it as it washed over her suddenly cold, numb limbs.

"The only safe place in this jungle tonight is up there." Her eyes followed to where his finger pointed, "In the canopy."

Dully she looked at the tree trunk and with great effort forced one foot in front of the other until she stood at the base.

"We don't have all night. In fact I'm pretty sure we only have a few hours of rest until the DaCostas start knocking at our door, so I suggest you get your ass in gear and climb the damn tree."

A small, smoldering flame of defiance sprung quickly to life and Skye fought the urge to turn around and tell Jagger to go fuck himself. She kept her mouth shut. It was time to pick her battles and she wasn't going to get in a pissing contest over where they should bed down.

Besides, she supposed he was right. There was no cave close by for shelter and while the jungle floor held many dangers during daylight, they tripled once darkness fell.

Her hands reached out, grasping the tree as hard as she could until her fingers found crevices with which she could leverage her weight. Skye began to climb, hoping like hell she'd be able to hang on and make it all the way without tumbling back to the jungle floor.

She almost giggled at the thought, feeling the hysterics riding so close to the surface. *That* would certainly be the icing on what had undoubtedly been one of the most trying days in her life.

She concentrated and hauled herself up using what last bit of strength she possessed, and tried to ignore the hot flush that spread across her face as she inched toward the canopy overhead.

Jagger was just below, and if he looked up, which she was sure he was doing at this very moment, he would have an unfettered view of not only her ass cheeks, but everything else in between.

She gritted her teeth, trying to keep her legs held tight together, which, while climbing, was really hard to do. After what seemed like forever she managed to pull herself up onto a natural platform, one that had been formed when the trees had come together and become one. It allowed about three feet either way of standing room, with natural barriers creating an almost cocoonlike room.

She could see their supply bags, including her precious satchel, hanging from a large branch. He must have scouted the location earlier in the day.

Skye turned to look down and froze at the look that hung on Jagger's face. His eyes glowed with sparks that lit them from behind and his lips were drawn back into a grimace that should have marred the handsome face, but didn't. As he jumped over the edge to land in a crouch, mere inches from her, the air shimmered and everything felt heavy, out of sorts.

Skye stumbled and took a step back, yelping in pain as her tortured, tired feet hit a sharp snag.

Jagger rose slowly, his large frame moving with the grace and fluidity of someone half his size. The man screamed otherworld and Skye froze at the intensity behind his eyes.

The man looked dangerous. The man looked *hungry*. And pissed off.

With her.

She continued to back up, casually taking in the immediate area around her, but it was no use. There was nowhere to hide, nowhere to run.

Not that she had the energy, anyway.

He took one step toward her and she flinched. Skye couldn't help it. As much as she didn't want to show an ounce of weakness, there was no denying the potent strength and underlying anger that fed the jaguar. His eyes swept over her, piercing, full of contempt and loathing.

Skye felt her heart jerk, chest tighten, and she swallowed painfully.

She couldn't help but feel hurt.

He reached for her and she held her breath, closing her eyes, expecting some sort of physical violence, but instead was pulled roughly into his arms.

The touch of his flesh was welcomed with reluctance. It heated her cold skin.

Skye stared up at him, confused. He pushed her back slowly, until her body was cushioned between the natural wall that the trees had formed and the hard body in front of her. She felt off balance, her torn and sore feet trying to gain leverage on the rough bottom.

Instinctually her hands braced themselves against Jagger's hard chest and she winced at the cruel laugh that fell from his lips.

Skye closed her eyes, wanting to banish the image of the disgusted look that graced his handsome features.

"Ever the little whore." Jagger's breath was hot against her cheek and she shivered as cold washed through her body. Words couldn't be hidden behind closed eyes and the despair that she felt inside was painful.

Why should she give a shit what he thought?

His hands gripped her cheeks, the fingers digging in until the whimper that was torn from her throat hung in the air between them. Skye could feel the tears behind her eyes, but she held on. There was no way in hell that she would cry in front of him.

"Just do it and get it over with," she spat out, her eyes opening wide as a spark of anger bit at her.

Jagger seemed surprised at her words, but only for a moment. Then understanding dawned and he smiled once more, the white of his teeth a soft glow amongst the dim gloom of night.

His eyes made a show of trailing a path down her body, but the curl to his lip left no doubt as to what he was feeling.

And it was anything but lust.

"Don't flatter yourself, Skye. If I wanted to fuck, I'd have you begging for it before your back even hit the floor." He laughed softly then, a sinister sound that grated on her last working nerve. "Don't get all excited. I'm not particularly fond of screwing the enemy's leftovers."

He turned her around before she had a chance to react, her mind stinging from the nastiness of his words.

"We need to sleep. I'm damn near dead on my feet, no thanks to you, and I've got a lot of shit to deal with tomorrow."

"What are you . . ." Skye's voice trailed off weakly. She felt like a rag doll that had been beaten down, trashed, and kicked to the curb. She just had nothing left.

Jagger pulled her down with him, keeping her back nestled against his chest. It wasn't for comfort, either. His arms were like hard steel bands that wrapped around the front, just under her breasts, holding her there firmly. Skye wasn't going anywhere.

Her tongue felt thick and her head was swimming from lack of food and water. Slowly her gaze wandered up to the satchel that hung just out of reach.

The weight of her mission and everything that had transpired over the last six months was incredible. Would she have the strength to carry it through?

"Lots to deal with," he whispered ominously against her ear. Skye couldn't hide the shudder that wracked her frame.

"And you're first up on the agenda."

Chapter 9

Skye wasn't sure how long she lay there, her body rigid against the warmth of Jagger's chest. She tried to ignore the feel of him, his muscles, the hard planes of his torso, the way his body rose and fell as he inhaled air deep into his lungs.

She was so tense it honestly felt like her body was going to snap in two. Her shoulders were sore, her neck in knots and her fists were balled together so tightly she could feel the wetness from the blood her nails had drawn.

The dizziness that had washed over her earlier was still circling inside her skull, making her feel weak, and to top it off her head was pounding so hard it felt like a truckload of jackhammers was having a freaking party.

She'd give anything for a couple shots of tequila. Or better yet an entire bottle dumped down her throat. She just wanted everything to go away.

What she wouldn't give to fall asleep and wake up in another life. In another world entirely. One that didn't include shifters, magicks, and demons.

The dead lump in her gut told her that fantasy was never gonna happen.

For the first time Skye was not only scared, she was beginning to lose hope. Even the months she'd spent in captivity being held by the DaCostas—*even then*—she'd never given up hope that the eagles would win.

That the portal would be recovered and sealed.

That humanity would be saved from the brink of a demon war.

But now?

Skye was just so tired and burnt out she didn't know what to think anymore. Was it even possible to win the war? It all seemed so incredibly hopeless.

She closed her eyes and fought the ache that had attached itself to her soul. It pulled at her, dragging her down. She hurt. Everywhere.

She needed to sleep, but was hesitant to fall under. She was scared.

Not of the jaguar that held her—although Skye was pretty sure she'd be changing her tune in the morning—no, it was the promise of something much more insidious.

Her nightmare from the evening before still hovered around the edges of her consciousness, the leftover images and feelings lingering, taunting.

Was Azaiel real? Were the nightmares more than what they appeared to be? She exhaled softly, trying not to move. Maybe she really was losing her mind.

Skye held on and did her best to keep her senses alive, her mind working even as she longed to close her eyes and rest. But as the minutes dragged by she could feel herself losing the battle. Jagger's heart beat a steady, hypnotic rhythm beneath her and the warmth from his flesh crept into the coldness of her own.

Eventually her mind began to wander and as she succumbed to the kiss of the sandman, a soft sigh of regret slipped from her mouth.

Jagger wasn't sure how much time passed, but eventually Skye grew limp as the weight of her body fell into the crook of his arms. Her head rested against his chest, but even in sleep, she held herself rigid. Her shoulders were hunched, her body held at an unnatural angle in an effort to avoid his touch.

She felt cold but he had no inclination to offer anything other than the prison of his embrace. He didn't trust her in the least.

He tried to ignore the scent that clung to her skin. He knew it was potent. Christ, it felt like she was drowning in *come fuck me* musk. He was angered by the response his body took.

He wanted her. Plain and simple.

Oh, he'd proclaimed his aversion to her charms, how could he not? She was obviously in collusion with the enemy. But the aching throb that lay heavy against his groin told another story.

Jagger felt another wave of loathing wash over him and this time it had nothing to do with Skye. It was toward himself and the weak betrayal of his body. He clenched his teeth together viciously and vowed that as soon as they got back to some sort of civilization, he'd find the first willing female that he could and screw her until his balls turned blue.

Tiredly his mind turned in circles. There was so much he didn't know and for the first time he felt a sliver of regret. He'd been selfish to disappear, to leave his family fighting a war without him.

He was the soldier, for Christ sakes, not Julian.

He closed his eyes and laid his head against the rough bark of the tree at his back, forcing his body to relax. The nocturnal sounds of the jungle soothed his soul, the clicks, hoots, hisses, and even the shrill call of the occasional howler monkey. They all melted together into a comforting lullaby, and eventually Jagger fell asleep.

At first he wasn't sure what had woken him. A feeling of unease. A blackness that slid over his skin. It awakened the animal deep inside and Jagger was instantly on guard.

His eyes flew open and his nostrils quivered.

The jungle was now silent, eerily so.

The black of night had given way to the hazy gray of early morning. Shadows shifted in the breeze that blew around him, looking sinister.

He felt his stomach muscles clench. The quiet ate at him. It wasn't normal.

He was instantly alert, and he pulled in the woman that he held with his arms until she was tight against his chest. There was something in the air but it was unlike anything he'd encountered before. The scent was subtle.

Skye moaned softly and her body began to shake in quick, jerky movements. Her head lolled to the side as her body continued to quiver and it took great effort for Jagger to hold her still.

Her eyes flew open, the blue roundness wide yet unseeing. He watched as her lips began to tremble, soft moans escaping.

His arms held her tighter but that just seemed to aggravate her even more, and her skull connected solidly with his chin as she continued to thrash about.

Son of a bitch!

Her fingers unfurled and the claws that ripped into his upper arms were sharp, deadly weapons. He looked down, not surprised to see long talons taking the place of her fingers.

Every hair on his body was electrified and his instinct to defend and destroy kicked in big-time. He began to pant and his body broke out in a thin sheen of sweat.

Skye's nails drew blood and he cursed under his breath. Fuck! He had no time for this shit. Jagger twisted his hips and pushed, effectively flipping Skye over so that she was now trapped beneath him.

She began to buck wildly, her strength surprising him. A chill slithered up his body and Jagger stilled, his head whipping around as the jaguar inside hissed in anger.

The space was empty. But he knew better. There was something there. It wasn't human or animal. Whatever the hell it was, it was definitely otherworld.

His eyes scanned the entire length of the canopy and his ears listened closely as he struggled to calm the woman beneath him.

The air seemed to dissipate, as if some force was sucking it out into a black hole. Frustration gnawed at him but Jagger kept still. He'd seen and dealt with many things in his life and knew the only way to defeat an unseen enemy was to keep a cool head and look for the perfect opportunity to attack.

Timing was everything.

Skye suddenly stopped moving and his gaze quickly

returned to her. Inside, the animal railed against him, wanting out, feeling panicky, as if under attack.

Her eyes widened in fear. Her lips began to move, whispered words falling from between dry lips, and he bent down closer in an effort to hear her.

She spoke in a language he'd never heard before, an ancient tongue. The rhythm was awkward, the sounds guttural and sharp. Her voice was rough, unlike the melodic timbre he'd grown accustomed to.

Her eyes were trained on a point behind him but they remained unfocused. As her voice rose the vivid blue receded, the color invaded by an insidious black that seeped into the orbs, leaving them dull, opaque.

She began to shake violently, her head thrashing from side to side, and Jagger began to fear for the woman beneath him.

"Skye!" he whispered hoarsely, using his legs to pin her down as his hands gripped her face hard. She continued to fight him, her body flushed with a fiery heat, the skin slick with her sweat.

The wind picked up and her hair began to snake out, catching the breeze as it whirled around the two of them. Skye continued to ramble wildly, the words nearly shouted. Her face had become a deep red and he noticed small slashes of blue returning to her eyes.

He lowered his head until he was nearly touching her and held her face between his large hands. "Fight it! Snap out of it!"

What the hell was going on?

His heart nearly stopped as the woman beneath him went rigid, her body arching against his. The veins in her neck stood out in stark relief and when she went limp, fear shot through him.

Jagger began to shake her violently, not thinking that his own strength could be damaging. She felt like a rag doll in his arms and frantically he felt for a pulse, feeling such a rush of relief when he found it that he began to shake as well.

He held her close to his chest, feeling the animal inside relax as the threat disappeared, retreating back to wherever the hell it had come from.

Skye's teeth began to chatter loudly and big, fat tears fell from her eyes. He looked down at her, surprised to see her focused on him. The blackness that had been there was gone, but was replaced with such pain and terror that it gripped him hard.

What was it about this woman that had him yoyoing like a wet-behind-the-ears teenager? One minute he wanted nothing more than to kill her and in the next, protect her with his very life.

He rolled over once more, bringing her with him, cradling her against his chest. There was no resistance.

He could hear her whispering and Jagger listened in silence as she repeated a phrase over and over again. It left him cold.

"Azaiel is coming. Azaiel is coming."

Who the hell was Azaiel?

He lay like that for several long minutes. Skye nestled into the protective shadow of his arms and he rested his chin on the top of her head. He could hear her heartbeat, its erratic pulse slowing until it banged out a slower, calmer rhythm. Her breathing normalized as well, and when she started to squirm, he let her go.

She pulled away, leaning against the tree bark, her shadowed eyes meeting his. She opened her mouth to speak and whispered, "Thirsty."

He held her gaze for a few moments, fighting the questions inside of him that demanded answers. He quickly stood up, retrieving a water bottle from one of the supply bags. He also grabbed four granola bars. He was hungry, but after an entire day without food, Skye must be damn near starved.

She took the bottle from him, draining it in several long gulps, and then ripped open the granola bars, eating them greedily.

His gaze fell to her fingertips and he noted that the clawlike talons were no more, replaced instead with long, elegant human digits. She caught his stare and sat up a little straighter, pushing her chin forward, her features now shadowed with a hint of insolence.

A spark of admiration glimmered in him; it was fleeting but there nonetheless. The woman was his enemy and involved in some seriously fucked-up shit, but there was something about her that pulled at him.

Hard.

Christ, the sight of her lips as she chewed hit him in the gut.

Jagger wanted to turn away but found that he couldn't. So he watched, eyes hooded, face a mask.

When she was done, she pulled herself up to her knees and looked at him expectantly. By now the sun was beginning to break through, and streaks of gold, red and orange bled across the morning sky.

The jungle sounds had resumed their loud, robust nature, the air alive with the shrieks of birds, monkeys, and anything else that went bump in the night. Things had pretty much returned to normal in this little corner of the world, but Jagger knew it was all a facade. Window dressing to hide what was really going on.

He looked at Skye in silence, her body barely covered by Declan's T-shirt, and while the anger was still there, riding just below the surface, there was a glimmer of excitement, too. It was something he'd not felt in years.

He frowned. What the hell did that say about him?

"So what now?" she whispered, her voice still rough.

Jagger rose to his feet, his frown darkening as he stood above her. "What's your connection to the Da-Costas? Why are they after you?" His face was shadowed as he moved closer to her.

Skye's eyes widened slightly and she looked at the ground. *So this is how it's gonna be*, he thought. He bared his teeth and crouched in front of her.

"I have questions and you will answer me, Skye, because if not," he said softly, dangerous, "the consequences will be very painful."

Her fragrant scent hung in the air, teasing him. His eyes darkened and he felt the animal inside begin to make noise. Oh, he'd enjoy making her talk.

Her delicate throat moved as she swallowed and he could see the internal struggle that was taking place. Her eyes shifted from his and then moved back again. She opened her mouth to speak, closed it and turned away before inhaling raggedly. She then looked him straight in the eye.

Skye squared her shoulders and seemed to have come to a decision.

"What do you want to know?" she asked softly, though her voice was still rough and dry.

Jagger's eyes narrowed and his gaze was piercing. Skye didn't flinch. There was a clarity present that brought a spark of life to the shadows that dulled the blue of her eyes.

"What the hell is your involvement with Cormac O'Hara?"

Revulsion, pain, and anger washed over her face as she bit her lip. She shook her head. "I'm not *involved* with Cormac, at least not in the way you think."

"Well, why don't you enlighten me? If you're not screwing him, what exactly is your relationship with the bastard? And what the hell is his connection to the DaCostas?"

He watched as Skye bit her lip, felt the snarl that rippled along inside of his mouth.

"Cormac is working with the DaCostas because they're both looking for something." She paused for a second, her tongue darting out to moisten her lips. "A valuable Aztec artifact that my people have guarded for eons."

Jagger looked at her, surprised. "Aztec?"

Skye frowned. "You really have no clue what I am or the history between our people, do you?" she snorted, and muttered, "Why does that not surprise me?"

"I deal in the here and now," Jagger whispered hoarsely, not liking her condescending attitude at all.

"*Really.* So that's why you disappeared for three months? Felt like a break from the here and now, did ya?"

"How the hell would you know any of that?"

"I was there last night for your family reunion, remember?"

Jagger moved so fast she had no time to react and his fingers dug into her arms cruelly. "We are not talking about me," he hissed. "Understand? My situation or anything about me is no concern of yours."

The small whimper that fell from her lips alerted

him to the fact that he was on the verge of crushing her bones beneath his iron-clad grip.

"Take your hands off me," she said, her voice low and controlled. Her hand started to shift, and he looked down at the deadly talons that were quickly replacing her fingers. Jagger threw her from him, disgusted in both himself and the anger that she provoked. Mostly because, deep down, he knew she was right.

He took a second, calmed himself and turned back to Skye. Her hand was back to its human form. "What exactly is this Aztec artifact?"

Jagger watched her closely, noticed the stain that crept up over her cheeks. Saw the way her eyes shifted away and then back to his.

"It's a small round disc," she said softly before looking away again.

"A small round disc? That's it? What the hell is so important that both the DaCostas want it, and a scumbag like Cormac?"

"I'm not sure exactly."

Liar, Jagger thought. He continued to watch her in silence. He'd bet his last bottle of Canadian whiskey that she knew exactly why they wanted the disc.

"My father hid it here in the jungle," she continued haltingly. "It was ours to protect. Cormac murdered him because he wanted to get his filthy hands on it."

Skye looked at him square in the face, her body trembling, but her voice was strong. "I will not let it fall into their hands. I need to find it before they do. Before anyone does."

Jagger took a few minutes, his mind shrewdly going over what she'd just revealed. The pain on her face was unmistakable, and God help him, he believed her when she said she wasn't working with Cormac or the DaCostas. But there were still a hell of a lot of loose ends that needed tying.

"Why did the DaCostas have Libby?" he shot at her.

She shook her head. "I don't know. They had some kind of grudge against your brother, I think." She shrugged her shoulders. "I wasn't there nearly as long as Libby, and truthfully, it's not like bonding was on our minds. We were focused on surviving."

"Who's Azaeil?" His eyes narrowed as her face whitened. Skye looked away.

"Where did you hear that name?" she asked finally. The fear in her eyes made Jagger's stomach muscles clench.

"From your lips. This morning." He moved closer to her, noting how she was trembling. Her hand rose shakily to push the thick rope of hair behind her ears.

"I . . . I don't—"

Jagger exploded, cutting her off. "You're treading on soft ground here. Don't play me. I will accept some of your half truths, *for now*." He glared at her, totally pissed. "But I want to know who the hell this fucker is. Because *he was* here, this morning, and if I'm going to have a hope in hell of protecting you from whatever shit you've gotten yourself into, I need to know everything."

Skye swallowed thickly and drew in a shaky breath. "He was here?" She blanched at his curt nod. "Did you see him?"

"There wasn't much to see, actually, but yeah, there was something here and I'm assuming it's Azaiel, since you mumbled something about him coming."

She closed her eyes and shuddered. "He's real," she said incredulously, shaking her head.

"What the hell is he?"

Skye opened her eyes and he felt a wave of trepidation run through him. She looked scared shitless. She looked resigned. But to what fate?

"He's visited me on and off since I was a child. I always thought he was a figment of my imagination. A bad dream that never went away." Her eyes were luminous, huge in her face as she turned to him. "But things have changed and I can't be sure, but I think he's a . . . *demon*," she said softly and then looked away before muttering something under her breath.

Only the keen sense of hearing Jagger possessed enabled him to hear. A few words spoken and the ominous ring to them left a hollow feeling deep in his gut.

"And he's coming for me."

Chapter 10

Fear, thick, malicious, and pungent clogged her airways. The taste of it was bitter and Skye turned from Jagger. He'd already seen and heard enough. He didn't need to know that she was shaking in her boots.

She glanced down at her bare toes and grimaced as her tummy rolled over for the hundredth time. That's if she actually *had* boots on. She needed to get dressed and get organized.

Skye focused on her satchel and tried to shake the hopelessness and anxiety that she felt. She would not think of Azaiel. Not now.

The bag hung from a tree not more than a few feet from her. The soft leather was well worn. It had been a gift from her father when she was a teenager.

Slowly she crossed the remaining space, her fingers reaching out to touch it. The feel of its softness tugged at the bittersweet place in her heart and the ache in her chest intensified.

It was snatched from her grasp before she was able to grab hold of it, and she turned around, a snarl erupting from between her clenched teeth.

"This goes with me," Jagger said, his voice commanding with a take-no-shit kinda attitude. "It's the only way I can keep you from spreading your wings and flying away."

The arrogant son-of-a-bitch. Skye wanted nothing more than to slam her fist into his perfectly sculpted nose.

"Fine," she said. *Fuck you,* she thought.

Skye whirled around, her eyes searching the immediate area, before turning back to him. "I need my clothes. I'm not trucking through the entire jungle in a T-shirt that barely covers my ass."

She felt the blush rising in her cheeks again as Jagger's eyes moved over her slowly. Too slowly. "Where are they?"

She watched in silence as he opened her satchel and withdrew the clothes she'd been wearing the day before. He tossed them over and she clutched them tightly to her chest, waiting for him to either turn around or get the hell off the platform. When he did neither she raised her eyebrows.

"I'd like a little privacy, if you don't mind."

Jagger laughed softly, his eyes glinting like emeralds in the early-morning light. "It's nothing I haven't seen before."

Skye's mouth went dry in less time than it took for him to speak. His voice was low, rough, and the expression on his face was dangerous. The air literally crackled with energy. Her heart skipped a beat, several in fact, and she felt light-headed once more.

Angrily she shoved aside all emotion. "Whatever,"

she said, and reached for the bottom of the T-shirt, intent on changing regardless of whether she had an audience or not. "It's not like I expect a jaguar to behave like a gentleman, anyway."

She turned around and began to lift the shirt from her body, ignoring the heat that scalded her skin as she thought of his sexy eyes devouring her naked flesh. She doffed the top as a mischievous smile tugged at the corners of her mouth.

Two could play this game.

Slowly she bent over, knowing that the roundness of her butt was on display at an angle that was both teasing and erotic. She grabbed her shorts and slowly pulled them up over her hips and then she grabbed her tank top, turning around as she pulled it over her head. She knew her breasts were on display, their full-ness emphasized as she moved her arms up over her head.

But the smile that still lay on her lips disappeared in an instant as she pulled the top all the way down, and was greeted by nothing more than silence and empty space.

He'd climbed off the platform.

Annoyance shot through her but was quickly pushed away. It was for the best. No need to rile the jaguar. He was one complication she could do without.

Skye quickly lowered herself off the platform and seconds later was standing at the base of the large tree. Jagger's dark gaze swept over her and he held up one of the supply bags.

Bitterly, she noted her satchel slung across his shoulders.

She crossed over to him and grabbed the supply bag, hefting it onto her shoulders. She turned and looked up past the canopy of trees, closing her eyes as she welcomed the first true rays of sunlight that penetrated the thick jungle ceiling. The warmth awakened the eagle deep inside of her, and she felt the same joy she did every morning as the sunlight caressed her cheeks.

Melancholy grabbed at her hard and she would have given anything to shift and greet the sun's kiss.

"We need to move out. I can smell the DaCostas. Their stink is riding the wind and we don't have much time."

Skye hunched her shoulders at Jagger's words, feeling the tension cloak her like a blanket. There was no escaping her situation. She couldn't just fly away and pretend that everything was peachy. In fact it was rotten as all hell.

She shot him a look. "I need to find the disc."

Jagger nodded. "I'll help you find this disc, and when we do I expect to hear the truth." He smiled softly, his teeth a fierce slash of white against his tanned skin. "I will accept nothing less."

He turned and indicated they head to the right, back to where they'd come from the night before. "We need to hook up with the others first."

"No!" Skye uttered the word before she had time to filter her mouth.

Jagger frowned and crossed over until they were merely inches apart. His male scent, a tantalizing musk, tickled her nostrils, awakening something inside of her that was totally inappropriate, considering the circumstances.

She wanted to look away but found that she couldn't.

And that pissed her off.

"We have a posse of fucking DaCosta warriors on

our tail, not to mention the whole Cormac connection. Who knows what the hell he has up his sleeve. Seems to me we need all the help we can get."

Skye looked away and said nothing. She knew it was a huge waste of time to argue with the man. She'd have to be smart. Bide her time.

Why not let them help her find the portal? Once she had it in her hands she'd escape. It was probably best that no one be around when she sealed it, however.

"Fine. I just don't trust Declan, is all. He does have Cormac's blood running through his veins."

Jagger exhaled before he spoke and when he did, the deadly serious tone indicated just how passionately he felt about the men. "Declan, Cracker, and my brother are honorable men. I don't give a rat's ass who Dec's father is. He's one of the good guys, and that's something you shouldn't forget."

Skye shrugged her shoulders and remained silent, pushing aside her anger at the impossible situation she'd found herself in. Christ, who would have thought, forty-eight hours ago, that she'd be working with a couple of jaguars, a sorcerer, and some dude named Cracker?

Skye actually giggled, earning a surprised glance from the jaguar. Her smile widened as she headed into the thick, already hot jungle.

Good, she thought. I'll have to do my best to keep him on his toes.

They hiked through the dense foliage for well over an hour, bypassing the waterfall and pond from the night before. Skye refused to look at it and tried her best to banish the image of their bodies sliding through the cool liquid. Her naked flesh against his hard body.

What the hell was wrong with her? She was in

crisis. The world was on the verge of destruction from demon forces unimaginable and she was getting all hot and bothered over some attractive man-meat?

He was a jaguar warrior to boot, an enemy, even if at the moment he seemed to be on her side. Most were not to be trusted. She'd have to be careful.

Skye pulled out another granola bar and grudgingly ripped it from the wrapper, shoving the entire piece into her mouth without thinking. She chewed it hard, ignoring the man beside her.

It was difficult, but she managed to focus her thoughts and eventually relaxed enough, so that the tight band of tension along her shoulders disappeared altogether.

They climbed higher and the air changed as the sun encroached and kicked the moon out of the sky. It was still early morning but the humidity carried with it the hint of rain. Skye inhaled deeply, loving the scent of the Caribbean Sea that drifted on the breeze.

She was secretly hoping the others had taken off and felt a huge stab of disappointment as they crossed a small river to find the three men waiting for them on the other side.

All of them looked at her as if she were an insect that should have been crushed beneath Jagger's boots.

She lifted her chin and met their gazes full on. She addressed them, her voice nonchalant. "Gee, I was hoping your manners would have improved a bit with a full night's sleep, but I can see that would be mistaken."

Cracker's pale eyes regarded her in silence. She held his gaze even though there was something about the man that put her on edge. He made her nervous in a way the others didn't.

She could tell he was still pissed that she'd escaped

from them before, after they'd rescued her from the DaCosta compound. But there was no time for bruised egos. She needed to take the bull by the horns, so to speak.

She needed to gain their trust.

Skye took a few extra seconds, even as the silence became a heavy weight that made the air hard to breathe.

"How is Libby?" she asked finally, noticing the whiteness around Cracker's mouth as he tightened his lips.

She refused to look away.

The older man spit to the side and answered gruffly, "Libby is fine. She's in Canada with Jaxon and their boy, Logan."

"Good. I'm glad to see she got her happy ending."

And she was happy for Libby. Happy enough that it hurt deep inside because she knew there was no such silver lining for her. Her happy ending was nothing more than a fantasy. How could it be anything but? She would seal the portal and spend eternity in the hell realm.

Yeah, some happy fucking ending.

Not for the first time Skye felt a tug of resentment rush through her, but she pushed it away quickly. There was no time for a pity party.

"You gonna share with us what went down at Carocal?" Declan shot at her.

Skye turned to him and spoke calmly. "I asked Libby to tell all of you that Cormac had killed me. I didn't want him or any of the DaCostas to know I'd survived."

Declan's eyes narrowed and he studied her so intensely that she began to feel uncomfortable. "It's you my father wanted, not Libby," he said softly, and Skye took a step back as the tall man crossed over to her.

A growl, low and angry, fell between them and Declan halted as Jagger shoved his way in front of her. "You will step back."

Declan raised his hands, a smirk grazing his handsome face. "Hey, I'm not interested in touching her. I just want to know what the hell my father wants with her." He shrugged his shoulders. "That's all."

The heat from Jagger's body washed over her suddenly cold frame and Skye felt a ripple of frustration run through her. She had no time for these games. The demon realm was knocking hard and it was up to her to slam it shut.

"Jagger says that I can trust all of you." She looked at each of them. "I don't. Unfortunately, I have no choice. Time is running out."

"Why don't you stop being so cryptic and tell us what the hell is going on?" Declan shot back.

Skye ignored him and kept her eyes focused on Cracker and the tall, brooding jaguar that stared at her from several feet away. He was Julian. She remembered him from three months ago. The resemblance between him and Jagger was unmistakable.

She spoke calmly, though inside her heart fluttered and she felt sick to her stomach. Even though she would tell these men only the bare minimum of what was going on, it still went against everything that she believed in.

"Cormac is after a disc, an ancient Aztec artifact that my people have guarded for thousands of years."

"Who exactly are your people?" Cracker asked. His eyes had narrowed but she sensed a sincerity in him that set her mind somewhat at ease.

"I am an eagle knight," she answered softly.

"A what?" Declan snorted.

Jagger shot a look at him. "Let her speak." His tone brooked no argument and Declan raised an eyebrow but remained quiet. He gestured with his hands for her to continue. "By all means."

"I'm a shifter, one of a few left." It was hard to keep the bitterness from her voice, and Skye didn't even try. "My people were hunted to near extinction hundreds of years ago." She glared at all of them. "By the magicks and the jaguars."

"Why?" Cracker's one-word question caused such a well of emotion to churn inside of her that Skye closed her eyes and drew on the strength deep within her.

"My people have been charged since the dawn of time to keep watch over certain artifacts, and for that reason we've been hunted. Destroyed by the likes of you."

Jagger made a sound at her side and for the first time she let her vision wander to him. He stood looking down at her with an expression that was hard to read. Did he believe her? Or did he think she was full of crap?

No matter. He moved a few feet away, his face dark, brooding.

"This disc that you seek, it's something the DaCostas want so bad that they'd get into bed with someone as untrustworthy as Cormac?"

Skye turned to Declan. His eyes were clear and shrewd.

She answered him simply. "Yes."

"It must be valuable," he continued. "What does it do?"

"It's a portal," Julian inserted quietly. Everyone

looked at him and Skye's gasp caught in her throat, nearly choking her. "To the demon underworld."

Fuck! How the hell did the jaguar know that? The bastard had done his homework.

"What?" Declan looked as surprised as the rest of them, and Skye ignored the glare from four sets of eyes as they all turned their attention to her.

"Is this true?" Jagger asked and for the first time a trace of something more than worry edged his words.

Skye considered lying. Hell, the eagle knights guarded several other ancient relics, but she realized there was no point. Julian had already guessed what they were after and by the way he was looking at her, he knew the truth as well as she did.

She exhaled softly and shook her head. "It's the portal they're after, yes."

"I've read stories about it and of your people. Thousands of years ago the jaguar warriors pretty much annihilated your tribe in order to get their hands on the portal. It was thought to be lost, as well as the lineage of the eagle knights."

Skye's eyes flashed and she looked at Julian hard. "Well, my people held on, *barely*, and were able to keep the portal hidden. But someone has betrayed us and for the last three years we've been on the run. Hunted again." She felt her eyes mist with the warmth of tears. "My father was our last hope. Only he knew where it had been hidden. But he was murdered before he could recover it." She paused for a moment, unable to go on as the memory of her father's death washed over her. "Now with Finn gone, it's up to me to find it and destroy it once and for all."

Julian held her gaze for several long, uncomfortable

seconds until finally she looked away. He knew too much.

"There is no one else," she said simply.

Skye ran her fingers through the thick hair at her neck. Things were moving way too fast and in a direction she didn't much care for.

"Not that I don't appreciate the history lesson and all, but seriously, what the hell are we gonna do about this portal or whatever the fuck it is?" Declan looked at all of them expectantly. "Damned if I'll let Cormac get his hands on—"

"This is not your battle to fight," Skye shouted. She was fed up and pissed off. Who the hell did these men think they were? This was her mission. It always had been.

"This became my business the minute you invaded my territory with two DaCostas hot on your heels." Jagger was angry. This she could see and a ripple of fear sliced through her at the look that clouded his green eyes many shades darker.

The power that hung on his frame was unmistakable and as he crossed the distance between them, his large body moving with a predatory grace, she shivered.

He stopped when he was just a few inches from her. Skye could see the pulse that beat steadily at the base of his neck. It was mesmerizing, and she found she couldn't take her eyes off of it.

His scent was intoxicating, and she felt the great raptor inside of her move, wanting out. Wanting to get away from a temptation that not only was a bad idea, it was also forbidden.

Her mouth went dry as her gaze climbed up and met his moss green eyes.

"If you want to survive this and retrieve this disc, I suggest you put aside any notion of a rogue mission, because you're stuck with me." He smiled at her harshly. "I will not see you harmed." His eyes narrowed. "I can't . . . I *won't* let that happen again."

Jagger's words puzzled Skye. She got the impression that he was no longer talking about her. She didn't have time to ponder them.

He opened the satchel and shoved the notes and maps into her hands. "What do these mean?"

Her fingers held the precious papers loosely and her vision blurred as she looked down at them. Her notes and scribbles could be seen clearly in the margins. She didn't have to read them to know what they said. Just as she didn't have to read them to know she was still no closer to finding the cave that she sought.

With or without the help of these men, the situation was hopeless. Why the hell hadn't her father trusted her enough with the location of the cave?

Not for the first time the bitterness of it all stuck in her mouth, and she wished for nothing more than a cool glass of water. Anything, to wash all of it away.

"I need to find a specific cave," she said haltingly, trying to control her emotions. Now was not the time for her to break down.

"A specific cave?" Declan laughed. "Would this particular cave come with a, I dunno, a flashing neon sign saying, *I'm here*?" He looked at all of them incredulously. "This is fucked."

"The Cave of the Sun? Is that it?"

Skye looked at Jagger, clearly surprised. "Yes," she answered him. "How did you know?"

"I saw it in your notes." Jagger's intense eyes bored into hers and she felt everything fade away, as if it were the only two of them there. "I might know of someone who can help us."

There it was. Crunch time. She either accepted his help and went with it, or tried to escape at the earliest convenience.

Her focus fell on the muscular arms held loosely at his sides, trailed along the intricate tattoo that peeked from beneath the T-shirt that he wore. He was so tall, strong, and incredibly male.

He was jaguar. He was her enemy.

Yet the overwhelming urge to slide up against his chest and let him wrap his arms around her was so intense she took a step forward. Their eyes connected and the energy in the air seemed to crackle.

Or was that her imagination?

"Yeah, I'm not into this whole flirting-in-danger thing, so why don't you two chill." Declan's sarcastic tone was more effective than a bucket of water and Skye shook her head as she took a step back.

Cracker spit into the ground, his mouth chewing hard on a dark clump of tobacco. "So," he said roughly, "we got a plan?"

Chapter 11

Jagger watched the conflicting emotions that ran across Skye's expressive eyes. He knew what she was feeling. The same ones were hammering away at the inside of him and he didn't understand them any better than she did.

He looked at the other men, decision made. "Skye and I will find this cave and retrieve the portal." He rolled his shoulders and kinked his neck. The corded bands of flesh that ran along the base of his skull were tight as hell. "I need the three of you to do what you can to neutralize the jaguars that are gunning for us."

His eyes flicked over his older brother and a fierce wall of pride threatened to come crashing down over him. The change in Julian was nearly indescribable. He looked about as far away from the boardroom as you could get.

It was all good. At least Jagger hoped that it was. He sensed a wildness that had never been there before.

An untamed edge that the jaguar thrived on. He knew it would explode eventually. Jagger just hoped that when it happened, any casualties would be limited.

"Don't take any foolish chances. See if you can dig up anything on Cormac. His location, his contacts, plans. Whatever. I want that bastard." His gaze passed over Declan. "No offense."

Declan laughed softly, his tone deadly. "None taken, but you'll have to get in line. The only one who's gonna touch that slimeball is me."

The two men nodded at each other.

"Anyone able to contact Jaxon? Maybe utilize some of the PATU information network? There's no way in hell all of this activity is going unnoticed." Jagger looked at them all expectantly.

"We're still hanging below the radar. Colonel Taggert is in, but for now we're working with little to no backup." Declan sighed heavily. "Ana, Jaxon, and Libby are holed up somewhere in Canada. They've been busy setting up new PATU headquarters, working with Taggert and a select few."

Jagger frowned at the news. He didn't like the situation at all. "Do you have a secure channel? Can I get a message to him?"

"We have a satellite phone, yes, but aren't due to check in for another twenty-four hours." Cracker made a face. "A precaution. We could try to get hold of him but Jaxon won't answer unless it's at the agreed-upon time."

"Understood," Jagger answered, clearly disappointed. "When you make contact tomorrow, tell him he can kick my ass in person soon enough." He smiled wryly. "And ask him to find out anything he can on some dude named Azaiel."

"Azaiel? What the hell kind of name is that?" Declan asked.

"Dunno," Jagger replied, his eyes darting back to his brother. "You have anything to offer?"

Julian shook his head and shrugged his shoulders. "I haven't a clue."

"Okay," Jagger said. "You got an extra sat radio?"

Cracker dug around in his bag and handed one over to Jagger.

"I'll contact you once I have a location for this cave. We can rendezvous there." He looked at all the men. "We good?"

"Jagger, can I have a word?"

Skye watched as Jagger moved toward Cracker and Declan. The three men huddled together and she tried to ignore the occasional glance her way. She had no clue what the hell they were discussing, but it obviously involved her.

She inhaled a deep, cleansing breath, carefully folded her notes Jagger had given to her and put them into the bag. She grabbed another granola bar and turned away. Skye needed to wrap her brain around the entire mess and make sure she knew what the hell she was doing.

She'd only had a few moments of solace before she became aware of Julian, standing a few feet away. Skye turned and studied the man closely. He was handsome, dark and dangerous like his brother, but there was something about him that was more aloof. Like he was holding back.

Jagger was no such animal. He was full frontal all the way.

Skye also realized with a start, that Julian had

no warrior tattoos on his arms. She searched closer, blushing when he cleared his throat.

"I'm not like my brothers."

"Oh, sorry, I didn't mean to . . ." Skye's voice trailed off because, truthfully, she didn't know what the hell she meant.

Silence fell between the two of them, interrupted by the occasional call of a bird or the shriek of a howler monkey. She could still hear the low voices of Jagger and the other two men, but they were too far away for her to make out their words clearly.

"Does he know?" Julian asked, his brow furrowed, his stare intense.

Skye stared up at Jagger's brother, her eyes large and questioning. "Does he know what?"

"That the only one who can destroy the portal is that which created it."

She arched an eyebrow. "What were you, the dorky kid who read history books for kicks? You really did your homework didn't you?"

Her tone was light but the shadows that darkened her eyes with unshed tears was anything but.

Julian ignored her comment and nodded his head toward the group of men conversing several feet away. "Does he know what you're planning?"

"Why would he?" she retorted, exasperated. "Aside from the fact that all of you seem to think I have this damsel-in-distress thing going on, I don't need your help to do what it is that I have to do. This is my fight, whether you want to believe it or not, and how I'm going to accomplish my goal is no one's business but my own."

"I see the way he looks at you. He won't like it."

Skye looked up at Julian, surprised. "I'm not sure what you mean."

Julian shrugged, but both his face and his tone were dead serious. "He wants you."

She laughed curtly. "Really . . . well, a quick fuck is about all Jagger's interested in, believe me."

She looked away as pain sliced across her chest, drawing in a quick breath. "I might even take him up on that." She laughed bitterly. "I mean, my days are numbered, right? Why shouldn't I be allowed to have a little comfort before . . ." Her voice drifted off into silence. She couldn't continue.

"I think you're very brave."

Skye made a face and shook her head. Her heart was bittersweet, her mind made up. "I'm not brave," she whispered.

I'm scared shitless, she thought.

Her cheeks puffed out as she exhaled hard. Angrily she wiped away the moisture from the corners of her eyes.

She turned from Julian. He unnerved her.

Seconds ticked by, and when she raised her head, Skye's eyes were like glass. She looked over to Jagger.

He glanced up and their eyes connected. It was like a physical blow to her gut and it took everything inside of her to remain calm, focused. Jagger's face was unreadable. His body language was tense, the energy in the air palpable. Thick.

It fed the hungry raptor deep inside of her soul, and Skye shook out her arms, smiling at the jaguar. Doing something was way better than sitting on your ass doing nothing at all. Even if the end was near.

It was time.

"Are you ready?" she asked, a challenge ringing in her voice.

Jagger nodded to the men and then looked back at Skye. Long wisps of caramel-colored hair clung in tendrils to her neck. The tank top that she wore did pretty much the same, the thin cotton melded to her lush curves.

If he closed his eyes he'd have no problem whatsoever picturing her naked, wet, her eyes full of desire and her mouth swollen from his own.

But there was no time. He needed to focus and find the portal. Only then would he have the answers that he sought, because he sure as hell didn't believe half the crap she'd told him. Something else was at play here, he could feel it.

And the woman in front of him held all the answers.

"Okay, let's do this." He closed the distance between them and indicated the direction he wished to go.

He grabbed the supply bag and the leather satchel that Skye was holding. He felt her watching him closely as he slung the two bags over his shoulders. She glanced at his brother Julian, and for a second the cat clawed just beneath his skin. Jagger had to fight the urge to growl, to warn away the other man from the blonde.

What the hell was up with that?

Julian shot him a quick look as if he could sense the turmoil that slithered just beneath the surface.

"So, where we headed, anyway?" Skye's husky tone effectively broke the awkward moment and Jagger answered her quickly, pointing toward the northeast.

"We need to head back toward the Cockscomb

Basin. That's where the jaguar reserve is located. If we can't find Nico there, then we'll try Monkey River."

"You're taking Skye to see Nico?"

Jagger turned to his brother, not liking the tone or the implication. He would protect Skye.

"Nico knows every square mile of this entire area, from the Carribean Sea to the base of the Victoria. If he doesn't know where this cave is located, then no one does."

"But he's . . . the last time I saw him, he was unstable." Julian's frown hardened even more. "You would trust him?"

Jagger did growl, low, rough, and the meaning was clear. *Back off.* "Nico will not harm a hair on her head. He may be crazy but he'd never attack someone." His gaze touched on the blue of Skye's. "Unless he was provoked."

"Nice," Skye muttered, stowing the other supply bag tight across her shoulders.

Jagger held his brother's attention for several more seconds. A myriad of emotions flew through him.

They'd never been super close, the two of them. As the oldest, Julian had been groomed from a young age to take over the helm of Blue Heaven Industries from their father. It had pretty much been a done deal when adolescence had come and gone, revealing no warrior tattoos.

Jagger and Jaxon, however, had both developed the warrior tats when they were on the cusp of change, and the subtle dislike his father had for that part of their heritage was not easily hidden. Jagger had fled the homestead as soon as he'd been able. Enlisted, trained for special ops, and had never looked back.

It was ironic to see how the call of the wild had

affected Julian. Right now, in this moment, with the heat of the jungle damp on their skin, the threat of battle imminent, his brother was just as much a warrior as if he'd been born with the very tattoos his father abhorred.

Still, brother or not, he didn't like anyone questioning his authority and decisions.

"Be careful," Jagger said gruffly, and then he turned away. He indicated that Skye follow; without a backward glance he led the way and the two of them disappeared into the jungle.

The going was rough, the air heavy with the threat of a storm. Jagger kept up a relentless pace, stopping only briefly for a rest, and if fresh water was nearby, they'd fill their bottles and then move on.

There was a sense of urgency he couldn't shake, and he was sure that Skye felt the same. She kept up, didn't complain, not even when he knew she was close to being dead on her feet.

Dusk was rapidly approaching. They still had a full day's hike to get to the Cockscomb Basin. It was between the Maya Mountains and the Caribbean Sea.

Jagger had been vigilant and knew they were safe for the moment. He sensed no other warriors or any traces of magick on the wind.

He began to scout for shelter, but it was Skye who pointed out what appeared to be ruins of some kind. They were obviously Mayan and as they approached in silence, he felt a sense of wonder. It never ceased to amaze him how time marched on, her trials and tribulations scarring the landscape, but something always survived.

They approached with caution and again his senses picked up nothing out of the ordinary. The birds, insects, and all the other noises that filled the jungle like a chaotic symphony signaled nothing out of order.

It looked to be some sort of ceremonial area, much of it reclaimed by the rain forest, but it would provide shelter for the night.

Skye stumbled as she walked beside him and his arm snaked out, catching her around the waist. She stilled, catching her breath, yet didn't pull away.

She'd long given up trying to tame the wild mane of hair that streaked past her shoulders in long wisps of golden smoke. The tendrils curled seductively, caressing the bare skin of her arms and neck.

Jagger had the insane urge to push the heavy mane away to cool the hot skin beneath it.

"We rest here," he said gruffly, not liking the softness that had unfurled inside of him. Things were about as bad as they could get. Christ, they were hunting down an ancient Aztec portal that was a fucking conduit to the demon realm.

There was no room for rainbows and puppy dogs.

Skye remained quiet, although she pulled away and walked over to a downed tree. He watched from the corners of his eyes as she sat down, grabbed a tin of food from her pack and opened it.

Jagger did the same, so busy trying to ignore the loud silence that he didn't taste the beans that he gulped down in minutes. The hunger pains in his gut began to ease, although the ache that formed in the pit of his stomach was a testament to the fact that he'd wolfed his food down like an animal.

He leaned back but was afraid to shut his eyes. Would she try to escape?

Jagger tilted his head and observed her as she finished the last of her tin. Her tongue darted out, quickly licking away a drop of sauce that had landed on the corner of her mouth. He was mesmerized at the sight and when she stuck her finger in her mouth, to suck away any lingering remnants that she might find, he felt his groin tighten in response.

All he could think about was her luscious lips wrapped tightly around his straining, painful erection.

And she had no clue as to the effect her simple actions were having.

"Come here," he commanded roughly. Her stare jumped to his, and he held it, her blue eyes wary and hesitant.

He could see that she was shivering. Her body had been through a lot over the past few days, and he knew that physically she must be damn near the end of her rope. That being said, he still didn't trust her enough to allow her to be away from his reach.

She raised her head, her elegant chin jutting out. "No." Her one-word answer was no surprise, but instead of impatience and anger, he felt a sense of pride in her belief that she could win over him.

His grin widened. The little minx had no clue what she was up against.

"Come here . . . *now*," he said once more.

He could see her brain working furiously, looking for a way out. He couldn't be sure if it was because she was so incredibly tired, or if she realized the futility of the situation. Maybe it was both.

No matter. He watched her closely as she got to her feet, pulling along a blanket that had been stuffed inside her supply bag. She stopped just in front of him and bit her bottom lip.

He smiled up at her wickedly, spreading his legs and indicating she slide in between them. Skye hesitated for only a second and then something flashed across the deep blue of her eyes. They darkened and a ghost of a smile tugged at the corner of her mouth.

A tingle of energy slid down Jagger's spine and he felt his mouth go dry. Anticipation shot through him, but it was quickly replaced with anxiety.

The feel of her ass against his crotch had his cock twitching excitedly and the uncomfortable heaviness that followed was painful.

His body immediately tightened and when she wriggled her softness against him and murmured, "Oh, sorry, just trying to get comfortable—the ground is so hard," he knew he'd made a terrible mistake.

Fuck.

What the hell had he been thinking? He should have tied her to a tree or something.

He tried to ignore the earthy scent that clung to her skin. By rights the woman should stink to high heaven. They had been trekking through the jungle for days. But she smelled incredibly delicious and he wanted nothing more than to run his tongue down the back of her neck, nibble his way around the delicate jaw, and claim her luscious lips as his own.

"Who is this Nico?" Skye asked, her voice slicing through his fantasy. She moved her body once more, a subtle grind, and he clenched his teeth. "Ah, that's better," she said softly.

Jagger blew out hot air. It was going to be one hell of a long night.

He took a few moments and forced his body to relax. It was hard. The warmth of the woman between his legs called to the animal inside of him. He could feel the possessive need, the *want* that lay there waiting to explode.

"Nico is jaguar. No one really knows where he comes from, what clan. His tattoos are unlike any I've seen before." Jagger controlled the shudder that tingled inside of him, but it was hard. Skye Knightly felt too damn good. "He used to belong to my brother's unit at PATU but left several years ago."

"Okay, I've heard you boys talking about PATU and I have no clue what the hell that is."

Jagger smiled at the indignant tone of Skye's voice. She sure as hell didn't like being out of the loop. "Paranormal Antiterrorist Unit. It's specialized and uses highly trained operatives, all otherworld. You know, people like us, non humans. Jaxon has headed the unit for the last seven years."

"And this Nico person was in this unit. Why did he leave?"

"That"—Jagger sighed—"is not my story to tell."

"Well, what did Julian mean when he said that Nico was unstable? Are we hanging our hopes on some nut job who's gone native and lives in the jungle full time?"

"I went *native* and my faculties are wholly intact."

Skye snorted. "I wouldn't be too sure of that."

"Look, I'll be the first to admit that Nico has issues, but it's not like we have much choice. If anyone knows where this freaking cave is, it will be Nico."

He waited as his words soaked in. His body was tight, uncomfortable. When she moved yet again, an exquisite pain shot from his cock and traveled up his body like a lightning bolt. It left in its wake a fire that singed every nerve ending along the way. It elicited a hiss from deep within his chest and he cursed under his breath.

Jagger didn't know what would happen if she kept

up her game of cock tease. Her round ass was an invitation he was finding hard to resist. The fact that her heart rate had sped up and her body was now flush with heat told him that she was not immune to the pull of desire that raged inside of him.

"You will not win," he whispered, low, against her neck. He knew exactly what she was up to.

Skye turned her head slightly, until their mouths were almost touching. When she whispered, the heat from her mouth caressed his lips like a kiss: "Who says I want to win?"

Her voice, husky, fanned the flames of desire to a level he'd not felt before.

Ever.

Fuck, Jagger thought as her lips reached for his. He held back for a second and then with a groan covered her mouth with his own. As her sweetness opened up to him, he pushed back the thoughts that lingered like a bad dream. He opened his mouth fully and his tongue plunged deep inside the warm wetness of hers.

Jagger ignored the voice that echoed deep within his mind.

No good can come of this.

Chapter 12

Dangerous slivers of desire swept across Skye's flesh and she shuddered as Jagger's mouth met her waiting, eager lips. Each pass of his tongue pulled at something deep inside of her, an ache that roared to life with a pulsating need that, while painful, carved trails of pleasure-spiked desire across her skin. It felt like every single nerve ending was electrified.

The intensity left her breathless.

All of this with just a kiss.

She groaned softly into his mouth, shifting her body until she was able to turn fully. Skye wanted every single inch of her flesh touching his. It was all she could think about. The incredible need to touch and to taste.

It was like a fever, this need to connect on every level possible.

With Jagger.

"Christ, but you feel good." His low, rough voice

sent a new round of pleasure spiraling through her body.

"So do you," she whispered against his mouth.

Her hands had crept up his body and Skye's fingers dug in as she straddled him, pushing her center into the welcoming heat between his legs.

He was rock hard and the hiss that escaped his lips as she ground her body against him excited and thrilled Skye. She took wicked pleasure in knowing just how much he wanted her. To know that his passion more than matched the molten heat that raced through her veins was an amazing feeling.

She wanted to lose herself in him. To forget everything that tinged the landscape black and threw a dagger of destruction into her foreseeable future.

A future that was on borrowed time.

She shook her head and cleared her mind from such thoughts. An image of Jagger naked and wet, shrouded in mist as the wildness of the jaguar slowly fled his body, flashed before her eyes. He'd been so untamed, so feral when she'd first laid eyes on him.

She smiled into his mouth as he growled deep from his throat, his breaths coming in ragged bursts.

Skye grabbed his face between her hands, nipping at his nose as she pulled away. His eyes, electric green, burned with a fire and intensity that at one time might have unnerved her. Scared her, even.

Yet now it awakened something inside that answered in kind.

Jagger Castille was all male. Rough, hard, powerful. And for this night, he was all hers.

She didn't give a rat's ass that he was jaguar. Not at this moment, anyway. Because in the coming days none of it would matter.

Skye traced her index finger along his chiseled chin, up along his jaw until her hand sunk deep into the glossy waves that caressed his neck. He was so damn beautiful, it almost hurt to look at him.

She reached down slowly, watching his eyes dilate as her lips hovered just above his mouth. She knew that he wanted her as much as she craved him, and that only fed the fires to an even hotter degree.

The noises he made were so animalistic, she couldn't help but smile wickedly as each one tore from the back of his throat.

In a time when everything seemed to be uncertain, the one thing she could control was the here and now. How ironic that Skye, an elite eagle knight, wanted to control a jaguar warrior.

Badly.

His eyes began to glow; sparks seeming to fly from deep within. Skye felt his hands ease their way around her body until they cupped the mounds of her ass tightly. He pulled her in tighter, crushing her against him with merciless intent.

Skye bit her lip as the ache that lay heavily between her legs intensified. Jagger pulled her slowly back and forth across his erection, and the friction from the material of her shorts was insanely pleasurable.

Her right hand slowly brought his head back toward her, while she kept his mouth aimed toward her own with her left. She wanted to taste him, and opened her mouth hotly against his, her tongue going deep and securing his mouth as her property in one careful swoop.

He tasted like the jungle. Hot, spicy, dangerous.

Inside her soul, the raptor was hungry.

They kissed, long and hard, each feeding from the other with an appetite that was insatiable.

"I want you so bad it feels like I need to crawl inside of you or I'll go crazy," Jagger whispered hoarsely into her ear.

Skye stilled at his words. The longing and need that colored his words was echoed inside of her. It was almost painful, this need to mate. To make love with a man who was her equal.

A man you'll have to give up.

The thought slipped into her mind, silent and sneaky. Skye savagely pushed it away. Tonight was hers and to hell with everything else.

She pulled her mouth from Jagger's, loving the way he tried to hold on, as if she were the oxygen he needed to live. She then righted herself, keeping her body balanced on his crotch as she straddled his groin.

"You are a fucking angel." Jagger reached for her hair and she let him fondle it between his fingers, her hands running up along his forearms as he did so. She could feel her nipples, hardened with need, straining against the soft cotton of her tankie and she laughed throatily, pushing his hands away as she reached for the bottom seam.

As the sultry jungle air touched the heated flesh of her breasts, coaxing the nipples into an even harder pucker, Skye shuddered. They were so sensitive that she groaned softly. Her breasts felt heavy, full of need.

Jagger inhaled deeply and he held her hands at her sides, effectively trapping her. His eyes were nearly black with desire as they fed from the exposed flesh that trembled beneath his gaze.

Long moments passed but he wouldn't release her. Skye began to move impatiently against him. "Let me go, I need to—"

He moved quickly, his tongue darting out to attack the turgid nipple closest to him. He circled the hardness, moving his tongue with a deft control that left Skye shaking.

"Oh God, that feels so good," she whispered as she closed her eyes and gave herself up to the sensations that were fingering their way out from her chest, to the soft ache between her legs. It was like a direct conduit, and only intensified when he closed his entire mouth over her nipple.

Skye arched into him, wanting to grab hold of his head, but her hands were still trapped at her sides. He wouldn't release her. It was like an exquisite torture.

He began to suckle, *hard*, and each time he drew her deep into his mouth, it pulled at her desire in such a way that it was painful. Yet wholly pleasurable.

"Please," she whimpered, "I need to touch you."

Jagger laughed wickedly and moved to her other breast, trapping the aching nipple between his teeth, scraping the sensitive peak provocatively. Skye squealed and ground herself against him, loving the feel of his hardness. She began to writhe in earnest as small sounds of pleasure and desire fell from her lips.

Jagger held her firm still, his open mouth and tongue devouring the rosy hardness like it was candy. He licked, nipped, and suckled, and then blew on each breast. The sensation was unlike anything Skye had felt before, and her head fell back as she gave herself up to its exquisite pleasure.

She'd had lovers in the past. Yet none had affected her on such a level as did Jagger. He'd barely begun to scratch the surface and she was putty in his hands.

"Jagger, release my hands." Her words were throaty

but she managed to get them out, and when he suddenly acquiesced, Skye immediately grabbed his head and brought his mouth back to her own.

"You taste like sin," she whispered against his mouth.

A smile spread across her own as she pulled away and slowly stood. The night's kiss against her heated skin spread a rash of goose bumps across her flesh, and her fingers fell to the hard nipples at her breasts.

God, she loved the way his eyes reacted when she touched herself. She massaged the aching buds and laughed softly at the exasperated curse that flew from his lips.

"You're fucking killing me."

Skye tore her gaze away from his and let her eyes wander down the hard planes of his chest. Savagely, she reached for the shirt that covered what she so wanted to see and practically ripped it from his frame, tossing it aside, where it landed on top of hers.

Her mouth immediately fell to his neck and she nipped and suckled the base, licking slowly, seductively, at the point where his pulse banged out a rhythm of desire. Her nipples scraped gently against the hair on his chest and she sucked in her breath as a new wave of sensation poured over her flesh.

Jagger's hands wove a trail of fire up and down her bare back while her mouth slowly slid toward his chest, until her tongue flicked a wet kiss against each of his nipples. They, too, hardened, and she rose slightly until her breasts were crushed against his.

Something then slid across her subconscious. A whisper of darkness.

Skye stilled. Her heart beat fast and heavy in her chest as a spike of adrenaline rushed through her veins.

"Don't stop now," Jagger uttered, his voice hoarse, edgy with need.

"I just, I . . ." Skye struggled to clear the fog of desire from her brain. Something was weird. Off.

It tempered the raw need that she felt, but only minutely, and when Jagger once more claimed her nipple, deep in his mouth, she threw her head back.

His hands were inside the waist band of her shorts and he leaned back, pulling the denim from her limbs and leaving her bare to his roving eyes. They were hooded, sexy in their regard of her nakedness.

Skye smiled at Jagger and slowly slid her hands down her belly. She spread her legs open and teased the sweet spot that lay hidden within the folds of her sex with quick, gentle movements.

The sweat that covered Jagger's skin in a fine sheen quickly beaded and the look on his face was so raw and intense that she stopped her actions.

His eyes began to glow and the tattoos that adorned the hard lines of his abs and left bicep seemed to move. She was transfixed to such an extent that at first she didn't note the change in the atmosphere.

"Don't stop now, baby," he whispered hoarsely, though his voice fell from his lips in layers, and her heart jumped. Something wasn't right.

Slowly, as if from far away, she felt the beginnings of panic intruding. Skye's head felt fuzzy and she shook herself, trying to right her body.

Her skin was no longer heated but cold, and a feeling of dread settled deep in her gut. The air around them began to fog as the warmth from the earth reacted to the suddenly cold temperature.

Her desire fled, the need forgotten. Something was desperately wrong.

Jagger seemed to be oblivious to all of this, and when he reached for her, his eyes focused solely on the exposed apex of her legs, she kicked hard and rolled to the side.

"What the fuck?" The words, ripped from his throat were furious.

"I can't, I . . ."

Jagger stood over her, chest heaving, erection strained against his pants, with his hands clenched tightly at his sides. His face had gone white and she could sense the fury that lay just under the skin.

Skye scrambled away, more confused than ever, looking around wildly.

"Something was"—she swallowed, trying to force the words out—"something was here."

Jagger's eyes narrowed and he scented the air. When he turned back to her, his face was tight with anger. "Lady, the only thing that I see is a cock tease."

Skye shook her head, but no words came forth. She had no clue what had just happened and couldn't articulate it. She dropped her gaze to the ground, shoulders sunken as she tried to cover her nakedness.

She suddenly felt exposed, cheap.

"You don't understand," she whispered.

Jagger suddenly bent low, his breath striking the skin of her cheek. "No I don't. I don't understand any of this. I'm not one of your flyboy eagles, and I don't like games."

She closed her eyes and turned her head away.

Jagger pulled away. "We're done. Get dressed."

Skye kept a wary eye on him as she gingerly reached for her clothes. In less than thirty seconds she was dressed, unsure of what to do next.

"Come here," Jagger commanded, yet this time

there was no desire, warmth. In fact there was pretty much nothing at all.

She hesitated, but the look that he threw at her quenched any desire to ignore his request. The man was pissed, and now that several moments had passed, Skye was starting to think that he had every right to be.

Her eyes swept the area once more and nothing seemed out of place. The jungle was just as it had been. Silent, dark.

What the hell was wrong with her?

She held her head high and walked over to him, surprised when his arms went around her. But this was no gentle touch. He had a rope tied around her waist before she even knew what was happening.

It was long and he motioned toward the tree where her bag lay. "You bed down there. If you so much as move an inch I'll be all over you." His eyes narrowed cruelly. "And trust me, it won't be fucking I'm after."

Skye stared down at the intricately knotted rope that was tight and secure and then she looked back at Jagger.

"You've got to be kidding. This is not necessary," she ground out from between clenched teeth as her own anger rose up from deep inside to answer his.

Jagger just shook his head, ignored her, and pulled his T-shirt back down over his body. He wrapped the other end of the rope securely around his hand, crossed to where the two of them had lain together and flopped down.

Skye stared at him for several long moments, trying to control the anger that left her limbs shaking.

Un-fucking-believable!

She began to walk toward her bag, but realized the

rope didn't allow enough distance to do that. For a few seconds, she stood there, uncertain, pissed, tired as all hell.

Skye felt her strength begin to fade, like air leaking from a balloon, and she knew she needed to rest. She glanced over at Jagger and made a face. He looked like he was resting comfortably.

As she slid her body up against what was left of a stone wall, she made a vow to make the bastard pay for his arrogance. Her fingers fell to the rope that was tied a little too tightly around her waist. It was no use. The knot was intricate and much too tight.

Skye rested her head against the hard surface and closed her eyes. She began to shiver once more and wrapped her arms around her body, looking for what little comfort that she could. Her blanket was over by Jagger, but damned if she was going anywhere near him.

It was going to be a long and miserable night. She sighed tiredly and tried to sleep.

She was almost there, too, when the voice that she feared above all others, more than Cormac or any of the DaCosta scum, slid through her mind.

Azaiel's seductive whisper was like a dark promise. Skye's eyes flew open, wide with fear. She wanted nothing more than to flee, to run as far and as fast as she could. To reach for the golden sun when it rose and to shift so that she could fly away from all of this madness.

"You are so close, my little bird, I can almost taste you."

The words spoken in her mind seemed as if underwater. She could understand them but they faded in and out, muffled. Skye swallowed thickly, trying her best to dampen the fear that clogged her throat. "I will never let you touch me," she whispered hoarsely.

There was no response, and for a brief moment Skye wondered if in fact she was going crazy. If the hallucinations she'd had since a young child were just slivers of a madness that was finally manifesting.

Dully, she once more rested her head and closed her eyes. It didn't matter. If he was real, she'd meet Azaiel once the portal was sealed.

In hell.

Chapter 13

Jagger was awake well before dawn. He'd managed a few hours of shut-eye, which was a fucking miracle considering he'd had a raging hard-on that wouldn't go away.

His eyes swept across to the tree where Skye slumbered still. A million curses slid through his brain but he remained silent. There was no use getting all worked up. He needed to conserve his energy. He'd get his hands on the goddamned portal and make her beg for it.

It was time someone taught Skye Knightly a lesson.

A slow smile lifted the corners of his mouth and he relaxed. He was more than up for the job. He shifted his body, hissing softly as the bulge between his legs throbbed with a need long denied.

Christ, was he up for it.

Once he was somewhat comfortable, he opened his mind up and listened. The nocturnal sounds of the jungle comprised a melody he would never tire of. It fed his soul in a way that was indescribable. It calmed him.

Again, his eyes wandered over Skye's still form. Her chest rose and fell in the rhythm of sleep. The woman was a mystery. One that, he was pissed to admit, intrigued the hell out of him.

He didn't trust her, didn't know anything about her other than the fact that, apparently, they were natural-born enemies.

He got to his feet and crossed over to where she lay. Hopefully, when he rendezvoused with Cracker and the boys, they'd have more information on her family, the Knightlys. He knew her father was dead and there was a missing brother, Finn, but other than that he was clueless. The whole eagle knight thing was a mystery to him and he didn't like any loose ends when running a mission.

In a fluid movement Jagger doffed his clothes and quickly tied the loose end of the rope up to one of the protruding branches of the downed tree to her right. He left it in an intricate knot, knowing it would be a cold day in hell before she was able to undo it.

He cracked the bones in his neck and rolled his shoulders as the mist began to crawl up over his long limbs. Within seconds his bones popped, limbs shortened, torso elongated, and a thick, shiny black pelt was left in place of his flesh. The jaguar barked a soft call, its long tail swishing back and forth slowly as its senses drifted on the languid breeze.

After a few moments the animal jumped over the long, tanned feminine legs at its feet and disappeared into the underbelly of the jungle.

The powerful cat roamed a great distance, hunting, tracking, but there was no enemy to be found. Neither animal nor human nor otherworld. And while this was a good thing, Jagger was on edge. He sensed something off, a slight kink in the ebb and flow of the vibrations that ran along Mother Earth.

Was it otherworld? He was frustrated because, truthfully, he had no clue, and other than a vague feeling, there was no evidence to be found.

His thoughts turned to Skye and her weird behavior the night before. Was there some merit to her actions? Had she sensed something he'd not been able to? Or was she just one hell of an actress?

The large cat scoured as much area as he could, seeking out any enemy that he might have missed. When the first fingers of sunlight began to tint the sky, jagged shards of gold bleeding through the early gloom, he turned and made his way back to where he'd left Skye.

Jagger knew they still had a good day's hike before they would get anywhere near the jaguar reserve. And that was at the relentless pace only someone with the strength of the jaguar or eagle could attain.

He shook off the eerie quiet of the jungle and took off running. There was no time to waste.

He approached the ruins where they'd taken shelter the night before and slowed as he came abreast of them. Skye's subtle, fragrant scent hung in the air like a seductive invitation. He began to pant, his nostrils quivering, and his tail twitched aggressively, snaking back and forth.

Jagger growled from deep in his chest as he glided over the soft earth. He rounded the edge of the broken-down stone wall, its sad gray countenance mostly covered by the myriad of greenery that made up the jungle floor.

He immediately caught wind of the scent of blood and swung his great head back and forth, panic nipping at him when he saw that Skye was not where he'd left her. The rope lay in tatters, covered in the unmistakable scent of her blood.

Jagger's vision narrowed as the panic he felt intensified to an overwhelming sense of fear. He had left her there, tied up and defenseless. What the hell had he been thinking?

The mist immediately crawled over the powerful body of the cat and seconds later a tall human form emerged and ran toward the edge of the ruins.

Jagger knelt down, his fingers touching the earth at his feet.

The ground was messed up, but as far as he could see there was only one set of footprints. He scented the air, but other than Skye's fragrance there was nothing to be found. He quickly donned his clothes, pulled on his boots, and followed the trail back into the jungle. It led in the opposite direction from where he'd been.

He raced through the thick underbrush, his mind and body focused on Skye. It wasn't hard: she'd made no effort to cover her tracks and the scent of blood and fear lay heavy in the air. He found her less than a quarter of a mile away, at the edge of a small waterfall that fell from a sheer rock face.

She turned to him and that was all it took. He was at her side in seconds, a deep scorching shame hitting him hard as he looked down at her.

Her long hair lay in a wild mess, the thick waves untamed in the humid, wet air. Her tank top, drenched from the mist that hung in the air, was shredded violently and barely covered her breasts. The ragged edges were ugly, like gaping wounds. Large dark stains marred the white cotton and he could see that it was blood.

His gaze dropped to the chafed and torn flesh at her waist, and the shame he felt intensified.

What had he done to her?

"I thought you'd left me," she said softly, her voice trembling. "Like everyone else."

Skye raised her eyes and met his, and the pain and misery that was reflected in their depths touched something inside of him. He reached for her, ignoring the flinch as she looked away.

"He came back and you were gone." She shook her head agitatedly. "I panicked."

"Who came back?" he asked, his voice rough and urgent as his eyes skimmed the area around them. His adrenaline spiked and he hissed loudly as he turned back to her.

"Azaiel."

Her voice trembled and something inside his chest constricted as he followed the progress of a single solitary tear. It wove its way down her cheek and fell to the ground. One perfect drop of sorrow that nearly killed him.

"I didn't expect it. Not so soon. I thought he'd gone away." She held out her hands. "It was different. He was there, outside of my head. I could *feel* him like before, only stronger, and I panicked."

Jagger saw that her fingers were still rigid with the long, deadly talons of an eagle.

"It was daybreak and I could feel my strength returning. My only thought was to get away, so I clawed at the rope, but it was so tight." She began to cry and Jagger truly felt like the biggest loser on planet Earth and beyond. "I could feel his hands on me and I . . ."

An ache clutched at him hard and he dropped to his knees, drawing her into the warmth of his embrace.

"There's no one here now, Skye. You're safe," he murmured against the softness of her hair.

None of this made sense. A fucking dream demon manifesting itself? Jagger shook his head.

"I just wanted to get away," she whispered, as if she'd not heard a word he'd said. "He kept laughing in my head and . . ."

She inhaled raggedly and he felt her body shudder violently. "I just wanted to make him go away but he wouldn't stop. The things he said to me, I don't—"

Skye stopped abruptly and was silent.

"Don't what? It's all right, he's long gone." Jagger's senses had picked up nothing and he was dead certain they were alone.

His gaze took in her long elegant talons once more, as they shimmered and shifted, returning to their human form.

"He'll never stop," she said softly, almost in a daze. "He's coming. We need to go. There isn't much time."

"Here, let me help you get cleaned up."

Skye ignored him and wriggled out of his grasp. He let her go without a struggle, afraid that he would hurt her again. The raw skin at her waist made him cringe.

She grabbed a remnant of material at her feet and plunged it into the water that swept by.

Jagger turned to give her some privacy as she finished cleaning her wounds. The occasional sniffle echoed into the silence, and when she was done, his jaw ached from tension and self-loathing.

They made their way back to their supplies in silence. Skye had no more clothes and he found an extra T-shirt in one of the bags. It was large, obviously her brother's, and she tied it at her hips, effectively hiding the chafed skin.

They ate quickly, filled up their water bottles back at the stream and began the long, arduous hike over Victoria Peak. With luck they'd reach the summit by nightfall, then head to the jaguar reserve, in the Cockscomb Basin, by morning.

If there was a god, Nico would be easy to find and hopefully direct them to the Cave of the sun.

Yeah, and I'm blowing lucky charms out my ass.

Jagger grimaced at the thought, but he had to prepare himself. There had to be hundreds of hidden caves and grottoes just in and around Victoria Mountain alone. The Maya mountain range, where they'd just come from was a whole other story.

He chanced a quick glance down at the woman, who was having no problems whatsoever keeping up with him. Her golden skin was covered in a fine sheen of moisture, her hair curled in long caramel-colored ringlets, and her clothes clung to her frame.

The air was incredibly humid and Jagger could feel rain. He'd been in the wild for at least three months. If his calculations were correct, it was mid- to late May, and the rainy season would be upon the region in the next little while.

Making their mission much more difficult.

Jagger pushed those thoughts to the back of his mind. He'd deal with it, if and when the situation presented itself. Right now, he needed to concentrate on getting them safely over Victoria Peak.

They continued to climb higher, pushing through the thick stands of mahogany and cedar that were abundant in this part of Belize. The pace set was relentless, and by early evening they achieved their goal: they reached the summit. The last bit of sun lay bright across the darkening sky, the view unfettered by the tall canopy below.

Jagger turned to Skye. She stood a few feet away, panting slightly from the exertion of the climb. Her face was raised, eyes closed, and the soft curve of her cheek was illuminated by the last dying beams of sunlight. All around her a fine mist from the clouds created an otherworld effect.

She looked ethereal. As if she weren't real.

The sight held him still.

His gut tightened and a knot formed at the back of his throat. Jagger gave himself a mental shake. What the hell was wrong with him? So the lady enjoyed a bit of sunlight.

A loud call echoed down at them and they both turned to the right. A large bird drifted lazily on the wind, its wings spread languidly.

His eyes immediately fell to Skye but she was focused on the raptor. As it swooped lower, he was able to ascertain that it was indeed an eagle. The wind was blowing in the opposite direction. He couldn't catch its scent. He didn't know if it was otherworld.

"Is that one of yours?"

She just shook her head and answered softly, "No. That one is free."

Skye turned toward him abruptly. "Can I have my satchel?"

They'd barely spoken all day and while his first instinct was to keep the bag, he found himself handing it over. He still felt like an utter ass for what had happened the night before.

He turned from her and looked out at the Maya Mountains. They ran along the western side of the

Victoria, and even cloaked in the dull gray of early dusk, they were magnificent.

"We'll camp here for the night. Make our way down into the basin by midmorning."

Skye ignored him and grabbed a bunch of papers along with a tin of beans before she settled herself into a small crevice carved into the ground. Atop the exposed summit, there wasn't much shelter, so they took what they could find.

They ate in silence, and as the long moments ticked by Jagger found himself growing more and more annoyed. He couldn't take the silent treatment any longer.

"Look, I'm sorry I left you the way I did this morning, but I couldn't take the chance you'd fly away."

Silence still.

"For Christ sakes, Skye, give me a break. You would have done the same thing if the positions were reversed."

Blue eyes pinned him with a look that could shred intestines.

"That's bullshit."

"No, it's the truth."

She shook her head and even though he could tell she was furious with him, Jagger preferred the anger to the total wall of silence he'd been treated to all day.

"You're so full of it your eyes should be brown, not green," she spat as she came to her knees.

The wind had picked up as the coming night began to blanket the horizon, and long wisps of her hair floated on the breeze. She pushed them away impatiently, chest heaving, eyes blazing with anger.

"Last night was about control and nothing more. You were pissed you didn't get a little action and took it out on me. Last time I checked, a woman still has the right to say no."

Her words stopped the automatic denial that lay on his lips. Truth was, he'd *wanted* to hurt her, humiliate her the way she'd done him.

She marched over and thumped him in the chest. Hard.

"But what more could I expect from someone like you?" She shook her head. "You're no different than the DaCostas."

The insult hit him hard and his reaction was quick. "*That* is something you'll not say again." The whispered words were a deadly warning.

One that Skye did not heed.

"Fuck you. I'll say and do whatever the hell I want." Her voice rose shrilly. "I'm done with the fear, the uncertainty, the chaos." She turned from him. "I'm done with all of it. I'll get my hands on that portal and end it, once and for all."

Skye shot a look of loathing at him. "And I don't need a fucking arrogant jaguar to accomplish my endgame."

Jagger grabbed her arms, even as he felt his own skin begin to burn. For a second the air around him shimmered and he had to fight like hell to hold his animal inside.

Skye Knightly pressed every single button he had going. Hell, she fucking smashed them.

"No? Seems to me you and your kind have been out here screwing the pooch for months. Christ, you couldn't even avoid getting caught by the jaguars. What makes you think you have what it takes to find this so-called portal?"

"That's low, even for you. The only reason the DaCostas were able to get their filthy paws on me was because—" Skye stopped abruptly and Jagger paused, feeling an edge of unease surpass the anger that he felt. She was holding something back. It was in the way her eyes darkened just before she looked away.

"Don't stop now."

Her body was tense. She was obviously hurt, tired, and God knows, he was getting sick of the constant battle between the two of them.

He felt his own anger deflate and let her go, pushing her away. "Actually, fuck it. I don't care."

"They attacked at dusk," she said quietly and he stopped. "Like the cowards that they are, they attacked when I was at my weakest." Skye snorted and shook her head. "Even then it took three of the bastards to bring me in."

He watched closely as her golden skin flushed dark and her eyes shadowed before she looked away. Her delicate throat contracted as she swallowed, but when she turned back anger was quite evident in her face.

Her mouth was closed tightly and she shrugged her shoulders. He could tell there was some sort of internal struggle going on.

"What aren't you telling me?" he asked harshly.

"I can't . . ."

"You can't what? Look, I don't have the time or patience for these games."

Jagger was beginning to think he was better off distancing himself from the blonde. He needed to get this mission done and get away from her. Because the truth was, he did care. A little too much for his liking.

And he'd learned the hard way that it was a road he didn't want to travel on. Someone always got hurt.

Her face went blank. "Whatever," she muttered under her breath.

He watched as Skye gathered up her satchel and the

extra supply bag. It was obvious she was going to leave but he made no attempt to stop her. His anger was a slow burn that left his gut roiling.

He was torn. On one hand the need to protect was nearly overwhelming, but the desire to protect his sanity, his *soul* was pretty high on his agenda. He'd let the little bird fly the coop for the night and deal with her in the morning.

It took too much energy to fight and he needed sleep badly.

He turned away from her and rotated his head in an effort to relieve some of the tension that scraped along the edge of his shoulders and down his spine. God, what he wouldn't give for a refreshing swim.

Still ignoring the blonde he grabbed food from his own supply bag and was about to relax when the merest of whispers tingled down his back.

Jagger whirled around, nostrils flaring, as a scent drifted up his nasal passages, one that he'd not expected to run across out in the Belizean jungle.

He immediately crossed to Skye, his hand snaking out to stop her cold.

"Be still," he whispered hoarsely.

Her head whipped up but his hand was over her mouth before she could speak. Skye began to struggle and it was all he could do to keep her restrained in his arms. When she bit his hand, he clamped down on the curse that lay trapped in his throat and applied pressure, his arms brutally strong.

Eventually she ceased her struggles, although Jagger was pretty sure it was more to do with the fact that she'd not eaten or rested properly in days.

But it was already too late.

Two shapes materialized from the gloom that

shrouded the entire area. One tall, obviously male, the other female. Their scent was otherworld and it was one that he knew well.

A deadly calm slipped through his veins. The situation had just gone from bad to worse. Only he knew how much the stakes had just been upped. The fact that the two mercenaries had snuck up on him like he was a wet-behind-the-ears freaking newbie was unacceptable.

Skye Knightly was too much of a distraction. If he didn't deal with that soon, she'd get them both killed.

"Jagger Castille, been a long time."

He clenched his teeth so hard his jaw ached. But first things first.

It looked like Jagger's past was about to bite him in the ass. Big-time. If only he'd had more time back in Michigan, when he'd first realized they were tracking him.

"Tag," he said calmly. "Was hoping I'd never have to lay eyes on your ugly-ass face again." He then turned to the woman, whose smile was empty, cold. "Dani, you're looking a little pale. Short supply of O-neg around these here parts?" The sarcasm of his words was hard to miss.

"Good to see you too." The female spoke softly. "Although I'm guessing, you're not quite as happy to see us as we are to find you out in this godforsaken corner of the world."

Power surged through Jagger's veins as he smiled at the two before him. They both had a major hate-on for all things Castille.

Especially the one named Jagger.

Chapter 14

Instant dislike ripped through Skye's body as she carefully observed the newcomers. She could sense the animosity, the hatred, emanating from the two of them, but there was something else. Something subtle.

There was a history between them and Jagger. She could tell that it was ugly.

The female, Dani, was obviously a vampire. There was no mistaking the sickening scent that clung to her skin or the otherworld glow that hung in the air around her.

Of course the fangs that half slid from between the plump red lips were a dead giveaway as well.

The woman's eyes passed over Skye, dismissing her instantly, to rest on Jagger as if he were a yummy piece of meat she wanted to enjoy. Skye's hackles rose and for an instant she visualized her fist connecting with the perfectly white skin, marring the paleness in some violent way.

The other one, Tag, was something else entirely. That he was otherworld was without question. Yet his scent was something she'd not come across before.

His eyes were flat, dead, and at the moment their black roundness was directed solely at her. The intensity behind them made her skin crawl.

She moved back without thinking, her body melting into Jagger's warmth. Her reaction drew a wicked smile from the man.

Bastard knew exactly how he made her feel.

"Christ, Dani, you could have sent a postcard, although I guess I should be flattered I'm worth a trip to the Belizean jungle."

What the hell was Jagger doing, baiting them? Did he have a freaking death wish?

"But really, a little overly dramatic, don't you think? Seems an awful long way to carry a grudge if you ask me."

His hands tightened around Skye's waist. "You need to shift and get as far away from here as you can," Jagger's voice was a whisper in her ear.

A low growl escaped from Tag's mouth and Skye felt her belly flip over when she caught sight of the deadly row of serrated teeth. She couldn't stop staring at them, not even when he licked his lips and hissed at her.

It was then that she knew. Tag was a demon.

Shit, this put a whole new spin on the situation. Demons were still relatively few and far between in the human realm, and not much was known about them.

"Oh, Jagger, you silly animal. Haven't changed at all, have you?" Dani looked at his arms, still pressed possessively at Skye's waist. A shadow passed over her face and when Dani turned her attention to Skye, the vampire made no effort at all to hide the contempt and utter disregard that she felt.

"Want to weigh in on that one, chica? Is Jagger still an arrogant son-of-a-bitch who thinks the world revolves around him?"

Skye remained silent, not willing to be drawn into whatever the hell was going on between the two of them.

Jagger was slowly trying to shift his body so that she was no longer in front of him, his hands urgent at her waist. Once more he whispered softly into her ear. "You need to get out of here, *now*."

The tension in his voice lent credence to the severity of their situation, and Skye felt a myriad of emotions wash over her. On one hand she'd love nothing more than to call to her eagle, shift, and get the hell away from everything.

Aside from the fact that it was impossible for her to do that once the sun had set, she was more than a little surprised to realize she didn't want to leave Jagger.

At least not here, alone, to face the two deadly otherworlders who stood before them.

The vampire began to move toward them, her long legs not seeming to touch the earth as she drifted across the ground. She stopped a few feet away and hissed, baring her perfect white fangs as she laughed at them.

"You really think you're going to be able to protect her?"

"*I really think* we need to finish things and leave Skye the hell out of it."

The vampire's eyes darkened. "You're such an arrogant prick. You actually believe Tag and I spent the last week hiking through this fucking jungle because

I wanted a piece of you?" She sneered and shook her head. "Typical, but that would be wrong."

An eerie fog began to drift over the hard, barren ground. It slid along the earth and rock like a snake, moving sensually as it crept closer, caressing the vampire like a lover.

Dani licked her lips and her voice dropped as a cool breeze lifted her long dark hair.

"A call went out on the wire a few days ago." The vampire nodded toward Skye. "There's a shitload of mercenaries crawling through this jungle looking for her. She's worth a small fortune. Tag and I aim to collect."

Skye's heart began to beat heavily inside her chest as adrenaline rushed through her body. A fight was imminent, and even though she couldn't call upon her eagle, she still had enhanced strength and fighting skills.

She wasn't going down easily.

"The fact that we've finally got Jagger Castille in our sights is just an added bonus," the vampire added as she licked her lips salaciously. "Unexpected, but I'll take it."

Jagger shoved Skye behind him. She felt the heat from his body against her cheek and she swore the air shimmered around his form. He was on the cusp of change, his energy dark and dangerous.

Jagger kept his voice light. "Hate to point out the obvious, but dude, you're gonna have to go through me first." He growled then. "And though I don't make a habit out of hitting women, I totally am looking forward to bitch-smacking your white, bony ass."

Dani's eyes narrowed into small slits. "This has been a long time coming, Castille. I've thought of nothing else since Iraq. Speaking of . . ." The vampire began to move again, while the demon held back, his eyes glowing brightly in the early-evening gloom.

"You took out half my unit, and for that alone you will pay. Eden's death was only a small reward." Her voice deepened and shook as her anger became palpable. "Although I did enjoy hearing her beg for your life, just before I took hers."

Skye felt Jagger go still. It was one of those moments where the scenery faded into nothing but background noise. The trees still existed, the earth was still warm at her feet, but everything was fuzzy, unclear. The world shrank and became small. So small that the only things she was aware of were the four of them and the deadly game they'd become embroiled in.

"You look surprised. Who did you think was responsible for your lover's death?" The vampire hissed and growled. "I didn't drain her, didn't even go for a nibble. Your scent was all over her and ruined my appetite. But it was *my* hands that choked the last bit of air from her lungs."

She began to laugh once more, the sound maniacal. It was harsh and echoed into the darkness. A mess of howler monkeys began to make noise, their excited cries echoing up from the canopy below, adding to the illusion of chaos.

The air changed; electricity crackled along invisible conduits, charging the atmosphere with an eerie glow.

Skye could feel Jagger's rage. It clung to him like a dark cloud. It was in the way his heart slowed to an ominous beat, the way he shook out his limbs in slow, exaggerated movements.

In that moment she could feel how lethal an animal he was, and she looked up at Dani in time to see something other then hate flicker across her face. Was it fear? Probably not, but the vampire sure as hell knew Jagger was primed and ready for battle.

A million questions shot through her mind but the loudest had nothing whatsoever to do with the impending fight.

It made her angry, the direction of her thoughts, and she shook her head in an effort to purge them from her mind, but it was no use.

Here she was, atop a freaking mountain for God's sake, with a vampire and demon standing only a few feet away, both of them gunning for her . . . and the only thing she could think about was the mysterious Eden.

Who the hell was she? And what had she meant to Jagger? The vampire had said they were lovers, but had it been more than that?

Skye tore her eyes away from the vampire as the demon began to make a series of grunting noises, not words exactly, but definitely some kind of chanting. She moved back a few paces, her eyes riveted to the beast as his form began to change. His body began to inch upward, the already tall form adding several inches in height and bulk.

Skye was transfixed. She'd never seen anything like it. Not even in her nightmares.

A hand gripped her forearm hard and she was pulled to Jagger's side. His face was deathly cold, his rage turning the green of his eyes into crimson red.

"Get to Monkey River and find Nico. If he's not there someone should be able to locate him in the reserve."

Jagger's voice sounded as if there were several layers to it. Skye could tell he was fighting to keep his human form for as long as he needed to.

He began to make a keening noise and mist encircled the whole of his body as he pushed her away from him violently. "Now," was all he said before the change fell upon him.

Everything happened quickly. Bodies became blurs. Growls and screams ripped through the night air.

Skye stumbled back several paces, regaining her balance quickly. She watched as a large black cat erupted from the mist in front of her. Its body aimed straight and true for the vampire.

Dani's fangs had elongated even more and the lethal weapons glistened in what little light there was. The vampire rushed at the jaguar and their bodies met in midair, the thud that reverberated in the night a testament to how hard they hit.

Skye started to run toward them, intent on helping Jagger any way that she could, but at the last minute sidestepped to the right, barely avoiding an assault from what was now a demon that was well over ten feet in height.

He whipped around, growling in anger and laughed down at her.

Skye held herself loose on the balls of her feet, hands fisted at her side. Desperately, she searched the immediate area for any type of weapon. When the demon began to laugh, he fed the anger inside of her until the flush of it crawled across her skin.

"Glad to see I'm so fucking amusing, dickhead," she shouted, trying to tame the fear that was banging at her. The beast was massive and unless a miracle occurred, she didn't see a way out for either her or Jagger.

Crap, the only demon fighting she'd ever seen had been old episodes of *Buffy*.

Skye gritted her teeth, her gaze alighting on a small

pile of rocks that fell away from a massive boulder to her left. She could hear the battle raging behind her but dared not turn from the demon.

His long, forked tongue slid from his mouth, as if testing the wind. Words slithered from between the jagged teeth and the stench made her nose wrinkle in protest.

"I can smell your fear, little bird." He laughed harshly as he moved toward her. "It only makes the game that much more pleasurable."

"Well, hell, glad to see I've managed to brighten your day, because so far, mine has been fucking peachy."

Skye edged over toward the rocks, her mind circling for a way out. When she was only a few feet away, the demon lunged at her, his long arms grabbing for her. She jumped, trying to clear the boulder, and felt a hot sting of pain slice across her calf as the demon's claws dug in deeply.

The cry that ripped from her lungs was harsh, but the pain was excruciating.

Skye's hands landed on the top of the boulder and she tried to pull herself up, but the demon grabbed her and threw her back as if she were nothing more than a rag doll.

She landed on her back. Hard. And she began to sputter as the wind was knocked from her.

There was no time to react. He was upon her.

The heat of his breath against her face was bad enough, but the stench had her belly turning over in protest.

"Damn, no one ever introduce you to a nifty little thing called mouthwash?"

"Dumb bitch. You think to bait me? I care not for what you think." He began to laugh once more, from deep in his chest. The vibrations shook her body and it felt like his words were not only outside of her, but in her head as well.

Skye shook herself, trying to clear her mind. If she could somehow distract the fucker long enough, maybe she'd find a way out of this mess.

"Cormac said he wanted you alive, but he didn't say we couldn't have a little fun with you."

The hissed words slipped through her mind and Skye recoiled in horror as the demon lowered his head until there were mere inches between them.

"A demon's kiss is something everyone should experience at least once in a lifetime." His wide mouth opened and the serrated teeth hung heavily in menacingly dangerous rows. They dripped with something akin to saliva, but the liquid was brownish in color.

Skye's eyes singled out a drop that clung to the teeth precariously, and when it fell toward her, she closed her eyes in revulsion, only to cry out in pain as the liquid slid across her cheek.

The burn was intense, the pain sharp, searing.

Skye began to buck wildly, her arms flailing out, and when her hand clamped down upon a rock she picked it up and threw it with all her might at the demon's head.

He roared in anger and swung his fist at her, striking her with an equally vicious blow.

Skye screamed in fury, frustration, and plain old fear. Her cheek was on fire and her calf felt like there were a thousand shards of glass ripping through it.

The demon began to lower his head and for that one brief second, Skye could honestly say she'd never been more terrified in her entire life. It was all encompassing. Immobilizing.

Frantically, she clawed at the demon, trying to arch away, but it was no use. Even with her enhanced strength the demon was much too strong.

When his mouth closed over hers, Skye nearly lost her mind. The terror that ripped through her was unlike anything she'd ever experienced.

The demon moaned into her and went still, but the pull that Skye felt deep inside of her intensified. Her skull was on fire and her head pounded. It felt like her very soul was being ripped from her body and the cold that seeped into her veins was sharp, as if she'd been dipped into the deepest, most frigid part of the Atlantic Ocean.

It was liquid ice.

She struggled still, but Skye's vision began to blur and even though she fought like hell, she began to lose hope.

A god-awful cry ripped across the darkness that had entombed her and Skye's eyes flew open. The cry had come from inside her mind and she knew without a doubt who it belonged to.

Azaiel.

The demon, Tag, broke away and looked down at her. The fear that hung on his distorted features caught at her.

"I knew not . . ." the demon mumbled, confused and deathly *afraid*. He then made a series of choking noises, as if he were being strangled from the inside out. His body began to shake violently and then he collapsed on top of her.

The weight very nearly crushed her and it was all Skye could do to push the body off of her. She rolled to the side, coughing, shivering, and feeling like she'd just died. Dully, her gaze landed on Jagger, still in animal form, his jaguar panting from exertion.

At his feet lay the limp body of the female vampire. From what she could see through the thick haze of fog that was slowly descending upon her, the vampire's head had been nearly torn from her body.

Skye was afraid of losing consciousness. Afraid that the demon's kiss would claim her, destroy her. Funny, considering where she was going to end up when she finally sealed the portal.

If she sealed the portal.

The feeling of sadness that washed over her brought tears to her eyes and she struggled to see through them, to focus on Jagger.

The cat jumped over Dani's body as the mist claimed it and it was Jagger himself who knelt over her. His hands touched her face, fell to her chest and then to the rest of her body.

"Why the fuck didn't you leave?" His words were laden with a pain she'd never felt before.

His whispered words tore through her and if she could, Skye would have done anything to ease his burden.

She stared up into eyes full of pain. They shimmered as the last of his jaguar left his body, the bright green orbs now solemn and dark.

"I can't . . ." The words came haltingly. " . . . shift after dusk."

Jagger cradled her closer, shaking his head. "Why didn't you tell me?" he asked.

Skye closed her eyes and whispered simply, "I didn't trust you."

"Of course you didn't. Why the hell would you?"

Jagger's voice rose and she flinched, though it went unnoticed as his anger kept pace. "Jaguars have been killing your kind for eons."

He paused then. "How did you . . . ?" He glanced at the demon at her side. His innards were exposed as sulfuric smoke escaped from every orifice. She could tell he was as confused as she was, but when Skye opened her mouth to answer, no words came out.

Her body was cold and she began to shiver uncontrollably, her teeth chattering against each other in a relentless rhythm. Her stomach was roiling, her head light.

When the seizure hit it was all she could do to keep her sanity.

Jagger shoved his finger down her mouth in an attempt to clear her airway and turned her onto her side. She struggled to breathe through the attack and the panic that punched her hard in the gut.

Was this the end? Is this what it felt like to die by a demon's hand?

The cold whisper that wove its way through her body left every cell aching and on fire with pain.

Her eyes rolled upward and then she saw nothing.

The only witness to the large man cradling the shaking woman was a lone wailer monkey that had made its way up from the canopy below. It had been attracted to the violence and dark energy in the air.

It paused, raised itself up on its back legs and then slowly slipped into the night, leaving Skye halfway between the dark and the light.

And a jaguar warrior, a man with no religious conviction at all, left holding her tightly, a prayer falling from his lips, the only sound to greet the now silent jungle.

Chapter 15

The first light of dawn was just breaking across the jungle when an exhausted Jagger finally stopped his treacherous descent. He'd pretty much used up all of his energy getting Skye down from the summit of Victoria Peak. It had been a long, arduous night but he couldn't afford to linger.

He needed to get Skye to Monkey River. Surely there would be someone who could help her.

Where the hell was Cracker when he needed him?

Jagger gritted his teeth, paused to take a long swig of water before forcing some of the precious liquid between Skye's cold lips.

Fucking demon! How the hell had he not known what Tag was, back in Iraq? The man's scent had always been off, but he'd just assumed the bastard was Dani's lackey. Her bitch-slap boy.

He should have taken them all out when he'd had the chance. Would have, too, if Eden hadn't been . . .

Jagger couldn't finish the thought. He couldn't go there. Not ever again.

Skye began to twitch violently and he held her tight, knowing the spell would pass. It seemed to be the way of it.

He was frustrated at the lack of knowledge he had in regard to demons.

He knew they existed. In fact several had been purported to be the targets in operations he'd quarterbacked. But the intel that had been gathered was sketchy at best. He'd personally never laid eyes on one before this night.

Jagger sighed tiredly. He had no time to dwell. He needed to get his ass in gear.

His gaze fell on the face cradled so close to his chest.

Skye had been in and out of consciousness for most of the night; her hoarse whispers were in an ancient tongue. She spouted things he couldn't make sense of and he couldn't help but wonder at the many layers that lay beneath Skye's facade.

He closed his eyes, but only for a moment. The face that had haunted him for months was always lurking about. Eden.

Her death was on him. Savagely, he drew air deep into his lungs. Dani had paid for her part. He'd long thought that if he could avenge Eden's death it would assuage the emptiness that ate at him every day.

But it did no such thing. It was still there, carving more and more trails deep into his soul.

Jagger was cursed and he knew it.

His tired arms pulled Skye in close to him as he secured the heavy satchels that hung from one shoulder. He would get her out of this mess, with the portal intact. He would protect her and keep her safe. She would not become another Eden.

And then he'd disappear.

He continued to move through the greenery on his long legs. He still had a hell of a lot of ground to cover and most likely wouldn't make it to Monkey River before nightfall.

Added to that was the fact he had a large contingent of DaCosta warriors on his ass, coming at him from the north with God knows how many more soldiers for hire, all of them gunning for Skye.

Jagger hiked for hours, crossing many small rivers that ran from the top of the mountain, cutting a path through the jungle and into the basin, where they dumped into some of the great rivers of Belize, the Swasey and South Stann Creek.

He was in the heart of the jaguar reserve before he realized things were not as they should be.

Jagger should have noticed sooner, but truthfully, he was incredibly fatigued. He'd been carrying Skye for nearly twenty hours and had had virtually no food or rest in days. He stopped abruptly, his senses fingering their way out as he sought to find the barest hint of an enemy.

But there was nothing, and an eerie cold began to settle alongside him. Jagger began to suspect that dark arts were at play. The rhythms of the jungle were out of whack. It felt like all life had been sucked from the very heart of it, leaving nothing but the breeze, the greenery. The enemy.

He'd not seen or sensed a single jaguar, ocelot, or puma. The amazing myriad of birds that normally filled the canopy high above him with their endless shrieks and squawks was missing.

They'd all fled.

He paused. Not even the local black howler monkeys trumpeted his presence.

The feeling of unease that settled inside him only confirmed that danger lurked about, hidden within the shadows between the trees. Carefully he scoured the entire area as he lowered Skye to the ground. She was still feverish and his fear that she would succumb to whatever the hell the demon had done to her was nearly paralyzing.

He needed to get to Placencia and get a boat to Monkey River. Nico had mentioned a local Mayan healer once who had made her home there. That had been several years ago, but at the moment it was his only hope.

He forced some more liquid down Skye's throat, cradling her head as she thrashed. He pulled her to rest against a downed tree trunk. They were along the banks of yet another small creek and he left her, sliding into the wet coolness in order to fill their bottles.

It was then that he became aware of another presence.

Jagger froze, his body tense, ready to fight. Slowly his eyes swept the immediate area, and without making a noise he leapt back up the bank, carefully placing the bottles near Skye. Reaching into the deep pockets of his cargos, his fingers encircled the deadly knife that lay there.

It had been charmed, a gift from Declan.

When he stood, all the fatigue and pain had fled, leaving behind only the anger and madness that fueled his jaguar in battle. The taut muscles of his arms and abdomen gleamed under a soft sheen of sweat. His tattoos stood out in stark relief against the dark skin, their intricate markings seeming to shimmer and move as he flexed his arms and rotated his neck.

Jagger crouched low, scenting the air, and as he did so the hair at the back of his head stood on end.

Something was there, just beyond the creek.

Silently he kept to the shadows that lined the bank, his body moving with stealth and determination. His mind went quiet, all of his senses focused on tracking the presence that he felt.

He slipped into the mess of vinery that caressed the edge of the creek and disappeared from view.

Jagger kept his body low to the ground and for a brief second debated calling his jaguar to him, but a noise ahead gave him pause. There was no time.

He held the knife loosely in his fingers and his eyes flattened to a dead, dull green as he inched forward. For once he was grateful there were no creatures around to trumpet his presence.

He watched as a large, black jaguar slid into view. Its massive head slowly turned before settling directly in front of where Jagger hid.

The animal barked a warning, emitting a growl that echoed in the quiet. It slowly began to move toward Jagger, its body downwind, and Jagger cursed silently at his inability to read the beast.

Was it a shifter? Or just a male protecting its territory?

The animal paused only a few feet from him, and when Jagger noticed the strange mist that began to flow over its flanks, his adrenaline kicked in.

Fuck. Definitely a shifter.

Jagger exploded from the greenery, his arms outstretched, the deadly blade aimed straight for the jaguar.

The two men met in midair and landed together in a pile of raw muscle, anger and curses.

The intruder was strong, his energy heavy, dark, but the two of them were evenly matched. The knife was knocked from Jagger's hand and he head-butted the bastard as hard as he could, twisting his body in an effort to get his weapon.

"Fucking Castille, you always were such a little prick."

Jagger froze. The voice was familiar. As was the arrogance and hostility.

He slid forward, intent on righting his body, when a fist slammed into the side of his cheek, sending shards of pain across his face.

"What the—" Jagger managed to get out before he was cut off.

"Next time you'll think twice before attacking the cavalry, asshole."

With great effort, Jagger held his anger in check and turned to the man who stood facing him.

The warrior's body looked as if carved from granite, every single muscle seeming enhanced, honed, hard, and lean. The scars that crisscrossed his chest and rib cage were whitened next to the dark skin that stretched tight across his abs.

The face, nearly feral, couldn't hide the handsome features, nor the cold blackness that rested in the eyes. The once neatly trimmed hair was long, unkempt, and when he smiled, Jagger could sense only the merest slip of humanity within.

It seemed he needed to look no further.

Nico had found him.

The small modicum of relief Jagger felt was tempered by the blast of anger that washed over him. His cheek fucking killed him, and the impotent need to act, to do something with the electric energy that rode him, had him clenching and unclenching his hands so strongly that his forearms ached.

Jagger took a second, controlled his temper, and ran his hand along his jawline.

"Heard you were still a jungle hermit."

Nico laughed harshly and began to pace in a circle as if the thought of standing still was too much to bear. He stopped suddenly. "Beggars, my friend, beggars . . ."

Jagger hated to admit it, but the warrior was right. He had no choice. Nico was about all he had at the moment.

"I need to find the Mayan healer you told me about years ago. She still around?"

"For the female?" Nico laughed softly, his teeth a slash of white in his deeply tanned face.

Jagger growled a warning and took a step toward Nico.

"You will not touch her."

"I have no desire to. She stinks of demon." The tall warrior's eyes narrowed. "The only reason I'm here is because Jaxon called in a favor." He spit into the ground. "Trust me. I don't give a flying fuck what happens out there, so long as it stays out of my jungle." His voice deepened and an unholy light lit his eyes from behind, emphasizing the glittering darkness within them. "And right now it's crawling with every kind of scum you can imagine."

"Yeah, well, my life hasn't been puppies and rainbows either," Jagger snarled. "This shit that's gonna hit the fan is about as bad as it gets. But right now Skye is priority number one."

Nico regarded him in silence. "What's priority number two?"

Jagger hesitated, suddenly not so sure trusting the warrior was a smart move. The ex-PATU soldier had spent the last several years out in the jungle, with no human contact except the occasional visit from his older brother, Jaxon, and the few times Jagger had seen him, they'd not been exactly friendly.

Many thought he was crazy, and after what he'd been through there had to be some merit to it. But did Jagger honestly think Nico would betray the warrior brotherhood? Betray his history with Jaxon?

In the end, loyalty to their common ancestry won over. "You ever hear of something called the Cave of the Sun?"

Nico's eyes narrowed. He stared long and hard at Jagger, his body tense. "That's what this is about?"

Jagger nodded, his mouth set into a grim line.

"I'll take you to the healer," Nico replied, a tic playing along the side of his cheek. "Then we'll go to the cave. But I'll warn you."

Jagger paused, eyebrows raised.

"You won't like what's there."

Jagger snorted. "I figured as much."

Mist once more crawled up Nico's body and Jagger stood back as the energy within crackled and sparks flew everywhere. The tattoos that adorned his body were different from any he'd ever seen. They moved and glowed as the magick began to take hold.

Nico was strong—one of the strongest warriors he'd ever come across, and that quality alone garnered much respect.

Jagger turned and led the animal back to where he'd left Skye. She was slumbering against the tree trunk, her arms held loosely against her midsection as if she were trying to wring some small bit of comfort from her cold body.

The cat inched forward, its great tail twitching back and forth in agitation. Jagger growled at it and the animal stopped, its canines exposed as it barked and hissed.

"She's mine."

The words slipped from Jagger's mouth before he even realized he'd spoken them. Two little words, but suddenly so heavy with meaning, emotion. Christ, he sounded like Tarzan, and from what little he knew about Skye, she sure as hell wouldn't be content as Jane.

Hell, she'd be kicking Tarzan's ass from here to Mexico.

He shook his head and ran his fingers through his hair. His eyes traced the gentle curve of her chin, the fullness of her mouth, and the delicate area underneath her ear. Somehow, in such a short time, this woman had insinuated herself deeply into his psyche. She'd given it meaning again, after he had spent months wandering the jungle aimlessly. Half alive. Half dead.

That was no longer.

Jagger quickly crossed to Skye and scooped her up in his protective embrace.

His body trembled as the force of his thoughts washed over him. How could he ever have thought to leave her when this whole mess was done and over with? He'd never met a woman like her before and he doubted there was another. She filled the ache inside of him so that he could breathe again.

She moaned softly, and as his arms tightened around her, he whispered, "You won't be getting rid of me so easily, my little bird."

The jaguar turned and crossed the creek, with Jagger following closely behind. They disappeared into the thick foliage that lined the opposite bank, and the jungle claimed them whole.

Many hours later they stopped at the edge of the town of Placencia. They'd been lucky and hadn't come across any of the commandos that had been dispatched to the jungle in search of Skye.

She had become more and more lethargic as the day progressed, and the urgency Jagger felt was becoming a physical manifestation. Nervous energy clawed at him. He could feel it building. The waiting was driving him fucking crazy.

He watched as Nico returned to his human form. The tall warrior took a deep draw of water and stretched out his long, lean limbs. "The healer, Mary, lives about a mile from here. I'll bring her back."

Nico swung his head back, the dark of his eyes glittering diamonds in the early-evening gloom.

"Can't we just take Skye to her?" Jagger was getting anxious. They'd come so far.

"That wouldn't be a good idea. She doesn't like strangers." Nico turned from him, "I'll do my best to convince her that your woman is worthy. I won't be long."

"You'd better do more than convince," Jagger muttered, but the warrior had already disappeared.

Jagger took a few moments to grab some food from his bag. Being a former black ops soldier, he was used to going days without sleep and food, but even he'd found the last few to be some of the most exhausting he'd ever had.

He ate quickly, holding the shivering Skye against his chest. A long strand of her hair fell across her face and as such breath was expelled from her body, it moved. He reached for it, his dark, rough fingers carefully rolling the silky strands between them. He bent down, nuzzled the soft skin along the side of her neck, and felt his animal tremble with emotion.

She moaned softly and turned into him, her arms going around his neck as her heated flesh pressed against his bare chest. He could feel her breasts, soft, curved, full, and his body began to tighten painfully.

What the hell was wrong with him? The woman lay in his arms, ill from the effects of demon poison, and all he could think about was how much he wanted to touch every inch of her. Kiss away her pain.

His body was rock hard and he clenched his teeth tightly, until the pain along his jaw became too great.

After a few moments he was able to relax, and blew out a deep breath as he sat down and leaned back against a tree, Skye nestled protectively in his arms.

He knew they weren't far from the Caribbean Sea. The smell of salt lay heavy in the humid air. It tugged at something inside of him, leaving a bittersweet melancholy in its wake.

Here, on the banks of the Monkey River, the jungle seemed untouched by the darkness that was slowly seeping into the local landscape. There was no smell of demon, shifters, or black magick.

It was as it always had been.

Jagger, more than anyone, knew how quickly reality could change, how much it was already changing.

He'd seen a demon, full on, and knew that they were slowly seeping through into the human realm. There was no other choice. They had to destroy the portal.

He looked down at Skye and murmured, "We'll get it done."

Jagger's eyes closed and though he appeared to be resting, he knew exactly when Nico arrived, and he definitely wasn't alone.

Quickly he rose to his feet. He'd wrapped Skye in a blanket and she lay on the ground, shivering still.

The tall warrior was quiet, and though he'd managed to find clothes, it did nothing to lessen the wild aura that shrouded his body. He turned to look down at the woman beside him and Jagger was surprised at the flash of warmth. She meant something to Nico.

The woman, Mary, was small, barely reaching Nico's chest. She was Mayan, with thick dark hair that hung to her waist in an intricate plait. Her skin was wrinkled with age and the eyes that stared out through the dark at him had seen a lot.

They were the color of dried tobacco leaves and she pierced him with a stare that seemed to look right through him. The woman made him uncomfortable.

After a few seconds she shuffled forward, past him, and knelt down beside Skye. Her hands held two large bags. Jagger watched as she slowly peeled back the blanket, running her hands slowly up and down Skye's shivering body.

She inspected the wound on her calf and then bent over her, sniffing around her ears, nose, and mouth.

Jagger was beginning to think the woman was loony, and when she carefully withdrew a long, slimy snake from the bag beside her, Nico had to physically restrain him.

"What the hell is she? A fucking voodoo witch?"

Nico shook his head, a ghost of a smile playing along his face. "Mary uses the ancient magicks. It might seem strange to you, but this is something she's done many times." Nico pushed him back. "You need to give her some room."

Jagger's hands remained clenched to his sides, his eyes riveted on the scene before him.

Mary hunched over Skye and let the snake slide from her grasp until it lay coiled in the middle of Skye's belly. As the animal unfurled its length and slowly moved along Skye's body, Mary began to murmur words and phrases Jagger had never heard before. And Lord knows, he'd spent a good bit of time among the Mayan and other indigenous peoples of Belize.

She sprinkled herbs, foul-smelling concoctions, in a circle around Skye and then rubbed something together between her fingers. Skye began to shake violently, and Jagger broke from Nico, his long legs carrying him to her side in seconds.

Mary glanced up at him and he stopped dead in his tracks. Her eyes were glowing, swirling rings of fire. She motioned to him and he fell to his knees, holding Skye still while the old woman cradled her face between the bony fingers of her hands.

When she lowered her head once more, Skye began to moan loudly and when Mary's mouth closed over Skye's, Jagger struggled to hold her down.

The keening sound that built from deep inside Skye was awful to hear. And when Mary drew away, spitting black, foul-smelling liquid into the dirt beside her, Jagger watched in shocked silence. Acrid smoke rose and every bit of greenery the liquid touched withered and died in front of his eyes.

The snake lay limp on Skye's flesh, its dark green color fading fast.

Mary repeated the procedure, again and again.

Eventually there was nothing more for her to draw from Skye, and when she was done, Mary fell back to her haunches, clearly exhausted. She wiped her mouth with a cloth, rinsed with a solution that was equally repulsive, and then turned to Jagger.

She didn't say a word but her eyes spoke volumes.

"Thank you," he said hoarsely, not really knowing what to make of what he'd just witnessed. His eyes drifted to Skye. She lay on her side, but her color looked healthier and the scent that had clung to her since the attack was no more.

Mary turned from him and grabbed the snake. He watched in silence as the carcass hung from her hands before she deposited it back into the bag. Without another word she crossed to Nico.

She paused and then spoke softly to the warrior, her hand gentle on his. When she turned once more to Jagger, her features softened and her large expressive eyes misted. She seemed incredibly sad.

She nodded her head and then disappeared into the darkness that lay heavy along the jungle floor.

"What did she say?" Jagger asked as he carefully tucked the blanket around Skye once more, thankful to hear that her breathing had returned to normal.

Nico had begun pacing again, his body coiled tight and his face dark. The energy that clung to him was frenetic and dangerous, off center. But then again, the dude *was* crazy.

"She called upon every god imaginable and asked for a blessing."

"Great, I'm guessing she thinks I'm about to get my ass kicked." Jagger grimaced. "Good to know."

Nico stopped his pacing and the two warriors stood

in silence, listening to the comforting sounds of the jungle. Each deep in thought.

"I need to hunt," Nico said suddenly.

Jagger watched the warrior slide into the darkness and then he went to Skye. He pulled her against his chest and settled in to rest. Tomorrow they would head out in search of the Cave of the Sun.

His thoughts turned to his enemies and he snarled softly into the night. He would not hesitate to kill any who stood in his way.

Chapter 16

Skye was awake long before Jagger. Her head hurt, her throat was dry, and every single muscle that she owned was either sore or cramped.

But she didn't dare move.

Being held by the tall warrior, tight against his chest as if she were a breakable, a china doll, was like heaven. Well worth any of the other discomfort.

She let her hand trail a soft path across the width of his shoulders, admiring the intricate tattoos that marked him as jaguar.

How weird was that? Had she lost her mind?

Maybe she had. But, hell, it just felt *so right*.

She sighed softly and snuggled deeper into his embrace, wanting the moment to last longer than it could.

Images danced in front of her, hazy weird things, and while she knew something profound had happened the night before, she wasn't quite sure what it was. Skye remembered the demon, the vampire, but most everything else was fuzzy.

Her hand rested against Jagger's chest and she could feel his heart beating steady, firm against her fingers. She turned her face and kissed his skin, her tongue slowly moving over his flesh.

He tasted wild, untamed, and she moved slightly as the softness between her legs began to pulse. It was a sinfully sweet pain, and as she continued to rub her legs together, it increased, drawing a small moan from her throat.

She could feel the response in his body, his hardness thickening against her thighs, and she smiled softly to herself. Her hand moved across the rock hard abs, up his arms, and when she looked up at his face she stilled.

Green eyes, dark and stormy, pinned hers with an intensity that took her breath away.

"Hey," she said softly.

He didn't say a thing. He didn't have to.

The air stilled around them and her mouth went dry. She wanted him. That was all.

When he lowered his mouth she met him with equal fervor, her tongue sliding between his lips and attacking aggressively. The feel of his warmth was incredible and she nipped at his mouth, her tongue circling madly.

His taste was wild. Intoxicating. It pulled at her and she felt the heat rush through her body, filling her veins with liquid fire.

"I want you," she said simply; there were no other words.

Jagger groaned against her mouth, his tongue plunging into her depths. He pulled her across his body until she straddled him, and his mouth fell to her breasts.

"Are you all right? Christ, I thought you weren't

gonna make it." He paused as if he'd said too much. "I mean, the demon . . . you're not in pain?"

"The only pain I'm feeling right now is the kind that hurts so good, it's sinful."

Their eyes met and held.

His were dark with need, and with a growl he pushed the thin T-shirt she wore up roughly. His hand claimed one breast while his hot mouth closed over her other nipple. He suckled the turgid peak, hard, and each pull drew a line of desire from deep within the folds of her sex.

"You're so fucking beautiful," he whispered against her soft flesh. The stubble that adorned his cheeks was rough, and as it scraped across the sensitive skin of her breasts she moaned once more.

Skye arched her back, her hands digging into his thick hair. She pulled him into her roughly and smiled when he chuckled at her display before treating the other nipple to the same wicked sensations.

She began to gyrate in his lap, her softness pushed hard against the hard bulge that lay between his legs.

"I've never felt like this," she said breathlessly. "Never wanted someone so bad that it hurts."

Skye's eyes widened. The sight of Jagger's dark head against the golden skin of her breasts was incredibly erotic. It fed her passion, inflaming her desire to a level she'd never reached before.

She didn't care that he was jaguar. The world was going to hell. Literally. It was time for Skye to take what she wanted and damn the consequence.

She grabbed the baggy top and pulled it over her head and then stood up.

She could feel the first rays of sunlight beginning to break across the morning sky. It sang to her, and the rush of power that filled her soul only enhanced the emotions and sensations that ran across every single nerve ending in her body.

Jagger lay at her feet, his body resting against a tree, his panting, naked chest heaving. The green of his eyes literally glowed, and Skye couldn't help but think he was the most incredible man she'd ever come across.

Strong. Wild. He was an animal, and one she had every intention of taming.

She smiled down at him, slow and seductive, and then grabbed the waistband of her shorts. Without hesitation she stripped them from her body and stood proudly before him, her golden skin alive and open to his hot gaze.

"Don't tease me, Skye." His eyes darkened. "I don't think I can take it."

The warning was there and she paused for a second, a blush coloring her cheeks. She'd brought him to the brink several times before, but this time was different.

"I want to make love to you, Jagger."

She took a step forward and began to pant as his eyes feasted on the blond patch of hair between her legs. His handsome face was focused entirely on her, and the look of hunger that adorned his features was laid bare to her. It was raw. Honest.

"Come here," he said hoarsely.

Skye took one more step and when his arms snaked out and grabbed her around her butt she nearly stumbled. Automatically her hands reached out and she braced herself against the tree.

Every limb trembled and if not for the strength of the man beneath her, she would have surely collapsed.

She looked down at him and her breath caught in her throat at the heated glance he threw up at her. His lips were drawn back and a growl ripped from deep in his chest.

"You belong to me," he said, and she could do nothing but nod. There were no words for what she was feeling.

His fingers trailed over the taut skin of her belly and he stopped near her navel. Skye looked down and felt something break inside of her as he reached over and gently kissed the flesh that was still raw from three mornings before.

Slowly he spread her legs until she was open to him—the part of her that was trembling, swollen with the need for his touch. And when his fingers sought out the wet heat hidden between the folds of her sex, she threw her head back, her mouth open, her breathing ragged.

His touch passed over her clitoris softly, and then again more aggressively, each time eliciting sensations inside of her that fired off into every direction imaginable.

He held her ass with one hand and thank God for that. Surely Skye would have melted into a pool of liquid nothingness. His other hand continued to caress her slick folds, teasing, tugging, and when she felt the heat of his mouth on her inner thigh, Skye thought she'd go mad from desire.

Small sounds erupted from the back of her throat and her fingers gripped the tree, the nails digging in hard.

She spread her legs even more and began to gyrate, loving the rough feel of his whiskers as they brushed against the softness of her thighs.

Anticipation was running rampant through her

body and as the moments ticked by, with her desire running hot, the need became nearly all-consuming.

"Please," she whispered hoarsely, shoving herself at him. Wanting him to do more than caress and tease.

She heard him laugh against her, his fingers rubbing along the inside of her wetness. The sensation was pleasing, but left her wanting a whole hell of a lot more.

"What do you *want* me to do, sweets?"

Her hips nearly buckled as he licked along the inside of her leg, his tongue long and firm.

"Jesus Christ, Jagger, I want . . ." Her voice trailed off as he continued to run his tongue along her inner thigh, circling the entire area.

"What do you want? I need to hear you say it." His voice was thick, heavy, and Skye knew that he was as close to the edge as she was.

"I want your mouth on me," she yelped softly as his tongue made a quick pass, dipping just along the inside of her center.

"I want your tongue inside of me."

The hand at her back dug in and he brought her close. Skye looked down at him, felt the cream of her desire begin to pool as the feral look on his face fed her like a bowl full of chocolate and cherries.

He growled softly, smiled a wicked smile, and then answered her call.

Jagger's tongue plunged deep inside her opening, working her over with a ferocity that brought screams from her mouth. Deftly he played with her clit, suckling the engorged nub until the pressure inside of her began to shake along her inner channel.

When his teeth scraped along the sensitive peak she

leaned back and her hands fell away from the tree, finding their way to the dusky nipples that stood erect and needful. She massaged her breasts as Jagger continued to pleasure her in a way she'd not thought possible.

His tongue was like magic and he fed from her like a hungry man. When he inserted two fingers deep inside of her while continuing his assault with his wicked mouth, Skye truly thought she'd faint from sheer pleasure.

Was it possible to lose consciousness from the act of lovemaking?

"Oh my God," she whispered. "I've just never . . . ever . . ."

She couldn't even articulate her thoughts.

Jagger paused against her. She could hear his ragged breathing and knew he was as affected as she was.

"That's because you were made for me and no one else."

His fingers began to work their way deeper inside of her, and when he curved them, found that special spot that lay hidden, she nearly collapsed.

Skye looked down again, her eyes drawn to the man beneath her.

"You will never belong to anyone other than me," he said again. His words were simple but she knew what they meant. He was a warrior; they played for keeps.

It was then, in that moment, that she knew.

Their future would never be a *together* thing. How could it? She had a mission to finish.

And it broke her heart.

Her sad thoughts melted away as Jagger continued to worship her body, his fingers, tongue, and mouth giving her pleasure beyond what she thought possible.

Skye feared she would rip apart, so intense was the orgasm that exploded over and through her.

Her hands fell to Jagger's head and she rested against him as her body continued to shudder from its release.

When she could stand no more, she slowly slid down until she was face to face with the man who had not only rocked her world, but had also changed her forever.

He grabbed her chin gently and brought her lips to his. She opened beneath them, wanting to crawl inside him, to caress and touch every inch of his body. She wanted to fulfill every wish and desire.

If only she had enough time.

Skye kissed Jagger with such passion that the ferocity of it startled her. Her arms wrapped around his powerful shoulders and she pressed every inch of her flesh against his.

He broke away, breathing hard. "You're fucking killing me, woman."

His beautiful eyes regarded her, hooded and full of need.

There was so much to say. Could she trust him enough? To tell him exactly how she felt? That amidst all this craziness she felt the same?

Was it fair considering her days on earth were numbered?

"Jagger, there's something—"

Her words were lost as a harsh voice cut through them.

"I'd throw some clothes on if I were you two. We've got a situation brewing and you've got *maybe* ten minutes before a nasty group of magicks crash your little love fest."

Skye stilled. She didn't recognize the voice but the scent was unmistakable. The man was jaguar and by the reaction in Jagger's face, she was guessing he was the mysterious Nico.

Jagger's arms tightened against her, effectively shielding her nakedness from the stranger.

"Turn your back. Give the lady a little privacy."

She heard Nico laugh softly, dangerously. "Well I've been standing here for a few minutes. It's not like I haven't seen the goods."

Jagger's hands tightened even more.

"You will turn the fuck around and show some respect." There was no arguing with his tone and the energy in the air tripled. It became dark and threatening.

She heard Nico moving behind her and chanced a quick glance back.

The man that stood staring at the two of them was something else entirely. He looked savage. Lethal. He looked pissed.

"If you want to make it to the Cave of the Sun, I suggest you get your ass in gear." Nico's dark eyes glittered through the gloom and Skye swore she could see his jaguar, just beneath the skin. "I'll get you there as promised, but then I'm done."

His eyes slid to Skye's and she swallowed thickly, sensing the danger that lurked just beneath the surface. This jaguar was volatile, unpredictable.

She held her chin up, refusing to look away even though the man unnerved her.

"I don't trust you," he said, baring crisp white teeth. Nico then grabbed their water bottles and disappeared.

Skye rested her head against Jagger's fast-beating heart.

"Don't mind him," Jagger murmured against her hair. "He's always been an asshole."

Skye didn't answer. Truthfully, her mind was on other things. There was so much left unsaid. She just didn't know if she had the balls to put everything out there.

"We need to go." Jagger kissed her quickly on her forehead and pulled her up, his hands caressing every inch of her along the way. They were gentle, but the light in his eyes was anything but.

"Jagger, I . . ."

"Sshh." He shook his head. "There's a lot that needs to be said, but we don't have the time."

He grabbed her clothes from the jungle floor where she'd tossed them earlier and handed them to her.

He flashed a smile that tugged at the very center of her soul. So much that it hurt.

Oh God, how she wanted him.

"When this is all over, I'm bringing you back to my place. We'll spend an entire week in bed." He winked. "And *then* we'll talk."

Skye looked down quickly and pulled her shorts up over her body. The bittersweet sadness that she felt was worse than anything she could imagine.

To find someone like Jagger, now, was tragically ironic.

Nico appeared from out of nowhere, it seemed, his presence cutting a sober path through a moment that really could not happen. There wouldn't be a happy ending for Skye; she might as well accept it and move on.

"We need to get going," Jagger said, and the urgency in his voice snagged her attention quickly. "They're not far."

The silent jungle bled through and Skye paused, her eyes scouring the immediate area that they were in.

Gold and red shot across the sky now and already the humidity clung to her skin, curling her long blond hair into thick waves. Hurriedly she tied it back, nervously aware of Nico's dark eyes on her.

He turned without a word and slid into the darkened interior. Jagger motioned for her and without hesitation, she grabbed her satchel, slung it across her shoulder, and followed suit.

There were no words spoken on the long, arduous trek. The pace Nico set was tremendous and it took everything in her to keep up. Skye didn't complain once, but when they finally stopped for a break, several hours later she fell to the ground, exhausted.

They were along the banks of a small stream, one of many that fell from the great Maya Mountains around them, weaving their way across jungle and rock as they ran toward the rivers that would eventually dump into the Caribbean Sea.

The air was heavy, thick with moisture. Skye knew there wasn't much time until the rainy season was upon them.

She watched tiredly as Nico left yet again, melting like a ghost into the trees that surrounded them. They'd covered a lot of area, making their way south, deeper into the Toledo district.

"Where's he going?" she asked, curious.

Jagger's eyes followed hers and they narrowed. "He's running a perimeter, there's something off out there." He rolled his shoulders. "Can't you feel it?"

Skye shook her head. "No," she murmured softly. But then again, she'd been distracted all morning by her thoughts. None of them pleasant.

"Do you remember anything?"

Startled, she looked up at Jagger.

"About the demon attack."

She held his gaze and answered, "Not really."

And that was a total lie.

She'd remembered the ferocity of the demon attack in minute detail as they'd trekked through the jungle. But it was the other memory that gave her pause.

Azaiel. His rage and power had been earth-shattering.

Skye wasn't sure what freaked her out more: the fact that she'd almost been cut to ribbons by a ten-foot freaking demon, or that she suspected Azaiel had destroyed said demon.

Was it possible? How else could she explain what had happened?

It scared the crap out of her to think that he had such an ability, to transcend dimensions.

Jagger studied her in silence and eventually she looked away. She'd never been good at lying.

"Nico seems a little . . ." When in doubt, change the subject.

"Crazy?"

Skye shook her head. "No, I was going to say 'damaged.'"

Jagger shrugged his shoulders. "He's got some issues. Hell, he's still the grade-A prick he's always been, but considering what he's been through, I'll cut him some slack."

"Has he said . . . I mean, did he mention anything about my brother? About crossing paths with another eagle shifter?"

"No, that hasn't come up," Jagger said gently as he crossed to where she sat. "Once we get our hands on the portal, I'll contact Cracker. Maybe they've come across him. Jaxon might have some intel as well. Even without the full arm of PATU available to him, he's got a hell of a lot of contacts."

Skye looked away, lips tight. She doubted she'd ever see her brother again. Hell, she didn't know if he was alive and even if he was, there was no time.

She had to shut down her emotions, because when she took the time to think about the state of her life and the role she needed to play in the coming days, it was just too much.

She bit back the bitter tears that threatened and tried to keep her composure.

"Hey, you all right?" Jagger's hand caressed her cheek and she leaned into the warmth of his touch.

"I'm fine," she managed to say. "I'm fine."

She was so not fine.

"Who's Eden?" The words slipped from her mouth and even she was shocked that she'd vocalized them.

Jagger's face went blank and she looked away, embarrassed.

"It's all right. You don't owe me anything." Skye tried to move from his embrace but was held firm. She felt tears begin to prick the backs of her eyelids and she struggled to hold them back.

What the hell was wrong with her? So he had a past. It's not like she'd never been with anyone before.

His fingers cupped her chin and he forced her face upward.

"Open your eyes and look at me," Jagger whispered.

Even though Skye wanted nothing more than to fade away and melt into the earth at her feet, she found herself looking deep into the green eyes above her. They were full of pain. And regret?

"Eden was a woman I was . . . *involved* with." He paused and inhaled deeply. She could tell he was struggling with his thoughts, trying to articulate what was in his heart.

"Jagger, really. It's none of my business."

She began to wiggle, trying to get away, because the truth was, she didn't want to hear about Eden.

"She was a member of my unit in Iraq, a young woman who was under my protection." His voice had changed, deepened, and Skye winced at the emptiness that colored his words.

"I should have stayed away from her, but I was weak and she paid with her life." He looked down at her then and her breath caught in the back of her throat, nearly choking her.

"Seems to me anyone going to war knows what the risks are," Skye whispered.

"I failed to protect her," he continued, as if he'd not heard her words. His eyes were stormy, the green similar to the dark moss that clung to the jungle rocks. "I should never have touched you."

Skye reached for him then and swept her lips against his in a kiss that was achingly sweet. "I touched you, remember?" she murmured against his mouth. "And really, I don't need a jaguar watching my ass, I'm more than capable of looking after myself."

A loud crackle echoed through the air. It sounded like muffled thunder. Jagger reacted instantly and shoved her to the ground just as a huge limestone boulder behind them exploded into thousands of fragments.

"Jesus fuck," he shouted, rolling to the side and taking her with him. "Go!" he shouted, pushing her away, the mist already crawling up his body. "Now. Shift, and get the hell out of here. I'll find you."

Another energy blast, one heavy with dark magick, shook the earth floor violently, downing several large mahogany trees.

"Now," Jagger shouted once more, his voice ending in a snarl when the animal inside of him took over, erupting with a fury as black fur began to ripple over his flesh.

Skye was up in an instant, the raptor clamoring for a way out.

She rushed forward, following the jaguar, and heard her eagle cry out as her body began to change.

The wind tore at her hair as she jumped high into the air. Her clothes fell to the earth and she welcomed the power flooding her cells as the great golden eagle was set loose.

Her wings caught the wind and she flew high into the sky, arcing into a circle before skimming the canopy below.

With a savage call, Skye turned and prepared for battle.

Chapter 17

Her eyes quickly homed in on three shadowy forms along the banks of the small stream, several hundred feet from where she'd just been. They were in a triangular format, moving forward slowly with predatory case. The one in the front, the leader, must have been the bastard that had shot the energy blasts.

They were charmed, their bodies somewhat transparent. To the jaguars below, the invisibility charm would most likely camouflage the enemy totally, making them extremely difficult to hunt.

As an eagle knight, however, Skye's enhanced vision was a definite advantage. Not only could she see in layers, her eyes had two centers of focus, meaning she could see both in front and to the side.

As she focused on the enemy spread out before her, she could also see Jagger to the right, his dark body slipping in and out of the tree cover.

She spotted Nico farther down, coming up behind the enemy, but he was too far away to be of any help. Even though Jagger would be able to sense the magicks, he wouldn't be able to see them in time.

She needed to up their odds of winning.

Anger sat low in her belly and everything faded from her mind but the hunt.

Skye was cresting the wind, her sleek body riding the air like a kite. She dipped her left wing, set her course and flew like a rocket toward the enemy closest to Jagger.

Her long, sharp claws lay open and as she skimmed the canopy, the wind flowing over her feathers, she tapped into the power of the sun and called upon the ancient Aztec gods Quetzalcoatl and Chalchiuhtlicue to give her strength.

She slid through the air, a silent, lethal predator, and as she approached the enemy, she let loose a war cry that echoed shrilly in the quiet jungle.

The magick within her sights glanced up at the last moment, not prepared for the deadly claws that scraped through flesh and bone. They ripped into soft tissue, and Skye tugged with all the strength she could muster. She then tilted her body slightly as she sailed by, the sharp talons digging in even deeper.

She was up and away before the bastard knew what had hit him, his cries of pain and fury following in her wake.

Shouts rang out and the two remaining magicks began to shimmer as their charm faded and then died out like a candle in the wind. The man she'd attacked had obviously been the one holding the charm in place, and it had evaporated as soon as he became injured.

No doubt he was using all his juice to mend the gaping wounds she'd left on his face.

She saw Jagger pause, his green eyes following her closely. Inside she was smiling wildly as she flew over him, rushing through the air like a golden bullet. The thrill of the hunt was exhilarating and she banked to the left, her feathers ruffling as she changed direction and headed back toward the fight.

She could hear a sizzling, crackling noise in the air as the magicks began hurtling bolts of white-hot energy, but it was the accompanying sound of gun-fire that struck terror into her heart. Her eyes quickly scoured the jungle below, and while she could see Nico rushing through the jungle in an effort to get back, she knew he'd be too late.

Jagger was almost upon the leader she'd injured and the magick's curses rang out, echoing alongside the gunfire, creating a cacophony of noise that was terribly out of place, here in the jungle.

With one more pass she could immobilize the bastard but Jagger was there. He'd look after the asshole. It was the other, the one with the gun, that concerned her more.

She called out to the jaguar as she whipped by and heard his answering bark. It was loud, aggressive. Totally pissed.

Jagger would just have to learn to deal. Skye Knightly was not the kind of girl who ever ran from a fight.

She flew lower, so low that her deadly claws could have easily snatched a small wailer monkey from the trees she passed over.

Straight ahead she could still see two forms moving quickly toward their fallen comrade. They seemed confused, scared—total newbies out in the jungle. She made a clucking sound deep from within her throat.

Dumb-asses.

They weren't her concern. There was a fourth. The one with the gun.

The sun on her back gave her a boost and she reveled in the power that rushed over her body. Searching carefully, she almost missed him, but a quick movement to her right alerted her and she barely avoided the shot that whizzed by. She banked to the left, her large wings catching a rush of air as she rode it to safety.

She circled once more, barely ahead of the barrage of bullets that were now sweeping the empty space just behind her. They glowed a deep reddish color, obviously charmed with some god-awful thing. Skye held on, determined to take the bastard down.

Her speed topped one hundred miles an hour as she shot forward, intent on circling behind her enemy. Skye then dipped below the top of the canopy, using it for cover as she continued forward, zigzagging crazily amongst the trees.

When she caught sight of him just in front of her, she called on the last bit of reserve that she had and increased her speed to such a level, Skye appeared to be nothing more than a blur.

The eagle knight called her battle cry again and extended her long, razor-sharp claws as she swooped lower, toward her target.

She whizzed by, knocking the gun from the magick's hands as she swept upward and then banked sharply, intent on a return pass.

As Skye narrowed again on her target she quickly became aware of a couple things. The first one being the target wasn't a man, but a female, a tall woman with flowing hair the color of midnight.

She also brandished a second weapon, a nasty-looking crossbow, aimed directly at her.

Skye didn't hesitate. Her large wings, spanning nearly nine feet, pulled her lower and her eyes locked on the target.

The woman held still and as Skye barreled in on course, she could see clearly, even from several hundred feet out, the woman's dark eyes and her lethal concentration.

She was almost upon the woman, her large body twisting in the air, trying to become an impossible target to shoot at, and when the heat flashed by, singeing the edge of her wing, she felt not pain, but surprise.

It was enough and she faltered, but at the speed Skye was going she knew she was going to crash.

Her golden body shot down through the canopy and she heard the roar of a jaguar as she slid into the darkened interior and disappeared from view.

Jagger felt his heart stop. Literally.

When Skye had flown past him, a crazy blur of golden feathers, his first reaction had been anger, disbelief. Why would she disobey his order and return? Was she fucking nuts?

He took off after her, although his anger had quickly bled through a spark of admiration when he'd come across the injured enemy. The tall man was cursing the eagle knight as he held his blinded eyes.

Jagger had made quick work of the asshole and moved on. There was no time to waste. He'd heard the shots and knew the danger had tripled, and the fear he felt for Skye drove him forward with savage intent.

Two more men of magick stood in his way, but they were inferior, and while he immobilized them quickly, they did manage to slow his progress. As he took off running through the jungle, his only thought was to get to Skye.

The fear that hung in his gut was sickening and it increased sharply as the echoing sound of gunfire rent the air.

He reached the battle just in time to see her hit and watch her veer crazily away into the thick trees that lined the bank of a small stream.

He bolted toward the tree line, hearing an answering war call as Nico arrived on the scene. He didn't look back. Nico could look after himself.

His body slid through the dense undergrowth that covered the jungle floor, large paws slicing through lush greenery. He scoured the area with his eyes and nose and followed her scent. It had changed subtly, but lay heavy in the air, agitating the possessiveness that he felt.

Jagger located her almost immediately; the flash of golden feathers called to him in a way that hurt. The mist slowly crept over his body and as the ancient magick took hold, stripping back fur and elongating bones, he tried his best to clamp down on the paralyzing fear that clogged his throat.

He approached the downed eagle, his steps soft on the moist earthen floor. Skye had landed deep within a bed of vinery, but he approached with caution. An injured animal was much more prone to striking out, and he'd seen the damage that her vicious claws could produce.

"Skye," he whispered softly. "Baby, you all right?"

The eagle slowly began to move, her large wings unfurling, and he held back as she maneuvered her way from the thick vines and hopped down onto the jungle floor.

She was magnificent. Took his breath away, and that was saying something.

When she'd first shifted days earlier, Skye had been an incredible sight in the air as she'd followed him through the jungle. But here, now, up close he could see the true beauty that was an eagle shifter.

Her golden feathers shone, seeming almost translucent as they caught what bit of sunlight there was down here at the bottom of the jungle.

He watched in wonder as she stretched out her wings in a graceful arc and stood, silent, before him.

"Come here," Jagger said simply as he took a tentative step toward her. He held out his arm, coaxing, pleading.

The fear that she would up and fly away was paramount and he still had no clue as to what her injuries were. She'd not shifted back to human form, so that told him all was not well.

The eagle cocked its head and as the eyes regarded him in silence, Jagger smiled to himself.

She was beautiful. Fucking amazing to look at. Her strength, spirit, bite-me attitude—all of it was there in plain sight. It tugged at his heartstrings.

The eagle shifter might not know it yet, but he had no intention whatsoever of letting her go.

As he moved closer, Jagger could sense her confusion and it gave him pause. He didn't want to frighten Skye, but again, the thought that she would leave him, now, forever, tore at him and he went with his gut.

"Here sweets, come here." He had to believe there was a connection between the two of them that she felt as well.

He motioned toward his arm, now fully extended, and when the eagle began to hop toward him, he stilled.

She maneuvered ever so slightly, gracefully jumping into the air and landing on his arm. Her long, deadly talons were gentle as she clung to his forearm, and he reached out a tentative hand, feeling deep possession rush through him as she let him stroke her feathers.

Jagger stared deeply into the eyes of his woman and felt such a rush of pride he needed to look away. To collect himself.

After a few seconds he turned and headed carefully back where he'd come from, toward Nico.

He found the warrior by the stream and when Nico turned around, the look on his face was priceless.

Jagger could well imagine the visual he presented. A tall, dark, naked dude, full of jaguar tats, coming out of the jungle with an eagle on his arm wasn't something you'd see every day.

Nico's eyes narrowed. "She all right?" he asked gruffly.

"I think so. She hasn't shifted back, so I can't be sure."

Nico grunted. "She sure as hell went in hard. That was fucking kamikaze." He took a deep swig of water and then laughed. "Something I'd do." There was a hint of admiration in the warrior's tone and Jagger looked at Skye with pride.

She sure as hell didn't listen, but would he change that? Hell, no.

Jagger took in the sight of the dark-haired woman on the ground. He sniffed the air and looked at Nico in surprise. "She dead?"

The warrior shook his head. "Nope."

"She's jaguar," Jagger said, his words ending on a growl.

"Yeah, I noticed."

"What the fuck is this world coming to? Jaguars working with magicks against jaguars."

The large eagle began to rustle, the talons digging into his skin. Jagger stroked Skye's feathers with his fingers, his tone reassuring. "Let's get you some clothes."

He nodded to Nico. "What are you going to do with her?"

Nico's eyes wandered back to the prone woman at his feet. "I haven't decided yet. She might have information that could prove useful." He shrugged his shoulders. "I think we'll let her wake up and see what the bitch has to say."

"It's not like we have all day." Jagger frowned.

"If she's not awake when we're ready to leave, I'll deal with her." The ugly truth fell from Nico's mouth and Jagger turned away, suddenly weary of all the violence and turmoil.

Would it ever end?

Jagger followed the stream back past the bodies of the two men who'd accompanied the dark sorcerer until he came upon Skye's clothes strewn about the jungle floor.

He knelt down and watched in silence as the eagle hopped from his arm. She flapped her wings, the long elegant appendages sweeping a large arc in front of him. Her eyes, blue as ever, regarded him in silence, and when the mist began to crawl along her body he moved back.

It enveloped her whole—long fingers of fog that crept up into the air at least ten feet. He found he was holding his breath and let it out in a rush as Skye emerged from the mist and walked toward him.

His eyes ate her alive and his heart began a slow, sensual beat that hit heavily, deep inside his chest.

He'd never seen anything so sexy, sensual.

Slowly his eyes traveled up her body, the long, toned limbs, past the juncture between her legs, and up along the flat belly until they rested briefly on her full, golden breasts. Her long caramel-colored hair hung in messy waves, blowing softly in the wind as her chest rose and fell.

The dusky nipples, erect and full, begged to be kissed, to be cherished and worshiped. His mouth began to water at the thought and his cock roared to life in answer.

Christ, how he wanted this woman. Any other time he'd have her on her back so fast, she wouldn't know what the hell had hit her.

A little problem, that. The whole time thing.

Jagger glanced down at the huge erection between his legs and shifted his body in an attempt to alleviate the discomfort. Seemed these days, he was nothing more than a walking hard-on.

"Are you okay?" he asked gingerly. He actually took a step back as she continued to walk toward him.

Skye rubbed her arm, her breasts swaying gently with the motion. "I took one for the team." She then cocked her eyebrow. "Care to kiss it better?"

Jagger stifled the groan that lay at the back of his throat. "I'd do much more than that, but we have no time."

Skye stopped in front of him. He looked down into her wide blue eyes and felt something inside of him break. A hard shell had been cracked, leaving a trail of soft mush in its wake.

He was a goner. There was no way around it.

Him. Jagger Castille. Totally fucking in love with the woman who stood before him.

His hand snaked out and plunged deep into the soft hair that lay at her neck. He pulled her into him until he felt every single naked inch of her body pressed up against his. When her arms encircled him with equal fervor and she ground her softness against his straining cock, Jagger thought he'd literally found heaven on earth.

Or hell, depending on your take.

His tongue plunged deep inside her mouth and he growled against her lips as he fed from her, stroking long and hard. Marking her as his.

It took great effort but he broke from her and held her tight against his body. The soft sigh of regret that fell from her lips was nearly his undoing.

He kissed the top of her head. "We've no time."

"I know," she answered haltingly.

"I'm not interested in a quick fuck."

Skye stilled at his words and leaned back until her large eyes locked on his. There was much there, hidden beneath the blue, and he ached to be able to discover all her secrets.

He would. Just not now.

"When this is all over, I promise you"—Jagger grasped her chin in his hands and kissed the soft skin along her jaw—"I will make you howl with pleasure until you can't think straight."

He felt her body shudder against his.

"Problem is, I don't howl, remember?" She turned into his hand, nuzzling his palm and then she nipped him. Hard. "But I do scream."

Her tongue flicked out and she licked him.

"We need to get dressed," he said hoarsely as he watched the smile spread across her face. His aching cock twitched and felt near to bursting.

She knew it, too.

He groaned and pulled her mouth to his once more, claiming her lips with a gentle ease that belied the fierce need inside of him.

They broke apart and he turned from her. With a grimace he glanced down at the aching erection that hung, heavy, between his legs.

From the corner of his eye he could see Skye, bent over as she pulled on her shorts. The sight of her silky smooth ass, curved and inviting, very nearly did him in. He clenched his hands together and grimaced as a hiss escaped from between his teeth.

He needed to find the fucking portal. Like yesterday.

He glanced down at the aching hard-on. If not, it was gonna be a long, uncomfortable trek.

Once they were both dressed, they gathered their bags and joined Nico back where they'd left him.

The warrior greeted them with a grimace.

"She's awake but not talking."

Jagger's gaze rested on the woman Nico had tied securely to a tree.

She was tall, athletic. She tilted her head and her large dark eyes regarded him in silence. Her long hair was loose, blowing into the breeze like snakes in the wind.

He could just make out the telltale markings along the side of her neck and he paused, surprised.

Not only was she jaguar, she was a warrior as well. It was extremely rare in his world to come across a female warrior, especially one on her own. The males developed their tats in their teen years, when they progressed from boys to men. A female warrior's tattoos only materialized when they had sex with their mate.

So where was hers? And what clan did she belong to?

He would have asked her, too, but Skye broke from his side and dashed across the small clearing, an unearthly yell breaking from deep inside.

She leapt over Nico, who was crouched on the ground in front of the mystery woman.

With a resounding thud, her fist connected with the jaguar's cheek. The hit was hard and he watched, shocked, as the woman's head snapped back and a second later fell forward.

She was out cold.

Skye turned to him, her breaths coming in spurts as she tried to clamp down on the emotion that was running through her.

"What?" she said defensively. "She had that coming."

Skye hiked up her bag and looked at the both of them, her voice commanding. "Bring her along. I'm not done with her."

She turned. "Let's get cracking, boys, we don't have all day."

Jagger watched as the most delectable ass he'd ever come across walked ahead of him, back into the jungle.

He looked at Nico, who seemed to be as shocked as he. The warrior shrugged and untied the unconscious woman, hauling her across his powerful shoulders.

A ghost of a smile played along Nico's lips as he followed in Skye's footsteps. "Christ, man, I wouldn't want to get on her bad side." He disappeared as well, his words hanging in the air behind him. "I wish you luck."

Jagger fell in behind and smiled to himself.

Bring it on, he thought.

Bring it on.

Chapter 18

They continued to hike through the dense jungle, across streams, larger rivers, and deep waterfalls. After what seemed like hours, Nico motioned for them to stop.

"The cave you seek is up the side of that mountain." He pointed to the largest one in the range. It looked fairly close, but Jagger knew how deceiving that was and how difficult the hike would be.

"We rest, leave at sunrise, and should be there sometime tomorrow afternoon." Nico's teeth slashed through the thickening gloom. "Unless we run into another hunting party."

They found a cave halfway up a steep incline next to a waterfall, one that was hidden beneath a heavy fall of mist. It would provide shelter and a safe place to spend the night. There was no sense pushing forward until they'd had time to eat and rest.

Jagger let his gear fall to the ground, his gaze drifting toward Skye automatically. She'd been quiet most of the way, avoiding his attempts at conversation.

"You all right?" he asked as he moved toward her.

"I'm fine," she said, but the tone of her voice indicated she was anything but.

"You sure? Nothing you want to talk about?" he prodded.

She nodded her head and didn't answer. Jagger stared at her for a few seconds and then moved away. Something was up, but Jagger decided to give her some space. A lot had happened in a short period of time and it was a lot to take in.

He crossed over to the female jaguar they'd brought with them. She'd regained consciousness an hour into their hike and had been on her own power ever since.

"You want some water?" he asked roughly, his dislike clearly evident.

She looked up at him. Her large dark eyes narrowed, and Jagger knew there was a lot going on behind them, but then she looked away without answering.

He smiled wickedly and took a long swig of the cool liquid, wiped the sweat from his brow and leaned in close. "Not very smart"—his voice lowered even more and the contempt he felt lined his words thickly—"for a jaguar warrior." He stepped away. "I won't offer again."

She ignored him and he walked over to Nico.

"You get anything from her?"

"No. She wasn't into polite conversation." Nico spit into the ground and looked back toward their prisoner. "Too bad, really."

"What's that?" Jagger asked.

"A female warrior is rare, worth something, but

she's obviously damaged goods. There's no reason to keep her around."

The meaning behind Nico's words wasn't hard to miss and Jagger sighed in frustration because he knew the warrior was right. The woman was not needed. She was the enemy.

It really left only one choice.

"Let me talk to her, see if I can get some intel. Maybe it just requires a woman's touch. It might give me the edge that we need." Skye walked between the two of them and looked at Nico. "You don't exactly inspire the warm fuzzies." She shrugged her shoulders. "No offense."

Nico grunted and shook his head. "None taken. Have at her, Kamikaze," he said. "But it wasn't me who jumped like Superman and clocked her in the head."

Skye blushed, the color warm against her cheek. Jagger fought the urge to lay his hand there, to feel the heat of her flesh against his.

"Well, she shot at me first." Skye looked over at the woman. "Give me a can of beans, some water and let me see what I can find out."

When she turned back, her blue eyes were hard, unyielding. Jagger could tell she wouldn't take no for an answer. "If she doesn't cooperate, I'll take her out myself."

Jagger retrieved his bag and handed Skye food and water.

"Don't expect much. If Nico couldn't convince—"

He was shut down by the disgusted look she threw him. "Don't you dare go there, Castille. I think I've more than proven myself."

Jagger kept a straight face but relaxed into a grin

when she turned away from him. He stretched out long muscles, closed his eyes, and opened his senses to the elements.

What he found was troubling.

He could sense discord in the energy that ran along the earth. The natural rhythm of the jungle had been sliced, damaged; harmony was broken. The unnatural quiet was so harsh on his ears that he fought the urge to cover them.

The animals had all but fled, because they could sense it, too: the evil that was slowly seeping into the local landscape.

It left an awful taste in his mouth and Jagger shook his head, fighting the savage urge to bark his anger.

Fucking magicks and their dark arts. Did they honestly think the human realm would benefit from the legions of demons that would escape?

His eyes flew open and he turned toward Skye and the prisoner, watching in silence as she settled down in front of the female warrior.

"I need to hunt," Nico said quietly, his eyes, too, on the women. "And scout. Could use some help."

Jagger rotated his shoulders, but it did nothing to alleviate the stress and tense muscles that lined his powerful frame. He needed to shift, to run free as a jaguar.

He knew it was the only way to alleviate, if only briefly, the burning need and want that fired every cell in his body.

"She'll be fine."

He looked at the older warrior and nodded. "I've no doubt of that whatsoever."

He could see Nico's jaguar shifting below the man's skin, and it only fed his animal's desire to be set free.

"Skye," he said roughly as he began to move toward the mouth of the cave. "We'll be back. If anyone crosses this threshold, do not hesitate to use the goodies Declan gave me. They're in my bag."

She cocked her head to the side but didn't turn to meet his eyes. "Be careful," she whispered.

Jagger hesitated, even as the burn began to sizzle across his skin, but there was nothing more.

He turned, pissed and not knowing why. What had he expected? A kiss and a pat on the ass?

He stripped, welcoming the magick as it wound its way up his body. His mind cleared as bones popped and elongated. He ran, his long limbs sliding into the thick black pelt of his jaguar.

Jagger joined the other warrior, who waited at the bottom of the waterfall, and without a backward glance disappeared from view, melting into the darkness that surrounded them.

In the cave, all was silent.

Skye regarded the woman before her, noting the tired circles under her eyes that marred the otherwise perfect skin. She winced slightly as the bruising on her face began to take root, a dark mottled blemish that ran along the length of her jaw.

"Admiring your handiwork?" the woman hissed. "The entire right side of my face is fucking killing me. Thanks for that."

Skye's eyes widened. "Um, last time I looked I was saving your ass. Nico would have ripped you apart. Besides, you *shot at me*, remember?"

"Don't flatter yourself." The woman held out her bound wrists. Skye rummaged around in Jagger's bag and found a knife. She quickly cut the restraints. "And just so you know, both the bullets and the arrows were charmed. You would have been fine."

"What are you doing out here, Jaden?" Skye asked as she handed the woman the beans. "It seems a little extreme even for you—I mean, don't you think your brothers are going to wonder why you keep disappearing from the resort?"

"First off, *my brothers* don't give a rat's ass what I do. I only hear from them when they want something." She laughed, a low harsh sound. "I'm pretty much on the bottom rung as far as they're concerned."

Her eyes deepened then with an intensity that was palpable. "You disappeared off the grid—what the hell do you think I'm doing out here?"

"But it's so dangerous. If your family finds out what you're doing . . . what you've been doing for years, they'll—"

"Yeah, I know. No more Jaden. I get that and I'm fine with it."

Skye studied the dark woman across from her. She'd not known Jaden DaCosta for long, had only met her on a few occasions, the first being when she'd been held prisoner at the DaCosta compound less than a year earlier.

She was edgy, dark; a woman whose emotions ran deep. Jaden's family wholly believed that she was deeply entrenched in the DaCosta agenda. Skye knew better.

Jaden DaCosta worked special ops for the government. To the outside world, she was the successful owner of one of the most posh resorts in Mexico.

Jaden had promised to help her find the portal. She had no intention of seeing her family get their hands on it. Whatever her reasons were Jaden hadn't shared, and even though she was jaguar, Skye trusted her.

Jaxon Castille had managed to get her out of the compound before Jaden had returned, and as soon as she was able, Skye had contacted Jaden at the resort she owned in Mexico.

She'd been secretly helping Skye, feeding her information, intel on the operations of the DaCosta clan and when she could, tips about the possible resting place of the portal. She'd definitely stuck her neck out and Skye could do nothing but admire her for it, because she knew that if her complicity was ever found out, the repercussions would be deadly.

"Are things that bad?" Skye asked quietly, not really wanting to hear the answer.

Jaden shook her head and looked away. "It's about as bad as it can get." She shook her head. "Worse, actually. Cormac is on the warpath, and he's put a bounty on your head. Every fucking mercenary from here to China is descending on this jungle, all with orders to find you or find the portal and *kill* you."

Skye grimaced and looked away.

"My brothers are in a frenzy to find it before Cormac. Dumb bastards think they can double-cross him." Her words were bitter. "I hope they all rot in hell."

"I'm close to it Jaden. I can feel it."

"I hope so, because I've been walking around with a sick feeling in the bottom of my gut for days." Her dark eyes bored into Skye's. "You need to get to the portal and destroy it once and for all."

Jaden took a long draw from the water bottle and then turned to Skye with a wicked smile in place. "I'd love to know how the hell you ended up out here with the youngest Castille brother. I thought he bit the bullet after the compound was attacked."

"It's a long story," Skye murmured.

"I'm sure it is," Jaden snickered. Her dark eyes remained fixed on Skye. They made her nervous.

"What?" Skye said, more than a little defensively.

"You *do know* that the Castille boys aren't keepers."

Skye frowned at that. "I'm not looking for a keeper, thanks." *It's not like I'll be around for that, anyway.* "You know them personally?"

Jaden's face darkened but her voice was light as she answered. "I've read both Libby and Jaxon's files. The only Castille I've ever met in person is the oldest." Her gaze drifted to a place just beyond Skye as she continued. "Once. A long time ago."

"You mean Julian . . . he's here, in the jungle."

Something flickered across Jaden's face, but was gone just as quick. "Julian Castille is an arrogant prick," she said, her face hard, and then she laughed. "He's still out here? I'm impressed. Thought he'd go running back to his plush office and endless parade of women." She snorted. "I can't see it. He's too white collar. Christ, the man is totally Hollywood."

"That doesn't sound like the person I met. Julian Castille seemed very intense, dangerous even." Skye shrugged her shoulders and stood up. "They all seem . . . so complicated."

"You don't know the half of it."

Skye paused. "What do you know about Jagger?"

In a way she hoped that Jaden knew nothing. There was no point, really, in knowing more, and as the words left her lips she wished she could take them back.

Jaden stood as well, stretching out long legs and

running her fingers through the curtain of dark hair that fell halfway down to her waist.

She turned to Skye and pursed her lips, exhaling slowly before answering. "I don't know much. He's the youngest, followed Jaxon into the military, where he was trained as black ops. I don't think he was ever attached to PATU, instead served his country in places like Iraq and Afghanistan." She shrugged her shoulders. "I know he resigned his commission several months ago and has been in the States ever since. Well, until recently, that is."

"You don't know anything about a woman named Eden, do you?"

Jaden shook her head. "No, sorry, who is she?"

Skye turned away. "No one."

"A word of advice?"

Skye stilled.

"Do not get involved with Jagger Castille. It will only bring heartbreak. Look at Libby Jamieson, at how she suffered because of her love for Jaxon."

"But they're together. Things worked out."

Jaden raised an eyebrow. "And you know this because . . ."

"I saw them together just before I fled Caracol. There's no mistaking how intense his feelings were."

"For now," Jaden said grudgingly. "But at what price? She lost years of her life and nearly that of her child."

Skye was silent as she studied the shifter. She got the feeling something else was at play but didn't push as she sighed softly. "It doesn't matter, anyway, it's not like I have much . . ." Her voice trailed off as she thought to herself, *time*.

"What are you not telling me, Skye?"

Jaden grabbed her arm and spun her around.

Skye smiled and shook her head sadly. "Nothing. Everything will work out and be fine once I get my hands on the portal."

Jaden thought the same as everyone else: that she was going to destroy the portal and life would return to the status quo. If only it were that simple.

Her mind turned to Jagger. What was she doing with him? It made no sense. She had nothing to offer him except pain. Skye did not want to be Eden number two.

She kept her face neutral and refused to look away from Jaden's eyes, asking instead, "So what's your plan? Can you not come clean with Jagger and Nico?"

"No." Jaden shook her head violently. "I can't trust a soul. No one can know I'm the mole in the DaCosta organization."

Skye made a face. "Okay, I get that. What's next?"

"I'll head back and try to buy you as much time as I can, but it won't be much. There're just too many mercenaries arriving each hour." She spat into the ground. "The entire jungle smells like a fucking paranormal melting pot." She raised her eyebrow. "And that's a stink I can barely stomach."

"Okay, let me come up with something. Jagger and Nico aren't dumb, they'll be all over your escape and—"

A sharp pain exploded along the side of her temple and Skye tilted forward as the world began to spin.

What the hell?

She tried to articulate her thoughts but her mouth didn't seem to be working. Her eyes tried to focus on Jaden, but the woman was nothing more than a blur.

"Sorry chica, but really, you had that coming."

Skye heard the words spoken and then everything went dark.

It was a dark moonless night, one meant for the predatory beasts that roamed the jungle.

Yet Jagger took no pleasure from his nocturnal jaunt. Things had changed. The darkness that was threatening could be felt everywhere. It seeped into the earth at his feet, and poisoned the air that he drew into his lungs.

It made him sick to his stomach to think that certain factions of all the paranormal beings—vamps, shifters, magicks—were actively looking to unleash the demon underworld in the human realm.

Were they fucking clueless? Did Cormac and his cohorts actually think they could control the beasts of the underworld?

Their arrogance and severe lack of regard was astounding.

Nico joined him then, his long, lean body slipping through the dark underbrush. The big cat grunted and turned back toward the cave.

It was time.

There was nothing out here to hunt. The entire area was eerily silent. The animals had all fled, and so far, there was no sign of the enemy. No hint of magick on the air, just the empty silence of the jungle.

Nervous tension sat low in his belly, and the need to get back to Skye rode him hard. Jagger took off running, his powerful frame eating up the distance in no time, and less than twenty minutes later the two males stood near the base of the cave where they'd left Skye.

He called the mist to his body and moved forward,

walking through a change that, while painful, was exhilarating as well. The raw power that his body possessed fed something in his soul that he would never be able to explain.

As he climbed the ledge and entered the cave, his exuberance fled.

Skye sat against the cold rock wall, rubbing her head and cursing under her breath. He quickly turned, scented the air, but it was useless.

The female jaguar was gone.

Long gone, by the minute traces of her scent that lingered still.

He growled and crossed to Skye, his hands reaching for her.

"What the hell happened?" he asked, trying not to sound accusatory but it was kinda hard. Hell, she'd been in charge of one prisoner. A *restrained* prisoner, to boot.

"What do you think happened? The bitch clocked me."

Skye's eyes were full of indignation and for a brief second his anger slipped.

"Are you all right?" He reached for her head and she tried to move away from his touch. "Be still," he growled, his tone brooking no argument.

Gently he felt along the base of her skull, fingers slipping through the silken hair. When they slid across the sizable goose egg, she yelped. There were no other injuries that he could see, and Jagger sat back on his haunches.

"You'll live," he said gruffly.

Skye looked up at him, her eyes indignant, cheeks pink.

"Thanks for pointing that out."

"How the hell did she escape?" Nico's voice echoed into the cave and they both turned as he entered.

Skye looked at the ground and muttered, "I don't know. She was eating. I thought we'd established some kind of rapport and then . . ." She shook her head. "She just attacked me and I had no time to defend myself."

Skye blushed and kept her eyes on the ground.

Jagger stared down at her. "It doesn't matter. She'd never have told you a thing."

"That's not acceptable." Nico said softly, his tone dangerous, his dark eyes focused solely on Skye.

Jagger glanced back at the warrior, not liking the insinuation in his words. "Back off," he growled. The need to defend Skye was overwhelming, and even though his gut was telling him all was not what it seemed, there was no time to dwell on it. "Let's bed down for a few hours and then head out. We need to get to that cave ASAP."

Nico shrugged his shoulders, his body language nonchalant, but the energy that fell from his powerful frame was dark. "I'll get you there by tomorrow afternoon and then, like I said before, I'm gone."

Jagger didn't bother to answer. He grabbed a blanket and tossed it to Skye and as she wrapped the softness around her body, he tried to ignore the ache that had settled deep inside of him.

He wanted nothing more than to take her in his arms and rest against her warmth, if only for a few hours. But something had changed. A new aloofness had taken hold of the blonde. He didn't understand it.

He sat down a few feet away from her, his body tight with want and need, the cold rock a hard pillow at his back.

His eyes closed almost immediately.

Nico paced along the perimeter of the cave for several minutes. His insides were all tangled up, and the need to move was a constant pain that would not go away. He glanced back at the two people who shared the cave.

They were both doomed. Love was an emotion that belonged on the pages of fairy tales. Out here in the real world, it complicated things. It ripped you apart and left you less than what you were.

Its betrayal ran deep.

He should know. It was the reason he rarely slept.

Nico continued to pace and his gaze came to rest on something that lay along the floor of the cave. His curiosity piqued, he quickly crossed over to within a few yards of Skye for a closer look. They were the bindings he'd put on the female jaguar's hands himself.

He reached down and gathered the remnants, fingering the edges carefully. They were clean and had been cut.

The obvious question was, who the hell had cut them? The female warrior or Skye?

He shook his head as his attention drifted to Skye once more before landing on Jagger.

Poor dumb fuck, he thought.

Nico turned away and tossed the bindings over the edge. He watched as they fell into the black nothingness that surrounded the cave, and inhaled deeply. The fresh, moist air tugged at the small part of his soul that was still alive.

He quickly pushed it away.

He didn't care. He *couldn't* care. He would lead them to the cave, like he'd promised. His debt to Jaxon Castille would be paid.

And he'd disappear forever.

Chapter 19

Jagger was awake well before dawn.

The air was heavy with the promise of rain and the jaguar reveled in the feel of the mist as it clung to his heated flesh. He felt a keen sense of melancholy as the familiar scents wove their way deep into his lungs.

So much had already changed out here and it pained him to know that so much was lost.

He clenched his teeth together tightly, letting the muscles work sharply along his jaw. He'd be damned if the otherworld forces at work were going to leave their putrid mark here in the jungle.

It would be over his dead body.

He jumped to his feet in silence, nodding to the warrior who stood a few paces away. Nico never seemed to sleep. Jagger wasn't even sure how he functioned.

"I'm going to contact Cracker and the boys," he said quietly.

Nico looked at him, his eyes glistening eerily in the

dark, and nodded back. "I'll have a look around while you're at it."

Jagger's eyes strayed to the still form wrapped in a blanket. Skye had fallen asleep almost immediately. He knew she was exhausted. The pace they'd set the day before had been relentless, and on top of the demon attack, he knew she wasn't at full strength.

She'd not complained once. Jagger had to admire the tenacity and perseverance the eagle possessed.

He stretched his long limbs out, but his eyes never left the blonde. The breaths she took were even, her sleep undisturbed.

No more Azaiel, at least for now.

He felt a slow burn tear at his gut as he thought of the faceless demon, or whatever the hell he was. He'd be damned if the fucker would have another shot at her.

Not on his watch.

Once the kinks had been worked out of his stiff legs, Jagger crossed to his bag and retrieved the satellite phone. He slipped outside and began to climb higher, until he was perched atop a large granite slab that jutted out from the earth into a natural ledge. He opened up the phone and quickly punched in the number.

Even though the call was being routed via a secure satellite, Jagger was still nervous about the possibility that it would be intercepted. However, there was no other way.

It was answered after the first ring.

"Yeah, Cracker here."

"Christ, you're sounding chipper this morning." Jagger smiled widely at the sound of Cracker's rough vocals.

"Must have something to do with the fact I've had my ass shot at several times over the last twelve hours, with all sorts of nasty things."

Jagger's smile slowly faded away. "Julian all right?" he asked quickly.

"Julian's fine, no thanks to the DaCosta bastards who've been dogging us for the last twelve hours, but I think we've pretty much neutralized 'em."

"Good to hear." Jagger paused. "Nico's led us to within a day's hike of the cave. We'll be there sometime this afternoon. You able to rendezvous?"

"We're not far behind you, cowboy, so that's a tenfour."

Cracker's answer surprised him. "How the hell do you know where I am, exactly?"

"We managed to snag us a wereshifter."

"And?"

"A mercenary from Africa. Seems there's some kind of bounty on the eagle shifter and the entire area is crawling with slimeballs, all gunning for her." Cracker laughed harshly into the phone. "He thought he'd buy his freedom by passing on a little intel. We took the intel but the poor bastard is rotting at the bottom of the river."

Silence greeted Cracker's words as Jagger took a few seconds to process this new information.

"He told us the eagle had been spotted near Placencia. We started heading your way immediately. Figured you could use the help."

Jagger sighed deeply. Things had just escalated.

He paused, his thoughts running in all directions. "You make contact with Jaxon?"

"Checked in yesterday, and I don't mind telling you, he's gonna kick your ass but good."

"Good to know." Jagger laughed softly at his friend's words. "He have any intel on Skye's family? On her brother Finn?"

"Said he'd do some digging, but he could only confirm his knowledge of their existence."

"What about the portal?"

"Again, he knows it exists, but even Jaxon's surprised Cormac and the DaCostas are after it. He and Ana are dealing with something at their end, and they'll join up as soon as they can."

Jagger's mouth slashed into a wide grin as he thought about his older brother, Jaxon. It would be good to see him. Regardless of the fact he'd have to cover his ass. Literally.

"We could use their help. Nico is bailing after we reach this cave."

Cracker grunted, but said nothing.

Jagger proceeded to give Cracker the proper coordinates of their destination and then quickly returned to the cave.

It was still dark. The moon was dead in the sky and offered no illumination at all. His eyes quickly swept the interior and he felt his heart jolt a little when they landed on Skye.

She was awake, and staring at him in silence. Even through the gloom his nocturnal eyes could see the need that lay there. It was primal, harsh.

It cut him, slicing a pain across his chest that only confirmed what he already knew. The woman had grabbed him whole. Lock, stock, and barrel.

Nico was still gone.

He growled softly and stepped toward her.

Skye's breath caught in her throat.

The predatory gleam that shone from deep in Jagger's eyes tilted her insides and left her feeling weak and breathless.

Crap! She needed to get hold of herself. There was no time for what his eyes were wanting. *There was no time for what she was feeling.*

"Don't come near me."

Her words were spoken fast and even she winced at the harsh tone that laced them.

Jagger's eyes narrowed but he didn't stop until he was standing less than a few inches from her feet.

His scent washed over her, pulling at something within her body that answered in kind. It was painful, slicing hard through her chest and it brought with it a hint of tears.

Angrily, she pushed all those thoughts aside, the ones that centered on the longing and aching she felt for this man before her.

"What?" she said, knowing she sounded like an insolent bitch, but helpless to stop herself. What was it about the man that brought out her worst behavior?

He continued to stare at her, the dark green depths of his eyes reflecting like mirrored glass, even through the darkness that fell between them.

"You lie."

Skye's heartbeat hit at the inside of her chest in a steady rhythm that she was sure he could hear. The man confused the crap out of her and she wished he would just go away.

"About what?"

He smiled then, the white of his teeth slashing through the blackness.

"Everything." His voice sounded dangerous. Low.

Skye felt faint. He knew? Her secret?

"I don't—"

He moved so quickly then, the blur registered *after* he was on top of her body.

"You want me as much as I want you. Why do you insist on denying your need?"

The warmth of his breath caressed her cheek and Skye could not look away from the intensity of his gaze.

"I do . . . want you," she whispered, "very much so. I just don't know if we should . . ." Her voice trailed off as a wave of heat ran across her skin.

She couldn't finish her sentence and forced herself to look away, closing her eyes when she felt his fingers encircle her head, plunging deep into the thick hair at her nape.

Her insides liquefied into a molten fire as he slowly turned her toward him, and when his lips stopped, a whisper away from hers, she felt the ache deep within her break, its painful longing fingering out in a well of need that was nearly overwhelming. She wanted nothing more than to wrap her arms around him, and lose herself forever.

"We can, little bird," he whispered, "and we will."

Skye stilled at the raw power in his voice. She was aware of the breaths being pulled from her body, the sound painfully weak as it echoed into the dark and silent cave.

When his lips swept across hers the moan that lay at the back of her throat escaped and with it a sob. Everything that she'd ever wanted was in front of her.

Jagger Castille was a man worthy of not only her respect, her allegiance, but of *her heart*.

How incredibly unfair to find him, the man who could complete her, at a time when the only way she could save him and the rest of the world was by giving up her own life.

She felt the tears as they slowly seeped from the corners of her eyes and when she would have looked aside, he held her still, his mouth slowly kissing them away.

And when Jagger claimed her mouth finally, she was done. There was no way she could fight him any longer.

She opened herself fully to him, her mouth relaxing as she welcomed him into her soft warmth.

He tasted incredibly rich and her lips quivered beneath his as a plethora of sensations rushed along her nerve endings. His tongue invaded her body, each pass along the inside of her mouth pulling heat from deep within.

She was flush with the intensity of it. Dizzy and weightless.

Her hands slowly crept up his shoulders, her fingers trailing a line across the powerful muscles that bunched there. The sensations were incredible and Skye would have loved nothing more than to drown in them, to forget everything except the touch, and taste.

When he pulled away and the heat was replaced with a rush of cool air, she looked up at him, her mouth opened slightly as she panted her disapproval.

Jagger looked down at her for several long seconds and she slowly calmed her body as the remnants of his kiss wove their way throughout her system.

His mouth was no longer tender, but tense, and his eyes narrowed.

"I won't have you"—he gestured with his hands—"here on the floor of some fucking cave out in the middle of the jungle."

He was angry. It was in his tone and the way that the green of his eyes seemed to glow with a reddish light.

He bared his teeth and the animal that lay beneath

his skin shifted, and for a second, Skye felt as if she were staring straight into the heart of the jaguar. It was both magnificent and terrifying.

"We'll do this right. When all this madness is done."

Skye swallowed thickly and began to speak, but the growl that escaped his lips effectively quieted her retort.

He bent over her. "And once I claim you as mine, Skye Knightly, I will never let you go."

His words shocked her and Skye could do nothing but stare stupidly at his back as he turned from her and disappeared out of the mouth of the cave.

Even though the air was hot and heavy with humidity a feeling of cold washed over her. Skye wrapped her arms around her body in an effort to give herself what comfort she could, pulling the wool blanket up around her limbs. Her teeth chattered and her body shook, all of it accompanied by such a heavy weight of sadness that she felt as if she were drowning.

All sorts of memories washed over her then. Images of her father and mother, Finn and herself, played like silent movies behind her eyelids. Happy times that would be no more.

She began to cry softly, her heart breaking at the future lost to her. At the memories she would never have a chance to make.

With Jagger.

Long moments passed. The only sounds that could be heard in the cave were her gentle sobs. As her sadness seeped into the very air that she breathed, Skye felt the strength that lay at the heart of who and what she was begin to take its place.

The eagles were a noble and proud group of knights who lived to protect the very things that would destroy humanity. They were selfless. Solitary. It was dangerous.

It was a legacy, one to be proud of and it was time for her to *own it*. Not just in theory, but in actions.

She threw the blanket from her still shivering form and jumped to her feet. There was no time for weakness. Not now. Not with the end in sight.

"Good, you're awake." The low, harsh words grabbed her and she turned in surprise. She'd not heard Nico slip into the cave.

His eyes were fierce. Something had changed and unease slid through her body.

"Where's Jagger? Is he all right?"

Nico stared at her in silence. When he began to move toward her, his long legs full of predatory grace, she stepped back but felt the cool wall of the cave at her back.

"Who are you, Skye Knightly?"

His question threw her, although the dislike he obviously felt was very apparent.

"I'm not sure what you mean," she answered haltingly.

He laughed then, softly, and Skye shuddered at the raw power that emanated from deep within the warrior.

"I think you know *exactly* what I mean."

He took another step toward her; she could feel the heat that emanated from his tall frame. His eyes burned with a fire that, truthfully, alarmed and frightened her. He was on the edge, this warrior, straddling the line between sanity and clarity in such a way that was unpredictable.

He could ruin everything.

She swallowed thickly but held her ground. "Nico, I

don't have time to play twenty questions." She decided to be honest. "Look, I'm grateful you're leading us to the Cave of the Sun, but let me be blunt. I think you're more than a little crazy and I don't trust you." She paused before adding, "So why don't you just ask me what it is you want to know?"

He growled softly and she could sense the anger that lay just beneath the surface. "You know what I find interesting, little eagle?"

She could only shake her head in answer.

"No?" He leaned in closer and Skye tried to turn away but she couldn't. The blackness that laced his words and burned in his eyes had her gut clenching, and for the first time she began to fear for her safety.

"I find it interesting that you don't trust me, when in fact you're the one with something to hide."

His voice lowered, falling in layers from his lips, and Skye flinched at the intensity of his gaze. He was close to turning. She could see it.

"I don't know what you're talking about."

Nico laughed. The sound was harsh, unfriendly. "No?" he said as he cocked an eyebrow. "Care to explain how the female jaguar escaped?" He leaned down toward her, and Skye held her ground. His voice was barely above a whisper. "I found the remnants of the female jaguar's bindings. They were cut. Clean and precise."

Skye tried her best to appear calm and kept her face blank.

"I don't like what you're implying. Why the hell would I let a jaguar warrior escape, especially considering she's hunting me?"

Nico grinned down at her, his handsome face fierce. "I was hoping you'd be willing to share."

Skye looked away and shrugged her shoulders as her mind whirled into a million thoughts. She'd never been good at lying, although lately, it seemed to be a skill she'd had no problem acquiring.

"Move away from her."

Jagger's growl erupted from the edge of the cave and Skye turned toward him, her heart pounding heavily inside her chest. The warrior stood with legs spread, a casual stance, really, but the anger and blackness that clung to him was unmistakable.

Nico whirled around and snarled as he took a step toward Jagger. Skye's throat constricted and she jumped forward. "Stop it! Both of you." She ran toward Jagger, her eyes beseeching. "We're so close to the end, we can't fall apart now."

Jagger's eyes shot sparks of energy and the green of them took her breath away. He didn't take his eyes off Nico, but his warm hand fell to hers as he pulled her in close to his body.

"Did he touch you?"

Skye shook her head. "No," she whispered. "No, we're good. I just want to go and find the cave."

Jagger looked down at her then, his face unreadable, and the emotion that welled up from deep inside of her was like a physical ache.

"You'll take us to the cave and then I want you gone." The words were directed at Nico. They were flat, cold.

Skye could feel the other warrior move behind her and by the way Jagger's arms tightened around her protectively, she knew Nico was close.

She held her breath.

"I have no problem with that," Nico answered softly.

The relief that washed over her was nearly incapacitating. Her legs buckled and Skye leaned into Jagger, resting her head against his chest.

Nico exited the cave, leaving the two of them alone with their silence.

"Are you sure you're all right? I shouldn't have left you alone with him. He's screwed up. Has been for a long time. I just never thought he'd—"

"Ssshhhh. I'm fine Jagger, really." Skye's eyes were captured whole by the intensity of his gaze. "I just need this to be over."

Jagger's fingers trailed softly across her cheek until they lay against her lips.

"Let's do this," he said quietly. He lowered his mouth and the pain around her heart sharpened. His lips caressed hers softly, teasing her with the merest whisper of pleasure before they were gone.

Skye turned from Jagger, hoping the sheen of tears had gone unnoticed. She quickly grabbed her bag, making sure all of her precious notes and maps were in place. When she turned back, Jagger was waiting, the intensity of his gaze more than a little unsettling. He cocked his head to the side and she moved to the edge of the cave.

It was still dark, a few hours away from dawn, but she had no problem navigating down. The jungle was silent, eerie. It was more than a little unsettling. Every single alarm bell was ringing deep within her. Nothing was right. Everything was wrong.

Yet there was nothing out there. The jungle lay empty.

Smart, she thought. All the animals had fled. They could sense the darkness that was slowly seeping into the very heart of the jungle. Sad thing was, if she wasn't able to stop it, there would be no place to hide.

Skye looked toward the last mountain to cross, the

one that sheltered the Cave of the Sun. It lay dark, silent, and forbidding. A shiver crossed her body and her heart began to beat against her chest as the adrenaline kicked in.

It was time. Before the end of this next day, she would hold the portal in her hands. She would fulfill her destiny by sealing it forever.

Skye squared her shoulders and avoided Jagger's gaze. She had no time to dwell on the what-ifs or the could-have-beens. She had no time for love.

She *would* do this.

And have the rest of eternity to think about regret.

Chapter 20

They hiked for hours through dense forest, cool rivers, and across waterfalls that fell hundreds of feet. The sun broke from the dark of night although it couldn't penetrate the fog and mist, which lay like a blanket and shrouded the entire area. The vibrant blues and greens of the jungle seemed dull, lifeless, as if a paintbrush of gloom had washed over the entire area.

Skye took a long draw from a flask of water and wiped the sweat from her brow. Her eyes remained fixed ahead, on a point near the summit of the mountain. It was where Nico had indicated the cave was located.

Nervous energy tugged at her and Skye had to concentrate in order to stop her hands from shaking. After shoving the water canister back into her bag, she flexed her fingers and cracked her neck from side to side. She was tense, on edge.

She found her gaze drifting to Jagger and felt everything inside of her still at the burning look of need and hunger in his eyes. She tried to swallow but found that she couldn't.

Jagger watched as Skye turned from him, his gaze resting on the delicate curve of her cheek and jaw. She was so beautiful it hurt him, *physically hurt him*, to look at her.

To know that she was only a few feet away and he had no claim on her, *yet*, was painful. The desire to brand Skye as his had been riding him hard all night.

It was something he could no longer deny.

Skye Knightly was the woman he wanted. He was ruined for anyone else. There would be no other.

A feeling of uneasiness washed over him then. As much as he desired Skye, he knew next to nothing about her and he couldn't shake the feeling that she was holding something back from him.

Would he end up as Eden had? Broken? Desperate for a love that couldn't be returned? Even now the guilt he felt punched him hard in the gut. If only he'd been stronger.

Bitterly, he pushed those thoughts away. He couldn't go there. Not now. He needed to remain focused and alert.

"The cave is there."

Nico stopped beside him. They were the first words spoken between them since they'd left predawn.

Jagger followed his direction and narrowed his eyes, but couldn't see an opening.

"To the right, just past the large boulder on the other side of the waterfall."

Jagger's gaze went to just beneath the summit. Low-lying mist curled lazily along the rock face, hanging over the water like a curtain. The jungle was still abnormally silent. Unease sat low in his belly and he shook it away as his eyes drifted over the entire area.

From what he could tell it looked to be at least another hour or so before they would reach the cave. He turned to Nico, but before he could speak, Nico continued.

"Be careful. The entire area is protected with ancient wards. I hope your little eagle knows how to navigate them."

Jagger nodded.

"Do not trust her." Nico's warning was whispered softly. "She has your heart, so she's basically got you by the balls. Don't think she doesn't know that."

Jagger's eyes narrowed menacingly. They glittered, glowing green as his anger began to churn. He snarled and felt the beast inside of him awaken. He didn't like the warrior's tone or meaning.

"I think it's time for you to go." Jagger bared his teeth and let the animal show briefly.

Nico held his ground and shook his head. His voice was bitter, resigned. "Bad times are coming. I can feel it. Nothing will be as it was, but one thing will always remain the same."

"I don't have time for riddles."

Nico snorted, his eyes cold and steely. "Betrayal tastes like shit and if you get enough of it, it'll drive you fucking crazy."

Jagger watched as the warrior turned and disappeared into the fog that continued to swirl in ribbons around him.

He felt like punching the crap out of something. Anything. Impotent rage began to burn in his gut, and he had no clue why. Jagger felt like he was on the precipice of something life-changing. He just didn't know in what direction it was headed.

Hopefully not to hell.

"Where's he going? Will he be . . . all right?"

Jagger turned to Skye. She stood a few paces from him, her long blond hair tied loosely at her nape. She was all golden sunshine, lush curves, lean lines, and soft skin. Even through this cold mist that hung over them like a gray film, she shone like a beacon.

"I don't know." His eyes moved to just behind her. "But we're here. The cave is just beyond that waterfall."

Skye turned to follow the direction of his finger and he took a few moments to drink in the beauty that she was. He felt the familiar burn, the itching beneath his skin as the jaguar craved the woman who was his. It was painful, but he relished it.

It meant that he was alive. That there was hope and a future he could grab on to. One worth fighting for.

He hiked his satchel as he sized up the best way to climb to the cave.

"Okay, you ready?" he asked Skye, feeling his heart clench as her blue eyes shone out at him. Her mouth was tense and he could sense the fear that lurked just beneath the surface. He couldn't blame her. Only a fool would approach the end of a mission and not feel fear.

But that was good. Fear could make you strong if used properly.

"Yes."

"Nico said the entire area is protected with wards. Otherworld I'm sure. I'm hoping you'll know what to do?"

He watched as she swallowed slowly, and ached to

run his tongue along the hollow of her neck, easing his way upward until he could claim her lips as his. Her eyes darkened and he smiled gently. She felt it. The physical connection between the two of them.

His groin tightened at the very thought, and images of her in front of him, legs splayed open, assaulted him.

"Our people have certain . . . protective magicks we've used for centuries. I will be able to get us through."

"Great." His voice was thick and he sounded drunk. He couldn't help it. His mind had gone to a place that he needed to stay away from. Even now, he could taste and smell her. His cock twitched painfully as he envisioned her warmth perched above his mouth. Of her hands in his hair as he fed from that secret place between her legs.

"We should go," he ground out from between gritted teeth.

The sounds of desire that had fallen from her lips had been enough to drive him crazy the other night, but now? They echoed in his mind and were pure torture.

"Are you all right, Jagger?" Skye asked and moved toward him.

"I'm fine. Let's do this." His answer was curt, and he exhaled slowly, holding back a groan as she bent over to retrieve her bag.

Something then slid over him and gave him pause, effectively dousing his desire with a cold, hard dose of reality.

It was ancient, black, and invading. Inside, the animal began to growl and Jagger scented the wind, turning his body so that his eyes could scan the immediate area.

The feeling rushed him and then was gone, but the whispered words that flooded his brain brought a snarl to his face.

She's mine.

The otherworld stink was unmistakable. It belonged to the phantom fucker from down below. *Azaiel.*

"Jagger? Seriously, you're starting to act as crazy as Nico."

He shook his head as his eyes skimmed the top of Skye's blond head. "I'm good. Let's go."

She paused for a second and then started up the trail toward the waterfall with Jagger close behind.

A line had just been drawn. The gauntlet thrown, and he was not backing down. Jagger would not let another touch Skye.

If this Azaiel thought to make a play for his woman he'd find out soon enough that a jaguar warrior would stop at nothing to protect his mate. He smiled viciously as he followed her upward.

Bring it on, asshole, he thought. *Bring it on.*

They climbed higher, carefully picking their way across the nearly sheer rock face until just over an hour later they approached the waterfall. The mist was cool against his face and Jagger noticed that Skye had lost her tie somewhere along the way. Her long hair blew in the breeze like caramel candy and he longed to grab hold of it, to bury his nose in its softness.

She turned then and caught his heated stare. Jagger felt a sense of satisfaction rush over him as her cheeks deepened with a rosy blush.

"I think the opening is on the other side."

He nodded and followed her. They slid down into the pool of water that welcomed the rush from hundreds of feet above, and Jagger grabbed her bag, holding it aloft so as to keep the contents safe.

When they made it to the other side, his animal began to make noise once more. Jagger couldn't be sure if it was the sight of Skye, her clothes wet and pasted to her body like a second skin, that excited the jaguar deep inside, or rather, the heavy weight of magick that blanketed the area.

Whatever it was, he had to force the animal back and concentrate. Skye was breathing hard as well, and as she began to climb up the other side, he searched along the rock face, looking for the opening that would lead to the cave.

He saw nothing and was beginning to lose his patience when Skye stopped abruptly. He very nearly slammed into the back of her.

"It's there," she whispered.

Jagger followed her gaze and felt impatience rush through him. He couldn't see shit.

Skye moved past the large boulder that stood like a soldier and he quickly followed suit. She carefully set her bag down, the fog swirling hard and fast around them.

Jagger inhaled deeply, all senses on full alert. The magick that coated the surrounding hillside was ancient, and though it didn't set off alarm bells, he couldn't help but pause at the power it wielded.

Skye closed her eyes and he stood back. He could feel little pulses of energy in the air, almost like a force field was in effect. Which in fact was what the magick was for. It would be enough to repel wild animals or humans with no knowledge.

The wind picked up, tossing the long strands of caramel into the air so that Skye's hair surrounded her head like Medusa's snakes. She looked wild, untamed. Fucking magnificent.

Slowly her hands drifted out on either side of her body, and he was mesmerized by the elegant fingers. She looked so fragile then, with the wind whipping around her.

His breath caught in his throat as gentle words began to roll from her tongue. Ancient, powerful words laced with a magick he could feel. They were not anything he'd heard before, and as her voice rose to crest the wind, the powerful emotions that rocked him were hard to contain.

She was his warrior woman and she tapped into a savage need inside of him. He'd never seen anything like it and felt pride for this woman who was before him.

Her hands began to make intricate movements, precise and detailed as they wove some foreign charm into the air. When Skye's body began to waver he stepped in close to her back, but she raised her right hand and halted him when he would have touched her.

The air was thick and it was hard to breathe. His heart began to accelerate as the fog swirled ever closer, slick with a mist that drenched their clothes and cooled their flesh.

And just when Skye's voice faded, her last words echoing softly into the wind, he saw it. The waterfall itself began to shimmer, to pulsate and move. He narrowed his eyes, and slowly, like a film had been pulled back, he was able to see the opening.

It was slim, the merest whisper of a passageway in the rock wall beside the waterfall.

"We need to hurry. I can't hold it much longer. I'm not powerful enough."

He looked at Skye, saw the exhaustion in her face,

and scooped her into his arms, grabbing her bag from the ground and ignoring the protest from her lips. Quickly his long legs ate up the last few yards to the opening, and as he slid through, he felt a subtle pressure. Almost like a pop, but then he was inside and the sensation fled.

It was dark, silent. Cold and damp.

For several long seconds the only sounds heard were the breaths from each of them.

Skye clung to his body, her arms tight around his neck, and as his eyes adjusted to the gloom, he nuzzled the top of her head, inhaling her scent deep into his body. It felt so right, having her in his arms, and the immediate ache that accompanied the thought hit him hard and fast.

His breathing increased tenfold and just as his body began to hum with a hot flush of desire, she pushed away, wriggling her limbs until reluctantly he let her slide from his arms.

"This is it!" she said, her voice full of wonder.

Skye grabbed her bag from him, rummaging inside, and a few seconds later artificial light flooded the cave.

He looked around and felt a keen sense of disappointment. This was it? There was nothing special that he could see. No markings, no artifacts. Just the cold gray walls staring back at him.

"Oh my God, they're beautiful!"

Jagger turned, perplexed at the look of wonder on Skye's face. He could see nothing and he remained silent as she slowly walked over to the farthest wall. Her fingers gently caressed the rock and as they passed over the hard surface he saw sparks fly and symbols appear beneath her touch, only to sink from sight as her hand moved farther along.

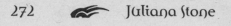

She turned then, her face alight with strong emotion.

"Aren't they amazing?" She laughed and he found himself smiling in return.

In two steps his long legs carried him to her side and he shrugged his shoulders. "I don't see what you see." His eyes looked down at her intently. "I see flashes of symbols, but it's only when your hand is near the stone."

Skye shook her head. "Gawd, I'm an idiot. Of course." She looked up at him, the blue of her eyes flashing, glowing eerily in the dark. "You're jaguar. You wouldn't be able to see."

She paused and he felt her excitement as if it was his own. Jagger broke into a grin and loved the way her eyes lit up as she looked at him.

"I wonder . . ." Skye's voice trailed off and when he felt the warmth of her hand on his own, everything inside of him liquefied. Seriously, he felt like he could melt into a puddle of need and want. The intensity of emotion that she tugged out of him was incredible.

He now knew exactly how Jaxon had felt about Libby.

He hissed softly as she cradled his hand and followed as she tugged him forward, not paying attention to her actions. Not caring, really. The fact that he was with her, that her warmth and touch was on his skin, was enough for him. For now.

"Look," she said softly, and his eyes lifted away from her face to follow the direction of her gaze.

He felt the energy tingle along his forearm but he wasn't prepared for the magnificent vision that appeared beneath his hand. The hand guided by Skye.

"What the . . ." His eyes widened at the intricate

display before him and he shook his head, smiling down at Skye in wonder.

"You see it? Now?" Her words were breathless and they trembled from her soft lips.

"It's amazing," he answered, and in truth, it was one of the coolest things he'd ever laid eyes on.

Ancient markings in a dazzling display of color were displayed across the entire rock wall of the cave. Many he recognized from books and drawings he'd seen in his youth, yet a lot were strange.

There were various pictures of eagles in flight, some in half shift, showing both their human and animal side. The jaguars that could be seen were depicted as dark and evil, but they only added to the drama of the markings, and he grinned at them.

Jaguars *were* dark, powerful creatures.

The markings and symbols shimmered against the hard surface as if they were holograms and the light that filtered between them was luminescent.

"What do they mean?" Jagger was curious.

Skye moved closer and kept her hand over his. He looked down, loving the look of concentration and wonder that consumed her features.

She bit her lip, cocked her head, and it was nearly his undoing. He wanted nothing more than to claim her lips and kiss her like she'd never been kissed before. His grin widened even more. He felt like a giddy freaking schoolboy.

Yet Skye was totally unaware. With her free hand she pointed to the various symbols that swept across the wall.

"They're not words or sentences so much as meanings, *warnings*."

Jagger's eyes followed the arc of her hand as she

continued to trace the strange and exotic drawings. She pointed to an exquisite rendering of the sun set in the mouth of a large eagle. It was encircled with symbols that shimmered and glowed beneath her caress.

"This"—Skye turned to him, her face flush with excitement—"is the symbol of my people."

She turned back, her eyes full of concentration as she murmured, "I wish Finn were here. He was always so much better at this kinda stuff." Her words ended on a soft note and Jagger felt her pain as if it were his own. There'd been no word about her brother and as far as they both knew, he'd perished in the jungle when the jaguars had first attacked.

She inhaled a shaky breath and whispered, "These symbols are my history." She looked up at him. "And yours. Our people were once united, but now . . ."

She knelt down and her hand slipped from his. Immediately, the shimmer and translucent images fled from his eyes, leaving only bare, cold gray walls.

Silence fell between the two of them and a sense of foreboding washed over Jagger. He shivered slightly and squared his shoulders.

"We need to go there." Skye stood and he followed her along a narrow passage that ran underneath the waterfall. It was icy cold and the artificial light illuminated the breaths that came from their lungs and lay in the air like small puffs of smoke.

The roar from the water could be heard as it slipped over the rock face on the outside and Jagger had a hard time shaking the feeling of dread that was fast rushing through his bloodstream.

He didn't like it here. He sensed some bad mojo.

As they trekked further along, light could be seen filtering through the gloom a hundred yards ahead.

Skye turned off her flashlight and the natural light was a much softer illumination, blanketing the cold gray in some bit of warmth.

She began to hurry and Jagger had to jog in order to keep up. When they entered a large chamber he stopped, surprised and amazed at the scene before him.

The entire cavern was alight with a radiant glow, and as far as he could tell there was no source for it. It was warm, comforting, and he looked at Skye, his heart stopping at the shadows that fell across her face.

"It's up there," she said softly.

He followed her gaze and could only shake his head in wonder at the artwork adorning the ceiling. This he could see, without any trouble. It wasn't concealed by magick.

The entire universe, it seemed, had been depicted with an enormous sun at its center. And in that center was an opening big enough to let something through. Something small.

Like an eagle.

A feeling of dread erupted inside of him, and he took a step toward her.

"You're not doing this alone." His breathing became heavy and his voice deepened, echoing loudly into the chamber. "I won't allow it."

Skye shook her head and her voice was tense. "There's no choice."

Jagger took another step toward her even as his eyes began to shrewdly inspect the cavern. He might be able to slip through the opening in his jaguar form, but how the hell was he going to get to it?

"Fuck!" he shouted, exasperated and pissed off. "I won't let you go alone." He clenched his hands together and his face darkened with emotion. His eyes glowed as a ferocious snarl erupted from deep within his chest. "I won't."

He nailed her with a look that brooked no argument. "It's not acceptable. There has to be another way."

His mind worked furiously, but as he glanced up at the opening again he bleakly wondered what it was he thought he could accomplish. He wanted to protect her and felt helpless at his inability to do so.

"There is no other way, Jagger." Skye bit her lip and shook her head. "I have to do this, otherwise . . ." Her voice trailed away until there was nothing but the heavy weight of silence between them.

He closed his eyes, not wanting her to see his pain. His weakness. Inside his soul, the great jaguar stirred, agitated and alarmed. "If anything happens to you . . ." he whispered roughly, not able to finish his sentence and articulate what his mind was thinking.

She closed the space between them in one quick movement and grabbed his face with an intensity that hit him hard. Her scent, so unique and exotic, clung to his skin like he'd been wrapped inside of her, and his body responded ferociously.

His arms went around her, pulling her into his hard embrace with a passion that reached to his core. This was no ordinary woman he held. She was otherworld. An eagle knight. He had to trust that she knew what the hell she was doing.

His lips glanced over hers like a soft whisper and when she opened beneath him, he groaned into her mouth. "Return to me," he said, and then he kissed her long and hard, until she broke from him, her breaths exhaling from her chest in a rapid rhythm that sounded almost painful.

He saw the sheen of tears that clung to her eyelashes. They looked like jewels sparkling against the glare of the sun. They tugged at him and yet his eyes hardened until he knew his animal was shining through.

He wanted her to know how dead serious he was.

"If you're not back here within the hour, I will rip this entire fucking mountain apart." He bared his teeth and growled. "Do you understand? I'll kill anything that stands in my way."

She tried to look away from him but he gripped her chin hard, and even though he knew he was most likely hurting her, he was barely able to stop himself from grabbing her and taking her the hell away from everything.

Screw the eagles and the jaguars and the dirty magicks who bedded down with the demons. Fuck them all.

His mental rant was short-lived. "I will come for you," he said simply, his eyes drowning in the huge expanse of blue that stared back at him in silence.

Skye nodded and grabbed his hand, gently prying his grip loose with her fingers. "I have to go; there's not much daylight left and I need to shift." She inhaled deeply and stepped back, turning from him as she began to shed her clothes.

Already the mist was crawling along her golden limbs as the ancient magick took hold. She could feel the raptor inside begin to stir and she moved away, calling to her animal, welcoming the power that accompanied the change.

I love you.

The words fell from her lips but the sound that erupted from her mouth was a chortled cry that echoed sharply against the walls of the cavern.

Her wings unfurled and with a sweep of them she rose gracefully into the air, circling around, her talons extended as she swept by her clothes and satchel. She easily scooped them up.

There was no way in hell she was going to greet the underworld in the buff.

She rose ever higher in the cavern, her shadow casting a macabre display along the wall, and without another glance downward, she disappeared through the opening.

Chapter 21

Skye shot through the opening, her body slicing through the air as she picked up speed. She was in another chamber, this one just as large as the one she'd left. There were no special markings here, no symbols etched into the limestone, but the glow that shrouded the room was magnificent.

It warmed her feathers, fed her power, and she continued to circle ever higher, instinctually following the light.

The chamber eventually emptied out into more of a narrow passage, and after a few moments she was forced to shift back to her human form in order to navigate safely.

She dressed quickly and then tucked the satchel under her arm. Skye followed the path set before her and climbed higher, her feet running up steps that had been carved hundreds of years earlier. The air was damp but warm, fed by the incredible light that lit the path.

The going was tough, the stairs steep, and the

magick that hung in the air was heavy. It tingled along her body, rushing over her flesh, energizing cells until her senses were hyper-alert.

She could hear her breath exhaling slowly from her body, her heartbeat steady and sure inside her rib cage. Moisture dripped from the walls on either side of her and she could literally hear it slide across the smooth rock.

The tunnel began to widen at this point. However, her eyes, long accustomed to the brightness of the sun, were no match for the brilliance of this glow. She winced, fighting the urge to shield them with her hands.

She was so freaking close.

"I'm almost there, Dad," she whispered as she began to jog, carefully jumping over several steps as the tunnel veered sharply to the right.

She'd just cleared the turn when a chill rolled over her body and her gut clenched in reaction. Skye stopped abruptly, crying out in pain as her bare feet skidded across the stone floor.

"Shit!"

A heavy feeling drifted across her mind, as if something or *someone* had snuck in for a peek. She shuddered at the creepiness of it and grimaced as her eyes scanned the area around her.

There was nothing but the eerie glow washing over the rock face.

Skye's arms crept up and she rubbed her shoulders. Tension hung just beneath her skin and her muscles ached with the weight of it. Her body was now slick with sweat and she tucked long wisps of hair behind her ears as she exhaled slowly.

She turned her head and listened for a few more seconds before she began to move forward cautiously.

She had no time to waste. Even now the jungle was

most likely crawling with a whole host of baddies, all with one goal. Her, or the portal.

She was damn sure no one was getting their hands on either one.

Fog drifted toward her as the passage narrowed and the elevation sharpened. She was no longer heading in a horizontal direction, but running up a steep incline.

The light was near blinding and she needed to shield her eyes in order to see properly. As she continued along, shimmering symbols began to dance in front of her, like mini-holograms. They floated amid the fog in a spectacular display that told her she was but steps from her goal.

Skye stopped. Just ahead was a large opening, its gaping mouth full of light, warmth, and mist.

It was protected by an invisible force field, a powerful one, by the feel of it. She could feel the energy as it sizzled in the air.

Skye concentrated and after a few seconds was able to "see" it. It was thickly woven, full of magick.

She closed her eyes and began to recite the ancient words she'd never spoken aloud before, sacred ones that had been passed down to both herself and Finn. She began to weave symbols in the air, back and forth, as the mystical language of her people fell from her lips in a bittersweet melody.

Her fingers began to work their way *through* the invisible shield and as the power inside of her awakened, it hummed along her limbs, shooting out from her fingers in an arc of color that shattered the wall before her.

Her heart was now beating a mile a minute, and Skye hesitated for a second as her thoughts turned to the man she'd left behind.

Her chest constricted and she had trouble breathing. She could turn around right now and run back to Jagger. She could tell him the truth and let him know that she'd picked him over her destiny.

She wavered then as she stood upon the precipice of the darkest moment in her young life. She thought back to all the eagle knights that had given their lives in order to protect the portal. They had sacrificed so much.

Her father, the protector of their time, had given his life to do just that, and Finn was dead, for all she knew. How could she fail them now?

Her fists clenched tightly at her sides and she ignored the pain she felt as her nails dug into the soft flesh there. A deep sadness welled up from her soul and she began to cry.

She was trying to be so brave. Wanted her father to be proud of her, and yet, all she could think about were the things that would never be. She'd never see the sun rise again, or fly through the fresh morning air.

She felt the pieces of her heart break a little more.

She'd never know the strength of Jagger's love, or the pleasure of waking beside him each morning. She'd never have a child.

The ache intensified and Skye was ashamed to admit how weak she felt in that moment. She didn't want her life to end. For Christ sakes, she was only twenty-seven years old! She'd not yet begun to live!

She sniffled and the sound echoed sharply in the cold dampness before fading away to nothing.

She stood still for a long time and then a spark of strength began to burn in her gut until it spread across her body, leaving her trembling. She felt it then. The power of her people. The power that was inside of her, and she knew she would be strong enough to carry through.

Skye inhaled deeply. Even now the jungle was crawling with the dark forces that Cormac had gathered. She thought of the creature that had attacked her only a few nights previous. Already, demons had begun to seep into her world.

Her fingers trailed across her lips. If she closed her eyes, she could still feel Jagger's kiss. She could still taste and smell him.

It would have to be enough to get her through.

Christ, get over yourself, she thought.

"Just do it," she said loudly.

She shook out her limbs and squared her shoulders and then plunged forward, her body sliding through the protection ward with ease, although the energy left her skin sizzling. It wasn't unpleasant and fled as quickly as it had come.

Once she was through, the mist began to swirl ever faster, its touch cool on her flesh. Skye began to shiver as her heated skin reacted, flush with goose bumps. She crossed her arms across her chest, trying for what bit of comfort that she could.

She couldn't see clearly, and even though the light was bright, everything seemed out of focus. She felt as if her equilibrium was compromised and she stumbled, her head whipping around as she tried to gain her bearings.

It felt like she was outside, no longer protected by the walls of a cave.

The wind picked up and whipped long tendrils of hair about her face. It made an eerie whistle as it flew along the floor, tickling her feet and trailing with it a scent that was frighteningly familiar.

Panic settled deep within her soul as she frantically searched through the film of mist that coated everything in sight. Was Azaiel here in this realm? Or had she left her sanity behind?

Skye.

Azaiel's voice whispered through her mind, softly, like a caress, and she shuddered as the heavy weight of him seeped into her brain.

Fear clutched at her sharply and her teeth began to chatter as she continued to try and pierce the wall of mist with her vision.

Where was he?

But more important, where the hell was the portal?

Skye felt nauseous and for a second was afraid she'd faint, but she gritted her teeth and began to pant as she used every ounce of energy she possessed to push the fear away. When it broke and slipped from her she cried out, the sound dampened by the thick air that continued to beat at her.

She took a few tentative steps forward and then stopped.

Skye let go of all thoughts, memories, fears, Jagger—anything that wasn't connected—and closed her mind to everything but the portal.

Her mind went blank for a few seconds and she tensed to such a degree that her muscles ached. It felt like every inch of her body was being held tightly in a vise, gripped hard and wrung out so thoroughly that nothing but emptiness remained.

But then the warmth of the sun caressed her cheeks, and in her mind she could clearly picture the ancient round disc. It shimmered as if enveloped in a mirage of light, and when Skye opened her eyes the mist had all but vanished, leaving her alone on the top of the mountain.

"What the—"

She turned in a full circle, seeing nothing but a blanket of cloud surrounding the small area where she stood. It felt like she was on top of the world, standing along the edge of the known realm.

The magick that slithered along her skin was familiar. It contained the signature of her people and the joy such a simple feeling evoked inside of her was unparalleled. It told her that the eagle knights prevailed. That even though many had fallen to their dark enemies, their spirit and will lived on.

The clouds began to give way, receding to where they came from, and she saw the dark opening that she'd just exited. There was nothing extraordinary about it. It looked plain. Simple, as if it had never felt the touch of magick.

She turned once more, her eyes following the mist as it pulled back from the earthen floor, like a carpet being rolled back. The sun, though low in the sky, continued to heat her face and she fed from its power.

In the distance an eagle called, its cry slicing through the silence like a sharp knife. Skye shuddered at the lonely sound and searched for it to no avail. She heard one more call and then there was nothing.

Sweat began to slip from her pores and even though Skye tried to still her fast-beating heart, she couldn't calm her body. She knew the end was near and the heavy weight of it sat hard inside her soul.

Her T-shirt stuck to her skin. She pinched it away, hoping some air would alleviate her discomfort, but then she let it fall back in disgust. What the hell was she doing? She was gonna spend fucking eternity in the darkness, deep within the hell realm.

It's not like anyone down there was going to care that she had bad body odor.

A wave of cool wind slid across her cheek, blowing a tendril of hair along her nose. It was time.

Slowly she took a step forward. And then another, watching as the fog continued to dissipate, like the tide receding at the end of the day.

When the shrine was finally exposed, she couldn't help but feel a little disappointed. It held none of the grandeur of either one of the inner chambers and consisted of rocks, both large and small, that had been thrown together to create a small hut.

She closed the remaining feet in a rush and stood outside the entrance, her eyes scouring the facade. Above the opening there was a simple etching in the rock that depicted an eagle in flight.

Other than that, there was nothing.

She was left with nothing more to do than slip through. With a wary look around, Skye did just that, her blond head quickly disappearing inside the dark interior of the shrine.

Inside it was dark and the floor uneven. She swayed and nearly lost her balance. The satchel she'd clutched, forever it seemed, fell to the ground at her feet. Everything was weird, as if the alignment of the sun and moon, of the very axis of the earth was off kilter.

Something was wrong. She could feel it.

She waited for her eyes to adjust to the dim lighting and when her vision fell upon the dais several feet from where she stood, her breath caught in her throat.

It was surrounded at each corner with tall urns, ones that should be burning forever with the light of the sun. This she knew.

Skye swallowed thickly as the fist inklings of dread began to roll over in her belly. Something was drastically wrong.

She stood dead center to the dais.

Skye could do nothing but shake her head in dismay, anger and fear.

"You've got to be fucking kidding," she whispered hoarsely into the room, but there was no denying what her eyes were seeing.

The dais was empty.

A million thoughts rushed through Skye's mind and she frantically began a search of the entire area. Panic joined in the fun and her breaths heaved from her mouth in sporadic bursts as she struggled to hold on to what little thread of sanity she still had going.

The portal was missing!

How in the hell was that even possible? Where the hell was it?

Cold sharp pains clawed their way through her belly and she doubled over in the corner, her stomach heaving as she retched.

She fell to the floor and passed a trembling hand over her face, feeling the cold fingers sharply against her heated skin.

Dully, her eyes wandered the room, but it was no use. It wasn't like there were secret compartments with the portal hidden safely inside.

It was well and truly gone.

And Skye had no freaking clue as to its location. A thought struck her then, and she grabbed her satchel, her fingers barely able to get it open because they were trembling so badly.

But as she quickly went over her notes and those of her father's she felt all hope begin to fade. Every indication led to the belief that the portal was in the Cave of the Sun.

The fact that it was missing meant one of two

things. Her father had retrieved it, but since he'd been killed and it was obviously not in the hands of the Da-Costas or Cormac, he'd hidden it elsewhere.

Or someone had managed to break the eagle magick that protected the cave and the shrine, and had successfully stolen the portal. If so, their identity was a mystery, as they'd not shown their hand and had not come into play yet.

Either way, she was screwed.

She didn't have a portal to seal, and while that meant that she was *not* going to hell today, she still had a jungle full of mercenaries gunning for her ass. She swallowed hard, her mind whirling frantically. Her odds of surviving the next few days were less than ten percent.

If she was lucky.

She slumped onto the floor and rested her head against the cool rock wall. It was still dark inside the shrine and, for a few seconds at least, she felt invisible. Safe.

Damn, if only she had Finn to talk to. Or Father.

Restless energy pummeled her and she felt dizzy as her heart continued to beat against her chest. She'd closed her eyes and was trying to plot her next move, when she felt the merest whisper of a cold caress, almost like a snake had just wound its way across her mind and slithered down into her chest.

She jumped to her feet, her eyes circling wildly, but there was nothing there.

"Don't go all crazy now, Skye. You need a plan."

She couldn't think clearly though, and shook her head as she grabbed her papers once more and shoved them back into the bag. Her fingers touched something solid and she fingered the stone eagle, a trinket she'd had forever.

Abruptly, she shoved it back into the bag. She needed to get to Jagger.

With one last look around, Skye exited the small shrine, welcoming the sun as it continued to squeeze out her last rays. She needed to hurry. In less than an hour she'd have no power to shift and she knew there was no way she'd be able to slip through the opening that led back to the great cavern.

She retraced her footsteps rapidly, her body sliding through the magick that protected the opening, and it seemed that in no time she reached the exit to the cavern.

But there was a problem. A huge problem.

The opening was no longer.

Something broke inside of Skye then, and she pounded her fists against the solid wall that greeted her, cursing, screaming, and not stopping until the scent of blood filled the air. Dully, she looked down at her bruised and bloody hands and stepped away.

She truly was alone. There was no way of getting to Jagger.

Slowly she turned around and retraced her steps. She had no clue where she was going or what she was going to do. But she had to keep moving, because if not, then surely she would go insane.

She felt her strength fade as the sun began her final descent. The cave itself seemed to lessen, as if its power fled along with the sunlight.

Skye could feel the darkness as it crept along the walls and reached for her, and almost immediately she was swallowed whole.

Chapter 22

Within seconds of Skye's disappearance through the opening, the ground began to shake and the cavern pulsated as energy sizzled in the air. A snarl ripped from his throat as Jagger turned in a circle, not understanding what was happening.

The air shimmered around him and as he looked up at the ceiling of the great cavern, the etchings and symbols that had been so plain seconds before misted into a golden arc, then fell down in a shower of golden mist.

Fuck, that can't be good.

They disappeared from sight, leaving him choking on a ball of fear. His only thought was to get to Skye.

The earth continued to grumble beneath his feet, moving and shifting as he ran the entire circumference of the cavern. The sick feeling that ate at him was a constant burn in his gut. Some heavy shit was about to go down. He could feel it.

His eyes scoured every inch of his surroundings and his rage continued to grow. He felt impotent, helpless, and these were emotions a jaguar warrior was ill equipped to handle. He was used to being in charge.

All at once the rock began to liquefy and he jumped back from the wall as panic joined the anger that ate away at him. Not for his own safety, but for Skye. He cursed loudly. Why the hell had he let her go like that? What the fuck had he been thinking?

It was Eden, all over again. *Her* death had broken him. But Skye? If something happened to her, he'd be done. Over. He may as well turn around and hand his ass over to the DaCostas, because his life wouldn't be worth shit if she wasn't going to a part of it.

"Skye!" he yelled in anguish.

What the hell was happening?

There was a keening sound that ripped through the cavern, so loud he fought the urge to cover his ears. All around him the walls of the cave continued to expand and recede as if made of gas.

And then, as if stretched to the limit, they thinned and the hole in the ceiling blurred and folded over, becoming solid once more.

Within seconds it disappeared and the rumbling stopped, leaving Jagger in the center of a cave that was less than ordinary, cold, and gray. The glow faded almost immediately, and the cavern was plunged into a heavy, thick darkness.

His mind worked frantically through several scenarios and his frustration continued to grow at the severity of the situation.

His nocturnal stare swung around, back to the entrance. It stared back at him, taunting him and his inability to protect his mate. Inside his soul the animal cried out in fury and a shot of adrenaline spiked his blood to a boil. He took off at a run.

The passage was as dark as the cavern he'd just left, but his eyes sliced through the gloom. Jagger let his senses fly, looking for anything out of the ordinary. But there was nothing.

He retraced his steps and found himself back in the original chamber beneath the waterfall. It was cold and mist began to rise from his body. The anxious bite in his gut heaved. Nothing had changed here, but then what the hell had he expected?

Cold determination ripped through him and he took off at a dead run, his long legs covering the distance in no time. He burst forth from the cave, his lungs inhaling the early evening air as his eyes scoured the surrounding area.

It was dusk and the fear he felt for Skye tripled. He knew she was without her eagle powers, and even though she was still stronger, faster than most humans, it wouldn't help her this night.

Because it sure as hell wasn't humans who hunted her.

He needed to find her, like, yesterday.

Hold on, babe, I'm coming, he whispered to himself.

Quickly he stripped his clothes and tossed them behind the large boulder that stood at attention near the opening of the cave. Mist clung to his skin. It curled along the ground as it hovered above the waterfall less than five feet away, mixing with the magick that climbed over his limbs.

Within seconds he'd shifted and the large black jaguar that erupted from deep inside the mist took off at a hard run. Jagger ran at a relentless pace, his powerful frame eating up the ground as he slipped over rock and then plunged into the surrounding vegetation thick with the heat of the coming rains.

His "bad mojo" alert was on high and his eyes were forever scanning from left to right. As he crested a small rise he stopped, inhaling the damp air deep into his lungs, but there was nothing.

Disappointment slid through him and he barked softly, the sound muffled by the humidity. His green eyes carefully studied the area around him, running over the summit, which was not far up from where he stood.

Mentally he pictured the inside of the great cave, and after a few moments he began to move again. Truthfully, he knew the chances of finding Skye were slim. He didn't even know if there was another exit.

He just had to trust that there was. To think of the alternative was not an option at this point. However, if left with no choice, he'd blow the fucking mountain to pieces.

He continued to stalk the night, his nose and ears leading him forward as he picked through many scents, and there were a lot to take in. The stink of otherworld filled his nasal cavity and his eyes turned to the canopy below.

It lay silent, deadly.

Not one sound echoed up to him. The animals had long fled and left nothing behind except the evil that was slowly infiltrating their home. They were down there, the enemy, and Jagger knew he had little time in which to get to his woman and get them both to safety.

He began to pant, his powerful canines flashing white, and without another thought he began the final climb to the summit.

The going was rough, as the entire area was full of dangerous crevices that disappeared into the darkness. Heat and humidity coated the rock face, making it slippery and extremely hard to navigate, but still he moved on. As the minutes ticked by and the urgent need to get to Skye rode him harder, he began to take chances, his great body literally flying over the dangerous terrain.

He narrowly missed falling and only avoided injury because of his razor-sharp claws, which he used to dig into the earth and pull himself up the bank of yet another stream with a waterfall. The entire mountainside was littered with them.

He'd just reached solid ground when he stopped short, his chest heaving and mouth open wide. A grumble rolled deep from within his chest and he swung his head to the right.

Skye's sweet scent drifted over him, riding the slightest hint of air. His nostrils quivered and with an excited bark he took off. The area was shrouded in a heavy fog that coated the land thickly, making it difficult to see, but he homed in on her scent and that was all he needed.

A few minutes later Jagger burst through the fog and immediately felt the presence of magick. Old magick.

He proceeded cautiously now, noiselessly creeping ahead, and when he felt a gentle barrier in the air, he paused, tail twitching back and forth as he began to pace along the invisible perimeter.

He stilled, feeling helpless and agitated as he continued to study the area. He could see a small structure off to the right, built of stone and quite rough in its design. His eyes began to glow as he noticed the eagle etching above the door.

Without thought he moved forward and was immediately zapped by an energy source that ripped across his black pelt. He hissed and jumped back. There was no way he could cross the protection ward.

It was ancient, powerful magick.

He stood there, uncertain, his rage building steadily as his eyes flew back and forth, looking for a way in. He turned in a circle, scented the wind once more, anxious, confused. He continued to pace along the perimeter and when he saw her he stopped, transfixed by the ethereal beauty and fragile sadness that clung to her.

Long strands of her hair snaked out into the air as the breeze lifted them into a halo that surrounded her head like a twisted crown. His heart ached and he growled loudly, again and again until she turned to him.

The look on her face tore into his heart and he rushed forward, crying out as once more the energy that held him out sizzled against his flesh. When he heard her voice, he sent a keening cry erupting from deep within, and his tail flicked back and forth in agitation.

"Jagger."

Her soft voice was hoarse and Jagger could do nothing but stare at her, his body and mind in agony over his inability to get to her. He cried out again, the bark rough, and he began to pace along the edge of the protection ward once more, his eyes never leaving Skye's.

He reached out with a paw and took the hit of energy that cut across him sharply, hissing again. It was no use. She would have to come to him, but Jagger could see that something was wrong.

Something terrible.

Slowly, she began to walk toward him. He could see she'd been crying and his heart ached with the need to comfort her. She paused just on the other side of the barrier, and as their eyes connected something broke inside of him. His body began to tremble with the ferocity of it all as a great well of emotion threatened to consume him.

"I hoped you'd come for me," she said haltingly. "It's gone." She inhaled shakily and could barely get her words out. "The portal is missing and I don't know what to do."

Jagger growled and dug his great paws into the soft earth, wishing he could force his way through, but the magick was strong. It was nothing he was familiar with.

Skye shook her head and he hated the sad shadows that clung to her eyes. She looked so beaten. Defeated.

"There's nothing left for me but you." She paused and he knew she was trying desperately to gain hold of her emotions.

Jagger continued to pace behind the barrier and when she held her hand against it the entire wall of air pulsated into a solid form that slipped away into a shower of sparks. Energy shot out in every direction and then she was there in front of him, great sobs wracking her frame.

She knelt down and wrapped her arms around him, burying her head in the thick fur at his neck. He hated the sounds of her tears, hated the fact that she was so riddled with pain. He wanted nothing more than to make it all go away.

Silently the mist began to crawl along the earth until it wrapped around his body and he felt her arms loosen as his body began to change and shift. The fur rippled away from his body, leaving the hard flesh of his human self in its place.

And then she was there, all around him, her scent and her touch coating his body in its unique aura. Her arms wrapped around his midsection and she held onto him as if the hounds of hell themselves were after her.

The need to make her his cracked a hole inside of him that he knew no one else could ever fill.

"Jagger, I've failed my father." Her voice was nothing more than a touch of whisper, and she trembled in his arms, struggling to articulate what she was feeling. Deep, heavy shudders wracked her frame. "I've failed him and my people. If only I'd gotten here sooner." She looked up at him and his heart constricted as he slowly took in her pinched features, her gray complexion, and quivering mouth.

"If only I'd escaped the DaCostas sooner, or gotten to Finn before . . ."

Her eyes were wide, their blue roundness nearly overwhelming as they shimmered beneath his gaze, filled with the pain of tears.

"Shhhhh, it's okay, we'll figure something out." Jagger rubbed his hands along her back and crushed her as close as he could.

"Jagger, you don't understand—"

He interrupted, his voice firm, wanting only to calm her frantic, pained state. "I understand the plan needs to be altered, but chica, there is always another way."

Skye shook her head, her eyes swinging away from his. "If only it were that simple."

She began to shiver violently and her fingers found their way to his chest, her sharp nails digging into his skin. "I don't know if the portal was moved or taken."

Her eyes again met Jagger's and he gently wiped the large tears that fell from them. "As long as it's missing, my life is stuck in limbo, like fucking Groundhog Day."

Her teeth were clenched and she was barely able to get the words out. "There's no one else. They're all gone. Dead. I just wanted it to be over. Finally." Her soft sniff tugged at the last thread of his heart. "I'm so tired of all this life and death, I wish . . ."

Her voice trailed into silence and Jagger's hands slowly made their way up to her shoulders, where he caressed and massaged her. He bent low and whispered along her skin near her ear. "What do you wish, Skye? Tell me, and if I can make it come true, I will."

Jagger felt her shudder violently as he spoke, and her energy faded as she collapsed against his body.

"I wish I was normal. I wish that I was anywhere other than in the jungle. I wish I'd never heard of the fucking portal or the eagle legacy." She pushed against him and he looked down into eyes that had darkened several shades. Jagger's heart began a slow, heavy rhythm, one that danced the beat of seduction.

It was crazy. Where his mind was going. *What he wanted to do.*

The world was going to shit, the entire jungle was filled to the brim with otherworlders gunning for their asses, the portal had come up missing, and yet all he could think about was making love to the woman that he held.

"What do you wish?" he asked once more, his voice gone low, rough.

"I wish that I could be that girl . . ." She paused and inhaled shakily, her fingers splayed against his chest. He watched her closely, his stare intent. The air around them changed, sparked with the energy their bodies were creating. It felt like a blanket of nerve endings had just been laid across his entire body.

Jagger knew he was on the cusp of something life altering and he was more than ready for it. Everything that he'd ever done had brought him here. To this moment. With this woman.

Skye Knightly belonged to him fully, even if she didn't know it yet.

"That girl?" he prompted, barely able to get his words out.

Skye nodded. "The one who has her happy ending."

The denim blue of her eyes shimmered as she regarded him. Her expression had changed. No longer was she sad, broken.

Her arms crept up his chest to circle his neck. She stood on her toes and he could feel her heart racing, beating in tandem with his own. The need to take her, to claim her as his, rushed through him so violently, Jagger's eyes blurred and the familiar burn of his animal ripped across his flesh.

He closed his eyes briefly, trying to control the raging desire and need that threatened to engulf him.

"Couldn't we, for this moment, pretend we're somewhere else?" Skye's voice was thick and her breath against his neck was doing crazy things to his body. Jagger groaned loudly and his hands gripped her shoulders hard.

"We could," he managed to get out. His body was on fire with such need it was painful. The erection between his legs was crushed against her abdomen and as she pulled at him, trying to get closer, he hissed.

"You're fucking killing me, Skye." His eyes blazed, the green depths morphing into a darker hue, one tinged with the glow of feral desire.

"Good," she said as she pulled him down toward her.

Jagger resisted. His mind was a mess of thoughts. "Are you sure?" he said hoarsely.

"I want you," she said simply, her voice tremulous. "I don't care about anything else right now. I need to forget everything." Her hands wound their way into the thick hair at his nape. "Can't you help me forget?" she whispered hoarsely.

"Once I claim you as mine, there will never be another." His hands grabbed her face and he cupped her jaw between them gently. "Do you understand? For a warrior there can only be one."

Her eyes were closed and she rubbed against him seductively, eliciting another hiss from between his lips.

His face darkened and he tightened his grip on her face. "I will kill anyone who touches you." He shook his head as his skin continued to burn. "I will never let you go." His statement was a warning, whether she knew it or not.

"Shut up, already," she said roughly, and the look in her eyes as they flew open took his breath away. "And kiss me."

Chapter 23

Her lips opened beneath his and when his tongue slipped inside, each pass pulled deep into her gut, enhancing the ball of need until it was a shivering mass of desire.

The ache between her legs intensified and she groaned into the warmth of his mouth as she encircled his neck and wrapped her legs around his waist, pushing her pulsating center into him as hard as she could.

But it was not enough. The ache only grew in intensity and she felt her body swell, deep within the folds of her sex, heavy with need.

When his mouth left hers and trailed a line of fire down to the hollow at her neck, she closed her eyes and her head fell back, limp and vulnerable. She felt the wetness of his tongue against her skin and she wrapped her hands into the silky length of his hair again, pushing herself up at his mouth.

"Christ, you taste so good."

Jagger's voice was rough and it fanned the flames of desire even more.

Skye groaned into his mouth and her tongue attacked his with equal fervor. It felt like she'd never get enough of him.

She trailed her tongue along his lips, licking and nipping, until she nuzzled the spot between his ear and neck. His scent was wild, heavy and tantalizing. As she inhaled him deep into her, she felt the raptor inside cry out with need, flooding her cells with an incredible urge to mate.

It startled her and gave her pause. Skye rested her forehead against his jaw, her breathing rough and uneven. What she was feeling was unprecedented. It was raw, honest.

And for once in her life she was giving in to the dark side. She was going to take what she wanted, and to hell with the consequence.

"You're so beautiful," she said softly and then leaned toward him, her fingers tracing the intricate tattoos that colored his abs. She followed the touch with the softness of her lips and smiled against his flesh when she felt him tense.

It was satisfying to know he was as affected as she.

She continued to trail kisses along his abdomen and up his rib cage, gently tweaking his hard nipples as she moved further along. Skye looked up at him then and smiled seductively.

"I wonder what you taste like."

As she bent down in front of him the hiss that escaped from between his lips was quickly followed by a groan as her fingers teased the head of his penis with a soft, quick stroke.

Skye rested on her haunches, her eyes drinking in the sheer male beauty that stood before her.

She'd seen Jagger nude before. Hell, the first night she laid eyes on him he'd been in the buff.

But the way he looked right now, his body hard and proud, aroused something so fierce that all the softness inside of her vanished. Her heart skipped a beat. Or two. Hell, it could've been three. It was enough to make her dizzy, and when her eyes focused once more, they greedily ate up the straining length of him, so incredibly male, so incredibly hard.

Skye leaned forward and paused, her eyes turning up to him quickly, and she smiled before opening wide and taking as much of him as she could, deep into her mouth.

"Holy Christ." The words fell from his mouth and she felt his fingers in her hair, holding her head in place as she began to suckle at him, to lick and tease him with the sharp edges of her teeth.

She loved the feel of him, how the flesh of his cock was so soft, yet the shaft beneath it was hard and unyielding.

Her hands crept around him and she cupped his straining ass as she continued to pleasure him. Each time she pulled at him harder, taking more of him into her mouth, and he swore when she licked and suckled along the length of his shaft. Slowly her tongue and lips wove a wet spell of magic along him, and when she claimed his balls as her own, taking first one and then the other into the warm cave of her mouth, she felt his fingers pull at her hair, *hard*.

"I can't take much more." Jagger was now breathing in rough spurts and barely able to get his words out.

Skye laughed against him and looked up once more, but the heat and animalistic need that she saw there quieted her. The air around them changed, shifted, and for that one second in time, she felt a connection unlike anything she'd ever experienced.

Every single cell in her body was on fire with a need that only he could satisfy. She craved him like the most decadent slice of chocolate imagined and when he slowly pulled himself out of her mouth she was silent. She ran her tongue along the edge of his cock one last time and when he drew her up along the hard length of his body, she could do nothing but whimper with a need long denied.

Once more his mouth ravaged hers and she cried out as his hands tore her T-shirt off over her head, freeing her breasts to his hands and mouth. He attacked one turgid nipple immediately, suckling the peak fast and hard. Skye felt each pull as it went straight to the aching center between her legs.

She was incredibly wet and began to whimper against him. A myriad of sensations rushed over her body, setting every cell of her flesh alive with a need that, while painful, was coated with pleasure.

Jagger lifted her into his arms and continued to feast at her breast as he moved from where they were. She was aware of nothing but the feel of him on her flesh, as if she'd been sucked into a vortex of desire and want and need.

When she felt the silky wetness of water against her skin she opened her eyes, her hands still buried in his hair.

He'd brought them to a small waterfall that fell languidly from twenty feet above them. It pooled in a basin and Jagger smiled down at her wickedly as he set her bottom on a ledge.

The water was cool against her heated flesh and it felt wonderful as it sprayed gently across her back.

"Jagger, I've never felt like this, ever."

He murmured against her flesh, "Babe, you ain't seen nothin' yet."

The promise in his words excited, enthralled her; she had been trying to squirm out of her shorts before he'd even set her down. Jagger laughed wickedly as his strong hands slipped inside the waistband of her bottoms.

He kissed her softly then. A soulful, sweet kiss that nearly brought her to tears, and when he bent down to carefully remove her shorts, Skye felt the tears leak from the corners of her eyes.

Her heart was filled to bursting with emotion.

His right hand held her firm, the strong fingers splayed across the small of her back. She instinctually spread her legs slightly and when his other hand carefully parted her outer lips, and he blew on the heated core that was hidden there, she groaned loudly.

"Every single inch of you is like a fucking banquet," he murmured against her inner thigh.

Skye began to gyrate toward him as the ache intensified.

"Christ Jagger, touch me," she said, her breathing ragged, "I can't stand it."

He licked along the inside of her leg and she shuddered against him as he laughed softly. "Some patience, little bird."

But she was having none of his teasing. Skye dug her fingers into his skull sharply and shoved herself at him, crying out in relief as the heat and strength of his tongue stroked against her wetness.

She brought her knees up, her heels holding firm against the ledge and she leaned back against the rock wall, looking down at him between her legs and loving the feel of the water falling over her breasts and down onto her thighs.

She began to tremble as he suckled at her engorged clitoris. Her belly clenched tightly and she began to make small mewing sounds as her body jerked at each pass and pull of his tongue.

The response was immediate and she felt the exquisite pressure begin to build deep inside of her, touching off a fire that singed each and every nerve ending as it rushed through her.

Her entire body was aflame with need, her breasts heavy and nipples hard.

"Jagger, harder . . . oh my God, I've never . . ." Her words stopped abruptly as she felt her body tighten and then the well broke and she felt a flood of liquid slide from her body as an intense orgasm ripped through her.

"You taste better than honey." Jagger's hoarse words rang in her ear as she wavered against his touch. His tongue licked and suckled every last bit of desire that glistened against her skin.

It was instant gratification. But it wasn't enough.

Skye trembled in his embrace and felt like crying.

She needed more.

But the jaguar knew this, and she watched, lips parted, as he slowly kissed her along the entire length of her body, nuzzling against her navel, up to her rib cage.

He worshiped her breasts, taking his time, teasing each turgid peak until she thought she would go mad. His teeth scraped along the hard, pebbled nipples and she hissed as the sensation shot straight through her, down to her core.

Skye could feel the pressure begin to build once more and she shook her head, her long blond tendrils of hair sticking to her skin.

"Every single inch of you fucking rocks." His eyes had darkened to almost black and the tinge of red that glowed from within was a testament to how close to the edge the warrior was.

She was breathing heavily, her chest heaving, as she struggled for calm, and she looked deeply into his eyes.

"I want all of you," she whispered hoarsely. Her gaze went to the straining erection. "Inside of me." Skye reached for his lips, sliding her tongue along the aristocratic lines. She nipped at him then, harder than she'd meant to, and whispered into his ear, "Right now."

Jagger's reaction was immediate. He hissed, and for a second his body blurred, but then his hands were all over her, and he turned her around so that she was on her knees.

Skye laughed wickedly and thrust her ass at him as she went down, enjoying the feel of his hardness against her there. She was aching for him.

She didn't feel the rough rock on her knees, or the cool water that fell upon her. Skye spread her legs and turned to look back at him, feeling her tummy roll over at the savage look of want on Jagger's face.

His eyes were focused solely on her heated wetness and she spread her legs even more, enjoying the feral look that stole over his features. He moved into position and when his hands grabbed her hips, drawing her back toward him, she bit her lip.

When she felt his fingers dig into her flesh, so hard it would bruise for sure, she cried out. She began to shudder with anticipation, loving the way he felt against her and when he roared loudly and plunged the whole of his length deep inside her, she screamed his name, their voices echoing together in the jungle air.

He filled her completely and she arched her back instinctually, cutting the angle in such a way she could feel his hardness scrape along her channel, hitting the sweet spot almost immediately.

"Christ, but you were made for me and no one else," Jagger said roughly as he began to move slowly inside of her, drawing himself nearly out and then plunging back inside her soft heat.

Skye began to whimper. There was no other way for her to express the feelings and sensations that were attacking her body in relentless precision. Every time he went deep a thousand sparks of electricity exploded, their sharp bands of pleasure fingering their way out until every inch of her flesh was on fire.

Jagger teased her until she was nearly in a frenzy; drawing himself out again and again. He would take her to the edge and pull back just when she was ready to plunge over.

"Godammit Jagger, I can't take this." Her body was humming, energy flowing from her body to his, and inside, deep within the recesses of her soul, the raptor sang a song that was ancient.

You are mine, I am yours.

The words whispered along the edge of her mind and as the pressure began to peak, as Jagger bent over and began to pound into her in earnest, she knew that there was no turning back.

Jagger was hunched over her, his large frame glistening with sweat as his body continued to dance to an ancient rhythm that was unique and all their own. His muscles strained as one hand gripped Skye's hip, while the other was splayed over her head, resting along the rock wall that hid beneath the spray of water.

When he snarled, Skye answered in kind and when she felt the sting of his teeth along her shoulder she shuddered. Her head whipped back and she could feel his cheek next to the crook of her neck as he held on, his mouth and teeth digging into her soft flesh.

"Jagger, you're gonna kill me," she said hoarsely as the pressure reached a crescendo deep inside of her. She felt his body strain as her channel tightened around him.

"You feel amazing."

She could barely hear his words as he began to up the tempo, his body pounding into hers in a hard-hitting symphony of passion.

Her orgasm erupted from deep inside and Skye screamed as the intensity of it washed over her in waves, each thrust taking her deeper into an abyss of pleasure. Jagger continued to pump his body into hers, a snarl erupting from deep within his chest as he came.

He continued to rock her gently, each pass slower than the last, until he finally collapsed onto her, his arms pulling her close as he withdrew, and they fell back into the pool of water.

Skye lay against his hard, heaving chest and there were no words.

She opened her eyes and watched the water fall from above and relished the feel of it as it slid across her heated body.

In the sky the sun was fading fast and she could feel the power that it gave her slipping away. Clouds were hanging low and they were growing thicker as the moments passed. They were dark, ominous.

She sniffed the air and knew that rain was definitely coming.

She flipped over, pushing away from Jagger and immersing her body in the silky liquid. The basin was shallow here and she took care not to scrape along the rock near the bottom. The water felt amazing, magical, and she wished it had the power to wash away everything about her. To truly make her into that girl she so desperately wanted to become.

When she broke the surface and shook the water from her face and hair she sighed. Her eyes found Jagger immediately and a thrill went through her at the look that graced his handsome face.

But it was gone already, the glow of their lovemaking, and a heavy weight once more was pressing against her chest. Things were not finished here.

Angrily, she kicked her feet and swam the few feet to the edge. But then what had she expected?

"Hey." His soft voice was there, sliding across her like velvet. His smell was all around and she shuddered at the intensity of her feelings for him. A jaguar.

Skye turned to him and let him gather her into his arms. The heat from his body felt wonderful and she relaxed against him, once more fighting the sting of tears.

He was the man she loved, and she had no freaking clue what the future was going to bring.

"I'm so tired," she whispered.

Jagger scooped her up and grabbed her scattered clothes along the way as he walked back to where he'd found her.

"What's that?"

Skye followed his gaze. "It was the home of the portal."

At that precise moment the first splash of rain fell across her face, quickly followed by another.

"Looks like shelter to me," he answered and nipped at her nose. "Can you get me through the protection ward?"

"As long as we're together I can get you through."

"Good. That means we'll be safe. We'll rest here this evening and then figure out the plan in the morning." He continued to nuzzle her neck and small shivers of delight were once more making their way across her body.

"Don't worry, Skye, we'll find the damn thing and end this once and for all."

Skye closed her eyes and let her body relax into the strength of his. Her euphoria had already faded. She didn't want to think about tomorrow, or finding the portal.

Because once that happened, she'd no longer have him.

They lay down together, under the dais inside the stone structure that had been built by her people. A jaguar and an eagle.

Skye couldn't help but wince at the irony in that and as she snuggled closer to him she cleared her mind of everything except the warrior who held her so tightly. Long moments passed and eventually she felt his breathing slow, as did the beat of his heart, and eventually he fell asleep.

She couldn't shake the heavy ball of dread that clutched at her midsection. Something bad was coming. She could feel it. This was so not over.

Eventually her exhaustion won out and she felt herself slipping away into the arms of the sandman.

She wasn't sure how long she slept, but when she awoke abruptly, darkness blanketed the area. Skye was instantly on alert. She felt uneasy, and even though Jagger's arms encircled her, feeding her body with his warmth, she was cold and shivering.

Gently, she turned and looked at him. He was relaxed and it amazed her how boyish he looked in repose. A smile tugged at her mouth and her fingers touched his lips as she slowly traced their outline.

He turned toward her touch and she felt a pang inside her heart at the gesture. She bent, meaning to touch his lips softly, smiling wickedly as she thought to wake him and maybe "play" once more.

Skye.

One word whispered and her world stopped.

Skye.

She stilled, blowing out a fine sheen of mist as the stone shelter became unbearably cold. It was filled with an arctic blast of chill air.

She wasn't surprised he'd come. In fact, on some level she'd expected it sooner. She wasn't even afraid. Carefully she sat up, disengaging her limbs from Jagger's.

Come to me.

A shadowy form stood not more than two feet away, staring down at the two of them. She fought the urge to cover her nakedness but instead rose to her feet, studying the figure closely.

He wasn't real, or at least, his form wasn't corporeal. *But he was there.* Skye could feel the strength and power that he wielded. It was thick, potent, invading the very air that she breathed.

She held her head high and as his eyes locked on hers, the very ones she'd come to know since she was a little child. She saw the fury that shadowed them and she swallowed heavily.

Azaiel.

He raised his hand, holding it out, palm facing her and she *felt* his touch at her cheek. It was hot and stung her flesh. It was a peculiar sensation, considering how cold she was. His eyes burned red and the slash of teeth that cut through the gloom was feral.

Follow me to the portal.

Skye looked at him in surprise. That had not been what she was expecting to hear. How the hell did he know where the disc was?

She shook her head. "No." The word slipped from her lips before she even knew it was out. The feel of Jagger was still soft against her skin and the pain in her heart made breathing difficult. *I want to live*, she thought, *there has to be another way.*

"No," she said again, this time her voice firm.

He was only a shadow man. He had no power over her.

He laughed then, the sound echoing harshly inside her brain and she fought the urge to cover her ears. Pressure began to build along the sides of her neck, erupting from the inside, and her hands went to her throat as her airway was blocked. She looked at him in panic and gasped loudly as she struggled to breathe.

Oh God, he was going to kill her! The thought burst through her brain and she staggered a few feet, dry raspy noises coming from her throat as she struggled to breathe.

She was released just as the inky black of unconsciousness rode the edges of her mind. She took great hulking gasps of air as she looked at Azaiel, her eyes flaming twins of hatred.

Shadow man indeed; the fucker was full of powerful mojo, even though he was nothing more than a wall of mist. Bitterly, she shook her head as an image of the demon, Tag, dissolving into a puddle of crap entered her thoughts.

He'd done that.

Disobey me and the jaguar dies.

A whisper of blackness flew through the room and Azaiel smiled at her, his lips slowly parting into a grin that left her feeling sick to her stomach. She whipped around, her fingers still massaging her sore throat and froze at the sight before her. Shadowy figures bent over Jagger, gray visions of evil that hung in the air, waiting to pounce. She had no clue what the hell they were, but their presence was enough.

The threat to Jagger was real.

"I'll do whatever you want," she croaked, her voice coarse from his attack. "But you have to promise me, Jagger will be safe."

He smiled at her, and she blinked as his features began to solidify before her eyes. They wavered for a second before blurring into mist once more.

You're in no position to ask for anything.

He held his hand out again and she shuddered as his eyes slowly drifted over her nakedness. When she felt the cold touch of him on her skin she hissed and stepped back.

His eyes burned heavily, the black depths sinking into a rush of gold.

Cover yourself and follow me.

Skye hesitated as panic began to join in the fun. If only she could find a way—

I will kill him, slowly, and take you regardless. Do not test me. I'm giving you a choice, which is not something I do lightly.

His voice was amplified inside her skull and she

wanted nothing more than to rip him from her brain, but she bent her head instead.

Skye quickly gathered her clothes, slipping them over her limbs as her mind raced ahead, trying to figure a way out of this.

None of this made sense. The fucking portal was missing, she'd just had the best sex ever with a man she could envision spending the rest of her life with, and the demon Azaiel, the one who'd visited her in her dreams and nightmares for decades, was nearly corporeal.

Giving her orders. Telling her he'd lead her to the portal. What the hell was in it for him?

"Why is it you're willing to lead me to the disc? How do you even know where it is?" she asked once she was dressed. "Seems to me you'd want it to remain hidden." She shrugged her shoulders. "I don't get it. You must know I plan to seal it forever."

Azaiel stared at her for several long seconds and she shifted her weight from one foot to the other. His silent stare made her uncomfortable, nervous.

A cold, dead smile drifted over his handsome face and she felt a ripple of alarm slide through her veins. Skye took a step back as the power inside of him slithered across his shadowy form, draping him in another layer that solidified him even more.

I've been waiting years for this moment, millennia, in fact. You'll find out soon enough.

He turned and his laughter echoed inside her head once more. The alarm bells were ringing and the intensity of it all was giving her a headache. His cryptic words did little to shed light on the situation. In fact they scared the crap out of her, but at the moment she had no choice but to obey.

Skye was gonna have to play fast and loose. There were too many balls in the air, and at the moment she didn't want to catch any of them.

She followed Azaiel out of the stone structure and didn't look back at Jagger. She couldn't. To do that would break her, and she had a long road ahead.

Chapter 24

Dark and light mixed together to form a low-lying fog that clung to the jungle floor like a silk blanket. It ebbed and flowed with the rain that had been falling steadily ever since the night before. Alas, it seemed the rainy season had finally found its way to Belize.

Skye was soaked, her hair plastered to her skin, and though it was warm, unbearably so, it only added to the misery she felt inside. They'd been walking for hours, it seemed, and after everything she'd been through over the last several days, Skye could feel her strength waning. She gritted her teeth as she pressed on. She had to keep her wits about her.

Yes, we're nearly there.

Once more Azaiel's voice penetrated her mind and she grimaced, ignoring him completely. She'd studied him closely as they moved through the jungle, her shadow man from hell.

He confused her and she didn't quite know what to make of him. Oh, he still scared the crap out of her and she tried to avoid his gaze. His eyes were dark, opaque, almost dead-looking. When they were focused on her, there was an intensity about him that made her very nervous.

There were many layers to her dream demon, and her gut was telling her that he was not at all what she thought he was.

She wished she had more of a handle on him, because time was definitely running out.

When they'd left Jagger the jungle had been dark, full of night's caress, but now she could feel the warmth of the sun as dawn broke, and she held on to that. She drew in the power that floated on the air and kept it close to her heart. She would gather as much as she could and use it when she had the chance.

If she got the chance.

Tiredly, she rested her eyes on Azaiel. Somehow she felt his power was tied to the portal. She just wished she knew how. She could feel his strength increasing, the closer they got to it. The air around him moved differently, coating his form with an energy that was vibrant, alive. Any other time Skye would have been fascinated by such a sight.

As it was, it did nothing but terrify her. He paused abruptly and Skye stumbled to a halt. Her stomach tightened and she felt sick to her stomach.

They were deep in the jungle, the vegetation thick and lush. Before them a great heap of tangled vines rose up, their long arms twisted into a cloak of greenery. Skye's eyes narrowed. Something didn't seem right here, and she moved forward cautiously, until she stood a few feet from the shadow man.

He looked at her and she was shocked to see that his eyes had changed yet again. The black had been shot through with gold, and it echoed in the streaks of darkness that now graced the blond of his hair.

Can you feel it?

She nodded her head, her eyes widening as she took in the pulsating mist that formed a halo around his entire body. She let her gaze travel the length of him and though he was not yet fully in this realm, he was definitely getting more solid.

Which meant he was *uber* dangerous.

She was going to have to be careful.

He pointed toward the intricate mass of vines and they began to transform in front of her, pulling back and sliding away from the ancient structure that they guarded. The magick that clung to them was powerful, *familiar*. It was of her people.

Skye took a step forward. She couldn't help herself. She felt a keen sense of wonder as she studied the stone dwelling laid bare to her eyes. It was beautiful. Like nothing she'd ever seen before.

Each stone was unique in color, size, and texture, and they'd been arranged in such a way that she could see an eagle and a sun guarding the entrance.

"Is this . . . I thought . . ." She stopped, her mind a jumble of thoughts.

This is the true Cave of the Sun, and it's where your father moved the portal many months ago.

Azaiel's eyes began to glow in earnest, and Skye was ashamed to admit that the fear that sat heavily in her belly was threatening to explode. Her knees trembled and it took every ounce of energy inside of her to remain standing.

It's time for you to claim your destiny, Skye.

A dark sense of foreboding seeped into her soul, but she quickly pushed it away. Skye squared her shoulders. The demon was right about one thing. It was time for her to end this.

She held her head high and walked past him, swallowing her fear as she paused before the entrance. She closed her mind to everything but what needed to be done and then slipped into the cool interior of the cave.

She pushed long, wet strands of hair away from her face and ignored the blast of cold that crossed her skin. Her wet clothes offered no protection from the damp interior and she began to shiver as she walked further inside.

The magick of her people was much stronger here and she basked in its power. It fed the eagle inside and her great raptor awakened, overwhelming her with its need to act. She smiled sadly and forced her animal to be quiet. This was not the time to battle.

The magick coated everything in a glow and she welcomed the warmth that soothed her cold skin. It was fashioned somewhat like the previous structure, but there was nothing of ceremony to announce that such a valuable artifact as the disc was anywhere inside.

Her eyes found a low-slung stone altar in the far corner. The closer she got to it, the faster everything faded to nothing, until all her eyes could see was the round disc. She stopped a few feet away.

She was aware of her heart beating heavily inside the walls of her chest and each time she inhaled air deep into her lungs, the sound amplified, hitting her from both within and outside her head.

Her eyes drank in every detail of the ancient relic and she was surprised to note the very modest aura that surrounded such an extraordinary object. It was a simple disc, really, bereft of any type of grandeur and quite plain, in fact.

To most people it would appear to be nothing more than a round piece of stone with some markings etched on it.

Skye couldn't help but feel a little disappointed. She wasn't sure what she'd expected, and as she took the final few steps that brought her to the stone ledge it sat upon, she shook her head, marveling that such an ordinary-looking disc could wield such power.

A cold wash of dread rolled over her as she stared down at the disc. It looked as if it had been placed there with almost casual indifference. But there was nothing casual about the situation, and the reality of what she was about to do crashed through her.

She buckled over, her hands going to her head as a million thoughts rushed through her brain.

"Ugh," she whimpered weakly, trying to push away the image of Jagger's smiling face.

Could she do this? Did she have enough strength to carry through?

Don't stop now. You're nearly there.

The words spoken were much clearer this time. Skye's head whipped up and she felt the earth tremble beneath her feet as her eyes took in the shimmering form that stood on the other side of the altar.

Winter's kiss fell from Azaiel's mouth as he smiled and she felt it drip into her body, like shards of ice melting into her soul.

His features hardened and Skye felt the cold inside of her feather outward. She shivered and tried to look away, but couldn't.

You need to touch the portal. Pick it up, Skye. His

tone was cajoling, as if she were a small child who needed guidance.

Irritation flashed through her. *No shit*, she thought.

Pick it up, Skye, he said once again, this time with much more force. *You are the one.*

"The one?" she said dully. Skye's brain felt weird and mushy, and she tried desperately to keep her thoughts coherent.

The one to free me. His voice whispered through her brain like a lover's caress and he smiled at her, his eyes swirling ribbons of gold and black.

Skye bit her tongue. The taste of copper filled her mouth and she tore her gaze away from Azaiel and settled instead on the disc. It had begun to glow from within and she fought the urge to grab it and hold it near her heart.

It was calling to her.

"I don't want this," she said as tears threatened once more and her gaze settled on the demon. "I wish . . ."

You must finish this. Do you want the legions of hell running mad in the human realm? Can you live knowing it was because of your weakness that humanity was destroyed?

His voice thundered inside her mind and Skye winced at the ferocity of it.

They are like maggots, the demons that live here. They will destroy everything in their path. Darkness will fall upon the earth and only those with evil in their hearts will survive.

His eyes swirled faster still and Skye found that she was mesmerized by them. Every minute that ticked by brought more substance to his body. It scared her because she didn't know what it meant.

"Why do you care?" she asked suddenly, as if a

small crack had opened and let some form of her own thoughts through. "You're demon. Why are you helping me seal the portal?"

Azaiel stared at her, his eyes electric, and she could feel the rage that radiated from deep within him. It was a tangible thing, thick and meaty in the air. In that moment she had a glimpse of the power that he possessed.

It was unlike anything she'd ever seen before.

His face darkened and the air around him crackled with energy. He paused, visibly relaxed, and she heard his voice in her mind once more.

You will open the portal now.

His voice commanded her and she found herself nodding, even though deep inside a scream erupted. One that echoed in her ears until it fell away, silent.

"Yes," Skye whispered. She felt strange, like she had no control over her thoughts or actions. "I need to open the portal."

Except something was wrong.

She wasn't there to open the portal. She was there to seal it.

"No!" she whispered hoarsely as she shook her head in denial. But it was no use. Azaiel was much too powerful.

The words that were buried deep within her mind, the ones her father had taught her, slipped away until there was nothing but Azaiel.

She stepped up onto the ledge and focused her mind on the disc. Gently she reached for it and when she picked it up in her fingers, the earth trembled. Electricity flew from the stone into her hands, running along her body like a conduit until it erupted into the air, showering the room in a hail of sparks.

The power was nearly overwhelming but she defied the weakness that pulled at her legs. Her breaths blew hard from her lips. Something foreign tugged at her mind and she tried to shake off the eerie sensation.

But it was no use, and after a few seconds, words she'd never heard before began to fall from her tongue.

Heat began to swirl up along her body and she felt dazed as the power from deep within her fed the disc in her hand, running back and forth between herself and the portal.

Skye's vision began to blur and it felt like she was watching the entire exercise from above. As if her brain had separated from her body. In her mind's eye she could clearly see herself clutching the disc and Azaiel standing a few feet from her.

His image began to pulsate as he wavered between the two worlds that she now straddled.

Terror hit her, but it only seemed to feed the power of the disc. It began to glow bright red and the heat was scorching against her skin. The wind rushed into the small stone structure and a great roaring began to infiltrate her skull. It sounded like the very depths of hell were loose inside her head and she cried out as an intense pain ripped into her mind.

A million screams were let loose and she closed her eyes in anguish as the pressure inside her head intensified until she thought she was going to come apart. Darkness crossed over, encircling her body, and a great sadness welled up from within. Anguish and pain like none she'd ever experienced before enveloped her, and Skye wanted nothing more than to fade away and forget all of it.

And then it was over.

Skye trembled, her limbs shaking violently as her teeth chattered loudly. She didn't know what the hell had just happened, but she was pretty sure the mission had just taken a header south.

Like way south, into the shitter.

Her skin began to tingle, and she was aware that she still clutched the disc hard against her chest.

Warm breath along her cheek startled her and her eyes opened. She tried to scream but couldn't. Her vocal chords were no longer working.

A hand, strong and warm with flesh that was fueled by blood, cupped her chin and turned her face upward.

Somehow Skye found the strength to wrench free from him and she stumbled back several steps.

"What happened?" Skye croaked. "*What* the hell are you?"

"Patience," he whispered into the space between them. His handsome face opened wide as he smiled at her. "Hand me the portal."

She ignored his command, her thoughts confused and whirling into a mad bucket of soup. "Oh God!" she said painfully. "What have I done?" Her hoarse whisper echoed into the silence and faded away as she stared at him in horror.

Her eyes were wild now. She hadn't sealed the portal. She'd let *something* out!

He laughed at her then, the sound booming. It grated against her skull and she felt anger begin to unfurl deep in her gut.

"I'm one of the fallen." He smiled once more. His voice was gentle, as if he were talking to a child, but his face was stern as he took a step toward her. "The portal belongs to me."

"The portal belongs to my people. It is our burden to bear," Skye said, her voice high as she continued to feed from her anger.

His manner changed in an instant and he snarled.

"The portal was made with these hands." She watched as he held his palms out toward her, saw the bizarre markings that crisscrossed the skin in crimson detail. "It belongs to me."

Azaiel's eyes were focused on her, the gold receding until they were opaque black. His voice softened and he smiled.

"*You* belong to me."

Chapter 25

Jagger awoke disoriented and full of the heavy weight of fear. For a moment blinding panic threatened to overwhelm him. He'd not felt this way since Iraq and he railed against it, forcing it away as he sat up quickly.

He groaned loudly. His head was pounding like a calypso band was having a party inside his cranium. His fingers gently massaged his temples as he cracked open his eyes for a peek around.

He was in some sort of stone hut. Though it was still dark he could feel the shift of the earth's cycle and he knew that dawn was close at hand. He inhaled the fresh crisp scent of rain and stood up quickly, feeling an urgent need to act, but puzzled as to where the hell he was and what was going on.

He shook his head violently and grimaced, not liking the creepy sensation that was there, like his brain had been fucked with.

He glanced at the ground and spied a bag lying up

against what appeared to be an altar of some sort. Quickly he crossed over to it, his fingers clutching the worn leather as he brought it to his nose.

He closed his eyes and breathed in deeply and as the scent that lay there invaded his body and mind he felt the jaguar inside react violently. Images began to waver in front of him, memories bombarding him. He pushed against them, growling softly at the plethora of emotions that washed over him like a tidal wave.

Long blond hair, electric blue eyes, and soft golden skin that belonged to a goddess rose in front of his mind's eye. Skye!

Jagger dropped the satchel and began to pant as his panic and anger increased tenfold. He dropped to the ground in a crouch, his eyes scouring the earth floor there, trying to make sense of what had happened.

His last memory was of the two of them, together, his body claiming hers as his own. His eyes frantically swept the room and he vaguely remembered an eerie gray mist that had invaded his dreams the night before. It left a bitter taste in his mouth, for it had been a dark, malevolent presence.

Realization dawned then: Fucking Azaiel. What the hell was he? How did he have the power to transcend time and the space between the two realms?

A new thought struck then and it was one that left him cold with fear. What if the portal had been found by Cormac? What if Azaiel and a thousand legions of demons were at this moment spreading their wings here in the human realm?

In one fluid motion Jagger stood, stretched out his long limbs, and squared his shoulders. A deadly calm settled over him as he let his animalistic traits rise to the surface. The hunter and killer that was as much a part of him as his humanity now had free reign. Electricity tingled along his nerves and he felt his jaguar react with vicious glee.

He cleared his mind of everything except Skye and focused.

Skye Knightly was as much a part of him as his right arm; all of her, every last delectable, infuriating, irritating, and wholly pleasurable piece of her. He would fucking rip apart anyone or *anything* that dared to lay a hand on her.

And he'd start kicking ass with whoever was lurking just outside the shelter.

His body tensed and inside the animal quieted. He slipped along the far wall, his body melting into the shadows, and he waited, ready to pounce.

A stranger slid into view and stopped several feet away. He was tall and of powerful build. Jagger's teeth flashed through the gloom and he inhaled the intruder's scent, his eyes widening at what it told him.

In a flash the stranger rushed him, and Jagger barely had time to react before the wall of muscle slammed into him. The force of the hit pushed him back, but Jagger's arms went around the man's shoulders and they both flew back into the hard rock wall.

Jagger growled loudly, feeling the burn rip up his skin as the jaguar threatened to erupt. He grunted and head-butted the intruder, his skull connecting hard with the other's head. He felt instant satisfaction as bone crumbled and the scent of blood filled the air.

The large man yelled and grabbed Jagger's hand, twisting it, as the stranger's eyes began to glow. His body, too, began to shimmer and Jagger fought his way through the pain in his forearm as the intruder's hand morphed into large, sharp claws. Avian claws.

The dude was an eagle. But the question was, whose side was he on?

The sharp talons gripped his arm tightly and as his blood began to flow and coat the air with its coppery scent, Jagger began to burn with the need to act. He needed to get to Skye. With a mighty growl he ripped his arm from the stranger's and twisted away, using the rock at his back to propel himself through the air until he landed a few feet away, in a crouched position, hands fisted and ready to fight.

"Who the hell are you?" Jagger shouted, rage coloring his words so that his voice fell from him in layers.

The stranger stood slowly, chest heaving, and his eyes flashed through the gloom. He held his arms up, they were still in half shift and the deadly talons stared back at Jagger.

"Where is my sister?" he said, his words laced with emotion. "Christ, if I'm too late . . ."

Jagger stilled and straightened up from his crouched position. His mind rushed in several different directions, but one thing was clear. He needed to get to Skye, and the man before him could either help or hinder.

"Are you Finn?"

The light cast by the flashlight drew eerie shadows across the man's features. Jagger studied him closely. He was golden, his coloring similar to Skye's, and his eyes flashed blue.

The eagle's features were tense as his eyes quickly scanned the interior of the stone shrine. They whitened even more and he turned to Jagger, a furious snarl coming from between clenched lips.

"What have you done to her?" His question ripped across the air and Jagger growled in reaction.

"If you're suggesting I've somehow harmed Skye, you're totally off." Jagger took a step toward the eagle. "She's mine and I'll do whatever it takes to get her back."

"Yours?" he asked, his voice low and deadly. "Care to elaborate, jaguar? How can an eagle knight *belong* to a jaguar?"

Jagger hissed and felt the burn once more ripple along his heated flesh. Every inch of his six-foot-six frame trembled with the need to act, and he flexed his fingers in anticipation.

"I don't have time for this," he said as he began to move toward the exit. "Believe whatever the fuck you want, but your sister is my woman. We're mated and I will do whatever it takes to protect her."

The man's face was pained and he inhaled a ragged breath as his talons receded and his flesh morphed back into its human shape. His blue eyes were piercing. "She was mine to protect and I failed." He exhaled harshly. "Did she open the path to the portal?" the eagle asked as he ran his hands through his thick blond hair.

"It wasn't here," Jagger answered, scowling as he continued. "I have no clue where it is, and at this point I don't care." He shot a look at the eagle. "I've got a bigger problem and its name is Azaiel."

The eagle knight's face whitened considerably. "Azaiel? He's here? In this realm? How is that even possible?"

"I don't know, but he came for her last night, used some of his fucking mojo on me and I need to get to her before . . ." Jagger exploded, his fury making him nearly incoherent. "If anything happens to her . . ." He couldn't go on, not wanting to follow where his thoughts were leading.

"How long ago?" Finn asked as he moved toward Jagger.

"I'm guessing a few hours at least, which means I don't have time to play catch up with you." Jagger moved around the eagle, dismissing him, his mind already pushing ahead.

"He's leading her to the portal."

Jagger paused and turned back to the eagle knight. "You know where it is?"

Finn stared at him and then sighed heavily. "I only just learned where the real Cave of the Sun is located, I hope we're not too late."

Jagger stilled at Finn's words, not liking the bleak look that hid behind the eagle shifter's eyes.

"What's going on that you're not telling me?" he asked sharply.

"You don't know, do you?"

Jagger's anger exploded. "Know what? I don't have time for these games. Can you help me get to her or not?" His breathing was rough and the animal stirred beneath his skin, causing a burn to ripple along his flesh.

The eagle clenched his hands and Jagger could see he was struggling with something. "It should have been me, but the DaCostas . . ." He turned eyes that blazed with anger toward him. "I'd kill every last one of them if I could."

"Yeah, get in line," Jagger snarled. "You were saying?"

"To seal the portal requires a sacrifice." He pinned Jagger with a black look. "Skye can only do that by sacrificing her soul."

"Well, what the hell does that mean?" Jagger asked the question even as the dread that had been kicking him in the gut went into overdrive.

"It means that if Skye succeeds in sealing the portal

she will never return." Finn's voice was dead. "She'll be trapped forever in the demon realm." He paused and his face went white.

In hell.

The eagle knight's words exploded inside Jagger's brain and for several long minutes he couldn't breathe. It felt like his world had been suspended. The pain was incredible and he felt the anguish gathering inside his heart as his soul cried out in denial.

He knew what she'd been keeping from him. She'd never planned on having a life with him because she wasn't coming back.

The fury he felt in that moment was unprecedented. If Skye were here in front of him right now, he wasn't sure if he'd kiss every inch of her in relief or fucking kill her.

He couldn't accept that she'd open his heart and then slam the door shut. He snarled loudly and turned away. It was simple, really.

He wouldn't accept it.

"I'm going after your sister. I don't give a flying fuck whether she's sealed the portal or not, because even if she has, I will find a way to get to her." Jagger clenched his teeth, welcoming the anger. "And when I do, hell will be the least of her worries."

Jagger felt his power erupt along his spine, flowing out to every cell in his body as mist wound its way along his flesh, bringing with it the heavy black fur of his warrior.

Finn was already morphing into his animal form as the two men erupted from within the dark recesses of the cave. To most in their world, it would have been a peculiar sight, a jaguar and an eagle, enemies for centuries and yet now thrown together by fate.

A strange fog cloaked the entire side of the mountain, mixing with the steady downpour of rain that fell in sheets between the thick stands of trees. The eagle soared just above the canopy with the jaguar following his lead until they were both swallowed whole.

Julian Castille rolled his shoulders in an effort to shed the blanket of nervous tension that slid across his dark skin.

The rains had come, finally, after teasing them for weeks and he relished the feel of it against his body.

"I hate this fucking jungle," Ana cursed loudly.

They'd hooked up with Ana and Jaxon hours earlier, and even though it was dawn, the heavy mist that clung to everything around them provided sufficient cover for her. He'd been surprised to learn years ago that vampires didn't sleep in coffins during the day. In fact they required little or no sleep. They just needed to avoid direct sunlight or they'd literally fry.

Jaxon was deep in conversation with Cracker, getting up to speed. He wiped the slick moisture from his face and turned from them to peer out into the dark, quiet jungle. He felt anxious, as if he was traveling the same route over and over again. Lately he'd been constantly on edge, as if waiting for something to happen. He just didn't know what.

"You all right, GQ?"

Julian nodded to Declan. "Yeah, just feeling the need to finish this once and for all." He studied the tall sorcerer, watching him as Declan observed the vampire. It was obvious to pretty much everyone but Ana how deep the sorcerer's feelings ran.

"And you?" Julian asked.

Declan laughed, but the sound was harsh, empty.

"Just fucking lovely." He shook his head and shrugged his shoulders. "I'll feel a whole lot better when I get my hands wrapped around Cormac's slimy neck."

Julian remained silent, watching a muscle work its way across the tight skin of Declan's jaw. Declan carried the sins of his father close to his heart and it was a weight that was tearing at him every day. Julian felt a certain kinship with him.

His father, while not the maniacal monster that Cormac was, was still a bastard nonetheless.

Sadly, no one could choose who their parents would be.

"The fucker has all but disappeared into thin air, and he's got the entire jungle crawling with badasses from across the globe and beyond."

Declan turned to Julian, his face hard, dark with the cold fury that lived inside of him. "I will track him down one day and when I do—"

His words were cut off as Jaxon shouted an alert. It was quick, precise.

Immediately all five of them went into battle mode and an unearthly quiet settled over Julian. He felt his pulse begin to race as his body shot adrenaline deep into his veins, goading the animal that lay underneath, teasing it with the hint of violence.

He clenched his teeth and held on, something he was finding harder and harder to do lately. Truthfully, he'd only just begun to understand Jagger's need to live as a jaguar for the past three months.

It was something that ate at him constantly and the longer he'd been in the jungle, the more animalistic he'd become. He'd evolved and was still on the fence about whether or not the change was good.

When this was all over, he wasn't so sure corporate

America was ready to deal with the new Julian Castille. If they thought the old version was a cold, selfish bastard, then the new version was the devil himself.

Jaxon fisted his arm and they all fell into the shadows that bordered the area they were in.

His brother signaled to the left and Julian felt the burn of his animal yet again. He clenched his fists at his side, pushing the tremors back until he was able to focus. The thought of a fight was enough to send him over the edge.

He enjoyed it way too much.

His mind emptied and he concentrated on the shadows that flickered amongst the fog and rain that had laid claim to the jungle overnight. Carefully he scanned the area as he inhaled the myriad of scents in the air.

Something was there and it tingled along the edge of his mind. He turned to Jaxon in surprise.

But there was no need of words. The relief and anger on his brother's face was enough.

A large black jaguar slipped through the underbrush and came to a halt several feet away. Its eyes glowed green.

Jagger had found them. And he wasn't alone.

The animal paused, turned its head to the sky and Julian followed its gaze, watching as a large eagle swooped in, its great wings cutting through the air and sheets of water in silence. As the raptor approached he felt a sliver of unease.

There was dark energy here. He turned back to his brother Jagger, watching the large predator as it began to walk toward them, mist crawling along its black pelt as the magick took hold.

Above, the eagle circled once more and then disappeared into a fog of twirling mist that enveloped it whole. Seconds later two men appeared before them. His brother, Jagger, and a tall blond man, who, he was guessing, was the missing eagle knight, Finn, Skye's brother.

Jagger looked at them, his face bleak, and Julian felt his belly tighten. He'd known Jagger was headed for heartbreak. Had Skye managed to seal the portal?

"So," Jaxon said softly. "You need a haircut."

"And some clothes," Declan said. "Again."

Julian watched in silence as his brother Jaxon crossed to the youngest Castille and gave him a hard hug. "Been way too long." The two brothers stared at each other, the silence between them full of words they couldn't articulate.

"Where's Skye?" Julian asked, wanting to know even though he dreaded the answer.

"My sister is gone."

All eyes turned to the blond stranger. He stood alone, aloof, and the energy that surrounded him was full of anger.

Declan moved to Julian's side and quipped, "Gone where? She on vacation? Out shopping, getting her nails done, dunno, maybe hooking up with Cormac, what?"

The stranger hissed and took a step toward Declan, and Julian immediately tensed for battle. He could feel the darkness brewing, percolating and waiting to explode.

Jagger shoved his way in front of the stranger and snarled at the sorcerer. "Screw you, Declan," he said roughly. "I don't have time for your freaking comedy show, and you'd best watch your insults."

Julian watched his younger brother struggle to gain

control of his emotions and not for the first time, he wondered if it was all worth it. To give your heart to another, to love unconditionally . . . what the hell was so wonderful about that?

"This is Finn, Skye's brother," Jagger said, nodding toward the tall eagle knight. "He knows where Skye is." Jagger winced slightly. "Or at least where we think she might be."

Julian's eyes narrowed. The tall stranger remained quiet and glared at them all.

Jagger exhaled heavily and asked no one in particular: "Got something for me to wear?" A hint of a tired smile played around the corners of his mouth. "I don't particularly feel like trekking through the jungle with my junk hanging out."

"Well as much as I'm enjoying the show, boys, I vote you cover up." Ana arched her eyebrows and ignored the dark look Declan shot at her. "We've got a lot of ground to cover and I for one don't need any distractions."

Julian went through his bags and threw some clothes toward Jagger and Finn. A shifter always carried extra clothing. He threw them each a pair of pants, thinking there was no point, really. They'd be as soaked as his in minutes.

"Is that all I have to do to snag your interest, lady? Walk around and be at one with Mother Nature?" Declan's tone was light yet the hunger and irritation in his eyes was anything but.

Ana didn't take her eyes from the men as she answered. "Snag my interest, Declan?" She laughed softly. "To do that, I would have to at least like you . . . a little bit."

Declan flipped his middle finger, but the vampire had already turned away from him.

Julian watched as Jagger pulled on a pair of ratty old jeans and then he walked over to his brother. He had no extra boots, however; the two of them were going to have to rough it.

"You all right?" he asked. He could feel the cold fury that sat heavy upon Jagger's shoulders. His brother was wired tight and about to explode.

"I'll be good once I have Skye back."

Julian frowned, hating to point out the obvious, but he felt the need to have some clarity. "You do know what she needs to do to seal the portal."

Jagger turned to him. His face was thunderous, black with anger, and he snarled. "Yeah, I do. So what are you trying to say? I just leave her out there at the mercy of some fucking dream demon?" Jagger was breathing hard, his breaths ragged as he shoved his finger into Julian's chest. "That I don't at least try to stop her from doing something totally insane? My God, there has to be another way."

Inside, Julian's cat began to growl and he felt the familiar burn begin once more. He paused, centered himself and pushed back. Now was not the time to fight against his own blood.

"Jagger, I—"

Jagger continued, cutting him off. "If one hair on her head is harmed I will tear Azaiel apart and burn his flesh from this earth."

"Azaiel?" Alarm ripped through Julian. He knew that name. It tugged at the edges of his memory and it frustrated him greatly that nothing tangible came up.

"He's the bastard that came for Skye last night."

Julian considered his words carefully. "You know this might end badly?"

Jagger snorted and turned away, but not before Julian got a glimpse of the true heart of the jaguar. It was fierce, hard, cold, and calculating. He could feel his brother's power and his own animal fed on it. Welcomed it, in fact.

"It will end how it ends," Jagger snarled back at him. "Either way, nothing will keep me from Skye."

"You ready to do this?" Finn asked. The eagle's face was intense and he kept clenching and unclenching his hands as he turned to the west. "The sacred resting place is not far."

Jagger nodded. "Okay," Jagger said to them all. "Let's go snag me a demon."

Julian eyed Finn closely and noticed the tightening of the eagle's mouth. It only confirmed what he'd already suspected.

Things were not as they seemed.

Chapter 26

nger exploded deep from within Skye's gut and she hissed at the man who stood before her. Her eyes blazed and she snarled.

"I belong to no one but myself."

She clutched the disc hard against her abdomen, her fingers hot from its power as it continued to surge into her flesh. She felt it sizzle along nerve endings and as it rushed to her heart, the fast-beating organ was hit with a bolt of electricity.

She stumbled back and nearly fell to her knees. Christ, she felt so faint. She took a second and sucked in a great gulp of air.

Azaiel looked at her as if he were humoring a child. He took a step closer but she scrambled away, turning around as she searched wildly for the exit.

His voice stopped her cold. It slid across the distance between them, wrapping her in its seductive lilt. She turned back, confused and scared at the hold Azaiel seemed to have over her.

"I have watched you since the moment of your birth. When you took your first step, started first grade." His hands tugged at a damp curl. "When you cut off that lovely blond hair of yours and dyed it magenta." He took a step closer and Skye could feel the heat of him, fresh against her skin. "I was there."

His eyes had an intensity that grabbed at her and she wanted to look away, but found that she couldn't.

"When your heart was broken by that arrogant Swede, who do you think it was that reached out from beyond and plagued him with a sickness that lasted for seven days?"

Skye could do nothing but shake her head. She didn't understand any of this.

"When you were held prisoner by the jaguars I kept you safe, and even as they tortured and attacked the other woman, you were spared the ferocity of their anger."

"But how?" she asked, "and why?"

"Because you belong to me. I knew the moment you were conceived that you'd be the one to free me from my prison." He smiled at her and in that moment she caught a glimpse of the true soul behind the man, or angel/demon.

Or whatever the hell he was.

He was full of ancient power, deep magick that was not of this world. He was seductive and incredibly attractive.

But he was not Jagger and her heart ached at the thought of him.

"Call it what you want but you're nothing more than a glorified stalker." Skye made a face. "It's creepy."

"You're so like her," Azaiel whispered then, his eyes

and face changing as something dark slid across his memories.

"Like who?" Skye asked, a macabre curiosity fueling her on.

"The betrayer, Toniella." His eyes focused and he held out his hand. "The one who tempted me from above with empty lies and the warmth of her body."

Her gaze fell upon the markings that had been etched into his hands. They looked raw, painful, and she wondered what they meant. He lowered his voice, and it was full of anger and . . . sadness?

"She was a blond vision of the sun."

Skye backed up yet again and felt the cool stone at her back. She was well and truly trapped with a pissed-off and jilted angel from hell.

She tried to hold still and not show any fear, but when he reached for her hair once more she shuddered and turned from him. She could feel the warmth of his body and the electrical pulses that encircled his tall form.

"Once we are far from here I will wipe the memory of the jaguar from your mind."

Skye turned to him then, feeding off the small spark of anger that still curled in her belly. "You can never take him from me." She licked her dry lips as the realization of what Jagger meant rolled over her. He was everything. To give him up? That was the hardest thing she'd ever have to do.

Yet she would give her life for him, again, if she had to.

"I will do whatever you want." Her eyes widened, full of unshed tears. "Only because you promised that no harm will come to him." She eyed his lips, so close to her own. "But he completes me. There will never be another."

Azaiel pushed away from her, his eyes intense as they studied her carefully. Something slithered across his mind; it showed briefly as a flash of red that lit his eyes from behind.

"What now?" Skye asked suddenly as exhaustion rolled over her tired limbs.

"Now you will give me that which is mine."

Skye's fingers were numb from holding the portal so tightly. Her mind was a wild jumble of thoughts that made no sense.

"Are you going to destroy it?" she asked softly. "I know you're the only one who has the power to do that."

Azaiel's face darkened and the earth began to shake underneath her feet. "Why would I destroy the one thing that gives me control over the legions of doom?"

God, she felt like she'd fallen into middle earth.

Nausea rolled inside Skye and she hissed sharply. Azaiel's eyes had lost the gold and were completely black. He was pissed, and done playing games.

Her time was nearly up.

"But you said you hated the demons and what they would do to the human realm if let loose here."

He smiled then, a wicked look that did nothing to warm the coldness of his eyes. "You were stronger than I thought you'd be. I couldn't take the chance you'd be able to resist my powers of persuasion." He shrugged his shoulders. "I would have said anything to get you to open the portal. Toniella taught me well."

Skye's right hand held the portal close, her grip tight as she felt the power, taken from the still hot stone disc, begin to move where it was coiled inside her. It was fresh, hungry, and unlike anything she'd experienced before.

Thanks for that, asshole, she thought. *At least you've left me with a little something extra to fight back with.*

"I don't understand," Skye continued, trying to buy more time.

"There's no need for you to understand. The portal has many uses." He laughed, the sound wicked and grating. "The least of which unlocks the hell realm. Its secrets are vast, incomprehensible."

He loomed over her, his countenance dark, angry. "Make no mistake, little bird, the portal belongs to me, as do you." He looked toward the exit. "We're done here."

Her left hand was hidden from his view, behind her back. Skye struggled to keep her face calm, devoid of any emotion, as she felt her bones begin to shift and elongate. The pain was immediate, and seconds later she felt the sharp talons unfurl.

The time had come. There was no turning back.

Outside the rain continued to fall, the fresh scent mixing with that of the jungle and invoking a deluge of memories. Jagger, her father, Finn . . . all of them mixed together into a collage of pain. Sadness, deep and searing, hit her hard in the chest, but she held on, pushing it away as her lips tightened in resolve.

A sound erupted from outside, a howl unlike any she'd heard before. Skye looked up in surprise as Azaiel turned to the exit, enraged. The air around him blurred in a strange mist of gold and black, energy shooting in all directions, sizzling and then burning away.

It was ugly and beautiful at the same time.

Skye saw her chance and took it.

She clutched the disc tight within her right hand and brought her left out, the long, vicious claws curled and sharp as razors. Her heart beat fast, pumping the blood through her veins as she felt the power inside of her erupt.

She pushed away from the wall, leaping up into the air as high as she could. Her left arm fully extended, she brought it down in an arc as Azaiel turned to her, his face thunderous, his body shimmering with power.

She felt her claws rip through flesh and bone and she screamed, her battle cry full of every single emotion inside of her. It was shrill, loud, and it echoed in the morning mist.

Azaiel reacted instantly, his arm swatting at her as if she were no more than an annoying bug. He slammed his fist into her chest; the force of it knocked her several feet into the air and she landed in front of the doorway.

Skye was up in an instant, her body feeding on the adrenaline that rushed through her, and she was outside in seconds. The rain slammed into her, the sheets of water nearly solid as they fell from the heavens in a torrent.

Time slowed then. She could hear her heart beating a furious rhythm, her lungs drawing in great gulps of air.

The entire area was surrounded by every kind of otherworlder imaginable. She stumbled forward, moving so that she was away from the structure, aware that Azaiel had exited as well. She held the disc tight against her body, her left claw in front of her, the deadly weapon held high.

To her right were several shifters and her eyes widened at the sight of Degas DaCosta. He scowled at her and licked his lips menacingly. To his side was Jaden and she looked tense, worried. They were surrounded by jaguar warriors, wereshifters, vampires and a few with the aura of demon.

Skye felt the panic rip into her mind and she struggled to keep a cool, calm head.

"So we meet again, little bird."

The voice slid at her from the murky area to her left. He was in shadow, and solidified in front of her. Everything else faded into nothing as she met the eyes of the one man she hated more than anything.

Cormac O'Hara smiled at her, his handsome face twisted into a wicked grin. "I knew you'd eventually lead me to the disc." His cold eyes flashed as he looked beyond her to Azaiel. "I see you've brought me a present."

Skye could feel Cormac's power. It floated in the air, a tangible, living thing. It was stronger than before, darker. He'd been dipping into some heavy shit and that meant that the playing field was muddied even more.

"You know not what you're toying with, sorcerer," Azaiel said as he moved closer to Skye. The weird gray mist that clung to him continued to swirl and she noted the wary looks from the demons present.

They were afraid of Azaiel. Cormac, in his arrogant stupidity, thought he could manage him. He had no fucking clue. However, if they wanted to get into a pissing contest, that was fine by her. This was the opportunity she needed to get the job done.

"I know exactly what you are," Cormac said softly. "Why do you think I allowed the eagle to let you escape?"

Skye began to edge away from Azaiel and through the rain she noted all eyes were focused on the showdown between Cormac and Azaiel.

She chanced one last look at Jaden and nodded as she focused and began to chant softly in her mind. Skye had no clue if the words needed to be uttered aloud; she only knew that she had to try. There was no more time.

She'd come to the end and no one was taking the portal from her. She was in control and would end it. Now.

Jagger slid to a halt, feeling the heavy magick as it crackled and slid through the rain. It rode the wind hard, slamming into his gut and when the sweet scent so unique to Skye rippled across him, he growled softly.

It mixed and mingled with a whole host of otherworld scents and the need to protect his mate bled deep from within his soul. Its strength was furious and he began to pant in an effort to control his impulses. He needed to focus.

They were close to a large gathering of all sorts of nasty creatures. His nostrils flared as the scents of many slithered down into his lungs, agitating the beast within him. He tensed, gripping the modified Glock Declan had provided in one hand and a charmed machete in the other.

Declan slid up beside him. "Cormac's here. I can sense him." The Irishman's tone was calm and menacing. "Looks like it's time for a family reunion."

Jagger squared his shoulders and warned the eagle shifter to his right. "Skye must be protected. I don't give a damn about the portal or any of that crap."

"Don't worry, jaguar. You get my sister and I'll get to the portal." The eagle exhaled and shook out his limbs as he stopped alongside him. "It never should have been her. It's time for me to end this, make it right."

His brothers nodded to Jagger and disappeared into the darkened interior, followed in succession by Cracker and Ana. The rain and fog had stolen what little bit of sunlight there was, leaving the entire jungle swathed in near darkness. Nervous energy clawed at him and tremors wracked his frame.

A scream ripped through the jungle and he reacted instantly, jumping forward with Declan and Finn at his side.

Silently they slid forward, swiftly cutting through the jungle, and Jagger was thankful the protection charm Declan had invoked was still working. From what he could gather, they were outnumbered by a huge ratio.

As he slid to a halt near the edge of a clearing he felt his stomach muscles clench at the sight before him.

Skye was dead center, encircled on all sides by a motley assortment of the freak show that had gathered. Relief flooded him as his eyes ate her up greedily, running the length of her body. He noted the half shift of her arm and the fact that she clutched a round stone artifact in the other.

The portal. If he could, he'd destroy the goddamn thing himself.

When his eyes slid to the tall man nearest her, he felt the blackened rage inside of him push to the surface and he growled loudly, wanting to kill, maim . . . do anything to get Skye away from him.

He knew without a doubt it was the Azaiel. His

body began to burn and his eyesight blurred as the beast inside of him threatened to explode. Jagger hissed at the pain that ripped across his body as he forced his jaguar into obedience.

"That one's mine," Declan said as he pulled abreast of Jagger. He paid no attention. All of Jagger's energy was focused on Skye and he felt alarm rush through him as he saw her begin to chant.

In an instant he knew what she was attempting and without another thought he rushed forward, yelling loudly as his machete sliced cleanly through the neck of the shifter closest to him, severing the head from its body.

All at once he heard the cries of his brothers and the power inside of him fueled his body. Everything except Skye faded from his view and he rushed forward, swinging his machete and firing off rounds from the Glock.

He was aware Declan had broken off to the right and that Finn was close on his heels. Other than that, the only thing he saw was the woman who meant more than his own life. And he would give it, if he had to, in order to protect and keep her safe.

He'd just cleared the perimeter, when he was knocked to the side. Snarling, he went with it and rolled, bringing his gun hand up and shooting straight into the serrated mouth of a large demon.

The head rocked back but the bastard held on, black liquid oozing from the gaping hole at the back of its throat as its heavy weight landed on his chest, nearly knocking the breath from his lungs. Jagger brought his other arm up and stabbed the end of the machete deep into its neck, trying to force it through.

Still the demon held on, its deadly teeth dripping

with black saliva that burned as it fell onto his skin. He heard another grunt and tried to twist his body as a jaguar warrior climbed up the back of the demon and smiled down at him.

He kept driving the machete deeper into the demon's neck while twisting to avoid the serrated teeth that snapped closer to his face. He was just about to try and fire the Glock when the warrior screamed in pain.

A large machete sliced his back and poked out through the warrior's chest. The jaguar grimaced and fell into death's grip as he tumbled from the demon's back. Jagger shot the demon yet again and used every ounce of strength that he had to plunge the machete clean through.

With a mighty heave he pushed the demon from his body, his eyes meeting Finn's. The eagle warrior looked fierce. "Get to my sister and toss me the portal. I'll cover you."

Jagger jackknifed his body and was on his feet in an instant, his eyes seeking out Skye as she stood pressed up against the stone shelter. Her lips were still moving and in that moment her eyes opened and met his.

The shock and surprise that flashed across her face was replaced in an instant with heart-wrenching sadness. She looked at him and nodded slightly, her eyes telling him good-bye.

The air around her began to shimmer and he saw her smile through the tears that fell freely from her eyes.

I love you, she mouthed and the pain that lashed across his chest propelled him forward.

He rushed toward her, feeling the heat of bodies flying at him, enemies that were downed by the strength of the eagle knight at his side. The rain continued to pour, blurring her image as his eyes filled with water. Or tears of rage.

He shook his head and kept on, his body building speed until he was there. In front of her.

Her eyes rolled up and he feared he was too late.

Jagger grabbed her and wrenched the portal from her hand, not hearing the scream of rage that echoed in the wet air.

All around him the battle raged, and he whirled around, gripping the hot, electric disc tightly in his fingers, searching with his eyes for Finn.

The eagle knight jumped over the fallen bodies of their enemies, leapt up high into the air as Cormac did the same.

Jagger saw his chance and tossed the disc into the air, watching as it rotated slowly. It began to glow in earnest, and as Finn's fingers closed around it, he was grabbed from behind.

Loud shouts and echoes of pain and terror rent the air as a great blinding light flashed across the jungle. It sizzled along an invisible conduit, showering the entire area in sparks of energy that glowed brightly.

Jagger pulled Skye close to him and covered her with his own body in an effort to protect her from whatever the hell was happening. He felt the heat at his back and he fell to the ground as the earth trembled and the smell of burning flesh rode the air.

Seconds later, all was quiet and he slowly lifted his head and looked around. The faces of those left standing looked shocked and they melted into the jungle, retreating like the cowards that they were.

Bodies lay strewn about and as he met the eyes of

his brother Jaxon, he knew something terrible had just occurred.

Skye began to stir and then went limp. She was alive though unconscious. He needed to get her to safety. He rocked her gently in his arms and stood up, holding her close to his chest.

Jaxon closed the distance between them, his expression pained, confused. "They're gone," he said. "I don't know what the hell happened. There was a flash and they disappeared into thin air."

Jagger felt his throat tighten as he asked, "Who?"

Jaxon paused and the pain in his eyes was beyond words. "Julian, Cormac, Declan, and the tall one with the fucked-up eyes." Jaxon shook his head. "What the hell did she do? Did she close it? Are they lost to us forever?" he whispered hoarsely.

"They're gone, but not to the hell realm." Finn limped toward them, his right leg bleeding profusely. He grimaced. "The portal is not sealed. It's still out there."

"How the hell do you know that?" Jaxon asked as he ran his hands through his hair.

"Only one of purity can open it and only an eagle knight can seal it." Finn nodded toward the still unconscious Skye. "My sister is still here; the portal is not sealed."

"Well, where the hell are they?" Jagger shouted, his frustration and anger making him hoarse.

Finn looked at him and shook his head. "I don't know where, or what," he said softly. "But it can't be anyplace good."

Chapter 27

Their plane was wheels up several hours later. It was funny, really, how quickly they'd managed to get out of the jungle. The place he'd called home for the last several months.

Jagger cuddled Skye, tight to his chest, where she'd been ever since he'd grabbed her in the jungle. He studied her face and his thumb traced the soft line of her cheek. She was feverish, still unconscious, and worry ripped at him relentlessly.

"How's she doing?" Jaxon slid into the seat beside him and Jagger remained tight-lipped as he shrugged his shoulders.

"I don't know," he managed, hearing his voice tremble slightly as Jaxon's warm hand grabbed his shoulder with a reassuring squeeze.

"She's tough. Hell, what she's been through . . . she just needs some time."

Jagger nodded. "Any word on Julian?" His heart was heavy at the thought of his older brother.

Jaxon sighed and shook his head. "We don't know anything. I've got my contacts on it and Cracker is interrogating a few of our guests, but so far nothing. We get back to PATU, I'll be able to dig deeper."

His brother rubbed weary eyes and grimaced. "Cormac is one slippery son-of-a-bitch, but we'll get him."

Jagger looked at Ana. The vampire was distraught. She'd curled into a chair and had not said a word since they'd left Belize.

"She gonna be okay?" he murmured, his mouth nuzzling the top of Skye's head.

"I don't know. She's taking Declan's disappearance hard."

Jagger leaned his head back and stared out the small round window, not seeing anything as his mind continued to circle.

"I'm taking Skye home with me." Jagger blew out a ragged breath.

Jaxon looked at him, surprised. "We could use you at headquarters."

"I need to take her to the cabin, at least for a little while."

"But she might need a doctor—"

"I will go with them."

Both men looked over at Ana. The vampire's eyes were bloodshot but they shone fiercely. "I'll make sure she's all right."

Jagger nodded and Ana looked away once more, her chin trembling slightly as she gazed out her window.

Jaxon stared at Jagger for several long seconds and then nodded. "Take all the time you need, but keep in touch. I have a feeling the shit's gonna hit the fan sooner rather than later, and we'll need every man we've got."

The ragged group of survivors made it back to the States several hours later. Jaxon left for northern Canada immediately, taking Cracker, Finn, and their "guests," the few prisoners they'd taken. Their destination was the new headquarters of PATU.

Ana accompanied him back to his cabin. She was very quiet and seemed almost morose. He'd never seen the vampire in such a state.

Jagger sighed heavily. It was a bitch to navigate, the whole love thing.

They'd been at his cabin for nearly thirty-six hours, and Skye was still dead to the world.

A fever raged through her body and she'd been held firm in the grip of a nightmare for most of it. Jagger hadn't left her side once, had been quite rude to Ana, in fact, when she'd tried to get him to rest.

Wearily he rose to his feet, stretching his legs as he crossed by the bed and stared out the window. Spring had fled and summer had come to his little paradise. Outside the sun shone, touching the wild array of flowers that bordered his property. Goldenrod and lilies grew in abundance.

He thought that Skye would like them.

He'd had so many plans for this place and after Iraq they'd been shoved aside. He'd been empty, half broken, until Skye had fallen into his life and changed it forever. But now? He had no clue what the hell had happened back in Belize and he didn't know if she was damaged or whole. His eyes followed the play between two squirrels, a ghost of a smile lifting the corner of his mouth as they tumbled about, foraging for food to store.

"Jagger?"

He whipped around at the sound of Skye's voice

and was at her side in a second. She looked weak and her eyes were dull, shadowed.

He grabbed the glass of water off the bed table and held it to her mouth, gently coaxing her to take the cool liquid between her lips.

"What happened?" she asked as she struggled to right herself. "Where are we?"

"Shhh," Jagger whispered as he sank onto the bed beside her and gathered her close to his chest. "You're safe with me."

He felt her shudder and then bury her head in the crook of his neck. "I had such awful dreams," she whispered against him.

"Can you talk about them?" he probed gently, not wanting to force her but desperate for any information on what had happened to Julian and Declan.

She inhaled deeply and pushed against his chest. As he looked down at her, Jagger felt his heart constrict. She meant everything to him.

"I was going to do it." She met his gaze, unflinching, and sat up straighter. "I would have done anything to keep you safe. You need to know that." Skye paused and took another sip of water.

"I was going to hell for you and I would do it again if I had to." Her eyes were intense as they bored into his. "You know that, right? To keep you safe from Azaiel I would have done anything."

"I know," he said simply.

"Is he . . . ?" Skye paused, a look of confusion crossing her features. "Was he destroyed?"

"No, at least I don't think so."

"And the portal?"

Jagger shook his head. "We're not sure what happened exactly, but your brother seems to think it's disappeared into the twilight zone or whatever."

Skye smiled then and in that moment Jagger knew he'd do whatever it took to keep the smile pasted to her face.

"Finn's alive. I don't remember much, but he was there . . ." Skye laughed softly. "He was there." Her face sobered and she quieted, the blue of her eyes glistening with emotion. "But the others . . . I have vague memories and recollections of what happened." She paused and looked up at him, her eyes intense and full of pain.

"The dreams I've been having . . ." She swallowed thickly and shook her head. "Is it true? Are your friends . . . your brother, Julian . . ." Her face darkened and she grabbed his arms tightly. "Are they gone?"

Jagger's hands moved up to her chin and he cupped her face between his large hands, moving until he was so close he could count the tiny veins that fed her eyes.

"They're gone, yes, but we'll get them back."

The two of them stared deeply into each other's eyes, all the pain and frustration and struggle over the past several days swept away as their longing for each other rose to the surface.

"I feel so guilty," Skye whispered as her fingers reached out and traced his lips.

"Why is that?" Jagger asked, although truth be told, he wasn't paying attention to anything other than her mouth.

"Because all around us chaos and uncertainty are the norm. People's lives are being destroyed, your brother is missing and yet . . ."

Her heart was beating faster now. Jagger could hear it, and inside, the cat purred quietly as his own began to beat in tandem.

"Yet?" he prompted, his voice low and rough, and he inhaled a shaky breath as his lips caressed the soft skin of her cheek.

"All I can think about is that I'm here, with you, and I'm never giving you up." Skye turned into him, pressing her body as close to him as she could. Jagger groaned as every single inch of him responded to the woman in his arms.

"No matter what," she whispered, her eyes transfixed by his own. "I'm yours. I love you, Jagger." She laughed then. "How freaky is that?"

Jagger lowered his mouth until he was inches from hers. "I don't know, why don't you show me?" He groaned and covered her soft lips with his own. The hunger inside of him for the woman that he held was one that would never leave him. As long as he drew air into his lungs she would be his.

He kissed her with an intensity that shook him to his core and his body hardened to the point of pain.

"You are mine," he whispered against her lips. He felt them tremble beneath his own and he groaned as she opened beneath him, her arms circling his neck. "Whatever the future holds, we'll deal. Together. Don't ever leave me again."

"I'm not going anywhere," she said as she offered herself up to the one man who was strong enough to tame her, strong enough to fight for her.

"Take your clothes off," she commanded, nipping at his neck and falling back onto the bed, giggling as he hurried to do her bidding.

Jagger laughed softly. "You must be hungry. Don't you want some food first?"

"I'm hungry," she growled, "but it ain't for food."

Jagger slid into bed pulling her along the length of

him. She pushed him down and he sucked in a painful breath as she rose above him, every inch of her golden flesh exposed to his hungry eyes as she straddled his body.

Her breaths were coming in ragged spurts and she licked her lips, reaching for him, claiming his mouth with her own as she sank down upon his hardness.

He heard her gasp against him, her body shuddering as his cock filled her fully. Their tongues met in a feverish dance and his hands grabbed her hips, pulling her into him as he thrust upward.

She broke from him, pushing herself up as she began to roll her hips and ride him with an intensity that tore at his heart. Everything was there, in her eyes, for him to see and as the pressure built inside of him, he clenched his teeth and held on.

There were no words, no sounds other than skin on skin and the creaking of the bed as they began to move quicker, harder. He felt the pressure building deep inside and as her head rolled back, his fingers gripped her hips hard and he brought her up and then back down again, over and over, until he felt his release take hold.

She looked down at him then and they came together, their orgasms rolling over them in waves until she collapsed on top of him.

Later, after he'd loved her again, they lay exhausted, their bodies intertwined and their hearts beating as one. Gently he caressed the softness of her cheek and pulled her into the crook of his body.

"What do we do now?" she asked.

"We live our lives, deal with whatever comes our way together."

"Sounds good to me." She nuzzled his neck and

even though she'd used him good and hard, he felt his body respond, and he smiled against her.

"I just . . ."

"What?" he prodded.

"I'm sorry, Jagger, so sorry about your brother." She rested her head against his chest, and he felt her sadness. It rolled off her in waves. "About where he is."

Jagger pulled her in flush to his body and kissed the top of her head, taking comfort in the fact that even amongst all the craziness, they had each other.

That had to count for something.

He wanted to ask, to know more than what her cryptic words told him, but he remained quiet. To know more would break him and he knew he needed to be strong in the coming days, not only for Skye but for his family.

The two of them lay there for several long moments and eventually the weariness took its toll. Jagger fell into a deep sleep that was long overdue. As Skye snuggled into his safe embrace, she tried not to think about what she'd seen in her dreams. She couldn't go there, not yet, anyway.

Instead she sent a silent prayer to the gods.

And hoped like hell there was someone out there listening.

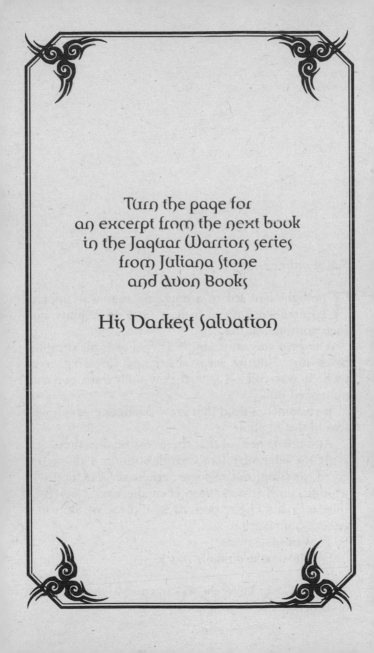

Turn the page for
an excerpt from the next book
in the Jaquar Warriors series
from Juliana Stone
and Avon Books

His Darkest Salvation

Six months earlier

The light had led to a darkness that was unprecedented—a flash of heat, a taste of sulphur, and then nothing but fire.

The pain was constant. It drifted over his skin like black mist, sliding across flesh and caressing every inch. It was full of an evil that both fed upon and nourished him.

It sustained a need that grew stronger every day he was in this hellhole.

And it *was* hell, of that there was no question.

At the edge of Julian Castille's vision a shape lingered, drifting, out of focus, ethereal. Watching . . . waiting, until it was time. Then she would carefully slice into his chest, peel back a piece of skin and resume her position.

To wait once more.

For the day he'd finally break.

Jaden DaCosta knew she was in trouble about ten seconds before the door opened.

It was in the air she dragged deep into her lungs and the electricity that ran along with it, pulsing, burning, as it slid down.

She whipped her head around, eyes scanning with quick, cool precision, and dove behind the sofa just as a click echoed in the darkened penthouse.

Her heart slowed automatically and she relaxed her limbs, calling the shadows to her as she slid forward on her belly. With her fingers she felt along her waist to cradle the edge of the charmed dagger that was there, and her senses sharpened as the animal inside awakened.

The door swung open slowly, sweeping across cool tiles and allowing a thin beam of light to fall into the dim interior. She could see a shadow reflected along the floor as long moments passed. It was impressive and she gritted her teeth in anticipation.

And then he was there, striding into the room as if he owned the place.

Jaden gripped the dagger tightly. She inhaled the stench of otherworld, yet it was somehow different, already fading fast.

The intruder paused, his tall frame humming with an energy that, while dark, was unlike any she'd ever come across. There was a familiarity to it and it tugged at something deep inside of her.

She watched in silence as he kicked the door shut, winced at the harsh echo of it as it slammed against the frame.

The man held still for a few moments and then his head swiveled around slowly. He scented the air and her breath caught at the back of her throat. Would he be able to smell through the charm that coated her body and masked her scent?

Who the hell was he? *What* the hell was he?

The stranger seemed to relax a bit and he rotated his neck, running his hands through the thick hair that hung in waves to his neck. Power clung to him, gripping his tall form hungrily, electrifying the air.

But it was tinged with a darkness that was hard to read.

He headed toward the kitchen area and the fridge door swung open at his command. Jaden could have saved him the bother. She'd already checked it out and no one had been inside the penthouse since Julian Castille had pulled a "Copperfield" and disappeared into thin air. All of the food was either moldy or dried up.

The shrill echo of a cell phone pierced the silence and she bit her tongue as her body jerked. The coppery taste of blood flooded her mouth and she narrowed her eyes as the stranger answered the call.

"Yeah." His voice was low, husky, with a rasp that sounded rough. He straightened and ran a hand along the back of his neck as he rolled his shoulders and listened. Jaden strained to hear, but even with her enhanced senses she couldn't pick up anything.

"I just got in." He sounded weary and she inched forward, trying to get a better look, but paused as he turned once more and headed toward her, stopping a few feet away.

There was something about the man that called to her and Jaden was finding it harder to remain calm and undetected.

She could just make out his profile, and her eyes took in the aristocratic nose, high cheekbones, and a mouth that even from this angle was to die for.

Inside, the cat erupted and she broke out in a sweat as her skin began to burn and itch.

Son-of-a-bitch! It couldn't be . . .

"It's bearable," he said, and she watched as he ran his hand over his chest. He nodded his head in answer to whatever was being said on the other end before whispering harshly, "Don't worry, I'm ready. Tomorrow we hunt."

He threw the cell phone onto the sofa, where it landed with a thud not more than two inches from her head. Jaden's heart took off like a rocket and was pounding so hard it was a miracle he couldn't hear it.

Julian Castille back from the twilight zone? Was it possible? Had the bastard managed to survive wherever the hell he'd been sent six months ago?

A fire of emotion erupted inside of her and Jaden had to use every single bit of power she possessed to keep it together. The man who'd haunted her dreams for years—three to be exact—stood not more than a few feet away, very much alive.

As much as Jaden loathed him, deep inside her soul the jaguar was singing, wanting nothing more than to mate. To claim once more the man who'd awakened her spirit and bonded with her jaguar. The man who'd given her one amazing night of pleasure and then had rejected her.

How pathetic.

Jaden felt her cheeks sting with the heat of humiliation as she recalled the look of disgust that had crossed his face when he'd realized what she was.

No one had ever made her feel like that before. Like dirt. Like less than dirt.

So many questions crowded her head, but she pushed them away so she could concentrate. Something was off. This wasn't the Julian Castille she remembered. Nope. Back in the day he'd been total GQ, hot for sure, but polished and boardroom-ready. This man? He was edgy, dark, and the word *sinister* came to mind.

She watched as he crossed to his bedroom and paused in the entrance, his head cocked to the side for a moment. He then padded over to the large bed just beyond and stripped the shirt from his body before slipping the jeans from his hips.

Jaden's mouth went dry. She couldn't take her eyes from him as he stood there, tall, fierce, buck naked, with nothing but moonbeams from the window caressing his taut, powerful frame. The dude had packed on some serious muscle since she last saw him.

She bit her lips to stifle the groan that now sat inside her mouth. Her jaguar was chomping at the bit, wanting out, and a wave of dizziness rippled through her brain.

Heat erupted between her legs, which only infuriated her more. How the hell could he do that to her? After all this time?

She closed her eyes, wanting nothing more than for him to disappear.

"If you want I can bend over and give you a real treat."

The words slid out into the space between them and Jaden's eyes flew open, her hand going for the knife as adrenaline flowed through her veins.

But it was too late. A flash of white teeth and a shimmering blur of air rushed at her. Jaden barely had time to roll to the side, and she jackknifed her body, landing in a crouch with the dagger held in front of her.

Only to feel the heat of him at her back.

Fuck!

She reacted instinctively and swung her hips to the side, hiking her right leg out, intending to drop him hard. But it was she who went flying, as large hands gripped her shoulders and spun her around like a top until she ended up on her back, splayed out like a total loser.

The knife clattered across the tiles and Jaden clenched her teeth and fought the urge to curse a torrent of foulness. She'd just pulled a total newbie boner and had no one but herself to blame.

Slowly her gaze moved up his long frame, skipping over the impressive display of manhood, up his taut belly, rock-hard abs, until she came upon a sight that was sobering, to say the least.

Jaden swallowed heavily and couldn't rip her eyes away from the macabre display of scars that crisscrossed, in perfect precision, just under his left pectoral, above his heart. It looked both raw and painful.

"Didn't anyone teach you it's impolite to stare?"

Jaden's eyes jerked up, to rest upon a face that was every bit as devastating as she remembered, if not more so.

Even in the dim light she could see the flair that lit up his golden eyes, eerily so, yet the smile that fell over his mouth didn't reach them. A shiver ran over her body.

Julian Castille was not the person she remembered. At all.

"I'm sorry . . . I . . ." she began, and actually blushed as she stammered like an idiot in front of him. "I didn't expect . . ."

"To find me in my own home?" Julian took a step back and Jaden carefully got to her feet. She eyed him warily.

"Where have you been?" she asked as she tried to move closer to where the dagger had fallen.

Julian's eyes narrowed. "I know you," he said softly.

Jaden's eyebrows arched and harsh laughter fell from her lips as she snorted. "Ya think?" she said sarcastically. Christ, was he brain damaged?

He regarded her in silence and a sliver of *something* flickered in the depths of his eyes, but quickly disappeared as his lips thinned.

"You're a DaCosta jaguar. You were there in Belize, just before . . ." His voice trailed off and Jaden was surprised at the layers of violence she could sense beneath the surface.

But then his words really sank in and the anger inside of her erupted. He honestly had no clue of their past? Of what they'd shared together?

"You've got to be joking," she whispered harshly, more to herself than anything. "You really don't remember who I am? Was I that forgettable?"

The air around him shimmered and before she could even blink an eye, Julian was there, at her back, his arm across her chest as he pulled her in tight to his body.

She had no time to react and dazedly wondered what the hell had happened to him. She was the warrior, not him. Yet it seemed he'd ingested a bit of superhero dust, wherever the hell he'd been.

"I know who you are." His breath was hot against her neck. "Jaden DaCosta."

She began to struggle, but even with her superior strength, he was just too strong, and several moments later she gave up, panting as she tried to calm herself.

His heartbeat was heavy against her ribs, the rhythm steady and strong, and the heat of him radiated throughout her flesh.

"Why are you here?" he whispered harshly, his breath warm against her neck as he nudged the hair that lay there with his nose. Small bursts of electricity fell across her skin and she shivered, pissed that she had no control over her body.

"Where have you been for the last six months?" she asked instead, spitting the words out from between tight lips.

His hand slid along her jaw and he gripped her, hard, his fingers digging in until he drew a whimper from her.

"Lady, you don't want to know where I've been. Not really. So why don't we stop playing this game and you tell me why a DaCosta jaguar is holed up in my place."

She felt his fingers dig in a little more.

"And no lies. I've not had the pleasure of kicking anyone's ass in a long time and really don't give a shit whether the ass is male or"—he ground his groin against her backside—"nicely rounded."

Jaden's mind whirled into a chaotic mess of thoughts. Could she trust him?

"I'm looking for something," she muttered, as her mind continued to process all of her options.

"Yeah, well aren't we all."

Confusion rolled over her. She had no clue where to go from here.

His hand slowly slid down her skin until it rested against the soft flesh that pulsed at the base. The beat was fast, hard, and Jaden was desperately trying to keep the jaguar at bay.

Her skin was on fire, aching, and it felt as if she was being ripped in two.

"You're a DaCosta. Convince me why I shouldn't just snap your neck and be done with it."

Something in the air changed, darkness slithered around them and she began to shiver as it clung to him and bled into her. It rippled along her skin until she felt nauseated.

Could she trust him? Did she have a choice?

"You didn't seem to care about *that* three years ago." Jaden winced as her thoughts slipped from between her lips, a whisper, yes, but vocalized nonetheless.

He stilled and she tried to ignore the hard planes of his body as he gripped her even tighter.

"Three years ago doesn't count anymore." His voice was soft at her ear, in total contrast to the tense feel of his body. "If I'd known then you were DaCosta I'd never have touched you."

Small ripples of pain and humiliation scorched her cheeks with heat and Jaden sought a place of calm. His words ripped into her harder than she'd liked. The man had been an invisible part of her life for longer than she cared to admit, and she'd been nothing more than the biggest mistake he'd ever made.

His hand slid from her neck, trailing a line of fire downward until he rested his large palm against her heaving chest. Her nipples were hard, erect, and she flinched as his fingers passed over them.

Julian's mouth was near her ear and his breath sent tingles of heat across her skin as he spoke, his voice low and sensual. "But it's a different world today, and right now you could be the devil's sidekick, for all I care." The air thickened, changed into something dangerous.

Jaden's pulse quickened even more and her eyes widened as his left hand traveled down to her hip. The unmistakable feel of his hard cock dug into her back and liquid heat began to pool between her legs.

What the hell was wrong with her? She should be kicking his ass but good instead of dancing on the edge. This game would not end well for her.

"It's been too long, Jaden."

Her tongue caught between her teeth as her name fell from his lips. The way he said it sent waves of pleasure rolling through her. It wasn't fair. She wanted to hang her head in shame at the betrayal of her body.

He tipped her head up until it rested against his chest and their eyes met. Long moments passed, and the only sound that was heard was their heavy breathing.

Then he smiled, but there was a cruelty in the depths of his eyes that gave her pause and put her instantly on edge.

"Yeah, way too long." He paused, and in that moment nothing existed but the two of them. "You'll do," he said roughly.

Then his mouth was upon hers, open, hot, and demanding.

And even though it was all wrong and dark and humiliating, deep inside, the cat began to purr.

Next month, don't miss these exciting new love stories only from Avon Books

Pleasures of a Notorious Gentleman by Lorraine Heath
A once unrepentant rogue, Stephen Lyons gained a notorious reputation that forced him to leave for the army. Upon his return he is given the opportunity to redeem himself, and Mercy Dawson will risk everything to protect the dashing soldier from the truth that threatens to destroy their growing love.

Wicked Nights With A Lover by Sophie Jordan
When Marguerite Laurent learns that she is to die before year's end, she desires but one thing—passion. But as she sets out to experience the romance of her dreams, Ash Courtland—the wrong man—threatens to give her a taste of the once-in-a-lifetime ardor she so desperately craves.

A Most Scandalous Engagement by Gayle Callen
When a scandalous escapade threatens to ruin Lady Elizabeth Cabot, she must pretend to fall in love with Peter Derby, a childhood friend. She never imagined the pretense would feel so real or that the man she's shared her past with could suddenly, irreversibly claim her future...and her heart.

Taken by Desire by Lavinia Kent
Anna Steele is not normally impulsive and Alexander Struthers is not one to seek true love. But when scandal forces these two into marriage, fighting the burning attraction that threatens to consume them proves more difficult than both of them could've imagined.

At Avon Books, we know your passion for romance—once you finish one of our novels, you find yourself wanting more.

May we tempt you with . . .

- **Excerpts** from our upcoming releases.

- Entertaining **extras**, including authors' personal photo albums and book lists.

- Behind-the-scenes **scoop** on your favorite characters and series.

- **Sweepstakes** for the chance to win free books, romantic getaways, and other fun prizes.

- Writing **tips** from our authors and editors.

- **Blog** with our authors and find out why they love to write romance.

- **Exclusive content** that's not contained within the pages of our novels.

Join us at
www.avonbooks.com